Runes

Book One

USA Today Bestselling Author

Ednah Walters

COPYRIGHTS

FIRETRAIL PUBLISHING

ALSO BY EDNAH WALTERS:

The Runes Series:
Runes (book 1)
Immortals (book 2)
Grimnirs (book 3)
Seeress (book 4)
Souls (book 5)
Witches (book 6)
Demons (Book 7)
Heroes (book 8)
Gods (book 9) June 14th 2016

The Guardian Legacy Series:
Awakened (prequel)
Betrayed (book one)
Hunted (book two)
Forgotten (book three)

WRITING AS E. B. WALTERS:

The Fitzgerald Family series
Slow Burn (book 1)
Mine Until Dawn (book 2)
Kiss Me Crazy (book 3)
Dangerous Love (book 4)
Forever Hers (book 5)
Surrender to Temptation (book 6)

The Infinitus Billionaires series
Impulse (book 1)
Indulge (book 2)
Intrigue (book 3) Coming 2016

TABLE OF CONTENTS

DEDICATION

This book is dedicated to my four daughters.
Follow your dreams and never let the word 'CANNOT' stop you.

ACKNOWLEDGMENTS

To my editor, Kelly Bradley Hashway, thank you for Weeding out the unnecessary words. I am so lucky to have found you.
To my beta-readers and dear friends, Catie Vargas and Jeannette Whitus, You ladies are amazing. You pushed and pulled me when I faltered. This book would not have been completed without you. You girls rock!!
To my dearest friends, Katrina Whittaker and Jowanna Delong Kestner, Thank you for always being there when I want to vent. Friends like you are hard to find!
Carolina Silva, THANK YOU, Thank you for taking my finished product and formatting it so perfectly, for being my sounding board on everything, and being the best PA an author could have.
To my daughter, MJ, thank you for listening to my crazy ideas and showing me how to bridge the gap between our generations.
To my critique partners, Dawn Brown, Teresa Bellew, Katherine Warwick/Jennifer Laurens, thank you for being there when my muse takes a vacation.
We are more than writing partners.
To my husband and my wonderful children, thank you for your unwavering love and support.
You inspire me in so many ways
Love you, guys.

TRADEMARK LIST:

Google
Nikon
Jeep
Frisbee
Sentra
Harley
Chex Mix
Vampire Diary
Supernatural
Lord Sesshomaru
Portland Art Museum
Tasmanian Devil
Warner Bros

GLOSSARY

Aesir: A tribe of Norse gods
Asgard: Home of the Aesir gods
Odin: The father and ruler of all gods and men. He is an Aesir god. Half of the de soldiers/warriors/athletes go to live in his hall Valhalla.
Vanir: Another tribe of Norse gods
Vanaheim: Home of the Vanir gods
Freya: The poetry-loving goddess of love and fertility. She is a Vanir goddess. The other half of the dead warriors/soldiers/athletes go to her hall in Falkvang
Frigg: Odin's wife, the patron of marriage and motherhood
Norns: Deities who control destinies of men and gods
Völva: A powerful seeress
Völur: A group of seeresses
Immortals: Humans who stop aging and self-heal because of the magical runes etched on their skin
Valkyries: Immortals who collect fallenwarriors/soldiers/fighters/athletes and take them to Valhalla and Falkvang
Bifrost: The rainbow bridge that connects Asgard to Earth
Ragnarok: The end-of-the-world war between the gods and the evil giants
Artavus: Magical knife or dagger used to etch runes
Artavo: Plural of artavus
Stillo: A type of artavus

CHAPTER 1. THE MAILBOX

"So unfair. My parents decided to limit my computer time again," Cora griped and rolled her eyes into the webcam. "But as usual, my best friend Raine has my back, so here I am with the next *Hottie of the Week*. Before I can give you his stats, I need a break, so I'll be back in a few." She pressed pause on the webcam, swiveled the chair around, and faced me. "Thank you. I'm starving."

I threw her a bag of potato chips, which she snatched in mid-air. Keeping the door between us, I dangled a can of soda her way.

"Come on. I'm not going to ambush you," Cora protested.

"Liar. Just remember, I'll unfriend you on every social network if you do it again, Cora Jemison," I threatened.

Cora pouted. "You're never going let me forget that, are you? One lapse in judgment, Raine. *One*, and I'm labeled a liar for the rest of my life."

"Just until we finish high school. Lucky for you, we've got less than two years to go." Melodramatic was Cora's middle name, which made her the perfect video blogger. I, on the other hand, hated seeing my face on video hosting websites, something she tended to forget when she got excited. "So, when will you be done? We have swimming, and I need to get online, too."

"Ten minutes, but I'm skipping today. Keith and I are going to watch our guys crush the Cougars. Go-oh, Trojans." She pumped her fist in the air. "Come with us, Raine. Please… please? You can help me choose my next victim for the vlog."

"I can't. I have an AP English report to write."

"Another one? That's, like, what? One every week? I knew sour-faced Quibble would be tough when he e-mailed you guys a summer reading list." She shuddered. "You should have dropped his class when you had chance."

"Why? I enjoy it." Cora made a face, and I knew what she was thinking. I needed a life outside of books. She said it often enough, as though swimming and playing an oboe in the band didn't count. I'd rather read than cheer cocky, idolized football players any day. Performing in the pep band during home games was enough contribution to the school spirit as far as I was concerned.

"Fine, stay at home with your boring books, but keep your phone with you," she ordered. "I'll update you during the game." She snatched the drink from my hand, opened it, and took a swig. "Thanks." She swiveled and rolled the chair back to my computer desk and turned on the webcam. "Okay, *Hottie of the Week* is in my Biology class. He's five-eleven, masculine without being buff. Don't ask how I know. A girl is allowed to keep some secrets, right?" She giggled and twirled a lock of blonde hair. "He's a member of the lacrosse team and has wavy Chex Mix hair, which is longer than I usually like on a guy, but he rocks it. Don't you just love that term? Chex Mix. Better than dirty blond, right? I stole that from Raine."

I closed the door and shook my head. Poor guy. By Wednesday, every girl in school would be speculating about his identity and his relationship with Cora, not to mention leaving snarky comments on her video blog. She thrived on being naughty, but one day she would cross the line and piss someone off.

Cora and I had been tight since junior high when I found her crying in the girls' locker room after P.E. She'd had such a hard time adjusting to public school after being homeschooled. Seeing her now, you'd never guess it. She was crazy popular, even though she didn't hang out with the in-crowd.

Downstairs, I got comfortable on the couch with my copy of *Grapes of Wrath* by John Steinbeck, tucked a pencil for scribbling notes behind my ear, and popped open my favorite spicy baked chips. Good thing Mr. Q had included the book on our summer reading list and I already read it once.

The ding of the doorbell resounded in the house before I finished my assignment. I grinned. Must be Eirik, my unofficial boyfriend. I jumped up, raced to the door, and yanked it open.

"About time you got he…"

I took a step back, my pulse leaping. In one sweeping glance, I took in the stranger's shaggy black hair, piercing Pacific-blue eyes under arched eyebrows, black leather jacket, and hip-hugging jeans. Either fate had conjured the poster boy of all my fantasies and deposited him on my doorstep or I was dreaming.

I closed my eyes tight and then opened them again.

He was still there, the only thing missing was a bow or a note with my name pinned to his forehead. Irrationally, I wondered how it would feel to run my fingers through his hair. It was luxurious and so long it brushed the collar of his jacket. His lips moved, and I realized he was speaking.

"What?" I asked. The single word came out in two syllables, and I cringed. *Lame, Raine.*

"I asked if you'd seen Eirik Seville," the stranger said impatiently in a deep, commanding voice as though he was used to giving orders, "and you shook your head. Does that mean you didn't understand what I said, don't know him, or don't know where he is?"

"I, uh, the third one." Could I be any lamer? Worse, warmth crept up my face. "I mean, I don't know where he is," I said in a squeaky voice.

"He said he would be at the house of..." he pulled out a piece of paper from the back of his biker glove, the fingerless kind, and read, "Raine Cooper."

"That's me. Lorraine Cooper, but everyone calls me Raine. You know, rain with a silent E," I said even though he didn't ask for an explanation. I tended to blabber when nervous. "Yeah, well, Eirik's not here."

"When do you expect him? Or should I ask when does he *usually* get here, Raine with an E?" the guy asked.

I bristled, not liking his mocking tone or the way he spoke slowly as though I was a dimwit. "He doesn't always come here after school, you know. You could try his house or text him."

Mr. Hot-but-arrogant shrugged. "If I wanted to use modern technology I would, but I'd rather not. Could you do me a favor?"

Use modern technology? Which cave did he crawl from? He spoke with a trace of an accent that had a familiar lilt. British or Aussie? I could never tell the difference.

He sighed. "You're shaking your head again. Did my question confuse you? Am I talking too fast, too slow, or is it me? I've been told my presence tends to, uh, throw people off."

I crossed my arms, lifted my chin, and stared down my nose at him. I was usually the calm one among my friends, the peacemaker, but this guy was seriously pushing my buttons with his arrogance. "No."

His eyebrows rose and met the lock of hair falling over his forehead. "No to what?"

"No, you didn't confuse me. And no, I won't do you a favor."

He rolled his eyes, plucked wraparound sunglasses from the breast pocket of his jacket, and slipped them on before turning to leave.

Yeah, good riddance. To copy Cora's favorite saying, 'he just lost hotness points'.

He paused as though he'd changed his mind and faced me, the corners of his mouth lifting in a slow smile. "Okay, Raine with an E, what do I have to do to make you play nice?"

Whoa, what a smile. I was still staring at his lips when what he'd said registered. I peered at him, hating that I had to look up at him. At five-seven, I was above average for a girl, but he was taller. Six-two or three I'd guess. Worse, my face stared back at me from the surface of his dark sunglasses, making me feel like I was talking to myself.

"Stop being rude and condescending for starters," I said.

He chuckled, the sound rich and throaty. Sexy. A delicious shiver ran up my spine. "I thought I was being extremely polite."

I snorted. "Right."

"Do I need to apologize?"

"Not if you don't mean it."

"Then I won't."

I debated whether to step back and slam the door on his face, but I couldn't bring myself to do it. One, it was rude. Two, I wanted to know why he was looking for Eirik. "Okay, shoot. What's the favor?"

"Tell your boyfriend that he and I need to talk. Today. In the next hour if possible."

That annoying, commanding tone got to me again. I mock saluted him. "Yes, sir."

He chuckled, then did something strange. He reached out and touched my nose. "Cute. Nice meeting you, Raine with an E."

Cute? Ew. I reached up to swat his hand, but he was already turning away. I followed him, not realizing what I was doing until I reached the driveway. Where was he going? He wore biker's gloves, but there was no motorcycle parked at the curb. He turned left, moving past our mailbox.

"What's your name?" I called out.

He turned, lowered his sunglasses, and studied me suspiciously. "Why do you want to know?"

"I don't," I said with as much distain as I could muster, "but Eirik will need a name to go with the message."

"My name won't mean anything to him. Just tell him the message is from your new neighbor."

My stomach hollowed out as though I'd jumped off a plane without a parachute. He couldn't possibly be my next-door neighbor. A week ago, the For Sale sign had disappeared, but I hadn't seen any moving truck to indicate someone was moving in.

Please, let his home be farther down the street. Several houses around my neighborhood had been up for sale the last year. Using a trip to our mailbox as an excuse, I continued to watch him. Nice walk. Too bad it was overshadowed by his arrogance. He passed the low-lying white fence separating our yard from our next-door neighbor's then cut across the lawn and headed for the front door.

Crap.

He stepped on the patio, turned, and looked at me, a mocking smile on his sculptured lips. I averted my eyes and pretended to sift the bills in my hand. As soon as he disappeared inside, I pulled my cell phone from my pocket and furiously texted Eirik.

"Who was that?" Cora asked from on top of the stairs when I entered the house.

I bumped the door closed with my foot and dropped the mail on the foyer table. "Our new neighbor."

She hurried down the stairs. "Eirik's old house or down the street neighbor?"

"Eirik's old house."

"Oh, I hate you. How come hot guys don't move next door to my house?"

"That's because you live on a farm in the middle of nowhere," I retorted.

"Yeah, whatever." She ran across the living room to the kitchen window and peered outside like an overstimulated terrier. "Where is he? Where did he go?"

I grinned. Trust Cora to provide me with comic relief. I collected my books, the empty bag of chips and soda can I had left on the coffee table, and followed her. "I told you, Eirik's place."

"Ooh, if he takes Eirik's old bedroom, he'd be able to see right inside yours and you his."

"And that's interesting because…?"

"We want to see him shirtless."

"Hey, don't include me in your craziness."

She made a face and mouthed the words I'd just said. "Oh, live a little, Raine. Seriously, sometimes I wonder how we can be so tight. You move slower than a slug when it comes to guys."

"And you go at warp speed."

Her jaw dropped. "Are you calling me a—"

"Male connoisseur… aficionado… nothing tacky." We laughed. Cora fell in love fast and often, and got bored just as easily. I was only interested in one guy: Eirik. He and I had been neighbors until last year when they moved up the hill to one of the mansions at the end of Orchard Road. I never worried about him seeing inside my bedroom. The thought of the new guy that close to me was, I don't know, unsettling. I dumped the soda can and bag in the garbage and started toward the stairs.

"It would be like old times," Cora continued, moving away from the window, "except with him instead of boring Eirik."

"Eirik's not boring."

"Is to. So what's Mr. Hotness' name? What did he want? Is he throwing a meet-the-new-neighbor party? First dibs on your plus-one." She looked at me expectantly.

I laughed. "No one throws that kind of a party around here. I don't know his name, and he was looking for Eirik."

"Pretty Boy knows him? He just lost hotness points," Cora mumbled.

"I heard that." I waited for her to catch up before I continued upstairs. "I don't get it. You and Eirik used to get along so well. Now all you do is snipe at each other every time you're in the same room. What happened?"

"He talks down to me, like I'm stupid or something."

"He does not."

"Does to. Today I asked him to help me with a math problem, and he looked at me like I was a slug masquerading as a human being. Then he smirked and told me to ask Keith. He can be so...” She growled, her eyes narrowing. “I wanted to smack him. I should have smacked him.”

Cora was smart, but she tended to act helpless around guys, which drove Eirik nuts. Deciding not to comment, I pushed open my bedroom door, and my eyes went to the window facing our neighbor’s. The wide window seat with its comfortable cushions was my favorite relaxing spot in the room. Outside, I preferred the wicker chairs on my side of the balcony. I was going to have to deal with my new neighbor whether I liked it or not.

Cora removed the cute little jacket she’d worn over her tank top, threw it on my bed, and walked to the window. She and I were about the same height, except she was skinnier and had bigger boobs. Throw in her blonde hair and gray eyes and you had every teenage boy’s fantasy. I was rounder with brown hair and hazel eyes, nothing to brag about, but I wasn’t at the shallow end of the beauty pool either.

“How does he know Eirik? Do you think he’s going to go to our school?” Cora asked.

“I don’t know *anything* about him, Cora.”

She threw me an annoyed look. “Only you can talk to a hot guy and forget to ask important questions. I would have gotten everything from him, including whether he has a girlfriend or not.”

She wasn’t bragging. Cora was amazingly good at gathering information, and she could be relentless when it came to guys, which is great for a vlogger. Sometimes it was funny, but other times annoying. Like now. I couldn’t tell her I’d been too busy making a fool of myself to say much to my blue-eyed neighbor.

“Are you done with my laptop?” I asked, settling on the bed. “I have to check a few things after I finish my report.”

Cora glanced at her watch. “Keith will be here in ten minutes, so I just need a few minutes to respond to comments; then it’s all yours.” She glanced outside then at me then back outside again. “It’s such a beautiful day. Let’s sit outside on the balcony.”

Oh, she thought she was clever. The weather was perfect, but I refused to be a groupie to that rude guy. “No, I’m fine in here.”

Cora pouted. “Pwease… pwetty pwease?”

I shook my head. “I want to focus on my work. You want to talk to my new neighbor, walk to his house and knock on the door.”

A thoughtful expression settled on her pretty face. “I might just do that.”

"Good. Just remember, you have a boyfriend," I reminded her.

She grinned. "Yeah, but I'm a mere mortal with a weakness for guys built like gods. I could feature him on my vlog."

I hope not. He looked like the type who could tear Cora apart if she dared. "You don't even know if he'll be going to our school."

"I would if you'd bothered to ask him." Cora sighed dramatically and settled on the window seat with my laptop. Occasionally, she stared outside. I was tempted to ask her if my new neighbor was outside, which bugged me. I shouldn't be interested in any guy period. I had Eirik—or I *would* if he could get his act together and ask me out. I hoped his feelings for me were just as strong as mine were for him. As for Cora, her restlessness made it impossible for me to focus. I was happy when Keith picked her up.

Less than an hour later, I grabbed by swim bag and raced outside. I had ten minutes to get my butt to Total Fitness Club for swim practice. I'd swum varsity since my freshman year, but high school swim season didn't start until next week. Off season, I swam with the Dolphins. Luckily, Matt 'Doc' Fletcher, my high school coach, also coached the Dolphins. Kayville might be a small town in northwestern Oregon, but we had three high schools and three swim clubs, and the rivalry was fierce. Most Dolphins went to my high school, too.

I threw my bag in the front passenger seat of my Sentra, ran around the hood, and saw the right front tire. I had a leak? It looked low. Could I take a chance and drive it? Maybe if I drove carefully and slow? Coach Fletcher was anal about tardiness. Worse, my attendance this past summer had suffered because of Dad.

My throat closed and tears rushed to my eyes. Not knowing whether my father was alive or dead was the hardest part of my nightmare. I still remembered the last conversation we'd had before he boarded the plane in Honolulu, the horror at the news about the plane crashing into the Pacific Ocean, the frustration as bodies were recovered and none matched Dad's. I was losing hope, while Mom still believed he was alive. How could he be after three months?

Our neighbors no longer asked us if we'd heard any news, but I'd overheard Mrs. Rutledge and Mrs. Ross from across the street gossip about Mom, calling her delusional. Prune-faced hags. I hated that we lived on the same cul-de-sac.

I kicked at the tire as though the simple act would ease my frustration, then pulled out my cell phone and checked for text messages. There was none from Eirik, which meant I couldn't ask him for a ride. *I hope he's at practice in case I need help with my car.* I texted him before calling Mom.

"Hey, sweetie." She sounded preoccupied.

"I have swimming, but I think my front tire has a leak and—"

"I can't leave work right now to drop you off. I'm dealing with a mini-crisis, too. Skip swimming, and we'll take care of your car when I get home. Call Coach Fletcher and explain."

"That's okay. I can still drive it. It's a slow leak and should hold until—"

"No, Raine. If you must go, hitch a ride with Eirik or Cora. I don't want you driving with a leaking tire."

"Cora's gone to the football game, and Eirik is not returning my calls. I can't miss practice, Mom. Coach has a big announcement to make, and today's the last class before tryouts for varsity." I'd be mortified if he knew why I'd been flaky the last several months. I still hoped no one at school knew about my father, except Cora and Eirik. "You know how he secretly uses summer club swim attendance to choose co-captains. I don't want to be the first co-captain to be dropped after one year."

Mom humphed, which warned me she was about to switch to Mother Bear mode. "I don't care how he chooses captains. You've earned it. I'll call him and—" There was a cracking sound in the background.

"What was that?"

"Jared dropped a mirror." There was mumbling in the background, then silence.

"Mom?"

More mumbled words reached me before, "I'm here. About the coach—"

"Don't call him. I'll take care of it."

"Are you sure?" She sounded frazzled.

"Yes."

"Okay. I'll try to be home early. Six-ish."

That meant seven or eight. My parents owned Mirage, a framing and mirror store on Main Street. With Dad gone, Mom was pulling double duty and often stayed behind to clean up and get the shop ready for the next business day. I rarely saw her anymore.

I texted Coach Fletcher, in case I didn't make it on time, then slipped behind the wheel. The tire pressure should hold. *Please, let it hold.*

I backed out of the driveway and reached out to shift gears when my new neighbor left his garage, pushing a Harley. Shirtless. I swallowed, drooled. His shoulders were broad and well-defined. His stomach ripped.

He glanced my way, and I quickly averted my eyes and stepped on the gas pedal. My car shot backwards instead of forward and slammed into something, jerking me forward. Panicking, I hit the brakes and looked behind me.

"Oh, crap." Of all the mailboxes on our cul-de-sac, I just had to hit the Petersons'.

Cursing, I shifted gears, moved forward until I got off the curb, switched off the engine, and jumped out of the car. Everyone had their mailboxes imbedded in concrete, but not the Petersons. They had to go overboard and use a fancy, custom-made miniature version of their house. Now the post leaned sideways like the Tower of Pisa, with red paint from my car all over the white pole. Their mailbox was totaled, the mail scattered on the ground.

Someone called out something, but I was busy imagining Mr. Peterson's reaction when he saw his mailbox. He was a big conspiracy theorist. The government and people were always out to get him. He'd believe I deliberately knocked down his stupid mailbox.

"That looks bad," Blue Eyes said from behind me, startling me.

"You think?"

He chuckled. "From that snarky comment, you must be okay."

"Peachy."

I picked up the mail. He moved closer as he helped, bringing with him a masculine scent hard to describe. It bugged the crap out of me that I liked it. Worse, the heat from his body seemed to leap through the air and wrap around me in ways I couldn't describe.

My mouth went dry. The instinct to put space between us came from nowhere, but I ignored it. Only cowards ran when faced with something they didn't understand, and my parents didn't raise one. Still, a delicious shiver shot up my spine, and a weird feeling settled in my stomach.

I waited until I was in control of my emotions before turning to face him. I tried not to stare at his masculine arms and chest. I really did, but all that tanned skin was so inviting and begging to be ogled. I'd seen countless shirtless guys before. Half the swim team spent time in tight shorts that left very little to the imagination, but their bodies were nothing like his. He must be seriously into working out. No one could be this ripped without hitting the gym daily.

"My face is up here, Freckles."

My eyes flew to his, and heat flooded my cheeks. I rushed into speech to cover my embarrassment. "I, uh, I was just leaving to go to swim practice and… and…"

"I distracted you. Sorry about that."

He didn't sound sorry. "You didn't."

He cocked his eyebrows. "Didn't what?"

"Distract me," I snapped and snatched the mail in his hands. "Thanks. I was checking my text messages when I should have been paying attention to where I was going," I fibbed.

Amusement flared in his eye, his expression saying he recognized my explanation for what it was: a lie. He had incredibly long lashes and beautiful eyes. Sapphire came to mind but…

Grinding my teeth at my weird behavior, I started toward the driver's seat, going for that space between us before I did something stupid like reach out and touch him or continue gazing into his eyes like a lovesick dimwit.

"Aren't you going to tell them you hit their mailbox? I mean, it's against the law to flee a crime scene and all that."

I glared at him. "I will talk to them when they come home from work. For now, I plan on leaving them a note. Not that it's any of your business." I searched inside the glove compartment for a notepad or anything to write on, but found nothing.

"I could explain to them what happened if you'd like," he offered in a gentle voice. "You know, share the responsibility. After all, I did distract you."

Seriously, how could someone so beautiful and tempting be so arrogant and annoying? I counted from ten to one then said slowly, "I don't need your help."

"Actually, you do."

"No, I don't." I marched to my house, conscious of Blue Eyes watching me. Sure enough, when I looked back, just before I entered the house, his eyes were locked on me, an amused smile on his lips. What was he so happy about? And why couldn't he just go away?

I pulled a piece of ruled paper from my folder and scribbled an apology with unsteady hands, then went to Dad's home office for a large manila envelope. Times like this, I missed him more. My eyes welled.

I blinked hard and put everything from the Petersons' mailbox into the large envelope before taping my note on the outside. I'd have to figure out how to pay for a new mailbox. Mom didn't like me working at the shop ever since I broke a few mirrors last summer, and jobs were hard to come by because of the bad economy. Something would come to me once I was calmer. Right now, I just wanted to get my butt to the pool and lose myself swimming.

I paused to calm myself before leaving the house.

Blue Eyes was studying the damaged mailbox like an insurance adjuster. Why couldn't he go bother someone else? Or at least put on a shirt?

"Excuse me." I skirted around him and propped the manila envelope against the crooked pole.

"I can fix this before they come home," he said.

I eyed him suspiciously. "Really? How?"

A weird expression crossed his face, but his eyes were watchful as though he couldn't wait to see my reaction. "Magic."

"Magic?" My hands fisted. I was in trouble, and he was messing around. "You know what? Stay away from me, Blue Eyes. Don't talk to me or even acknowledge we know each other when our paths cross again. "

"Blue Eyes?" he asked, eyebrows cocked.

"That's me *playing nice.*"

He laughed. "Look, Freckles—"

"Don't call me that." I hated that nickname. It was a reminder of the hated spots on the bridge of my nose and the teasing I'd endured in elementary school. I slid behind the wheel, started the car, and took off. I was careful not to drive too fast even though I wanted to floor the gas pedal.

I could see Blue Eyes watching me as he grew smaller and smaller in the rearview mirror, until I left our cul-de-sac and turned right. My day had just gone down the toilet.

***

I was twenty minutes late for practice and still pissed off at myself for overreacting to my nosey new neighbor. So he had a hot body and an attitude? Big whoop. He was the least of my problems. I had my family to worry about, my position as co-captain to defend, and a guy I was crazy about to convince I'd make a great girlfriend.

"Did you fix your flat?" Coach Fletcher asked when I walked to the pool deck.

"I'll take it to DC Tires after practice." I slid in the pool and joined the thirty members of the Gold Team. Silver and Bronze swam at five.

We had eight lanes, but two were reserved for club members, which meant we shared lanes, taking turns pushing off the wall and looping each other. I didn't see Eirik. He rarely skipped practice, so that was weird.

Following Coach Fletcher's instructions, I finished my freestyle warm up laps while the others worked on their backstroke. I attacked the water like it was my enemy, although I wasn't sure who I was ticked off at, me or my new neighbor. When I started studying the male swimmers and comparing their bodies to Blue Eyes, I knew I was definitely my own enemy.

"Since all of you swim for the Trojans, don't forget we have Ultimate Frisbee tomorrow afternoon at Longmont Park. We'll meet in the north field at four o'clock," Coach Fletcher said at the end of practice. "I sent your parents e-mails last week, so no excuses. This is supposed to be for the team, but we'll meet some of the new swimmers and discuss a few things. Tryouts start on the seventeenth, which is sooner than we usually start. Why, you may ask?" He grinned and paused for effect. "We'll be hosting Jesuit High and Lake Oswego on the twenty-ninth at Walkersville's swimming pool."

Everyone started talking at once. Others high-fived each other. The two schools produced the best swimmers every year and often won at state championships. We'd never hosted them before.

"In the meantime," Coach Fletcher continued, "I'll need volunteers to work with some of the new swimmers. Any takers?"

No one raised a hand. Coach Fletcher crossed his beefy arms and studied us with piercing black eyes. He was a short, stubby man with a receding hairline, who preferred to shave all of his hair, but took extreme care with his beard and moustache. "Come on, guys. I need volunteers."

I looked around and saw Eel's hand shoot up. 'Eel' was Jessica Davenport, our senior co-captain and our swim team bad girl. Sighing, I raised mine. A few more shot up.

"Good. You'll each work with a student the last thirty minutes of practice every day. If they need extra coaching and you want more time, let me know and I'll okay the use of the pool after hours."

"I have pep band practice every other Friday and won't make it to practice," I reminded Coach Fletcher after everyone left.

"We'll have someone sub for you. Where's Cora?"

"She wasn't feeling well when I saw her after school," I fibbed. Coach Fletcher's expression said he didn't believe me. I wasn't surprised. I sucked at lying.

"Tell her to text me."

"Sure. Did Eirik text you?"

"Yes. He explained his situation."

I frowned. "His situation?"

Coach ignored my question and looked at his watch. "If you plan to take your car to the shop, you'd better get going."

It was six fifteen, and DC Tires closed at seven. I didn't bother to shower, just changed and raced to my car. The air pressure held up again, thank goodness. At the shop, while they fixed the leak, I checked my text messages and responded to Cora's, which were funny. The game was close and could go either way, but she sounded like we'd already won. Cora had a way with words.

There were no texts or missed calls from Eirik, which was beginning to worry me. He never missed practice, and he usually answered my messages and calls. Did his absence have anything to do with the 'situation' Coach Fletcher had mentioned?

It was seven when I left the shop for home. I looked at my rearview mirror, convinced I'd heard the sound of a motorcycle start, but there were only cars behind me.

I entered my cul-de-sac, and the first thing I noticed was the Petersons' mailbox. The wooden post no longer leaned sideways, and the tiny house looked normal as though I hadn't hit it. Weird.

As soon as I parked, I hurried to the mailbox and studied it. There were no dents. No new nails hammered in. Nothing out of place. I touched the surface to see if it had been repainted. It was dry as the day Mr. Peterson had unveiled it. I pushed at it to see if it would lean sideways, but the vertical pole anchoring it to the ground was firm.

Where had my new neighbor found a replacement? The Petersons bragged about ordering the miniature mailbox house from some fancy homeowner's website, so there was no way Blue Eyes had bought it locally. Had he used magic? Yeah. Right. There was no such thing as magic.

CHAPTER 2. MORE THAN FRIENDS

The scent of food greeted me as I entered the house. Mom was home early, as promised, with takeout. Cooking wasn't her thing.

"I'm home," I called out, closing the door behind me and dropping my gym bag by the stairs. "Mom?"

"Be down in a sec."

I went to the kitchen and got a bottle of water from the fridge. As I guzzled it, I glanced out the window at my neighbor's house, my humiliation returning. I had to go over and thank him for fixing the mailbox. My pulse leaped at the thought, and my mouth went dry.

Think about Eirik… Think about Eirik…

I yanked the cord and closed the slats, then sneaked a cookie from the cookie jar. Chocolate chip, yummy. My favorite.

"Hey, sweetheart," Mom said as she entered the kitchen.

I shoved the rest of the cookie in my mouth, turned, and almost choked. Her colorful, flowing skirt, gauzy duster, and matching headscarf were way over the top. Mom was a throwback to Woodstock. She had a flamboyant Boho-chic style, which matched her bubbly personality. But at times, I wished she'd dress like regular mothers. You know, wear jeans or normal pants and tops.

Unlike my boring hazel eyes and dark-brown hair, Mom's green eyes and pitch black hair gave her an exotic appearance. She was also tall with a perfect figure for someone who didn't work out. Me? How should I put it? My ass had a mind of its own, and my chest quit on me years ago.

"I'm sorry you had car troubles, sweetie." She kissed my temple and enveloped me in perfume and other scents that defied description but I'd always associated with her. She leaned back and wrinkled her nose. "Eek, your hair reeks of chlorine."

"I didn't have time to wash it. You know, I had to take the car in," I reminded her.

"You drove it after I told you not to?"

"I know I shouldn't have, but I had to go and the leak was slow. Really." I braced myself for a lecture.

She shook her head and cupped my face. "Why do you have such little regard for your life, sweetheart? Do you know what could have happened? I'd hate to lose you in a senseless accident, Raine."

Like Dad. "I'm so sorry, Mom. I didn't think. I drove slowly. I was even late because of it."

She sighed and stroked my hair. "What did the shop say?"

"They fixed the leak. Did you see the e-mail about Ultimate Frisbee from Coach Fletcher?"

She frowned. "No. When did he send it?"

I sighed. Mom rarely used her computer. In fact, I'd reached the conclusion that she hated technology. She did inventory for the Mirage by hand and had piles of thick ledgers gathering dust in the den. "I don't know, but it's tomorrow afternoon at four."

"Do we need to take something? Drinks? Dessert?"

Smiling, I shook my head. "It's Ultimate Frisbee, Mom, not team dinner. How was the store?"

"Other than the broken mirror, business as usual. Go shower. I'll keep the food warm." She stepped back, reached down, and lifted a large paper bag from her hand-made crocheted bag. "Sweet and sour chicken, your favorite, and beef and broccoli for me." She dug inside a bag and pulled out an egg roll, which she dangled teasingly.

I snatched it and munched on it as I headed upstairs to my bedroom. After showering, I changed into sweatpants and a shirt and headed downstairs. Halfway down the stairs, I noticed Mom in front of the mirror in the living room. She was muttering to herself while studying her reflection.

"I can't do it without Tristan. Our daughter needs both of us." She swiped at the wetness on her cheeks. She'd never cried since Dad's plane crashed.

"Mom?"

"Ah, there you are," she said without looking at me. She moved away from the mirror and hurried toward the kitchen. "Let's eat."

I frowned, hustling after her. "Are you okay?"

"Yeah. I wish your father would hurry up and come home."

My throat closed. "Have you heard something?"

"No, sweetie, but three months is too long for him to be missing."

Even though he was listed as a missing person and his case was still open, he could have been at the bottom of the ocean for all we knew. I hated to be negative, but every time I visited the website the airline had created for victims of the flight and found nothing new, my confidence dipped. I didn't know where Mom got her optimism.

She removed the boxes from the microwave and poured herself a glass of wine, which she immediately sipped. "So, what do you want for your seventeenth birthday, sweetheart?"

"I don't know. The usual." I liked my birthday celebrations low key. I hung out with Eirik and Cora, watched my favorite TV series, and pigged out on pizza and cake. "What is it you and Dad wanted to tell me when I turned seventeen? You made it seem like it was important."

"Oh, honey." A haunted look entered her eyes. As though she didn't want me to see her expression, she put down her wine and unwrapped the chopsticks. "We'll explain after your dad comes home."

"Why not now?"

She smiled, reached out, and gripped my chin. "Always impatient. You get that from me. Your father is the patient one." She let go of my chin, picked up her drink, and sipped. "The story can wait. You're only seventeen anyway." She cocked her head, green eyes sparkling. "Let's do something fun together for your birthday, just the two of us."

What did my age have to do with anything? I forced myself to focus on her last statement. "Like what?"

"Mani-pedis. I can call Caridee."

Caridee Jenkins was Mom's manicurist. I never liked people touching my feet, but maybe this once. "Okay. When?"

"Let's see. I have to work tomorrow, and you have the Frisbee thing in the afternoon. Do you have plans for the evening?"

"I was planning on hanging out with Eirik and Cora."

Mom laughed as though to say, what else is new? "Let's have her come over on Sunday afternoon. We could get facials, too."

"Can a facial remove freckles?"

Mom's back stiffened, and her eyes narrowed. Uh-oh, I knew that look. It meant a lecture was coming. I braced myself.

"Lorraine Sarah Cooper, you should be ashamed of yourself. Don't ever do anything to get rid of your freckles." She touched my nose. "They are beautiful, like a sprinkle of gold dust."

I rolled my eyes. She was so biased. My skin would be perfect without them.

When we finished eating, Mom yawned and eyed her bulky bag. As usual, I knew she couldn't wait to disappear upstairs to take a long bath and relax. She worked hard and deserved it. "Go on upstairs, Mom. I'll lock up."

"You sure?"

"I have this covered."

"You do, don't you?" She kissed my forehead and picked up her bag and wine glass. "Goodnight, sweetheart."

"Night, Mom."

Left alone, I checked my phone one last time. Eirik still hadn't returned my calls or answered my text messages. His silence had pushed me past worry to ticked-off. I sent him one last text, then wiped down the counter and left the house for my neighbor's.

My heart picked up tempo with each step. What if he hadn't fixed the mailbox? I'd look like an idiot thanking him for something he hadn't done. Lights were on downstairs and upstairs, but as I got closer, rock music reached me from the other side of the house.

I followed the sounds to the garage, where Blue Eyes sat on a wooden box and tinkered with a greasy thingamajigger that looked like something one pulled out of a robot. I couldn't tell where the music came from, but I recognized the classic rock tune. Not bad.

He didn't glance up or move, yet the music stopped. Magic? No, I shouldn't even think like that. It was illogical. Magic didn't exist.

"I thought we agreed to stay away from each other, Freckles."

I'm not letting him get to me. Not this time. "I plan to, but you fixed the Petersons' mailbox, so I'm here to thank you."

"Courteous? You? What happened to the snarky girl I met earlier? Raine with an E?" He looked up, a wicked smile curling his lips. "I liked her."

I ignored the dig. "How did you do it?"

He wiped his greasy hands on a cloth. "Magic."

"Don't start. Magic is not real."

"Says who?"

"Me. Science. Logic."

"Okay, Freckles. We'll play this your way. We'll say I was inspired, and there're no heights a man can't reach when..." he got up, leaned closer, and whispered, "inspired."

I stepped back. He was overwhelming up close. Vibrant. "Uh, well, I just wanted to say thanks and see how much I owe you for replacing it."

He pulled a folded manila envelope from the back of his pants and offered it to me. It was the envelope I'd used for the Petersons' mail, but the letter I'd taped on it was missing.

"Where's my letter?"

"Check inside. It was a very sweet and sincere apology."

Part of me was outraged he'd read my letter, but I wasn't surprised. He was rude. "So how much do I owe you?"

He pushed his hands in the front pockets of his jeans, giving me a glimpse of skin around his waist. I quickly averted my eyes before he could catch me ogling him again.

"Let's see," he said slowly. "Fixing the mailbox, your car, sitting through tea with the two nosey ladies across the street, and listening to their gossip makes that—"

"You fixed my car? There was no dent on it."

"Scratches. Mrs. Rutledge and Mrs. Ross believed you deliberately crashed into the Petersons' mailbox. The scratches would have confirmed it, but I convinced them they were mistaken."

"Convinced them how?"

"By drinking lukewarm tea and eating rock hard scones." He shuddered.

I smiled despite myself. "Okay. So how much do you want?"

"I don't want your money, Freckles." His voice became serious. "But one day I'll need a favor and you'll drop everything for me."

Put that way, it sounded ominous, like he already knew what favor he planned to ask. I shivered. "As long as it's within reason."

"I've been told I'm a reasonable guy." The smile he gave me was slow and so wicked my breath caught. I stepped back.

"Well, uh, goodnight." I hurried away, but I was aware of his eyes on me.

His laughter reached me when I stopped to check the rear end of my car. Did I really have scratches? How and when had he fixed them? Maybe the motorcycle I'd heard after picking up my car hadn't been a figment of my imagination. He probably went to DC Tires and spray painted over the scratches. One phone call tomorrow should confirm it.

Magic my butt. He was just screwing with my head.

***

A weird rattling yanked me from a bad dream. I sat up and stared around in confusion, not sure whether I was still dreaming, but the dull hum filling my room was as familiar as the hated freckles on the bridge of my nose. My bedroom was the only room in our house with a vintage fan that droned all night like a plane's engine. According to Mom, the fan belonged in the junkyard or some metal sculptor's masterpiece. I disagreed. The fan was one-of-a-kind, like something straight out of a steampunk book, my latest craze.

I glanced at the clock on my dresser. Almost midnight. I'd barely gone to bed. Sliding under the covers, I closed my eyes and tried to force myself to fall asleep.

The rattling came again, and realization hit me. Someone was throwing pebbles at my window. Only one person could wake me up in the middle of the night and get away with it.

Eirik.

I flung the covers aside, ran to the window, and looked outside. He stood under the tree, shafts of street light bouncing off his golden locks, his faithful companion—a Nikon camera—hanging around his neck.

"I'm coming up," he called.

"No, you're not."

"C'mon, Raine." He started up the tree right by the house where the balcony ended.

"You didn't answer my calls or texts," I griped.

"I didn't have my phone. I still don't." For a six-foot-one guy, he was agile. But then again, he'd been climbing up this particular tree since elementary school. I still couldn't do it without scraping something. He landed on the balcony like a lithe jungle cat and flashed his famous sweet smile, amber eyes begging. "Let me in, please."

I crossed my arms. "Why should I?"

He rolled his eyes. "You're dying to know where I've been."

I was, but I had to take a stance. If I'd ignored his calls, he'd be pissed. He had a terrible temper. "Not interested."

"I'm sorry I didn't return your calls and texts. I was pissed, and my cell phone flew right out of my hand and hit a wall."

I frowned. "You mean you threw it."

"If you must be so literal," he said then added, "Uh, my parents are back."

The pain in his voice killed all my protests. His parents were cold, standoffish. They were the least loving people ever. I unlocked the window and stepped back, flipping on the light on my computer desk.

As soon as he stepped inside, I hugged him. He wrapped his arms around me and buried his face in my hair. Eirik and I had been inseparable since we were kids. We grew up together and played in our backyards, which were connected before his parents decided one day to add the stupid fence. We'd shared everything, and in third grade, we'd even promised to marry each other. He was my best friend, and there was not a thing I didn't know about him. His parents had adopted him when he was a baby, but instead of showering him with love and attention, they'd spent most of their time traveling and leaving him with nannies and a housekeeper. He'd spent most of his waking and sleeping hours at our house as a child and that hadn't changed. Sometimes I wondered how my loving parents could be friends with his.

"How long are they going to be around this time?" I asked, stepping back.

"They're not. They are talking about moving back home."

Home was somewhere in northern Europe. I panicked. Dad was still missing, and I refused to lose someone else I loved.

"No. You can't leave. We promised we'd graduate together, go to college, and—"

"Hey… hey…" Eirik gripped my arms and peered into my eyes. "I've spent the last several hours trying to convince them to let me stay."

"What did they say?"

"They'll think about it."

That wasn't good enough. "I can't lose you too, Eirik. Not now."

He chuckled, lifted his camera, and snapped a picture of me. "I'm not going anywhere, worrywart, and your dad will be back. Your mother believes it, and if you haven't noticed, she tends to be right about everything." He bumped my arm with his, then placed his camera on my computer desk. "So, can I stay?"

"Like you need to ask." He used to curl up on the window seat with a blanket, but then he turned thirteen, shot up, and the window seat became too small.

He pulled the rollout bed from under my bed and plopped on top of it. Other than Cora, most people at school assumed Eirik and I were a couple because we did everything together. Not that I cared what anyone thought. I had no interest in other guys, and he hadn't shown interest in any other girls. He and I would be so great together.

I threw him two pillows and lay on my tummy, so I could look at him as we talked. "You should move in with us. Mom can talk to your parents if you'd like."

"No, I have it covered."

He sounded confident, so I nodded. "Okay. About the new guy in your old house, he came looking for you."

He frowned, amber eyes narrowing. "Torin?"

So that was his name. Torin. It suited him. "Yeah, dark hair, leather jacket, and a Harley." *Dipped in arrogance,* I added silently.

Eirik frowned. "He didn't do or say anything to piss you off, did he?"

"No. Why do you ask?"

"You wore a weird expression just now." Eirik put his hands behind his head, and I found myself comparing him to Torin. Both guys were hot in their own way, though Eirik with his blond locks and amber eyes could be considered pretty. Physically, he was leaner and paler, masculine without being overpowering. Torin was taller with a wide chest, narrow hips, and ripped stomach. The guy had zero fat.

"Do you want the lights off?" Eirik asked.

For a moment, I stared at him, my mind a hot mess. I shook my head to rattle my brain back into place. "No. So, what did Torin want?"

He shrugged. "I don't know. I guess I'll find out tomorrow. Why are you staring at me like that?"

He was a sucky liar and tended to fidget, like now. "Like what?"

"Like I'm Pinocchio and you're the Wicked Witch of the West."

"Who's Torin?"

Eirik shrugged. "He's related to one of my parents' travel buddies, I think. They were worked up about his sudden arrival, which for my parents is pretty unusual."

Yeah, nothing ever ruffled their feathers, which meant Torin's people must be important. "So you've never met him before?"

"Nope." He frowned. "Why the interest?"

"You're fidgety, and that usually means you're hiding something."

He gave me an innocent smile. "I'm clean."

"Yeah, right. How long have you known about your parents' plans to move back to, uh, where's their native home? Sweden? Norway?"

"Denmark. I've known since last month." He sighed dramatically. "Can we go to sleep now?"

"Not after that confession." I sat up. "You knew for a month and said nothing to me? Why?"

He rolled his eyes. "Because I knew you'd stress about it."

"I don't stress."

"*And* drive me insane like you're doing right now," he added. "You're like a dog with a bone when you go after something."

"That is so insulting." I hit him with a pillow. He grabbed it and yanked, catching me off guard. I lost my balance and landed on top of him.

"Get off me," he grumbled.

"No." I wiggled to get comfortable, rested my cheek on his chest, right under his chin, and wedged my hands between him and the mattress. He smelled good. He always did. "How come I'm always cold and you're always so hot?"

"That's because you're a girl and I'm... me."

"Meaning what?"

"Nothing," he said quickly. "Just go back to your bed, Raine."

"Why?" I asked, pouting. "I'm comfy."

"I'm not."

I lifted my chin and studied him. He stared back at me with calm, intelligent amber eyes that could be warm one second and impossible to read the next. He had amazing cheekbones and a jaw that could have been sculpted by a master. His hair was a perfect blend of gold and brown. Chex Mix hair. He'd inspired me to come up with that expression. He really was beautiful, and any girl would be lucky to have him as a boyfriend. So why wasn't he officially mine? He'd never indicated he wanted us to be more, yet I've caught him staring at me with a weird expression.

"We've slept together before," I reminded him.

"We're not young anymore."

"No, we're not." His amber eyes darkened, and an insane idea popped into my mind. "Kiss me."

He frowned. "Why?"

"I ask you to kiss me and you ask why?"

He grinned. "Absolutely. You don't do anything without a reason." His eyes narrowed. "I know what you're doing you sneaky little... You're trying to get out of wearing the *T-shirt of Shame*."

He could be such a tool sometimes. Why I desperately wanted him to kiss me now was beyond me. Still, his lack of interest hurt. We'd made a pact that by our seventeenth birthday, if we hadn't kissed someone, and I mean seriously kissed with open mouth and tongue, we would wear a T-shirt with the words *Seventeen and Never Been Kissed.* He'd turned seventeen six months ago and worn his T-shirt without an ounce of shame because that was the kind of guy he was. Bold and cocky, but in an endearing away, unlike a certain neighbor. Girls at school had thought it was a joke and stopped him in the hallway, in class, outside school, everywhere to kiss him. The whole incident had started out funny, but it became annoying fast.

"Raine?"

"Okay, you busted me. I don't want to wear the stupid T-shirt." I pushed off him, turned off the light, and crawled back into my bed. I could hear him move about as though trying to get comfortable.

"If I thought you meant it, I'd kiss you," he said.

"Oh, shut up." He was humoring me now.

Another stretch of silence followed, and I wondered what he was thinking. "You are in a crazy mood tonight," he said.

He had no idea. "Do you remember the pact we made when we were ten?" I asked.

"Which one? I lost count after the one about not having sleepovers when you grew boobs."

I giggled, remembering that conversation. "So, why are you here?"

"I don't know. What pact are you talking about?"

We'd vowed to always discuss anything that bothered us. Torin bothered me in a way I didn't understand, yet I couldn't see myself discussing him with Eirik.

"We said we'd apply to the same colleges our junior year," I improvised.

"Don't worry about it. We *will* go to the same school."

If only I could be sure of myself the way he was. "I think we should choose now and go for early decision. Berkley maybe or... Where are you going?" I asked when he sat up.

"Can't you see it?" He pointed outside.

The light from the upstairs bedroom in Torin's house was flickering on and off. Three flashes, pause, one, pause, three. It was a signal Eirik and I had developed and used whenever one of us wanted to talk. "How does he know our signal?"

"I don't know," Eirik said, sounding pissed.

"Wait." But Eirik was already across the room. He opened the window. I followed as he scrambled down the tree. I could see a silhouette in his old bedroom. Torin. The flickering light stopped. Seconds later, Torin opened his front door and stepped outside.

How did he move so fast? Or was there someone else with him in the house? A parent perhaps? I couldn't climb the stupid tree, so I peered at them from the balcony. Their voices didn't carry, which only added to my frustration.

After a few minutes, Eirik came back and stood at the foot of the tree. "Throw down my keys."

I frowned. "Why?"

"I'm heading home. My mother called him."

I glanced at Torin. He was leaning against the porch pole, his arms crossed and eyes on Eirik as though making sure he left. "I'm coming down there."

Eirik shook his head. "No, Raine. You'll break something."

"I'm not using the tree." I closed the window behind me, grabbed his keys, shoes, and camera, and crept along the hallway. There was no sound from my mom's bedroom, but she was a light sleeper. I frowned, hating the fact that I was starting to think of the bedroom as hers instead of hers and Dad's. Downstairs, I found Eirik waiting outside the front entrance. "What's going on?"

"I don't know, but I've got to go." He looped his camera around his neck and slipped on his shoes.

"Why did your parents call *him* and not me?"

"Because they always assume I'm at the old house whenever I'm not home." He took his keys, and for a moment, he stared down at me. The silence stretched. I was so sure he'd kiss me, especially when his eyes went to my lips. Instead, he stepped back, lifted his camera, and clicked. He grinned when I scowled. He clicked again. "Night, Raine. See you tomorrow."

I walked down the driveway and watched him drive off, then glanced at Torin's house. He stood on the porch, still leaning against the pole, except his eyes were now focused on me.

What was his game? I wanted to march over there and demand answers, but I was too pissed. I turned, entered the house, and crawled into bed. Sleep eluded me for so long and when I finally slept, I had a weird dream I was being chased by something invisible.

***

The scent of fried eggs reached me when I woke up. Dad. He often cooked a special breakfast on my birthdays. Excited, I ran downstairs, taking two steps at a time. I stopped when I reached the kitchen and saw Mom at the stove turning scrambled eggs in a pan. Disappointment rolled through me.

"Happy birthday, sweetheart," she called out, bangles jiggling on her wrists, her hand-made stone necklace and matching earrings bearing the same weird symbols. "Eggs and toast coming up."

Smoke drifted from the toaster. I popped the toast out. "Do you need help with anything?"

"No, I'm doing fine." She turned off the stove and turned to study me. "When are you wearing your shameful shirt?"

I frowned. "*T-shirt of shame?* What... how did you know?"

"Sweetie, you're my only child. Of course I know everything you do, including bets you make with your friends or when they sneak in and out of your room instead of using the front door." She glanced toward the stairs. "When's Eirik coming downstairs?"

I opened my mouth, then closed it without saying a world. No wonder the table was set for three. "Since you know everything, you should know the answer to that question."

She chuckled and glanced at me from the corners of her eyes. "Speaking of the T-shirt of shame, you and he haven't kissed or—"

"No-oh." Images from last night flashed in my head, making me blush. "He was feeling kind of sad last night. His parents are thinking of moving back home to Europe, and he's trying to convince them to let him stay here and finish high school."

Color drained from Mom's face, leaving her pale. "Really? I must talk to Sari and Johan."

"Eirik said you shouldn't."

Mom walked to where I stood and rubbed my arms. "I'm so sorry, sweetheart. I know how close you two are."

"Can he live with us if they let him stay?"

"I don't know." She stepped back. "That depends on his parents. If they don't mind, of course he can stay with us." She picked up a toast and scraped the burnt parts into the garbage can before scooping the eggs onto two plates. The top side of the eggs looked undercooked.

I tried not to cringe. She was trying, so no matter how gross it tasted, I'd eat it. "About tonight, I'll need money for pizza and drinks."

"Okay. Remind me to add money to your debit card, too. Oh, and I'll buy the cake."

"Double chocolate with whipped cream frosting," I said.

She laughed. "Double chocolate it is. Get my wallet, sweetie, will you?"

I rummaged inside her hand-woven bag, found her wallet, and placed it on the table. After pulling out some bills, which she handed to me, she picked up her plate.

"I'll be home early with the cake. Happy birthday." She touched my cheek, turned, and walked away, forking her eggs. She disappeared upstairs.

The eggs were so terrible even pepper couldn't save them. I reached for a toast and smeared it with jelly. I was munching on a piece when Mom reappeared downstairs.

"Bye, honey. Love you."

My mouth was full, so I signed 'I love you'. The door leading to the garage closed behind her. I gave her five minutes, then dumped the rest of my food in the garbage and poured myself cereal. I finished eating, tidied up a bit, and headed upstairs.

I had two text messages, one from Cora and the other from Eirik. He must have gotten a new phone or salvaged his old one. They were on their way. I still had to finish my AP English report, but my heart wasn't really in it. It was my birthday, and I wanted to do something fun with my friends.

After a quick shower, I changed into a pair of sweatpants and a T-shirt, grabbed my laptop, and settled on my window seat before I remembered Torin. I found myself studying his house. The white slats covering the windows were closed. I wondered how he knew things like the light signal. Could he really do magic? Stupid question. Of course not. Magic wasn't real.

To prove it, I called DC Tires. No one remembered seeing a guy fitting Torin's description at the shop or any scratches on my car. Maybe he'd sneaked by them and fixed the scratches when they weren't looking. Why should I care whether he'd lied or not? If he wanted to pretend he could do magic, that was his problem. Pushing the matter aside, I went online and started my rounds.

First, I stopped by the website of Flight 557 and checked the latest news. There was nothing to give me hope. Next I checked my e-mails and stopped by social and book-related sites. Usually going through new releases, fan fiction of my favorite books, and checking which books were being turned into movies held me spellbound for hours. This time, I kept glancing out the window, hoping to catch a glimpse of Torin.

Annoyed with myself, I moved to my bed and forced myself to stay there even when I heard his voice mingle with Mrs. Rutledge's annoyingly chipper voice. Just because I was bored didn't mean I had to spy and eavesdrop on my neighbors. When the doorbell chimed, I sighed with relief, closed my laptop, and ran downstairs.

CHAPTER 3. RUNES

"Happy birthday," Cora sang when I opened the door.

"It's almost noon," I griped.

"I know. Sorry." She hugged me. "How does it feel to be seventeen?"

"The same way I felt yesterday," I said. My eyes met Eirik's. He stood behind her with a gift box tucked under his arm, his Nikon in his hand, and a sheepish grin on his face. "Is that for me?"

He lifted it out of my reach. "Yes, but you can open it later. Where's your *T-shirt of Shame?*"

I slipped out of Cora's hug and pointed at the front of my T-shirt. "Right here."

Eirik peered at the writing. "Are you kidding me? What language is that?"

"Latin." I grinned.

Cora read the writing and laughed. "Good one, Raine. I knew you'd find a way around it. It was a ridiculous idea to begin with."

"Why? Because you weren't qualified to participate?" Eirik asked, smirking. He gave me a hug. "Happy birthday."

"Just so you know, we're late because of *him*." Cora pointed at Eirik.

Eirik crossed his arms. "How is it my fault?"

Cora glared at him, then focused on me. "You know my parents took my keys, right? I didn't have a ride and made the mistake of calling him. He mumbled something and hung up on me."

"I did not," he protested. "The phone fell and before I could call her back, she called and started yelling. She sounded like a crazy person, so I turned off my phone. When I got to her place, she took forever to get dressed."

"I so loathe you, Eirik Seville," Cora ground out.

Eirik smirked. "You *so* adore me, Cora Jemison. You're just pissed I got Raine a present and you didn't," he said the last word in a sing-song. "So, what's the plan, Raine?"

I sighed. I hated it when they fought. It was senseless.

"We're going to the mall for her present,' Cora answered before I could. She looped her arm through mine and pulled me away from

Eirik. "I'm tired of buying you books. Every time I get you something else, you gush, and I never see it again. And *he* refused to tell me what he bought you." She glared at Eirik.

"Because it's none of your business," Eirik retorted, going toward the kitchen. The kitchen was his favorite place in my house.

"Did you hear something, Raine? I thought I heard a buzzing sound." Cora dragged me toward the stairs. "Why don't you change, so we can leave?"

I glanced down at my T-shirt and sweat pants. "What's wrong with my clothes?"

"Everything. It's your birthday. Spruce up a little. Even Pretty Boy," she waved toward Eirik, "dressed up for the occasion."

"I heard that, Smarty Mouth," Eirik called out, his head inside the fridge as he searched for leftovers.

"Dressed up" meant Eirik wore a dress shirt instead of his usual threadbare T-shirts. His trademark black canvas and trendy, ripped jeans were the same. I stopped, forcing Cora to stop, too.

"We're going to have a little chat." I gripped her arm and led her to the kitchen, where Eirik was selecting a large, shiny apple. He rubbed it on his shirt. "You too, mister. Focus on me." They stared at me expectantly. "It's my birthday, and I won't put up with your crap. No snarky remarks for the rest of the day. Get it? You two will be nice to each other if it kills you."

Cora stared at me with big eyes. "Wow."

"Not the response I'm looking for, Cora."

She raised her hands in surrender. "Okay. I'm not going to let him get to me."

"Good." I turned and cocked my brow at Eirik.

"Fine. She starts it, you know," he added, then took a large bite of his apple and chomped on it. Cora huffed and moved to the window.

I shot Eirik a warning look and mouthed, "Be nice." He rolled his eyes. "Now that we have an understanding, can I open my present?"

He pushed the box out of my reach on the counter. "Not yet. What do you have to eat around here other than apples? I smell eggs."

"Mom cooked some this morning. Birthday breakfast."

Eirik shuddered and made a face.

At the same time, Cora said, "Was it edible?"

The two had slept over at my place often enough over the years and tried Mom's cooking. I wagged my finger. "No wisecracks about her cooking either. She tried and that's what counts. Let's head downtown to the Creperie for lunch, then the video store to pick up a movie for tonight, and then the mall."

"What is it this time? Another *Vampire Diaries* marathon?" Eirik asked with a pained look.

I frowned. "I thought you liked *Vampire Diaries*."

"Yeah, you said Elena was hot," Cora added with a bite, but she was still staring outside.

"She is," Eirik said. "But the way she moons over the brothers? Not so hot."

I rolled my eyes. "I was planning on *Supernatural*."

The cheer I'd expected when I mentioned the hit series about two brothers who hunted demons was missing. Instead, Cora turned and exchanged a look with Eirik, who shook his head. My gaze volleyed between them. "Okay, what's going on?"

"Nothing," Eirik said quickly and selected another apple from the bowl. "The Winchester boys and pizza sound great."

"You can't lie if your life depended on it, Eirik. What is it?" I narrowed my eyes and shot him the same look Mom often gave me when she wanted me to confess.

He pointed at his mouth, which was full, then at Cora.

Cora glared at him. "Coward. Okay, Raine. This is the problem. For the last two years, we've celebrated your birthday in front of the TV eating pizza and cake."

"Three years," Eirik corrected and took another lusty bite of the apple.

Cora nodded. "Yeah, three. This year we're doing something different."

I blinked. "We are?"

"Yes. We're going to L.A. Connection," Cora said.

"Dad would never allow…" I remembered he wasn't around to say no. "I don't know. I'll have to ask my mother."

"Call her and see what she says," Cora urged.

I wasn't sure I wanted to go to a club. "Can I at least think about this?"

"No," Cora and Eirik said at the same time.

Okay, they were serious about this. I knew a lot of teens hung out at L.A. Connection on weekends. Even Cora often went with Keith.

Eirik wasn't big on the club scene, but maybe he didn't go because of me.

"Okay." I picked up the phone in the kitchen, which was near the window and glanced outside. Torin was raking leaves. No wonder Cora kept staring outside.

"Yummy, isn't he?" Cora whispered.

He was, but I couldn't say anything with Eirik close by. I speed dialed Mom's number. "Mom?"

"What is it, sweetheart?"

"Can I go to L.A. Connection with Cora and Eirik tonight? Just for a couple of hours," I added.

There was silence then, "Just a second, hun."

The others watched me eagerly. I made a face and turned toward the window as I waited. Torin had stopped raking and was shoving leaves into large garbage bags. He paused to wipe his brow, then lifted the bags and carried them to the curb like they weighed nothing, his walk graceful. As though aware he was being watched, he pivoted on his heel and looked toward my house. I turned my head before he could catch me watching him.

There was still silence on the line. "Mom?"

"Okay, Raine. We'll give this a try and see how it goes. You don't leave until I get home, and you must be back by eleven. No going anywhere else but the club and no drinking."

I rolled my eyes. "Yes, yes, no, and I don't drink."

"I know, but peer pressure can make kids do crazy things. I'll see you tonight, okay?"

I put the phone down. "She said yes."

Cora rushed to hug me, hopping with excitement. Eirik lifted his camera. "Smile."

I forced a grin, and he snapped pictures. Me in a club? This was going to be interesting.

"Can we go now? I'm starving," Eirik said.

"Give me a second." I ran upstairs, changed into skinny jeans, ankle-length boots, and a light jacket. I was about to leave when I glanced outside. Cora and Eirik were talking to Torin, their laughter filling the air. No, Cora was laughing while Eirik looked uncomfortable. What were they discussing? Not that I cared.

Suddenly, Torin looked up and stared straight at me before I could duck out of sight. My heart tripped. I wanted to look away, but I couldn't. A tiny smile tugged the corner of his sculptured lips. Then he shifted his attention to Cora. I blew out a breath I hadn't known I was holding. Not sure whether to join them or not, I headed downstairs and waited until Cora and Eirik were on their way to the Jeep and Torin was back to raking leaves before I went outside.

"What's going on?" I asked. Despite my vow to ignore Torin, he fascinated me.

"I'm starving," Eirik grumbled again.

"You're always starving," Cora teased from the back seat. "I wanted to meet your sexy neighbor. Torin St. James. Even his name is sexy. He's going to our high school, starting Monday."

Once again, my traitorous heart reacted, but I faked disinterest. "That's nice."

Eirik mumbled something that sounded like, "It's not."

I glanced at him and frowned. "Have you met his parents?"

"He doesn't have any," he said in a tone that was hard to describe.

"Everyone has parents, silly," Cara said and pushed Eirik's head. "He's a senior, relocated here to be closer to a friend. He didn't say what friend. I wanted to ask him whether he meant a girlfriend, so I could hate her. Have you seen his eyes, Raine? Gorgeous. Sapphire can't begin to describe them."

Eirik snorted.

I angled my body so I could see both of them and signaled Cora to stop with the gushing. She gave me a naughty grin that said she was just messing with Eirik. Seriously, she could be so childish sometimes.

***

Lunar Creperie was packed, the aroma of fresh crepes, pastries, and coffee in the air. Located a block from my high school, the restaurant was a popular hangout for students. Kayville was home to three high schools—two public and one private Christian school. Ours was the largest and the only school located in the historic downtown Kayville, so we owned *the Creperie* as we often called it.

Well, not *owned* owned. We just acted like the place belonged to us. We had our corners, the jocks and the cheerleaders, the preppies, the Goths and other rebels, and the swimmers slash band geeks—that was us.

"Hey, Seville." Tim Butler, a curly-haired guy, who played tenor saxophone in the band and was a backstroker on the swim team, waved us over. He was with his girlfriend and two other couples. We staked the table next to theirs and went to place our orders.

A prickly feeling told me we were being watched, so I turned around casual-like and gave the room a sweeping glance. My eyes met the topaz pair of Blaine Chapman, captain of the football team. Blaine was already being courted by scouts across the state. He forked his fingers through his wavy brown hair and gave me his famous I-know-I'm-hot smile before glancing down at his girlfriend, Casey Riverside. Casey was head cheerleader and the girl guys fantasized about and other girls would love to hate. Only no one could hate her because she was so nice and sweet. Blaine and Casey were Kayville High's perfect couple.

With them were two blondes and a guy with silver hair, all of them strangers to me. They were staring at us. I checked behind me to confirm it. Yeah, Cora, Eirik, and I were the only ones at the counter placing orders.

Cora stayed behind to talk to a friend, and Eirik went to get our drinks. As I walked to our table, I glanced at the strangers again. Their gazes didn't waver from me, their expressions hard to describe. Unease slithered up my spine.

Throughout lunch, I was aware of their eyes on me. I tried to ignore them, but it wasn't easy. They left the Creperie before we did, but as soon as we stepped outside, the feeling of being watched returned. It continued while we were at the mall, yet every time I checked, I couldn't see anyone.

"You okay?" Cora asked when we entered a jewelry store.

"Yeah, why do you ask?"

"You keep looking around as though you're searching for someone."

"I have this weird feeling that we're being followed."

Cora frowned. "By who?"

"By whom," I corrected and winced when she glared at me. "I don't know. Let's just get done here and go home."

But it was another hour before we left the mall. By then it was close to four, time for Ultimate Frisbee. Eirik was still at A2Z Games, and we had to practically drag him out of there. We headed toward Longmont Park in North Kayville.

In the last two years, we'd had about eighty swimmers vie for spots on the varsity team, and this year was no different. About fifty students were already waiting at the park when we got there and more continued to arrive. A third of them were new faces fresh from junior high. I recognized some from the Silver and Bronze teams at my club.

Longmont Park was one of the many parks in and around Kayville. It had a ballpark, a playground, fields used by Kayville Rec Center for recreational sports, and park pavilions for barbecues and parties. Today, like most Saturday afternoons, it was busy with families. We parked on the road and started for the pavilion where Coach Fletcher and the other students were already waiting.

"Raine Cooper."

I spun around and frowned when Blaine waved.

"Wait up," he said as he sauntered toward me. With him were the three strangers from the Creperie. Up close, the girls with their blonde hair and light-blue eyes looked like they could be sisters. The silver-haired guy had dark-brown eyes that almost looked black. Something about him gave me the creeps. I gave a tiny smile, happy that Cora and Eirik had waited with me.

"Raine is co-captain of the swim team and the fastest butterfly swimmer," Blaine said, surprising me. I had no idea he knew anything about me. He turned and flashed his mega-watt smile at Cora. "It's Cora, right?"

She blushed and nodded.

"Her best stroke is…?" He cocked his brow.

"Breast," Cora said with a giggle.

Blaine snapped his fingers. "Right, breaststroke. And what do you do, Seville?" he asked, staring at Eirik's camera.

"I'm the towel boy," Eirik said even though the swim team didn't have towel boys. "The most important person on the team."

Cora threw him an annoyed look. I barely kept a straight face.

"Think you're funny, Seville?" Blaine's famous topaz eyes darkened. He made a face, ignored Eirik, and pointed at the guy with him. "Andris Riestad. Maliina and Ingrid Dahl. They're exchange students from Norway and plan to join your swim tea—"

The loud purr of a Harley engine filled the air and cut him off. We all turned to stare at the biker. Dressed in all black—jacket, jeans, boots, and helmet, he turned onto the road that cut through the east and west fields and rode toward us. I frowned. Usually, you heard the sound of a motorcycle from afar; then it grew louder as it drew closer. This one had started suddenly as though it had appeared from thin air.

The guy parked at the curb and removed his helmet. Torin. I should have known. He ran a finger through his raven hair, our eyes meeting across the students staring at him. A spasm kicked my chest, and warmth rolled through me.

A low growl came from my left, and I turned to find the source. Andris Riestad was staring at Torin with hatred, mouth turned up, eyes narrowed. But what had me gasping were the weird tattoos on his hands. They spread to his arms and disappeared under his rolled up sleeves. They appeared on his neck, then on his cheeks and forehead, the ends of each tattoo disappearing under his hair. They'd started gray and darkened until they were black, the contrast between them and his skin striking.

I turned to see if the others had noticed, but everyone was staring at Torin. One of the Dahl sisters, Maliina or Ingrid, I couldn't tell which, turned and gave me a quizzical glance. I gave her a stiff smile, my gaze shifting to Andris.

She realized what I was staring at and grabbed his arm, drawing his attention to the markings on his skin. She whispered something in his ear. He studied me curiously. The tattoos faded fast as though he'd pulled an eraser switch. He smiled and winked. The girl looked at him then me, her expression changing and becoming thunderous.

I stepped back and reached for Cora's hand, something about the girl's reaction sending panic through me. Other than the weird tats, something was off about these new students.

"What's Torin doing here?" Cora whispered.

I shrugged. "I don't know. Let's go."

"No," Cora protested. "Let's wait for them."

I was sure she meant Eirik and Torin, who were talking, but I wanted space between me and the exchange students. Now.

"They'll catch up," I said and hurried away. Cora followed.

"All this new eye candy," she said, barely containing her excitement. "This year's going to be exciting." She glanced behind us and added, "Andris can't take his eyes off you."

I glanced back and cringed when he winked again. My gaze shifted to Torin, who was staring at Andris as though he wanted to rip his head off. They knew and hated each other from the look of things.

"Let's get started," Coach Fletcher called out.

We moved closers, some people sitting on the benches and the ground, the rest standing.

"This year, we have about a hundred students who've shown interest in joining the swim team." Applause and whistles followed. Coach Fletcher raised his hand and everyone went silent. "Trials will begin a week from Monday, which means you have one week to fill out swim forms. Returning swimmers know what I'm talking about. Newbies, you'll find the forms at the school website under 'sports'. Permission forms must be completed and signed by your parents and the medical form filled and signed by your doctor after a physical exam. No one will be allowed in the pool without proper paperwork on file. Make sure you read the requirements, which includes maintaining a certain grade point average. If you're failing a class, come and see me. We have tutors on the team who can help. All this information is available online. Tell your parents to expect an e-mail about a general meeting for Q&A with me." He glanced around and grinned. "Right now, let's have some fun. I'll call out team captains, who'll choose a team color and teammates." He held a box with different pieces of colored fabric.

We formed eight teams, though some people chose not to play. Eirik, Cora, and I all ended up on different teams. Using sweatshirts and jackets, we split the field into two and marked the end zones. The students with longer pieces of fabric wrapped them around their heads like bandanas while others, like me, tied them around our arms. With eight teams playing for fifteen minutes each, we rotated, giving players a break every fifteen minutes.

Our coach loved Ultimate Frisbee, so this wasn't the first time we'd played. Usually, we just had fun, but this time was different. The game became intense in no time. My team, Eirik's, and Torin's won the first round, placing us in the top four for the second round. Cora's team lost, placing hers in the bottom four.

Standing beside Cora, I watched Torin intercept a throw and force a turnover. He was fast and aggressive, and he could jump. He could play basketball if he wanted.

"He's good, isn't he?" a voice said from behind me.

I recognized Andris' voice, and my stomach clenched. "Who?"

"St. James."

I shrugged. "He's okay."

"How do you know Torin, Andris?" Cora asked.

"He and I go way back," he said mysteriously, giving her a brief dismissive smile before studying me. He didn't even bother to try to hide his interest. I fidgeted even though there was nothing he could do to me in front of all these people and in broad daylight. Everything about him bothered me. He didn't have a European accent even though Blaine claimed he came from Norway. In fact, I couldn't detect an accent at all. He could be from anywhere.

"How well do you know St. James?" he asked, glancing at me.

I didn't answer even though I knew he was talking to me. Cora prodded me sharply with her elbow. I glared at her.

"We just met him," I mumbled.

"And Seville?"

This time, I studied Andris. I didn't like his nosiness. "What about Eirik?"

"Are the two of you together?"

"Why do you want to know?" I asked rudely, and Cora sunk her elbow into my side again. I grabbed her arm, but Andris spoke.

"Just checking out the competition. So you and he…?"

"Are none of your business." My team was on again. I practically dragged Cora away.

"What's wrong with you? He likes you and you were so rude," she wailed.

"I don't like him." I searched for Eirik. He was talking to a group of girls to our left. I recognized three of them. "Stay with Marj and Eirik and away from Andris."

"Seriously, Raine." She shook her head. "No wonder you never date. You have trust issues."

"I don't. I saw weird tats—"

Someone yelled my name.

"I've got to go. Please, stay away from Mr. Norway." I took off.

This time, one of the Dahl sisters was on the opposing team. It was the same girl who'd shot me a mean look after the tattoo incident. I didn't let her presence bother me. Andris was where I'd left him, although he was no longer alone. The other sister was with him. Cora had reached the girls with Eirik and was laughing. Relieved, I searched for Torin. He was at the other end of the field guzzling water, his eyes on me. Somehow having him around was reassuring even though I couldn't explain why.

Halfway through the game, I jumped to catch the Frisbee and someone pulled an interception. One of the Dahl sisters. One second she was on my right, the next in front of me, catching the Frisbee. She passed it and smirked triumphantly.

Ignoring her, I started to run toward the other end of the field. She cut me off and whipped around so fast all I saw was a blur of red before something cracked my ribs and pain ricocheted across my chest.

The force of her kick propelled me backwards, but I didn't try to stop my landing. I couldn't. I was struggling to breathe. Every attempt to inhale sent sharp spears of pain across my chest and up my spine. All I could do was take short, shallow breaths. I tried to glanced down but couldn't. It hurt too much. As for the girl, I saw her reappear at the other end of the field just before I hit the ground.

I didn't exactly land on the ground. Someone broke my fall. I tried to turn my head to see who it was, but I couldn't move. Every movement filled me with pure agony. My chest burned, and my vision blurred. I must have broken several ribs, or even worse, my sternum.

"Can't... breathe..."

"Hang in there for me."

Torin. I felt rather than saw him lower me to the ground.

"Easy, Freckles. You'll be okay in a few seconds."

Black dots appeared in my vision, and I knew I was blacking out from lack of air. A weird sensation started on my arm and raced toward my shoulder. It spread across my chest, up my neck and face, and then darkness swallowed me.

When I came to, Eirik and Cora were beside me, their faces wreathed with concern. But the best part was the lack of pain. I could breathe. How?

"Are you okay?" Eirik asked.

"What happened?" Cora asked at the same time.

I struggled to a sitting position. Where was Torin?

"Is she okay?" Coach Fletcher yelled, and I looked up to see him hurrying toward us.

"She's fine," Torin answered from somewhere behind me. "She lost her balance and fell."

What a liar. I wanted to call him out, but first I needed to stop them from fussing over me. I hated the attention. I started to get up, but Cora and Eirik grabbed my arms and helped me up like I was helpless.

"I'm fine," I insisted. "Really."

Coach Fletcher stopped in front of me and studied my face. "Did you bang your head?"

"No."

He glanced behind me and asked, "St. James?"

"No, she didn't. She tripped and landed on her butt. She's fine." Torin's voice was firm and confident. Or maybe it was a man thing because the coach believed him instead of me.

"Okay. You sit out the rest of the game, Raine. Drink plenty of water. Are you playing, Seville, or can another player take your spot?"

Eirik hesitated, his eyes shifting to Torin. Something passed between them. Then Eirik said, "I'm in." He touched my cheek. "You okay?"

I nodded. "Really, I am."

He smiled and took off. Cora gripped my arm as though afraid I'd keel over. I just wanted to shake her off, so I could grill Torin about his lies and demand to know how he'd healed me. I hadn't imagined my cracked ribs or the pain. Then I wanted to find the Norwegian bitch that'd attacked me and slap her.

I pressed on my ribs. Not even a spasm of pain.

"You scared me, Raine," she said. "You looked like you'd passed out or something. Come on, let's sit under the pavilion, and I'll get you some water."

I didn't want water or to sit. I needed answers from Torin. "Could you give me a moment with—?"

The sound of a motorcycle engine filled the air, and my eyes went to the tree where Torin had parked his Harley. He was taking off. Just like last night, he'd moved from one place to another in a matter of seconds. My eyes followed him, not sure whether I should be afraid or grateful that he'd healed me.

How had he done it? Or maybe I had imagined the pain. Even as the thought flashed through my head, I knew I hadn't. Torin had healed me. How? Magic? No, that was ridiculous. There was no such thing as magic. Or maybe there was. I swallowed, a new kind of fear rolling through me.

What was Torin? Was he good or evil? It was obvious the others were like him.

I searched the field for Andris and the two blondes. They were entering Blaine's car. Why were they leaving? The games were still going on.

The one in red, who'd cracked my ribs, looked toward me and smirked. I shivered. There was so much venom in her smile. I had just acquired an enemy who moved like something from a superhero movie and had superhuman strength to boot, yet I didn't know why.

CHAPTER 4. THE BIRTHDAY GIRL

"Are you sure you're up to this?" Cora asked for the hundredth time.

I rolled my eyes. "Can you tell her that I'm fine, Eirik?"

Eirik stared straight ahead. In fact, he'd been quiet and preoccupied since we left the park. "Eirik?"

"Hmm?"

I exchanged a glance with Cora. A naughty grin crossed her face. She leaned forward and whispered, "Do you want to make out with us when we get to Raine's place?"

"Sure," he said. We laughed. He snapped out of it and frowned. "What?"

Cora only laughed harder.

"Are you okay?" I asked.

He pulled up outside my house and let the engine idle, his way of saying he wasn't staying. Still scowling, he said, "I'm fine. Why do you ask?"

"You've been rather quiet since we left the park." I hopped down from the Jeep. "So when are we leaving tonight?"

"Eight," Cora answered. "Eirik's driving." She tapped Eirik's arm. "You're driving me home, so don't take off. Raine, come with me." She gripped my arm and pushed me toward the house.

Eirik didn't complain about Cora's bossiness, which was unlike him. He must have taken my orders to be nice to Cora seriously. He reached for his camera. He was always taking pictures, and I was usually his main subject. Even at the park when he wasn't playing, he'd kept busy snapping pictures. I wondered if he'd captured the moment that girl kicked me. I paused to ask, but Cora kept tugging.

"Move it, missy. I have two hours to transform you, but right now I want to know what I have to work with," she said.

"Transform me?" I unlocked the door and allowed her to push me upstairs.

"Because your idea of dressing up is jeans, boots, and whatever top you have lying around in your closet. Your mom, on the other hand, has style. Your dad was a class act and… I mean, he *is* a class act." She sighed. "I'm sorry, Raine."

"Don't be." My chest tightened as I walked to the closet and opened it. For a moment, I stared at my clothes through blurry eyes.

"Raine?"

"I, uh, I have white jeans. Anything that glows under a disco light is fine, right?"

"Usually, yes, but it's your birthday and we're going to the club. Damn it." Cora hugged me from behind. "I'm so sorry I brought up your father. I don't know how to deal with this."

"Me neither." My voice shook. "Mom believes he survived the crash, but I'm losing hope. I don't want to mourn him because… because…" I couldn't finish the sentence.

"It'd mean he's gone." Cora's arms tightened around me.

I wiped the wetness from my cheeks and took a deep breath, then turned and faced her. She was crying, too. I tried to smile, but my tears started to flow again. "Can we promise not to mention him for the rest of the day?"

"Night," she corrected. "And the answer is yes. I'll focus on prettying you up." She nudged me aside.

"Prettying me up? That's insulting."

"Yeah, well, your understated style might work for school and the mall, but not the club. Not tonight," she said as she flipped through my dresses and sighed. "Just like I thought. Nothing in here. You know what? I'll come early with outfits, makeup, and hair stuff."

"Outfits?"

"Dresses."

"I don't like wearing dresses, and I have a perfectly decent blow drier, curling iron, and—"

"Just wash your hair and leave everything to me. Be back in a few. Love you." She sailed out the door and left me standing there slack jawed. Then I realized what she'd done. She'd deliberately distracted me from the issue with my dad, which meant she didn't mean to make me wear a dress. Thank goodness.

By the time I reached downstairs, Eirik's Jeep was out of sight. Good. Now for *the talk* with a certain neighbor. I reached for the doorknob and froze.

What was I doing? I'd vowed to stay away from Torin and his talk of magic. He had weird powers. I shouldn't even be thinking of confronting him. What would I ask him? How would I start? What if he was evil? From the way he moved, I couldn't outrun him.

Swallowing, I paced and debated my next move.

No, I refused to cower just because I was scared. If he were evil, he wouldn't have healed me. He *had* healed me. I hadn't imagined the pain.

Taking a deep breath, I opened my door and slowly walked down our driveway. My heart pounded hard as I started down the sidewalk and headed for Torin's front door. I paused before hopping onto the porch. Once again, I gave myself a pep talk before pressing the doorbell.

No response. *Okay, leave. You tried.*

But I couldn't leave now that I'd made it this far. I pressed the doorbell again and angled my head to listen for movement from inside. Nothing. The garage door was open and I'd seen his Harley, so I knew he was home. Maybe he was asleep. Relieved, I turned to leave.

He yanked the door open. "Can't stay away from me, can you, Freckles?"

"Don't flatter…" My voice trailed off when I found myself staring at his bare chest. Not that I was complaining, but did he have something against shirts? "Yourself," I finished weakly.

He chuckled, drawing my attention upwards, past the water droplets on his chest to the wet hair caressing his shoulders. At least he had a legitimate reason for walking around shirtless this time. Still, you'd think he'd put on a shirt before answering his door.

"Can we talk?" I said.

His brow shot up. "About?"

"The incident at the park."

He looped a towel I hadn't noticed around his neck, crossed his arms, and leaned against the doorframe. His eyes narrowed. "What incident?"

"You know, when that girl attacked me and—"

"You tripped and landed on your lovely ass?"

"Lovely…?" My face warmed. "That's not what happened and you know it," I protested.

"That's what I saw."

"Liar."

He straightened his body, the smile disappearing from his face. Aye, he was intimidating when he stopped smiling. Antagonizing him would get me nowhere.

"Forget I said that. Can you, uh, finish getting dressed, so we can talk? Please?"

He sighed and gave me a look that said he was humoring me. "Fine."

I released a breath I hadn't known I was holding. Since he'd left the door open when he disappeared somewhere inside the house, I peeked in and blinked at the emptiness. When Eirik's family lived here, they'd decorated the large living room with rich, earthy colors—brown, tan, and dark green. Torin's idea of décor was one leather couch and a table. There was nothing on the walls. No side tables. No TV. No pictures.

"Nosey, aren't you?" he said, appearing suddenly.

I jumped back, my face flaming.

"Uh, I, uh…" I couldn't come up with a single excuse.

He stepped on the porch, closed the door behind him, and lifted his arms. "Is this better?"

"Much." The plain, black T-shirt hugged his chest and arms. Whatever soap he'd used—or was it shampoo?—smelled nice. He walked across the porch and leaned against the top porch rail, his arms and legs crossed. He was barefoot. There was something extremely sexy about a barefoot guy in jeans.

"Do you want me to wear shoes, too?" he asked, sounding annoyed.

"No." Once again, heat rushed to my face. I crossed my arms and hugged myself. Now that it was time for answers, I wasn't sure where to begin. "What are you?"

Torin chuckled. "What kind of a crazy question is that?"

"The kind you ask someone without a medical degree, who saved your life in a matter of seconds," I said. "You healed me today, Torin. I don't know how, but I know you did."

He shook his head. "That's an active imagination you have there, Freckles." His eyes narrowed. "Or you must have hit your head after all."

Frustration bubbled to the surface. "I didn't imagine everything that happened to me at that park. The Dahl girl kicked me in the chest and broke my ribs. I remember the pain, not being able to breathe. I thought I was dying just before I blacked out. When I regained consciousness, the pain was gone. I don't care how much you deny it. You healed me, Torin. So, uh, thank you."

He frowned as though he didn't like my explanation or my gratitude. I couldn't tell which. "Do you know how insane you sound?"

"Insane is what I thought you were yesterday when you said you could use magic to fix the Peterson's mailbox, yet you did, and my car and now my ribs. How did you do it?" A slight narrowing of his gorgeous eyes was the response I got. I swallowed and bit my lower lip. "Are you like them?"

He straightened his body and shoved his hands in the front pockets of his jeans. "Like who?"

"Andris and the Dahl sisters. You move like her, the one who kicked me. Last night I noticed how fast you moved from your bedroom to the front door after you signaled Eirik, which reminds me. How did you know that signal?"

Silence.

Now he was staring at me as though I was a lunatic, which I wasn't. I knew what I saw last night, and the pain I'd felt at the park had been real. He was stubborn, but so was I.

"Okay. Forget about the signal for now, but you can't deny that you're different. That you can do things normal people can't."

No response.

Getting frustrated, I added, "I swear, I won't tell anyone."

Another stretch of silence followed. I could hear the wheels turning in his head as though he was deciding how much to tell me. I'd almost given up hope that he'd respond when he shrugged.

"Is that the best response you can give me? A shrug?"

A smile lifted the corner of his mouth. "Are you always this pushy?"

"Answering a question with a question won't work with me, and no, I'm not pushy. I'm the most easygoing person I know."

He snorted with derision. "Who told you that? Seville?"

I ignored the dig. "Listen, I'm trying really hard not to freak out about this. Put yourself in my shoes and imagine how I feel. Please, just tell me how you did it and I'll leave you alone."

He rolled his eyes as though to say he didn't believe me. "It's just magic, Freckles. Nothing special."

"What kind of magic?"

"The good kind."

"Do you use tattoos, too?"

He frowned. "Tattoos?"

"They appeared on Andris."

Torin blinked. "You saw them?"

"Yes. They were all over his body. They looked kind of, I don't know, cool."

He swore under his breath.

"What? Wasn't I supposed to see them?"

"No. They're not tattoos. They're runes, and Mortals aren't supposed to see them." He grimaced as though he'd revealed too much. He glanced at his watch. "Don't you have a birthday party to go to?"

"Mortals?"

Torin's blue eyes narrowed. "Excuse me?"

"You said *Mortals* aren't supposed to see them."

"No, I didn't."

"Yes, you did. What does that make you? Immortal?"

"Is that true?" He pointed at my T-shirt.

I looked down, and a wave of embarrassment washed over me. I still wore the T-shirt with *Seventeen and Never Been Kissed* written in Latin. I crossed my arms, blocking the words even though he'd read them. I lifted my chin, hating the fact that I was once again blushing. "No, it's not true. About the Mortal and Immortal—"

"Never been kissed? Really?" A wicked twinkle entered Torin's eyes. "What's wrong with Seville?"

I bristled. "This is just a T-shirt I found at the bottom of my closet, and there's nothing wrong with Eirik. We kiss all the time."

His grin turned into a chuckle. "Sure you do. Tell him to act quickly before someone snatches you from right under his nose."

I was beyond embarrassed now. Defending my relationship with Eirik wasn't going to do me any good since Torin already saw through my lies. Bet his magical abilities had something to do with that.

"You're only using my T-shirt to get out of answering my questions."

His gaze moved to my lips. "I'm starting to see why Seville's never kissed you. You talk too much."

I growled. "Ugh, you're so annoying. Believe whatever you want." I walked around him and hurried down the steps. How had our conversation moved from him to me?

"Happy seventeenth birthday, Freckles."

I kept going, needing to put some distance between us. Whatever he was couldn't be good if he had to hide, which meant no more talking to him or going to his house or letting him get under my skin.

Inside my bedroom, I peeked out the window. He was back upstairs, seated on the window seat. Eirik's old window seat. He blew me a kiss and grinned. Magical powers or not, he was still the most aggravating guy I'd ever met.

I yanked the curtains, something I'd never done during the day, then removed the offending T-shirt and shoved it in the garbage. A shower didn't make me feel any better. I needed to live a little, starting tonight.

Being seventeen and never been kissed sucked.

***

"Ready to see the result?" Cora asked me hours later.

I nodded, turned, and studied my reflection. She'd blow-dried and curled my hair, and guilted me into wearing one of her outfits—a white and sea-green organza dress with double spaghetti straps and asymmetrical hem. It appeared to move when I moved. On my ears and wrist were green earrings and a bracelet, birthday presents she'd bought for me earlier at the mall. My makeup was flawless. For once, my eyes had more green than brown.

"Well?" Cora asked.

"I love it, though I feel like I'm looking at a total stranger." I stepped into medium-high heeled sandals, the only footwear I had that weren't ballet flats or boots, and went back to studying my reflection in the full-length mirror. "You sure this is not too much?"

Cora sighed. "You look amazing, but you don't have to take my word for it. You need a second opinion? You'll get it. Let's go."

Panic washed over me. I wasn't ready to see anyone. Eirik had dropped off Cora and left. That left Torin, and I'd never ask his opinion on anything. Cora, on the other hand, was bold enough to brave it. Excitement skidded under my skin.

"Where are we going?" I asked.

"To see your mom. She's in her room waiting to see the results."

Torin indeed. I was becoming too fixated on that guy. Making a face, I tucked a wavy strand behind my ear and left the room. Cora knocked on Mom's door and pushed it open when Mom told her to come in.

"We're done, Mrs. C," she said.

"Oh, sweetheart. Look at you." Mom walked toward me, her hands clasped in front of her chest. "Turn around."

I did and chewed on my lower lip as I waited for her verdict.

"My baby grew up when I wasn't looking," she mumbled, her eyes overly bright.

I sighed. "Mom, it's just the dress, and it's not even mine. I borrowed it from Cora."

Mom chuckled, cupped my face, and kissed my forehead. "It's perfect on you. You did an amazing job, Cora. You should be a stylist. You know what flatters a person."

Cora blushed. "Thank you, Mrs. C. She just needs to wear green more often. It enhances the color of her eyes."

"It does, doesn't it?" Mom grinned.

"Uh, thanks for talking about me like I'm not here," I mumbled.

Mom fluffed my hair, grabbed a tissue from her dresser, and dabbed at some of the lip-gloss. "You look beautiful. Not that you don't always. It's just that you never care about styling your hair or wearing makeup."

"We have to go, Mrs. C," Cora said.

I sighed with relief when Cora spoke before Mom could expand on how I downplayed my looks. It was a recurring lecture.

"Of course. I already spoke with the guys, so they know I will hold them accountable if anything happens to the two of you. No drinking."

Cora giggled. "It's teen night on Fridays, Mrs. C. No alcohol."

Mom nodded. "Good. Are you spending the night here, Cora?"

"Oh yes. We'll have plenty to gossip about later tonight."

While Mom and Cora continued their exchange, I wondered which 'guys' Mom was holding accountable. Who was downstairs? I hadn't realized Eirik had come back. Obviously he wasn't alone. Who was with him? My heart kicked up a notch.

Mom kissed my cheek, whispering, "I added more money on your card, so take it." Then she added louder, "Have fun. Be back by eleven."

I went to get my cell phone, wallet, and jacket, and followed Cora downstairs. Eirik was in the kitchen wolfing down pizza, until he saw me. He dropped the slice and got up, his gaze admiring, his usual wisecracks missing. I guessed that meant he liked my outfit. He looked gorgeous in casual wear, but I couldn't see the person behind him, except for an elbow on the counter. Eirik wiped his hands on a napkin as he closed the gap between us.

Finally, I got a clear view of the guy behind him and disappointment coursed through me. Keith rose from the stool. I hadn't known he'd be coming with us.

I waved. "Hey, Keith."

"Hey. You look amazing."

"Thanks." I focused on Eirik. "Still not going to saying anything?"

"He will," Cora said, punching his arm as she and Keith walked past us, "after he picks up his tongue from the floor."

Eirik's gaze didn't leave mine as the door closed behind Keith and Cora. Finally, he glanced over my shoulder to the top of stairs. "Bye, Mrs. C."

"Take care of my baby, Eirik."

I rolled my eyes. "I can take care of myself, Mom."

"I will, ma'am," Eirik said as though I hadn't spoken and offered me his arm.

Outside, Keith and Cora were already inside Keith's Mustang. Eirik closed the door after I settled in the front passenger seat of the Jeep. Then he did something he'd never done before. He touched my lower lip.

"I should have taken you up on that offer last night," he murmured in a husky voice.

I grinned, instinctively knowing he meant the kiss. From his words, he sounded like it wasn't going to happen now. A bit disappointed, I asked, "Does that mean you don't want to anymore?"

"I don't want to mess your makeup."

"You're silly."

He crossed his arms along the Jeep's open window and studied me. "You are beautiful, make up and fancy hairstyle or not."

"Really?" He'd never told me I was beautiful.

He chuckled. "Of course you are, but I don't know if this new Raine would raid the fridge in the middle of the night to feed me or stay up all night and take care of me when I'm sick."

I giggled. "Of course I would. You're my best friend, and I'd do anything for you."

"Hey, let's go," Cora yelled through the window of the Mustang.

Eirik hesitated as though he wanted to kiss me despite his words, then he looked at his watch and raced around the hood to the driver's side. In minutes, we were heading west on Orchard Road. Eirik had the top of the Jeep up and warm air cranked.

We drove past Walkersville University, the local Christian college whose pool we used for swim meets, then turned left on Fox Street. The club, L.A. Connection, was at the corner of Main Street and North Bonnet. The parking lot was already packed, but the larger one behind the building was nearly empty. It didn't look like a busy night. On the other hand, it was only eight, too early for clubbers. In fact, whenever Cora went dancing, she never left until ten.

"Just a second." Eirik grabbed his camera from the backseat. "Don't put on your coat yet."

"It's cold," I complained, but didn't wear the coat and posed.

"You look amazing," he said, pressing the button.

"Thank you. Take one of me and Cora." She and Keith were walking toward us arm-in-arm.

"Later." Eirik took my hand.

The bouncer at the door stamped the back of our hands and waved us through without asking for our I.D.s or asking us to pay. Eirik must have taken care of everything. He was that kind of guy. His next birthday would be my treat.

The foyer was empty, which was surprising considering the cars in the parking lot. To our right were restrooms, and to the left, a broad doorway led to a lounge. A few couples lost in their private worlds sat around the room. Eirik didn't claim a table for us. Instead he headed toward the flashing lights farther ahead, where a long shimmering curtain separated the lounge from the dance floor.

Two young men, one with a punk haircut and electric blue side bangs and the other with a Mohawk with blond highlights, blocked our path.

"Password?" Mohawk asked.

Cora and Keith glanced at each other with bewildered expressions. I looked at Eirik, who shrugged and said, "Lorraine Cooper?"

Punk exchanged a grin with Mohawk, and they stepped aside, yelling, "The birthday girl is here."

Screams of "Happy birthday, Raine," greeted us as we entered the dance floor. The Beatles' rendition of "Happy Birthday" filled the room. Balloons and streamers rained down from the ceiling on us and the students already on the dance floor. Despite the flashing neon lights, I recognized swimmers from the park, my band mates, and Keith's lacrosse teammates and their girlfriends.

I tried not to cry as people sang and waved or hugged me. Eirik leaned close until our foreheads touched. "Happy birthday, Raine."

Then he pressed his lips to mine.

Maybe it was the moment, the music, the flashing lights and the crowd, but the kiss was perfect. Sweet. I put my arms around his neck and held him close. He grabbed my hand and somehow managed to lead me across the crowd to a set of stairs leading to a VIP lounge.

It had birthday banners and streamers. Marjorie 'Marj' LeBlanc, Catie Vivanco, and Jeannette Wilkes gave me hugs. They were juniors like me. The three of them moved to Kayville a year ago and bonded when they joined the swim team. Marj and Catie also played in the band while Jeannette and Eirik were editors at the Trojan Gazette, Kayville High's newspaper.

"Were you surprised?" Marj asked, speaking louder to be heard above the music.

I nodded and rubbed my arms, feeling chilly despite my jacket. "I still don't know how they pulled it off."

She pointed at Eirik, who was staring at the dancers below and laughing with Catie and Jeannette. "He asked us a week ago to help with the decorations, said it was a surprise for you. You have no idea how hard it was not to say anything this afternoon at the park. Have fun." She hugged me again and went to get her friends. They disappeared downstairs.

"How could you keep this a secret?" I asked. "You suck at secret keeping."

He gave me another peck then draped an arm around me and pulled me closer. "Magic."

"Don't joke." That was one word I didn't want to hear tonight.

"We started planning a month ago, reserved the place, and this morning worked with the club's party organizers to get everything ready. We have the place until ten, so let's go dance."

"What if I'd said no this morning or my mother had refused?" I asked as we headed toward the stairs.

"We would have sneaked you out, blind-folded you, and brought you here against your will." Eirik pulled me to the dance floor.

The Beatles were replaced by modern artists, and the crowd went wild. Bodies rocked, arms flailed, and hips swayed to the rhythmic music pounding through the room. Having an amazing dancer for a partner helped, too. Keith hated to dance, so Cora and I shared Eirik.

It was a while before I noticed them—Andris and the evil sisters. Panic flashed through me. Who had invited them? I gripped Eirik's arm, leaned in, and said, "Let's take a break."

"Okay. I'll get us drinks," he said.

"I'll go upstairs and rest my feet." I wanted to observe Andris and the Dahl sisters from above, not run into them. They were still by the curtains.

Eirik insisted on escorting me upstairs, where a few people were already seated. Some were making out, while others stared at the dancers below and sipped their drinks. Darrel Portman, the lacrosse player Cora planned to feature on her vlog next week, and his new girlfriend were all over each other. He changed girlfriends often. He paused long enough to eye me curiously as though seeing me for the first time. I'd gotten a lot of that look tonight. Maybe Mom was right about wearing makeup and styling my hair. Or maybe the fact that Eirik and I finally kissed was the cause. I'd never been happier.

Eirik left me near the table reserved just for me and disappeared downstairs. I searched for Andris and the two sisters among the dancers. I couldn't see them until the strobe replaced the colored disco lights.

One Dahl girl wore a one-shoulder, red sheath, mini dress that left little to the imagination, while the other's flowing white dress made her look other worldly. I couldn't see Andris. Even though he was dressed in black and probably blended better than the two blondes, his silver hair would stand out.

"So this is where the birthday girl is hiding," he said from behind me, and I stiffened. Before I could move, he'd gripped the rail on either side of me, neatly boxing me in, his body too close for comfort.

Heart pounding, my first instinct was to push him away, but something told me he'd expect me to react that way. Taking a deep breath, I faked an indifference I didn't feel. "What do you want, Andris?"

"You," he breathed in my ear. "Join me, Raine."

I cringed. His hot breath on my ear gave me the creeps, but I wasn't ready to turn and face him yet. "I just left the dance floor," I said, deliberately misunderstanding him.

"I don't mean dancing. I'm talking about my team."

"Team?"

"Me, Ingrid, and Maliina."

Were they some kind of a coven? What I knew about magic came from fiction, and it was all about witchcraft, death, and mayhem. "I'm not interested."

"You don't know the perks yet," he said.

I turned to face him and crossed my arms. "Why would I be interested in joining you after your friend tried to kill me?"

He grinned. "Maliina was just jealous. She's my mate, or as you Mortals say, my girlfriend." He reached out and touched my hair. "You could be one of us, Raine."

In his dreams. I pushed him away. Maybe the element of surprise was on my side or the need to get away from him gave me extra strength, but I pushed him hard enough that he lost his balance and landed on the table. I moved away from him, my mind racing. He had referred to us as Mortals as though he wasn't, just like Torin had earlier.

"What's going on?" Darrel yelled, standing up.

"Is this man bothering you, Raine?" another lacrosse player asked and drew closer.

I imagined what could happen if they dared to fight Andris and his magical runes. He was probably faster and stronger than Maliina.

"No, he's not," I said. "He was just leaving."

"Only if you come with me." Andris straightened his trench coat and extended a hand toward me. "One dance, Raine."

"I think she told you to leave," Torin's voice came from somewhere behind Andris. I searched for him in the shadows. I had no idea when he'd appeared or how much he'd heard, but I was relieved, which was totally wrong. He was just like Andris, an immortal wizard, witch, or whatever magical term they used.

Grinning, Andris turned and faced Torin.

Darrel and the other guy spoke again, but I'd stopped listening to them. I strained to hear the exchange between Torin and Andris. The pounding music made that hard, so I moved closer.

"Nice of you to join us, St. James," Andris said mockingly.

Torin grinned, red, blue, and green lights flashing across his handsome face. Like Andris, he was dressed in black. "Outside. Now."

"Why? You're no longer my superior." Andris sounded almost belligerent.

Torin didn't respond. Instead, he turned and started for the stairs as though he expected Andris to obey him.

Andris hesitated, glanced at me, and shrugged. "Later, gorgeous."

I shuddered with revulsion. As they continued downstairs, I debated whether to follow them. They were not mortals and had powers, two reasons to stay put and pretend they didn't exist. Below, Eirik made his way past the dancers with our drinks. I should wait for him, forget about Torin and Andris. He was normal, my best friend.

When Eirik stopped to talk to someone, I reached a decision. I grabbed my coat and raced down the stairs after Torin and Andris. I wasn't sure why I was doing it. I just had a bad feeling about those two.

Halfway down the stairs, I saw Torin push the emergency door. I searched for Eirik to see if he'd seen me. He had and waved. Crap. I pretended not to see him and hurried toward the emergency exit, which was now closed. I pushed it, but it didn't budge.

"That door only opens during emergencies," someone yelled in my ear.

I turned. Mohawk from the welcoming committee grinned.

"But two guys just opened it," I explained.

He shook his head. "That's impossible. An alarm would have gone off."

Unless Torin and Andris had used magic to open it. Frustrated, I almost bumped into Eirik when I whipped around.

"What's going on?" he asked.

"I need to use the restroom. I'll be right back." I pressed a kiss on his cheek and didn't give him a chance to say anything before I took off. The lounge was now packed with giggling girls in sequined tops, skinny jeans, dramatic makeup, and teased hair. Their dates checked them out on the sly while ordering drinks from the bar. I spotted a few familiar faces from school.

I kept going. Outside, I turned left and headed toward the back of the building, where the emergency exit was located. As I got closer, muffled voices reached me, not thuds of fists slamming against bodies like I'd expected. I slowed down, angled my head, and listened.

"Come on, St. James. Half the swim team's on it."

"You don't know that," Torin retorted.

On what? I crept closer.

"So a few might slip through, big deal. No one cares. They're just Mortals."

"I care," Torin retorted. "I have no intention of taking another detour to Land of Mist because you can't follow orders. Control her, Andris. She pulls another stunt like she did today and I'll personally escort her there."

"You can't threaten Maliina. She's my first mate."

A thud vibrated through the wall as though a giant bolder had rammed into it, and I jumped. "Listen, you bastard. I don't care if she's your first, second, or hundredth mate. I gave up ten years of my life because you don't know how to listen," Torin snarled. "Control her or lose her. Get it?"

What did he mean by he gave up ten years of his life? How the heck old was he?

"Why are you taking this job so personally, St. James? Jealous I saw the Cooper girl first? Or is it because her father is—"

"Her family situation doesn't interest me," Torin cut off Andris, but my ears twitched and my heart pounded. What about my father? "This is a job, like thousands we've done before," Torin continued. "We finish here and move on. We don't make stupid mistakes. She saw your runes at the park today."

Andris chuckled. "You know me. I get pissed, they appear. I get aroused…"

"Spare me the details. Find a way to disconnect your emotions from your runes."

"You're a cold bastard, St. James. Incapable of feeling anything."

"There's no room for love and sentiments in this business, just rules and punishment if you break them. No more turning Mortal girls, Andris. Everyone on the swim team is off limits, and I mean everyone, until it's time."

A chill crawled under my skin. Turning Mortals into what? They couldn't be vampires because they were not scared of daylight and I'd seen them eat regular food. Werewolves? Aliens? Demons? Or maybe I'd been reading too many paranormal books and was becoming paranoid. What did they want with the swim team?

I waited to hear more. Instead, a bright light lit up the alley. Just as suddenly, it disappeared. The silence was spooky as though something bad was about to happen. I peered around the edge of the building and blinked.

They were gone. How?

Then I noticed the runes on the wall of the building. They glowed as though written in neon ink. Maybe they could walk through walls. Had I really seen the emergency door open earlier? Torin had put his hand on it, and I'd just assumed he'd meant to push it open. Maybe they'd walked through the solid surface while I was distracted by Eirik.

The runes on the wall shimmered and grew faint as though the wall was absorbing them. I reached out to touch them when I felt a presence and tensed.

"Where is he?" a woman snarled behind me.

I yanked my hand back, my stomach dropping, and slowly turned around.

CHAPTER 5. THE BLACKOUT

Red sheath dress, thigh-high boots, furious expression, she was also the one who'd nearly killed me. Andris' first mate.

"Maliina," I said weakly.

"Where's Andris?" she asked.

"He's, uh, not here," I stammered and took a step back. *She's not human... She's strong... She has powers... Run... Scream...*

Despite my thoughts, I couldn't move. My knees knocked, and my throat seized up. She moved closer, and I took another step back, the back of my foot hitting the wall. I had nowhere to go, but face her. My stomach dipped when light bounced off something in her hand. She had a weapon. It looked like a letter opener except it was sharper with a thinner blade.

She was going to kill me this time. I just knew it. My breath hitched. "Maliina, I didn't come out here to—"

"You think I wouldn't notice you left after he disappeared."

"I wasn't meeting with him if that's what you think."

She closed her eyes, then snapped them open, her pale-blue eyes glowing eerily. "Don't lie to me. His essence is here. Is he going to turn you?"

"Turn me into what?"

"One of us."

"What are you?"

"Don't play dumb with me, Mortal," she moved closer, her body starting to glow as though neon lights were imbedded under her skin. "I might have been human once, but that doesn't mean I'm stupid. There's something different about you. What are you?"

Too distracted by her glowing skin, I didn't respond to her senseless question. As the light on her skin grew brighter, I realized it came from the runes on her body. Like Andris, she had one on each cheek and her forehead. A tear rolled down her cheek, and I almost felt sorry for her. Despite all her witchy powers, she was just a girl in love with a jerk.

"Maliina, Andris was meeting Torin, not me," I tried to reassure her.

"Liar," she yelled. "Torin and Andris can't stand each other. They can't be in the same room without trying to kill each. You *will not* take what's mine." She raised her weapon.

"No, don't!" I screamed, lifting my arms and covering my head. Any second, I expected a jab or a cut, excruciating pain. Instead the light from her runes grew stronger. I peered at her and gasped. She was cutting herself.

"Don't! He's not worth it. No man is worth…" Then I realized what she was doing. The letter opener wasn't a regular weapon. It was a sketching tool of some kind. She was tracing runes on her skin. The new ones glowed so bright I squinted to see her. Her face was distorted as though it hurt, but the look in her eyes was vengeful.

"You'll be sorry you crossed me," she vowed. Then she shimmered and became transparent, until I could see through her. The next second she was gone, the rustle of leaves the only sign she'd been there a moment ago.

I slumped against the wall trembling, my mind completely blank. Then everything rushed back—Maliina telling me I was different, the conversation between Torin and Andris, the runes on the wall. Something weird was going on in our town, and somehow I was part of it. Not just me, the swim team, too.

I hurried back into the building and went to the restroom. My reflection in the mirror shocked me. My pupils were dilated, and my forehead was shiny with sweat. I pulled a compact from the pocket of my coat, repaired my makeup, and headed back to the dance floor.

"You took forever," Eirik said when I found him dancing with Cora.

"Sorry, I needed fresh air." I tried to find Torin, Andris, and his mates, but I couldn't see far while on the dance floor. The look on Maliina's face stayed with me. The girl was crazy and after nearly killing me at the park, I was scared of what she might do. Part of me wanted to tell Eirik everything. He and I had never kept things from each other.

My new neighbor is an immortal who uses runes to do magic, and he and his kind are after the swim team. Yeah, I could just imagine Eirik's reaction. He'd think I'd gone crazy.

I wanted to go home and analyze what I'd heard, maybe stop by Torin's and ask him what was going on. No, that would be stupid. I was staying away from him, even if it killed me. Besides, I couldn't leave. Eirik and Cora had worked hard to make my birthday memorable.

I tried to push everything from my mind and enjoy the moment. I really did. Luckily, Eirik didn't notice I was distracted. The crowd on the floor doubled as more students left the lounge and joined us, giving me the perfect excuse.

"It's too crowded down here. Let's go upstairs."

Eirik wrapped his arm around my waist and walked with me upstairs, which was just as crowded. At least Keith and some of his lacrosse friends were at our table. One of the guys gave up his seat for me after offering his lap first, which earned him a mean look from Eirik. I loved his protective boyfriend routine, even the way he leaned down and planted a possessive kiss on my lips to let the guys know I was with him.

I was grinning when he grabbed his camera and headed back downstairs to take pictures. Having a boyfriend was awesome, but the other guys' reactions were even funnier. All of a sudden, I became interesting. Seriously, I would never understand guys.

Cora left the dance floor and joined us. She sat on Keith's lap and joined their conversation, which seemed to center around sports. I pretended to follow the discussion while I watched the dancers and searched for Torin. I couldn't explain how I knew he was down there in the shadows, watching. I just did. I couldn't spot Andris and his women either. Good riddance.

A kick drew my attention, and I glared at Cora. It wasn't the first time she'd kicked my shin. I wasn't in the mood to yell and call it conversation.

As though responding to my thoughts, the music stopped and the lights went out. Silence hung in the air like an ominous fog. Then a buzz rose as people started talking at once. Glowing LCD screens appeared as people used their cell phones to see their surroundings. Beeps of text messages, ring tones, and panicked murmurs came next.

"Let's get out of here," Keith said.

"No, dude," one of his friends said. "Down there is an accident waiting to happen."

Eirik was down there. I removed my cell phone from my pocket and dialed his number. "Where are you?"

"I'm okay. I'm trying to get to the stairs. Stay up there and wait for me."

"Okay. Do you think it's just the club?" The look on Maliina's face flashed in my head again. Could she have done this?

"I don't know, but if you look down, you'll see me waving."

I glanced down. Unfortunately, he wasn't the only one using his cell phone as a light source or waving. Others called out their friends' names or waved, too.

"Don't turn off your cell phone," I warned him.

"I won't," he promised.

A voice rang out, "Everyone, stay calm and stay where you are. Do not attempt to leave the dance floor and rush to the entrances until the generator kicks in. Lights are off across town. Once they come back, move in an orderly fashion and exit the building using both the front entrance and the two emergency exits in the back."

Seconds passed and became minutes. The crowd below grew restless.

"Don't touch me," a girl yelled.

"You groped me, you jerk," another one called out.

"Hey, that wasn't me," a guy snapped.

"Son of a..." A thump accompanied the words.

Fights broke out. Screams and thuds filled the dance floor. Starting to panic, I searched for Eirik, but I couldn't see him. Worse, our connection was broken. I tried calling him again just as the colored LED lights above the floor and the strobe lights behind the DJ's booth crackled as though coming back to life.

Everyone froze, their eyes staring up in anticipation. The lighting system short-circuited or something, and the crackling stopped. The lights went out again.

Chaos broke as people screamed and surged toward the exits. Frantically, I called Eirik. He didn't pick up his phone. I texted him, then leaned over the balcony rail. It was impossible to identify anyone. The screams grew louder. People wailed in pain as they bumped and tripped over each other. Panic hit me like a cement truck.

"Eirik!" I screamed.

"Stay up there," I thought I heard someone yell, but I wasn't sure whether it was him or someone else.

Heart pounding, I kept searching. Cell phone LCD screens zigzagged the air as people shoved and stumbled. They were following each other blindly. Some of the students on the balcony started for the stairs. Cora and Keith followed. I didn't know whether to leave with them or wait for Eirik.

"Come on, Raine," Cora begged.

"No." I recognized Torin's voice. It came from somewhere below. "Stay up there until everyone leaves, Raine. It's too dangerous down here."

I tried to find him but couldn't.

"Eirik is down there," I yelled. "I tried calling him, but he's not answering his cell."

"I'll find him for you. Just don't move," he ordered.

Someone touched my elbow, and I turned. It was Cora.

"Torin said it's safer up here and that we should stay," I said.

Cora looked at Keith, then me, and then back at him, thoroughly conflicted. "Can we stay with Raine?" she asked.

Keith surprised me when he nodded. Cora and I clung to each other and stared in horror at the scene below, both of us shaking. The pandemonium below continued, screams mixing with sharp screeches of pain. At least the emergency exits were open. I tried to locate Torin and Eirik with little success. The rest of the balcony crowd headed downstairs.

"Do you think Torin will find him?" Cora asked, her voice sounding funny.

"Yes." From what I'd overheard in the alley, Torin was an honorable person, uh, Immortal or whatever he was. Cora sniffled, and I realized why she'd sounded funny. She was crying. I didn't blame her. I was fighting tears, too. Tonight would haunt me forever.

"Do you think...?" she started to ask but stopped.

"What?" I asked.

"Do you think some of the people we invited are hurt? Because if we hadn't invited them..."

I squeezed her shoulders. "Don't think like that. We're not responsible for this. No one could have predicted we'd have a blackout." I glanced down. Through the emergency exit, I saw people moving around, headlights coming and going. Police sirens filtered through. Where was Torin? He was taking forever. If Eirik got hurt...

My phone went off, and I reached for it with an unsteady hand. Tears rushed to my eyes when I saw who it was. I brought the cell phone to my ear. "Mom!"

"Where are you, sweetheart? The lights just went off, and I thought it was only our block, but they say it's the entire county. Are you okay? Please, tell me you're okay." Her voice shook.

"I'm fine, Mom. I swear I am. I'm still at the club, but I'm fine."

"Oh, thank goodness. Are Cora and Eirik with you? Her mother tried to call her number, but she didn't pick up her phone."

I swallowed past a block in my throat and swiped at the wetness on my cheeks. "Eirik was on the dance floor when the lights went out. A friend is looking for him. Cora is with me. She's fine. I'm not sure what happened to her cell phone—"

"I have it, but my battery died," Cora murmured and sat up. "Oh, no. I have to call home."

"I've to go, Mom." I could see Torin's silhouette at the top of the stairs.

"Come home, sweetheart. Please."

"I will, as soon as I find Eirik. Don't worry, Mom. I'm okay." I pressed the phone into Cora's hand, got up on shaky legs, and moved toward Torin. "Did you find him?"

"Yes." As if he knew I was crying, he cupped my face and wiped the wetness with his thumb. For a moment, I let him, needing the connection with another person. "He was protecting a girl who'd been knocked unconscious. He took her outside and is waiting for the EMT. I'll take you to him." His hand dropped from my face and I felt so alone, which was ridiculous. "Let's go."

He led the way downstairs, surprising me again when he held my elbow until we left the building. Cora and Keith followed closely behind. The parking lot was half empty, but people were seated on the grassy patches around the parking lot.

"He's over there." Torin pointed at Eirik, who was by a girl on a patch of grass bordering the parking lot. Her eyes were closed as though she was asleep. Eirik had bruises on his face.

I turned to thank Torin, but he had already disappeared. I sighed. Maybe it was better that way. He didn't really belong here. Cora was crying while Keith held her. I indicated to Keith where I was going then hurried to Eirik's side. He took my hand and pulled me down beside him.

I wanted to scold him for scaring me, but I couldn't. He had a nasty cut above his right eyebrow and on his lower lip and discolorations on his cheeks and bloodied hands. It was as though someone had turned him into a soccer ball. Chances were he'd used his body to protect the unconscious girl.

I touched his forehead, though I was careful not to touch the cut. "Does it hurt?"

"It's nothing."

It didn't look like nothing, but he appeared uncomfortable with my attention. I focused my attention on the girl he'd rescued. I recognize her from the swim team. Kate Hunsaker. Her swimmer nickname was Shelly. I wasn't sure where the nickname came from, but our team was big on nicknames. She was a sophomore, didn't say much or socialize with anyone in particular, but she was an amazing breaststroker.

I glanced around. She wasn't the only one hurt. About a dozen or so people were on the ground, some with their parents and others with friends. Some of them I recognized from the swim team, others were just regular students.

"Is she going to be okay?" I asked Eirik.

"I don't know," he said, sounding so sad. "By the time I reached her, she'd lost consciousness. I tried to carry her, but it was impossible with the crowd shoving and panicking."

"So you protected her with your body," I whispered and rubbed his arm. When he winced, I let him go. "You're a hero, Eirik."

He shook his head. "I helped one. Torin helped a lot more."

"What do you mean?" I glanced around the park even though I knew Torin was gone.

"The emergency exits were jammed. He broke them down."

I hesitated, told myself it didn't matter, but I couldn't help myself. "How?"

"I don't know. People were banging on the door from the inside, and then it was lifted off its hinges from the outside. I didn't see it happen, but Condor recognized him from the park and mentioned it. Chances are he opened the second one, too."

Condor was a senior butterflyer. I knew I should stop questioning Eirik, but once again curiosity got the better of me. "What is he?"

Eirik glanced at me and frowned. "What do you mean?"

"Torin. He's different, isn't he? Like Andris and the girls."

Eirik frowned harder. "I don't know about different, but he's the kind of guy you can count on in an emergency. Who's Andris?"

Obviously Andris hadn't made an impression on him. "Exchange student from Norway. We met him at the park."

"Aah, he was with the two blondes?"

Go figure he'd remember the girls. Men. By the time the EMT appeared, strapped Kate to a gurney, and put her into an ambulance, her parents had arrived. There were about five people with serious injuries but more with minor ones who needed attention, too. Kate was the only one unconscious. Instead of going home, we piled in Eirik's Jeep and followed the ambulance to Kayville Medical Center. Cora came with us since Keith had to leave. His mother kept calling. We called home and explained where we were headed.

"Oh, sweetie." I could tell my mother really wanted me home.

"We'll wait with her parents just for a little bit, Mom. They're all from the swim team, and we want to make sure they're okay."

Mom sighed. "Okay, but be careful. Come home as soon as you can."

Inside the ER, the first person I saw was Torin. He was seated at the farthest corner inside the waiting area. My stomach flip-flopped, and my heart picked up tempo. Why was he here? He hardly knew any of the injured people. I changed my mind when I saw the people seated at the corner by the ER entrance—Andris and his girls. Maliina shot me a smug smile. I so wanted to march over there and smack her. Was she behind the blackout? Maybe they were all behind it. From the conversation between Andris and Torin, they wanted something from the swim team. Most of the injured were Trojan swimmers.

I was aware of Torin's eyes on us, hating the unsettling effect his presence had on me. My grip tightened on Eirik's arm. I rested my head on his shoulder after we sat. By the time everyone settled into the waiting room, there were almost two dozens of us mixed with parents. But half of us weren't hurt. We were there to keep vigil. The show of solidary didn't surprise me. Coach Fletcher always insisted we were more than a team, that we were a family. I never believed him until now.

Most of the injured had sprains and cuts that needed stitches, but nothing life-threatening. Kate had a fracture on her right leg, several cracked ribs, and bleeding in her brain. They rushed her into the operating room as soon as they arrived. Mrs. Hunsaker was in tears, and she wasn't the only one. Kate's best friend, whom I'd seen last year during meets, was in tears, too. Mr. Hunsaker appeared stoic, but it was obvious he was just being strong for his wife.

He stood and came to where I sat with Eirik. A nurse had already cleaned and wrapped up Eirik's bleeding knuckles and stitched the cut on his brow.

"Thank you for protecting my daughter, young man," Mr. Hunsaker said and pressed on Eirik shoulder when he started to get up. "No, don't get up. What's your name?"

"Eirik Seville." Eirik offered his left hand, and the man shook it gingerly.

"Mr. Seville, I'm Seth Hunsaker, Kate's father, and over there," he indicated Kate's mother, "is my wife Sally. We would like you to know you're welcome at The Oyster Bar any time."

"I, uh, thank you, sir. I did what anyone would have done in a similar situation."

"That's where you are wrong." Mr. Hunsaker glanced at his wife, then asked, "You swim with Kate?"

"We all do." Eirik indicated the swimmers in the room.

"Thank you." Mr. Hunsaker looked at us, his eyes bright. "All of you, for being with us here tonight. It means a lot to us."

As he walked back to his wife's side, the students who didn't know Eirik had protected Kate stared. My gaze connected with Torin's, the unsung hero of the night. I wondered how he felt being ignored. His expression didn't change, even when Cora went over and sat by his side. She stayed with him until it was time to leave.

It was one in the morning when they wheeled Kate from the operating room. We weren't allowed to see her, but the doctors talked to her parents and a nurse told us to go home. She was stable.

The streetlights were back on, I noted as we drove away from the hospital. Cora insisted on going home and was half asleep when we dropped her off.

"Are you coming in?" I asked when Eirik walked me to the door.

"Not tonight. I just want to go home and crash."

I touched the Band-aid above his eyebrow. The purple discoloration on his cheek looked worse. I wanted to kiss him, but I couldn't when he had a busted lip, so I kissed his cheek, instead. "Goodnight. Thanks for the wonderful birthday surprise."

He grimaced. "It ended on a shitty note."

"Don't think like that. It was beautiful, and I'll always remember it. And you were awesome tonight."

He frowned, obviously uncomfortable with the compliment. "I'll call you tomorrow." He gave me a brief peck on my forehead and walked away.

Mom was asleep on the living room couch, candles on every surface in the living room and kitchen. I blew them out, pausing when I saw Eirik's present, which I still hadn't opened. I tucked it under my arm and woke up Mom.

"You're finally home." Her eyes roamed my face as though looking for injuries before she hugged me. "What time is it?"

"Late. Come on, Mom."

"What happened to the girl who got hurt?" she asked.

"Her name is Kate Hunsaker." I explained her condition as we staggered upstairs.

The first thing I did when I entered my bedroom was peer at Torin's house. It was in total darkness. He had disappeared after the doctors spoke with Kate's parents. Was he home? Why was I worried about him? I was sure he could take care of himself. Besides, I had Eirik, my unofficial—or was it now official?—boyfriend and best friend. My life was perfect. Torin and his mysterious background didn't fit in it.

Closing the curtains, I sat on the bed and opened Eirik's present. I smiled at my favorite chocolate and a framed eight-by-ten picture of me. It was a memento from the years Mom tried to make me a carbon copy of herself. I was probably nine or ten and wore a Gypsy inspired outfit and a matching headscarf with beads. It was one of the first photographs Eirik had ever taken of me. He'd even signed it. Smiling, I placed it on my nightstand. I'd always treasure it.

I went to the bathroom to brush my teeth and crawled into bed.

***

Caridee came to our house for my birthday mani-pedis and facials, but all she talked about was the blackout.

"My cousin Camille knows Gaylene, who knows Chief Sparrowhawk's sister-in-law. The chief thinks someone went to the substation and threw the switches on the circuit breakers."

"We've never had a blackout before. Who'd want to plunge the town and neighboring county into total darkness?" Mom mused.

I didn't dare say anything, but a certain jealous exchange student came to mind.

"Kids playing pranks," Caridee said. "Sally Hunsaker's little girl got hurt real badly. They had to operate on her last night."

Mom reached over and gripped my hand. "Raine told me. She and the swim team stayed at the hospital with Kate's parents until the poor girl was out of the operating room. Trojan swimmers are very supportive of each member, you know. One of them, Eirik Seville, is the one who found the Hunsaker girl, protected her with his body, and carried her to safety," Mom repeated what I'd told her last night. I was surprised she remembered. "Because of him, that dear girl escaped serious injuries."

"How brave of him." I imagined how Caridee would embellish the story in the coming weeks. Eirik deserved a hero's recognition, even if it was through the grapevine. "I heard they were planning to operate on her again."

"Why?" I asked.

Caridee shrugged. "I don't know. Complications after surgery are pretty common."

My stomach churned. If Kate didn't make it... No, I couldn't afford to think like that. "Why does Chief Sparrowhawk think someone was behind the blackout?"

"He found something. Gaylene didn't know what exactly, but she said it was solid evidence someone messed with the switches."

After she left, I went upstairs and called Eirik. He sounded like he'd just woken up. "Kate is going in for a second surgery."

He cursed. "Do you want me to come over?"

"No, I, uh, I've tons of things to do. Maybe later." My eyes went to the box of assorted chocolates and the photograph. "I love my birthday presents. Thank you."

Despite saying I had things to do, we talked for a while. As soon as I hung up, I curled on the window seat with my laptop and went online to investigate runes.

The amount of information was staggering. Runes had meanings and stories behind them. They were alphabets used in ancient times for writing, divination, and magic by people from northern Europe, Scandinavia, British Isles, and Iceland. Andris, Ingrid, and Maliina were from Norway, which made sense. Did that mean Torin was from Europe, too? It might explain the British accent. Were they witches and wizards? It might explain their use of runes. It didn't explain why they called us Mortals.

I looked out the window at Torin's place. The slats were still closed. Maybe I should warn him that the police chief was investigating the blackout in case Maliina was behind it. No, I wasn't helping her. If she'd messed with the switches, she deserved to pay for whatever happened to Kate and the others. There'd be no journey to Land of Mist, which Torin had threatened Andris with, just good old Oregon prison and an orange jumpsuit.

I researched Land of Mist. There was no connection to runes, just books and online games. Wherever Land of Mist was, it was a horrible place to Torin's people.

Sighing, I put the laptop down and crawled out the window to the patio. Sometimes I wished I had a door like Mom and Dad. I'd begged them to add one when I turned thirteen, but they'd said no. It was better this way. No boys sneaking up into my room at night, Dad had said. Yeah, like that had ever stopped Eirik.

I leaned on the rail and inhaled. It was warm for fall, but knowing Oregon, the weather could turn chilly any minute. Most of our neighbors were indoors watching Sunday football. I could see inside the Rutledge's house through the open windows. Mr. Rutledge and Mr. Ross were watching football in the living room while their wives did something at the kitchen counter.

I glanced down and frowned. Had someone vandalized my car? Against the dark-red color, it was hard to tell. I crawled back inside my room and ran downstairs. Mom yelled something, but I didn't stop. I ran outside and gawked, my anger shooting up at the squiggles.

Who had done this to my poor car? Why?

I walked around and tried to wipe off the graffiti with the sleeve of my sweatshirt, but it didn't come off. Against the car body and the roof, the colors almost blended. Almost. On the windows and the tires, they looked garish. Maybe a carwash would get rid of them.

I started for the house, paused, and turned. No, they couldn't be. No freakin' way. I walked back to the car, but I was too close. I walked backwards to the middle of the cul-de-sac and squinted as I studied the graffiti again.

They weren't random drawings. They were runes, written in groups of threes, some across, others vertical. Who could have done this? Maliina, of course. But how had she found where I lived? What was her problem? Just because she hadn't hurt me last night didn't mean she had to put a whammy on my car. What were the runes supposed to do? Make my car flip, burst into flame while I was inside it? Torin needed to control that girl. It was obvious Andris couldn't.

I marched up to Torin's porch and rang the doorbell. No answer. He could still be sleeping or in the shower again. I banged on the door. Not a sound came from inside. Instead, I caught the reflection of Mrs. Rutledge and Mrs. Ross as they watched me from the porch. They gave me a look that screamed stalker. Bet they knew the number of times I'd talked to Torin since he moved in.

"He's gone," Mrs. Rutledge called out.

My stomach dropped. "Gone where?"

"Portland. He said he had a weekend job." Mrs. Rutledge smiled as though she enjoyed knowing something I didn't. I sighed. Cougar crush was so sad.

"Thanks, Mrs. Rutledge."

Back in the house, Mom was folding laundry. She frowned when I grabbed a brush, threw it in a bucket, and reached for a bottle of cleaning detergent.

"Are you okay?" she asked.

"Yeah." I turned on the water and poured a generous amount of the detergent in the bucket.

"What are you doing?"

"I'm going to clean my car."

"Now? Why don't you just drive it through a carwash?"

And play straight into Maliina's hand? I shuddered at the thought. I didn't think so. "No. I need to burn off some energy."

She studied me. "What's going on, Raine? I saw you go next door."

"We have a new neighbor. I went to, uh, say hi."

"That's sweet. Is it a nice family?"

"I only met their son, Torin. He'll be going to our school."

Mom grinned. "Is he hot?"

"Eew, Mom. He's…" *Superhot, mysterious, and magical, and he confuses me.* I turned off the water.

"He's what?"

"He's just a guy. I gotta go, Mom."

Outside, I scrubbed my car until my arms hurt. Using a water hose to rinse it off, I stepped back. I had done it. The squiggles were gone. Feeling better, I took the bucket and brush inside and came back with my keys.

No! My heart sunk. They were back. The water had just hidden them briefly. How the heck was I going to get rid of them? I kicked a tire.

"What happened?" Mom said, hurrying toward me. "I heard you scream."

"Someone vandalized my car, and I can't get rid of the drawings."

Mom stared at the car then me. "Oh, sweetie."

"Just look at it." I waved toward my car, so frustrated I wanted to cry.

Mom put her arms around my shoulders. "Raine, your car is spotless. In fact I've never seen it this clean."

"But…" Then realization hit me. She couldn't see the runes, while I could. Why?

"Did you get hurt last night at the club and forgot to tell me? You've been acting strange today." Mom pressed the back of her hand to my forehead. "You don't have a fever."

"I'm fine. I guess I'm just worried about Kate. I mean, if she hadn't come to the club for my birthday party, she'd not have been…" My voice shook to a stop, tears rushing to my eyes.

"Oh, honey." She gave me a tight hug. "You can't think like that. Things happen, and most of the time, they're beyond our control. Come on. Go lie down while I warm us something for dinner."

I cooked whenever I could, especially on weekends, but I didn't have the interest and I wasn't hungry. In fact, I hadn't felt like eating the whole day.

Back upstairs, I texted Eirik. "Can I get a ride to school tomorrow?"

"Sure. What's wrong with your car?"

"It won't start for some reason," I fibbed, the urge to cry washing over me again.

"I'll come over and take a look at it."

"No, it's… the truth is I just don't feel like driving myself anywhere."

There was silence; then he said, "I'm coming over."

It was hard not to tell him everything I'd overheard and learned about Torin and the others. He would think I was crazy. He couldn't see the runes on my car, so I had no proof.

My worries about Maliina and her plans for me escalated when Eirik showed me the pictures he'd taken last night and I realized something. Kate Hunsaker had worn a dress similar to mine, except hers was white and blue.

Could Maliina have mistaken her for me?

CHAPTER 6. MARKED

"Remind me never to hitch a ride with you again," I teased Eirik when he slid behind the wheel again and placed his camera on the tray between our seats. It was the second time he'd pulled over to take pictures of deer.

He grinned. "I couldn't resist. Winter background can be a bit tricky. Fall colors, I can play with."

I rolled my eyes and sat back, studying the scenery as we sped toward downtown. It wasn't that I didn't appreciate nature. I did. Vibrant fall colors were everywhere, reds mixed with yellow and orange. Of all the seasons, I loved fall the best. I just wanted to get to school as soon as possible. I couldn't explain the anticipation.

Okay, now I'm lying to myself. I wanted to see Torin. Last night, I'd stayed up late after Eirik left, hoping Torin would come home. He hadn't, so I wasn't sure whether he'd be at school or not. I had to know what the runes on my car meant and how to get rid of them. Andris and his harem would be no help, which left Torin.

We stopped at the traffic light on Main Street, then turned left toward school. Most brick buildings in downtown Kayville were old, the streets lined with mature trees. The hills and valleys surrounding the city were covered with miles and miles of vineyards. Kayville might be a small town in the middle of Oregon wine country, but we had everything any city had. We were also only about an hour from Portland.

Students hurried across Riverside Boulevard from the parking lots while others poured from the school buses lining the street. Eirik found a spot to park. While he aimed his camera at something and clicked, I reached in the back of his Jeep for my backpack. A distant purr of a motorcycle engine sent excitement through me.

Torin.

No student rode a Harley to school. A few had scooters and bikes, but majority either drove cars or took the bus. He entered the boulevard, and students turned to watch. A few pointed. Black helmet, black jeans and jacket—he looked like a renegade hell bent on disrupting the peace. I grabbed my backpack, joined Eirik, and started across the street toward the school. Eirik reached for my hand.

"You have to give it to the guy," he murmured, chuckling.

"What?" I asked.

"Torin. He knows how to make an entrance."

Torin parked at the curb, and the purr of the engine died. Still astride his bike, he removed his helmet, tucked it under his arm, and adjusted his sunglasses. As if possible, more girls stopped to stare. Eirik and I had reached the same side of the street when Torin reached for his backpack from the bike's side saddle, turned, and looked directly at us.

Eirik nodded. My stomach did that senseless crazy dance I was beginning to associate with him. I averted my eyes and stared straight ahead, even though I was dying to look at him again. Still, I was aware he was behind us during the short walk to the building. My heart pounded, and I was lightheaded. Then I realized why. I was holding my breath. That was so lame.

Next second, I froze at the foot of the stairs leading to the school's entrance, and he almost bumped into me. He said something I didn't catch because my eyes were on the massive doors of the school. Runes crossed the bottom red wood and the top glass panel.

What was going on? Were Torin and his friends marking their territories like a pack?

"What is it? Why did you stop?" Eirik asked.

"It's nothing," I said slowly and glanced at Torin. He seemed just as surprised, which meant he hadn't done this. That left Andris and his team. I was dying to ask Torin what the runes meant, but I couldn't with Eirik around.

"You look like you've seen a ghost," Eirik said.

"I'm fine. Let's go." My grip tightened, and I moved closer to him. As we approached the door, I tensed, expecting something bad to happen. Nothing did.

Inside the foyer, students stood in groups, catching up on weekend news. The snippets I caught seemed to focus on the incident at the club. I cringed. Torin disappeared toward the office while Eirik and I headed for our lockers.

"What happened out there?" Eirik asked.

"I thought I saw someone."

"Who?"

I hated lying to him, but I couldn't explain seeing things no one else could see. "My dad, but it was just a trick of light."

Eirik frowned, but he didn't say anything. We walked in silence until we reached the hallway, where his locker was.

"See you at lunch?" he said, but it came out as a question.

"Of course."

He peered at me. "Should I be worried about you?"

I punched his arm. "No. I didn't sleep well last night. That's all." He shot me a questioning look. "You know, worrying about Kate."

He nodded. Then he cupped my face, lowered his head, and kissed me. When he lifted his head, my eyes connected with Torin's. He was watching us. My gaze not leaving his, I went to my toes and returned Eirik's kiss with more enthusiasm, going beyond the casual lip action we'd shared the last two days.

"Get a room," someone said as he walked by.

Eirik wore a dazed look when I leaned back. Behind him, Torin turned and walked away. I stared after him, feeling like an idiot. I couldn't explain why I'd kissed Eirik so passionately in front of Torin.

"Wow," Eirik mumbled. "That was… uh…"

"Too much?" I asked, knowing I had gone too far. I wasn't ready for our make out to go beyond light kissing and holding hands.

"No, it was perfect. See you at lunch."

Cora was waiting for me by my locker. She looked like hell.

"Hey," I said, rubbing her arm. "You okay?"

"No. Haven't you heard?"

"What?"

"They don't think Kate's going to make it," she whispered, her chin trembling.

"Oh, no." We hugged. "A friend of Mom's said she was undergoing a second surgery yesterday. She also said someone caused the blackout."

"Really?" She sounded so hopeful as though blaming someone else eased her guilt. She had no reason to feel guilty. Neither did I, yet I did.

"Chief Sparrowhawk thinks so." I put my backpack away and removed my folder and the books I needed for my morning classes. "So if you're still blaming yourself, stop it. Whoever messed with the switch at the substation is responsible for this."

She sighed. "I wish that could make me feel better. Later, Raine."

Cora's English class was at the end of the west building. I stared after her, knowing I had to be strong for both of us. I went toward the stairs and my first class of the day. Most math classes were on the second floor. I thought I caught a glimpse of Andris and Maliina at the end of the hallway, but I might have been mistaken. My thoughts returned to the runes on the school entrance. Why would anyone put them there?

Stares and whispers followed me when I entered math class. Or maybe I was imagining things. I slid into my seat and pulled out my textbook. Across the aisle, Sam Rasmussen stared at me with a weird expression. He sported a bruise on his chin and right cheek. He was at my party on Saturday, and I didn't know whether to apologize for his injuries or not. I gave him a tiny smile, but he didn't return it.

"Raine Cooper," Frank Moffat said as he lumbered into the classroom. Frank was tall and big with curly brown hair and beady gray eyes. He was also one of Blaine Chapman's jock buddies and a known bully. Since he wasn't in my calculus class the first few weeks of school, I assumed he'd either changed classes or he was after blood.

"I heard your birthday party bombed. Everyone was dying to get out," he mocked.

My face grew hot. Seriously, some people were just too stupid to realize when a joke was tasteless. I stared at my books and ignored him.

He grabbed a chair, straddled it, and crossed his arms along the back. "Next time, make sure you tell people to bring flashlights."

This time, a few snickers echoed around the room. I glared at him and tried to come up with something to say, anything in my defense, but my mind went blank. I hated confrontations and could feel my temper rising. I bit my lower lip and tried to control myself. He grinned.

"What? You're going to cry? I hope it's for the people who were hurt trying to run away from you."

Knowing I'd say something I'd regret if I stayed, I got up and hurried out of the class, bumping into a student and almost tripping. The nearest bathroom was down the hall, so I gunned for it, locked myself inside a stall, and tried to control myself. My eyes smarted.

I wasn't a crier and often avoided unpleasantness, but this morning was different. Everything that had happened over the weekend came crashing down. It wasn't my fault there was a blackout.

The blame belonged to whoever had caused it. The more I thought about it, the more pissed I became.

I glanced at my watch. I had less than a minute to get my act together before the second bell or I'd get a tardy slip. I left the stall, splashed water on my face, and pat-dried it with tissue. I entered the class, and my feet faltered when I saw Torin. What was he doing in my class?

"Nice of you to join us, Miss Cooper," Mrs. Bates said, her eyes narrowed on me. "One tardy slip. Three strikes and you attend my Saturday class."

Mrs. Bates was an amazing calculus teacher, but she was über strict. Looking at her, you wouldn't guess it. She was petite with graying brown hair and warm brown eyes. Her rhinestone glasses were often perched at the top of her upturned nose. She could pass for a sweet librarian, until those brown eyes turned cold and narrowed at you, like now.

"I was already in class, Mrs. Bates. I just needed to—"

"Cry?" Frank asked.

I lifted my chin. "Throw up."

"Are you okay? Do you need to see the nurse?" Mrs. Bates asked.

"I'm fine now." My gaze met Torin's. He grinned with approval. Smiling, I walked to my desk. My victory was brief though. Frank and Sam started whispering. I didn't know whether I was the subject or not, but it was distracting.

"Would you like to take over my class, Mr. Moffat?" Mrs. Bates asked halfway through the class while studying him from above the rim of her glasses.

"No, ma'am. I think you're doing a fine job," he added cockily.

"Oh, thank you. Then why don't you share with the class whatever it is you feel you must discuss while I'm teaching?"

"Since this is my first day in your class, I think you should know that some of the students in here have *gas* problems." Muffled laughter filled the class. "Can I change seats, please?"

"No. You stay in your assigned seats unless you want to be kicked out of my class." Mrs. Bates glanced at me then consulted her notes and went back to teaching.

I wanted to die. Frank Moffat had just ruined my morning. The implication that I was passing gas in class was beyond humiliating. Who did he think he was? I was still pissed when class ended. Collecting my things, I tried to escape my embarrassment.

"Mr. Moffat and Miss Cooper," Mrs. Bates said, "stay behind, please."

I exhaled and stared down at the feet walking past. I knew which boots belonged to Torin. He hesitated near my desk before continuing toward the door.

"What's going on between you two?" Mrs. Bates asked.

Frank scowled. Since football players were treated like royalty, he probably hadn't expected to be called out.

"Miss Cooper?"

I shook my head. "There's nothing going on."

"Mr. Moffat?" she asked.

"She started it. All I mentioned was her party over the weekend, and she verbally attacked me."

I wanted to call him a liar, but suddenly I felt drained. I just wanted the meeting to be over. The school always gave football players a pass anyway, so whatever I said wouldn't matter.

"I made it clear on the first day that I will not tolerate insolence from students, bullying, or any behavior that disrupts the smooth running of my class. If you have a problem, resolve it before class or take it to your counselors. Now get out of my class, and let me not hear about this again."

The day went downhill from there. Lunch brought respite. Eirik took one look at me and asked, "What happened?"

I shook my head, not wanting to go into detail. "Let's just say I had a horrible morning. I can't wait for this day to be over."

"Me, too," Cora said, sitting across from us. Keith took the seat next to her. "Everyone is blaming me for what happened at the club."

"Me too," I said.

"Weird. No one's said anything to me," Eirik said.

"That's because you were the hero of the night and have battle wounds to prove it." Cora pointed at the steri-strip covering his wound. Then she appeared to shrink, her gaze on something or someone behind me. "Here comes one of my tormentors."

I looked behind me to see Frank Moffat. He was limping and looked pretty pissed, or scared. I couldn't tell the difference. I braced myself. Both Eirik and Keith stood, ready to take him on. Frank didn't appear to notice them, his gaze volleying between me and Cora. As he got closer, I noticed the runes on his right cheek. Was he another Immortal?

"Lorraine Cooper," Frank said, stuttering, "I'm sorry for picking on you in class and accusing you of terrible things. You didn't deserve any of it." He glanced at Cora. "Cora Jemison, I'm sorry for calling you names. I promise to never pick on you again." His body shook, and he turned and walked away.

"What was that about?" Cora whispered.

Maybe Frank wasn't one of *them* after all. Maybe the runes had made him apologize, which meant someone had drawn them on his face. Someone bold and not easily intimidated. I glanced around the room, but I didn't see Torin. For the first time, I saw the powers of the runes as positive, as something I might actually be interested in.

"My name is Frank Moffat," Frank yelled from the middle of the room, each word strained as though he was being forced to say them. People turned to stare, the room growing quiet. "Most of you know me as the Trojans' running back. A few of you know me as something else, a… a…" he jerked as though he'd been prodded again. "A bully."

"What's wrong with him?" someone at Blaine Chapman's table asked, his voice carrying.

"I pick on smaller and quiet students," Frank continued. His girlfriend jumped up and hurried to his side. She tried to pull him away, but Frank ignored her. "I'm a douche and a…"

Laughter filled the room and swallowed the rest of his words. Even his jock friends were covering their mouths and trying hard not to laugh. So much for loyalty. His girlfriend, now red-faced, ran from the cafeteria. Blaine and another player marched to the middle of the cafeteria and grabbed Frank's arms.

He was still yelling, "I'm so sorry for being a douche," when the P.A. system crackled and the principal's baritone rang out.

"All students report to the auditorium at the end of this period. Do not go to your next class. Head to the auditorium immediately."

We looked at each other and went to dump our leftover lunches. I usually love Hawaiian haystack, but I'd barely touched mine.

"What do you think's going on?" Keith asked.

"Going by luck today, something horrible," Cora answered and slipped her arm around his waist as we walked to the auditorium.

I didn't say anything, but I agreed with her. The day had started crappy and despite the humiliating apology from Frank, I had a bad feeling in the pit of my stomach. Interestingly enough, no one seemed to care about the reason for the unexpected assembly. Frank's confession was the topic of conversation in the auditorium, until Principal Elliot walked on stage.

"It has come to our attention that certain students have taken to harassing the others because of an incident that happened over the weekend during the blackout," the principal said. "We will not tolerate bullying of any kind or form. If you see anyone being intimidated, report the incident to the office immediately." He paused.

Cora and I exchanged a glance. News traveled fast.

"On the heel of that, we have some sad news to share with the student body. Katherine Hunsaker was at a party during the blackout and was rushed to the hospital with intracranial bleeding on Saturday night. Doctors did their best to stop the bleeding. Instead of getting better, Katherine became worse. The surgeons did their best to help her. Sadly, Katherine was pronounced dead less than an hour ago."

Everyone started talking at once. Cora and I reached for each other. Someone got up even though the principal was still talking. The haze of tears made it difficult to see who it was at first, but I recognized the swagger. Torin. I blinked and saw his face. He looked furious. Then three more people got up—Andris, Maliina, and Ingrid—and I knew something bad was about to happen.

"Counselors will be available to talk to students who need help coping with this loss," Principal Elliot continued. "Katherine represented the best this school has to offer. She was one of our fastest swimmers. She was also a member of the student council and a regular tutor at…"

"Cora, I'll be back," I whispered. She nodded and leaned against Keith's shoulder. I'd never particularly liked Keith. He always came across as too standoffish for the fun-loving and sensitive Cora, but I was beginning to see a new side of him.

"What's going on?" Eirik asked as he got up to let me pass.

"I need fresh air."

"Do you want me to come with you?" he asked like a dutiful boyfriend.

"No. Fill me in later." I didn't want him following me.

Outside, the front hall was empty. I checked the wide hallway on the left and right, but no one was there. Where did Torin and the others go? Turning to go back inside the auditorium, I saw them through the corner glass window. They were across street in the eastern parking lot. From the looks of things, Torin and Andris were having a heated argument.

Moving closer to the window, I winced as their fight became physical. One punch from Torin sent Andris in the air and across a hood into some poor student's windshield. It cracked as though hit by a demolition ball, but Andris bounced off it like a ping pong ball. He rammed into Torin. The two skidded along the parking lot, leaving a crack on the ground. Maliina and Ingrid moved closer as though waiting for a chance to pounce. Would they gang up on Torin?

I didn't want to get anyone in trouble, but someone had to stop them before one of them got seriously hurt or they wrecked the entire parking lot and more cars. I checked around me for security, but the hall was empty. My mind raced with indecision. The fight outside intensified. Andris threw Torin, and he landed on the fender of another car, leaving a dent so huge I was surprised every bone in his body wasn't broken.

The decision to find the school cop disappeared when Maliina's hands moved and light reflected something in them. She was carrying two knives or the weird thin blades she'd used to sketch runes on her skin. They were planning to kill Torin.

I raced out the door, down the lawn, and across the street. Thuds grew louder the closer I got to them. I also noticed the runes covering every visible part of their bodies. Did the runes give them superhuman strength?

"Stop it," I yelled.

The two guys froze and looked toward me. Not Maliina. She sent a knife sailing toward Torin, who was pinning Andris against a car door.

"Duck," I yelled.

Torin didn't move. He kept staring at me with a look I couldn't define. The knife sunk into his chest. I gasped, but he didn't even flinch. Blood spread on his black shirt.

"How can she see us?" Ingrid asked.

"I told you he healed and marked her," Maliina said with a sneer.

Without looking down, Torin gripped the handle of the knife, yanked it from his chest, and threw it down. Without missing a beat, he marched toward Maliina.

"Torin, don't," Andris yelled.

Confused, I watched the red and white blur that was Maliina as she tried to get away, but Torin was faster. One second they looked like the Tasmanian Devil in Warner Bros cartoons, the next he'd grabbed her from behind. He gripped her jaw and twisted, snapping her neck in one smooth move. I opened my mouth to scream, but my throat had seized up. Cursing Torin to Land of Mist, Andris caught Maliina before she hit the ground.

"Why?" Andris yelled.

"I warned both of you to leave Mortals alone," Torin growled as he started toward me.

I staggered backwards, needing to put space between us, so scared I could hardly think. Pain shot up my arm. I looked down, trying to find its source, and saw the knife protruding from my shoulder. It was a replica of the one Torin had pulled from his chest. Maliina must have thrown both knives at the same time. Weird, I hadn't seen the knife sail toward me or felt the pain when it pierced my skin. I'd been focused on Torin.

Tears rushed to my eyes, and wooziness washed over me. I hated the sight of blood, even though only a blot of red discolored my light-blue top.

"Easy, Freckles," Torin said calmly. "Let me remove it."

My head whipped up. "No. Touch me and I'll scream."

"Don't," Torin warned. He spoke with the authority of someone who was used to giving orders, and I found myself obeying and hating myself for being scared of him. What had Maliina meant by 'he marked her'?

"I just want to help you," Torin added softly.

"No. You're crazy." I shuffled away from him. I glanced at the others. Ingrid cradled Maliina in her arms while Andris etched runes on her arm. "You're all crazy."

Torin smiled. "Come on, Freckles. You know we're not. We are... different. That's all. Let me remove the knife, so the wound can heal."

I shook my head, my heart pounding so hard I could hear each beat on my temple. Worse, the arm with the knife was beginning to go numb. "No, the nurse will remove it and..." The last thing he'd said registered. "Heal? What do you mean?"

"The runes will heal you," he said gently.

"I don't want—" I looked down and gasped, as a fresh surge of panic rolled through me. Runes inked my skin. Where had they come from? I pushed back my sleeve and saw more. Before I realized his intentions, Torin grabbed the handle and pulled the knife from my arm.

I flinched, expecting pain. I felt nothing even though blood gushed from the wound and darkened my sleeve. Then it stopped spreading. I stared, too afraid to move or breathe. With a trembling hand, I pulled up my sleeve to reveal where the knife had pierced my skin. The wound sealed until nothing was left. No scar or bruise to show I'd been stabbed. The runes glowed then disappeared.

Shaking, I looked up at Torin in horror. I was a freak. "What have you done to me?"

"We'll talk later. Right now, go back to school." He shrugged off his jacket. "Wear this to cover your shirt until—"

"No." I pushed the jacket away, my stomach churning. "You did this to me."

He shook his head. "Freckles—"

"You marked me."

"I didn't."

"Liar. How do you explain the runes or my body self-healing? You've turned me into one of you, a freak."

"You're not a freak, and I won't let you become like me." He said it like he was something ugly and unpleasant, an abomination.

I stared at him unblinkingly. "What are you?"

Blue fire burned in his eyes as though he was struggling with his thoughts.

"What did you do to me?" I yelled.

He shook his head and spoke softly. "You would have died on Saturday if I hadn't healed you, Raine."

"You don't know that," I said through clenched teeth. His face faded and then zoomed into focus. I was about to faint. Worse, the smell of blood mixed with the shock of seeing the runes on my skin made me nauseas.

"Look at the cars," he begged, waving toward the casualties of his fight with Andris: dented hoods and fenders, crashed windows, and broken mirrors. "A kick from one of us can snap your spine in two or crush your ribcage like it did on Saturday."

I didn't want to hear his explanation or forgive him. "I didn't ask you to heal me, Torin."

"I know," he conceded, sounding so sad, anguish on his face.

"Then remove them." I stuck my arms out. "Do something and get them out of me."

He shook his head. "That's not how we do things."

"I don't care how you do things. Find a way to remove them." I staggered past him then remembered. "And that includes the ones on my car."

Confusion flashed in his eyes. "Your car?"

"Yes, my car. I can't even drive it because I'm scared it might explode. If she," I jabbed a finger toward Maliina, "is responsible for the blackout and caused Kate's death, she'd better stay dead or I'll report her to Chief Sparrowhawk myself." I walked past him, but he reached for my arm. I jerked away. "Don't."

"Take the jacket, Raine. Or you'll have to explain the blood to the school nurse and your friends."

I hated the fact that he was right. I had a tank top under my shirt, but wearing it would violate the school's dress code. To make things worse, some of the students had left school and were coming toward the parking lot. I grabbed the jacket from his hand.

"You're welcome," he said.

"Bite me." I hurried away, hating the sticky, wet blood on my skin. I yanked the jacket on and didn't look back until I heard the roar of his Harley. He rode away as though hell was on his heels. Andris was gone, too, but Ingrid was helping Maliina to her feet.

The evil bitch couldn't even stay dead. Go figure. Breaking each other's neck must be part of their daily smackdown. The two women turned to stare at me. I couldn't see their expressions, but I felt their hatred.

Yeah, right back at you.

Ingrid left Maliina's side and moved from car to car at a super-speed, pausing to mark them with her rune pen. I assumed she was fixing the cracks and dents their men had left behind. Shaking my head, I continued toward the building. I was never, ever going near them again. Next time, let them kill each other for all I cared.

Students were leaving the auditorium and talking excitedly when I entered the building. I managed to weave my way to the restroom, changed, and stashed my shirt in my locker. I didn't want the cleaning people finding it in the garbage can. I was already freaking out about what was happening to me without worrying about the school starting another investigation. I hurried to my next class.

CHAPTER 7. MAKING CONNECTION

"Do you need to see a counselor, Cooper?" Mr. Allred, my physics teacher, asked. He was the second teacher to ask me that very question since the assembly, and it was becoming annoying. My problems couldn't be solved by talking to a school counselor.

"No, I'm fine." Or I was going to be once I knew how and why my new neighbor had runed me. Marked me. Turned me. It didn't matter how I said it. I was a freak. The only thing stopping me from a total meltdown was what he had said. "I won't let you become like me."

He'd better keep his word.

Cora didn't mention the leather jacket or my tank top after school. Grief-stricken, she barely talked to me before taking off with Keith. Eirik was more observant. Even though I removed the jacket before entering his car, his eyes narrowed on it. He didn't say anything until we pulled up outside my house.

"Is that Torin's?"

I nodded, feeling guilty even though I had no reason to be. "I had a nose bleed and bloodied my shirt when I went outside during the assembly." I pulled out the shirt and showed him. He made a face. "I know, disgusting. Torin loaned me his jacket to cover up my tank top. You know school rules. No tank tops."

"That explains why you disappeared. I checked the hall, but didn't see you."

Weird. He should have been able to see me through the window. The others, according to Ingrid, were invisible to everyone but me. Yeah, lucky me. "Are you coming in?"

"No." He glanced at his watch. "I have my physical in thirty minutes."

"For the swim team?"

"Yep. Want to come and hold my hand?" he teased.

I grinned, forgetting my problems. "You poor baby. Sorry, I can't. Mom hasn't made my appointment yet, and you know how it is. If she's not there, the nurses won't let me past the waiting room." I stepped down from the Jeep and closed the door.

He rolled down the window. "Listen, Raine. Be careful around Torin."

I frowned. "Why do you say that?"

"I know my parents know his family, but I get weird vibes from him. Just be careful."

Vibes didn't begin to cover it. "Okay."

I watched him drive away, then removed my cell phone. I called Mom and reminded her about my physical. After she promised to make an appointment with the doctor, I grabbed a bag of spicy Doritos, soda, a notebook, and a pen, and headed back outside.

Homework would just have to wait. I needed answers, and since I couldn't summon the runes to appear on my skin without hurting myself first, that left the ones on the car.

I sat on the curb and copied the garish writings. The roar of Torin's Harley filled the air after a while, and my heart leaped. I pretended not to hear it and didn't glance over when it stopped. I continued to focus on the runes. There appeared to be six of them in a repeated pattern of threes, but the middle one was the same in all of them.

"What are you doing, Freckles?"

My stomach did that annoying flip-flopping thing. I wanted to ignore him. I really did, but I just couldn't. He slid next to me and peered at my book, bringing with him his warmth. It wrapped around me so deliciously I wanted to purr.

Don't let him get to you. He was the rude and cocky Immortal with superhuman abilities who'd runed me. He smelled good, too. Okay, so there was something about him that called to me. I could either whine about it or just ignore it. I needed his help.

"I guess you're ignoring me now," he said. "What happened to the gutsy girl who begged me to bite her in the school parking lot?"

"I did not beg." Only he could take something said in anger and flip it. "I'm copying the runes before you remove them."

He chuckled. "Who said I can remove them?"

"Me. One of *your* people painted them."

"Why would they do that?"

"Because she hates me." I glanced at him and wished I hadn't. Without his wraparound sunglasses, his eyes drew me in. He really had beautiful eyes and incredibly long eyelashes. My eyes strayed to his chest. He hadn't changed his shirt from earlier, and the blood from the stabbing wound was still there.

I pointed at the spot. "Can you get rid of that by drawing runes on your shirt?"

He glanced down and frowned as though surprised it was there. "Yeah, or I can do this."

He stretched his T-shirt so it plastered against his masculine chest, and my inner hound wagged its tail in appreciation. The blood on the fabric quickly disappeared. He grinned, looking pleased with himself. What a show off.

"How do you do that?"

"*I* control the runes on my body; will them to do my bidding. Unlike the others, I don't need to sketch new ones all the time."

Yep, he was definitely showing off. "Can you look at any rune and know what it means?"

He rolled his eyes as though the task was too mundane for someone with his abilities. "Before I answer that, how are you planning to decipher the codes?"

"Codes?"

"The message behind the rune patterns you have so, uh," he leaned closer, his arm touching mine, "sloppily drawn."

I sucked in a breath as I adjusted to the sensations shooting through my body from where our arms touched. My heart pounded. I wanted to move away and break the contact, but I couldn't. Truth be told, I longed to wrap myself around him and greedily absorb these new sensations. Now if only I could breathe before I passed out.

Then what he'd said registered. He'd called my sketches sloppy. Somehow my mind tended to process things a lot slower whenever I was around him, and it had to stop.

"Well?" he asked.

I exhaled and muttered, "I'll check online."

He laughed, and I wasn't sure whether he knew the effect he had on me or if my squeaky voice was the cause. Either way, he was laughing *at* me. Anger boiled to the surface. One minute in his presence and I wanted to deck him.

"Go away, Torin." I got up.

He jumped up. "It amazes me how Mortals think they can decipher messages from the gods."

I cocked my brow. "As in I'm the Mortal and you guys are some kind of gods?"

"Close, but yeah."

I counted backward until I was calm enough to speak without hurling my notebook at his head. "Why are you such a douche?"

His brow shot up. "Me? I'm the nice one. You're the... impossible one. One minute you're thanking me for healing you, the next you're yelling at me for doing it."

"You marked me with your stupid runes," I said through clenched teeth.

He pretended to think about it. "If I marked you, Freckles, I'd be under your skin. You wouldn't think of anything or anyone but me twenty-four-seven."

I'd thought of him nonstop ever since we met. Heat warmed my face.

A low grin spread across his face. "You've been thinking about me, haven't you?"

"You wish."

His eyes twinkled. "Bet you think about me when you kiss Seville."

I opened my mouth, then closed it with a snap. I didn't think I could speak without saying something I'd regret. "I loathe you."

"There's a thin line between—"

"Leave me alone." I marched toward the house, trying to escape my feelings.

"I can tell you what the runes mean," he said, following me.

"Yeah, like I'd believe anything you say now." I opened the door, entered, and turned. "Nice chatting with you, Torin. I'd say don't ever speak to me again but that would be pointless because you're always around, stalking me, waiting to play the hero. Whatever game you're playing, it's not working. I already have a hero, and he's... he's Mortal and amazing. When we kiss, I don't think. I feel." I slammed the door on his face and grinned. The grin turned into laughter. The play of emotions on his face as I'd berated him would go down in history. Shock, confusion, and amazement. I'd bet no girl had ever slammed a door in his face.

I threw out the empty Doritos bag and soda can and headed upstairs. While my laptop rebooted, I settled on the window seat. As though he'd been waiting for me, Torin sat on his window seat and studied me across the space. When he smirked, I faked interest in my computer and clicked on a browser.

"You know you'll eventually ask for my help," he said.

I ignored him, wishing our houses weren't so close.

"I will make you beg," he added.

Yeah, good luck with that.

"Most runes are not even found in Mortal books, let alone on the Internet," he continued.

It wasn't what he'd said, but how he'd said it that got me. "What are you?"

"What do you think I am?"

Annoyance coursed through me. "You have a nasty habit of answering my questions with questions."

He pushed the lock of hair from his forehead and grinned. "How else will you learn anything if I don't challenge you?"

On Saturday he couldn't even admit he'd healed me. Ignoring him, I Googled runes and clicked on the first link that popped up. It took me to a page with more links. One particular title caught my attention, and I pressed it. The article focused on the meaning of runes, but it was more detailed than the ones I'd read before.

The words under each symbol were in a language I didn't understand. In parenthesis were translations in English. The words wealth, joy, and gift popped out at me. I studied the symbols on my notebook and compared them with the ones on the screen. I found one that matched. It meant goddess, but no name was given. Which goddess?

"So what am I, Freckles?" Torin asked, sounding awfully close.

I glanced out the window and found him under my tree. "Annoying."

He chuckled. "You're cute."

I winced. Puppies were cute. Kittens playing with a ball of yarn were cute.

"You can do better than that," he said.

I sighed, hating myself for being curious enough to give in. "A witch?"

He made a face.

"Demon? Wizard? Warlock? Am I getting warmer?"

"Colder than Hel's Mist."

"What's that?"

"I'll tell you after you guess what I am."

I kept a straight face. "Rumpelstiltskin?"

He rolled his eyes. "Be serious."

"Werewolf? No, that might have explained the superhuman strength if I didn't know about the runes. Vampire crossed my mind, but you don't sparkle."

His eyebrows shot up. "Sparkle?"

"Yeah, like Edward. He's superhot and perfect."

Torin scowled. "*You* have seen vampires?"

"Of course. On the screen, in my dreams. What are you doing?"

"Climbing your tree."

I swallowed. "Why?"

"I like getting close and personal when talking to a beautiful woman."

My cheeks grew warm, and I looked behind me. "Who?"

"You, Freckles." He stopped at one of the top, sturdy branches, leaned against it, and studied me. "You should see yourself through my eyes, Raine Cooper. Gorgeous, fascinating, stubborn, funny, but I wouldn't have you anyway."

Oh, wow. No guy had ever complimented me with such conviction. My cheeks shot past warm to hot, which meant my face was red as beets. "You're kidding, right?"

"No, I'm not. Don't you think you're beautiful?"

"I meant does that old line really work anymore. *I like getting close and personal when talking to a beautiful woman,*" I repeated, imitating his deep voice and wiggling my brow.

He laughed again. I found myself smiling.

"Like I said, you're a hoot," he said. "FYI, up close and personal has gotten me a lot of play."

"Dimwits." The conversation I'd overheard between him and Andris flashed in my head. They were after the swim team, and it wasn't to help us win state. "Are you a merman?"

"As in male mermaids?" He made a face as though he'd swallowed a rotten egg. "Have you seen the weeds on their feet and hands, their slimy, green skin? I'd rather live in the Mist."

Okay, so mermaids and mermen existed in his world, wherever that was. "Where's this Mist, and what makes it so terrifying?"

"Land of Mist is where the un-heroic go when they die."

"Un-heroic?"

"People who die of old age and diseases."

Weird belief. "Have you ever dealt with a terminally ill person?"

Torin shuddered. "I try to stay away from hospitals. Sick people give me the willies."

What a baby. "They're the bravest and most heroic people in the whole world."

He frowned. "You've worked with such people?"

"No, but I visited Cora's grandmother before she died. She had cancer. If there's a place for heroes, that's where she belongs."

Silence followed my outburst. When I glanced at Torin from the corner of my eye, he was frowning. "Can I, uh, climb over to your balcony?"

"Why?"

He pulled something brown from his back pocket. "I want to give you this."

Jumping on my balcony and crawling through my window was Eirik's thing, and I wanted to keep it that way. "Come around to the front door."

He mumbled something.

"What?"

"Front door it is." He pushed the book back into his back pocket and jumped to the ground. It was a long drop with thick branches, but he didn't hit anything and landed gracefully like an alley cat.

He was leaning against the wall when I opened the front door. The way he handed over the book, it was as though he was giving me his most precious possession. "It has all the runes known to the gods."

"Thank you." The brown leather cover had an intricate symbol. Carefully, I turned it and flipped through the pages. The pages were made of light-brown, leathery material. The black ink was starting to fade, but I could still make out the runes. There was no numbering, but I'd say the pages were less than a hundred. "Which gods are you talking about?"

"I'm not going to make things easy for you."

"Meanie," I mumbled, still studying the pages.

The first pages had about a hundred runes, but the rest showed combinations of some of them in twos, threes, fours, and fives, their meanings written in a weird language. There was no English translation.

"What language is this?"

"Language of the gods. Once you find your runes, I'll explain what they mean."

Could I trust him? Half the time I wasn't sure whether he was mocking me or testing me. "Can we get rid of the ones on my car?"

"Sure, but you might not want to once you know what they mean."

"That means you know what they mean."

"Yep."

I groaned. "Why can't you just tell me?"

"If I do, you won't learn anything."

He was right. Dang it. "Why is it important to you that I learn anything at all?"

"So you can understand the ones inside you and how they got there."

"They healed me, and *you* put them there," I retorted. He didn't respond. "You're not going to deny it?"

He shrugged. "What's the point? You won't believe me."

"Damn right." He continued to watch me with an expectant expression as though waiting for something. "Do you, uh, want to come in?"

"Oh no. I want my jacket back."

"Oh. Just a second." I grabbed it from the table by the door where I'd left it and checked the inner sleeves. There were some spots of dried blood. "I should take it to the drycleaners first to remove the bloody smudges."

"I'm not scared of a little blood, especially yours." He took the jacket, then reached out and touched my nose like he'd done the first time we met. "Later, Freckles."

"A quick question," I said, wanting to detain him a little longer, even though I knew I shouldn't. "Which god rules the Land of Mist?"

"Hel."

I scrunched my face. "If you didn't want to answer me, you should have just said, 'I'm not telling you' in your usual pompous way. Thanks for the book, but you're still on my douche list." I started to close the door, but he blocked it with his foot. "What now?"

He grinned as though enjoying a private joke. "Land of Mist is ruled by a goddess, and her name is *Hel* with one L."

"Oh."

He cocked his brow. "Am I still a douche?"

I wrinkled my nose. "Oh, yeah. Did you rune Frank Moffat and force him to apologize to me and Cora?"

He grinned.

"Did Maliina mess with the lights at the substation?"

He stopped smiling. "No. I checked it. It was a glitch."

"Then why were you fighting Andris? I assumed it had something to do with the lights and Kate getting hurt."

"It had. Can I go now?" He walked backward, a wicked smile lifting his sculptured lips. "Or if you want me to stay, just say the word."

I snorted and closed the door, but I still heard his laughter. Shaking my head, I went back upstairs to my computer and research.

Hel with one L...

Hel was the daughter of Loki. Her home, named after her, was cold and misty. She took care of the souls of people who died of old age and diseases, just like Torin had said. I also found a nice article on Odin and the origin of magical runes.

Odin had gone in search of wisdom and became trapped by a tree. For nine days and nights, he'd hung upside-down, helpless to free himself. Maybe he'd meditated or something, but finally he'd found enlightenment and wisdom in the form of symbols. After sketching these signs on the trunk of the tree, Odin had freed himself. Back in Asgard, the god taught the knowledge of runes to his loyal companions and Mortals who fought the forces of darkness.

I sat back and grinned, savoring my accomplishment. Finally, I was getting answers. Torin and his people believed in Norse Pantheon and used rune magic. I guess that meant they were the good guys. I wished I knew more about his people. Greek mythology was big in literature. Norse? Not so much. Other than the stories of Odin, Thor, and Loki my parents had read to me when I was a child, I had zero knowledge about Norse gods and goddesses. It was time to re-discover Norse mythology, but first things first. I needed my car back, which meant understanding the meaning behind the runes on it.

I opened Torin's book and got busy. Once again, I could only identify the symbol of a goddess. She might be Hel for all I know.

An hour later, I was ready to throw the stupid book across the room. Without the translation into English, the book was useless. Going to Torin for help was like waving a white flag and screaming surrender. I wasn't ready to beg for his help yet.

Taking a break, I went downstairs, shoved a tray of frozen lasagna in the oven, grabbed my backpack, and started on my homework.

***

My cell vibrated hours later. "What are you doing?" Cora texted. "Just finished homework. You?"

"I haven't started. Don't feel like it. Want to go to The Hub for lattes?" she asked.

"Sure, but I can't drive."

"I got my keys back. I'll be over in a few."

I changed my top and put on some gloss, before grabbing a jacket and heading downstairs. The scent of lasagna filled the air. I reduced the temperature to keep it warm. The French bread would wait until I got home.

Cora honked her car horn, and I ran outside to join her before Mrs. Rutledge came out to complain about the noise. Cora looped around our cul-de-sac and took off with squealing wheels.

The Hub was a video store at the corner of 2nd West and Baldwin Street. As usual, it was packed with students, including the ones from Walkersville. The store also sold books and was thriving, despite the disappearance of national bookstore chains. The fact that it sold comics, manga, offered free wi-fi, and sold beverages was a big draw.

A couple left a corner table just as we arrived, and we hurried to claim it, placing our jackets on the chairs and bags on the table.

"I'll get us drinks. Caramel macchiato?" I asked.

"Grande." Cora slumped on the chair and stared into space. She was taking Kate's death pretty hard. I placed our order, added a blueberry scone, and joined her. She was on her cell phone. "Keith," she explained before I asked. "He's still doing volunteer work at the hospital. I don't understand why when he already has an academic scholarship to U-Dub."

"I wonder if he'll play for the Huskies." U-Dub, or University of Washington to non-Pacific northwest people, had one of the best lacrosse teams in the Pacific Northwest Collegiate Lacrosse League. Their recruiters came to our high school every year. "Do you think we should start volunteering more? You know, before we apply to college?"

Cora made a face. "We do enough. More than enough actually, and Ms. Lila will write glowing recommendation letters for us. Besides, until swim season is over, our evenings are taken."

Ms. Lila Chavez was the head of the English as a Second Language program for adult literacy at our school. In the last two years, we'd volunteered at the ESL program during summer and off swim season. But I knew students who'd built homes on Indian Reservations, South and Central America, even Africa, which made our civic services unimpressive by comparison.

"Your mom is still involved with the Habitat for Humanity, isn't she?"

"Yes, but I'm not crawling out of bed on Saturdays to build some stupid house." She got up and headed toward the manga section. I followed her and browsed, until we found some of our old favorite manga.

"Why did we stop reading these?" Cora waved a copy of a manga about a girl who was transported to feudal Japan, met a handsome half-demon, and journeyed with him to find pieces of a magical jewel.

"The anime was more fun. You had a crush on Lord Sesshomaru, like, forever," I teased.

"He's still my hottest hero."

We grabbed a few copies, turned the corner and almost bumped into Maliina and Ingrid. I turned to walk away, but Maliina said, "Hey, Raine, Cora."

Cora looked at them in confusion, obviously not recognizing them. "Hey."

"I'm Maliina, and she's Ingrid." Maliina waved toward Ingrid, who smiled. "We met at the park during Ultimate Frisbee. We are new to the swim team," she added when Cora still stared at her blankly.

Cora's eyes widened. "You're exchange students from Norway. You have a friend with silver hair."

"Andris," Maliina said.

Cora glanced at me and grinned as though remembering Andris had been staring at me at the park. If only she knew why. "I remember now. How long have you guys been in Kayville?"

"Just a few days and we already love it." Her accent seemed to be stronger, which was probably for Cora's benefit. "But I think we'll be more at home when we start swimming next week and connect with some girls. We don't know many people, and our host family has only boys."

"We can show you around," Cora offered and glanced at me. I shook my head, and she scowled. "Raine and I know all the cool places. Not just here, but in Portland."

Maliina grinned. "That would be wonderful. Were you guys leaving?"

"No, we just got here," Cora said. "We have a table up front and just ordered drinks."

"But we'll be leaving soon." I grabbed her arm, intending to pull her away from the two evil Immortals and somehow warn her against associating with them.

Maliina grabbed Cora's other arm and laid it on thick. "We drink coffee, but nothing fancy like you guys have here. Can you recommend something?"

"Excuse us, Maliina," I said and tugged Cora's arm.

Ingrid made a face. "You don't want to help us?"

"Of course we do." Cora threw me a surprised glance and yanked her arm from my grasp. As Maliina led her away, Ingrid hesitated as though she wanted to tell me something, then followed. This was a nightmare. Cora taking these two under her wing was a disaster waiting to happen, which meant I had to find a way to stop her.

While Cora helped them choose a beverage, I took our mugs of macchiato back to the table and went for the scones. Maliina kept glancing my way as though to check what I was doing. I loathed the girl. Sipping my drink, I plotted her demise. The fact that the runes would only heal her and bring her back to life didn't stop me from being creative. I bet she wouldn't stay dead if I chopped off her head. She might even run around like the Headless Horseman.

"They're going to try macchiato, too," Cora explained when they joined me.

"Nice." I smiled even though I didn't feel like smiling. Since there were no seats available at our table, I'd hoped they'd sit elsewhere. Fat chance. The two Immortals curled up on the floor beside our table, all chatty and smiley. Luckily, Cora didn't take her generosity too far and offer them her seat.

"Your favorite style is breaststroke, right?" Maliina asked, laying it on thick.

Cora nodded. "Yeah. You?"

"Butterfly."

"You'll be competing against Raine. She's our best butterflyer. At state, we usually have two relay teams, the main team and subs. The best swimmer in each stroke makes the first team."

Maliina grinned. "May the best swimmer win, Raine."

Bring it on, I wanted to say. "Sure. We should leave, Cora."

"Not yet." Cora lifted her drink and sipped. "Ingrid, what's your stroke?"

Ingrid glanced at Maliina before answering. "Breaststroke, but I could use some help. Do you think you could help me?"

"Doc always pairs us with anyone struggling with their technique," I said, not liking the direction of the conversation. It sounded rehearsed. "I'm sure you'll get all the help you need, Ingrid. Remember, tryouts go on for a week before he decides who makes the team."

"He already told us that, but I'm talking about this week. I really need help. Someone recommended you, Cora," Ingrid said.

This was ridiculous. What did they want with my best friend? "Cora—"

"It's okay, Raine," Cora said. "We can't use the pool at school because the season hasn't officially started, but we can use the club's. We are members and can sign Ingrid in."

"That's great," Ingrid said. "Can we start tomorrow evening? Maybe after dinner?"

Cora squinted as though mentally checking something. "It'll have to be after seven. Seven thirty? Where do you live so I can pick you up?"

"I think it's better if you two meet at your club," Maliina suggested. As Ingrid and Cora exchanged phone numbers, she shot me a triumphant glance. Whatever they were planning, it wasn't going to happen. Not while I was around.

"So what do you guys do when not swimming or drinking coffee in quaint little stores?" Maliina asked, focusing her attention on Cora again.

"We hang out, go online. I have a vlog, which I update every week and visit every day to interact with my fans. Raine and I were discussing about volunteering more. We help adult immigrants learn English, but we might do more. Build homes for needy people."

I rolled my eyes. Whatever happened to not waking up in the mornings on Saturday?

"We'd like to help, too," Ingrid said.

Maliina nodded. "Count us in. What do you do for fun?"

"We go to the movies, concerts in Portland. Cliff House on 14th North has arcade games, bowling alleys, and rock walls if you're into rock climbing. Friday nights at L.A. Connection is teen night, so that's another cool place to hang out." Cora frowned. "We were there last weekend during the blackout."

"Isn't that where a student died?" Maliina asked as though she didn't already know. "I heard there was a party or something."

Cora's chin trembled, and I knew she was about to start crying again. Whatever game these two were playing had to stop.

"Cora, we should go," I said.

"We threw Raine a birthday party," Cora said at the same time. "Kate died at the hospital, but she was hurt at the club. She was really nice."

Maliina reached out and gripped Cora's hand. "I didn't know she was a friend."

"She was one of us. I mean she was on the swim team." Cora stared at her hands, a tear rolling down her face.

Maliina knelt beside her chair and hugged her. "Did you know her too, Raine?"

I wanted to punch her, but I couldn't without explaining why to Cora. I stood and gathered my things. "Let's go, Cora. I promised Mom I'd have dinner ready by the time she gets home. Your drinks are ready, Maliina. You can take our seats."

Frowning, Cora stood and picked up her jacket, keys, and coffee. "Nice talking to you."

"See you at school," Maliina said, moving to the seat I'd just vacated.

"Don't forget to text me about tomorrow," Ingrid added.

Not if I could help it. I ushered Cora outside.

"Ohmigod, Raine. What's wrong with you?" she asked. "You were totally rude to them."

"I don't like them."

"You don't know them well enough to dislike them," she retorted. "I don't understand you."

"It's simple. They're liars. I saw them at the club on Saturday. They came to the party, Cora. Andris even asked me to dance, but back there, they acted like they didn't know Kate was hurt at the club."

Cora frowned. "Then why bring her up?"

"Because they are *not* nice. I saw them after I turned down Andris, and Maliina was a total bitch. She acted like I was after Andris."

"You hate him." Cora was quiet as we drove home. "Is Ingrid as bad as Maliina?"

"I don't know."

Cora pulled up to my house and stared into space with a pensive expression. She glanced at me, a stubborn light in her eyes. "Okay, this is what I'll do. I'll coach her tomorrow night and then call it quits."

It was better than nothing, but I planned to be there too, just in case Maliina showed up.

"Okay." We hugged, and Cora drove off.

I glanced at Torin's house as I walked toward my door. The lights were on downstairs. Should I tell him what happened with Maliina and Ingrid? It was obvious they were using Cora to get to me. I paused, thought about it, and reached a decision. This was my problem, not Torin's.

CHAPTER 8. DAMAGE CONTROL

"Thanks for making dinner, sweetie," Mom said when she walked into the kitchen. She picked up a toast of garlic bread and took a bite. I'd just pulled out the tray from the oven. "Oh, crunchy. How was school?"

"Terrible."

She frowned, putting the toast down. "What happened?"

"Kate Hunsaker died."

"Oh, honey. Come here." She gave me a hug, then leaned back and rubbed my arms. "You should have called me."

I shrugged. "The principal talked to us, and there were grief counselors for those who needed one. Some stupid guy confronted me and Cora in class and said it was our fault. You know, because of the party." Mom's back grew stiff, her green eyes flashing. I couldn't believe I'd said that to her. "That was before we were told Kate died."

"Who's this guy? What's his name?"

"It doesn't matter, Mom. He's an idiot."

"People are always lashing out when they grieve." She peered at me. "Listen to me, sweetheart. I feel terrible Kate died, but it wasn't your fault or Cora's or Eirik's. If the blackout was meant to happen, it was going to happen. If it was her time to die and move on, nothing and no one could have stopped it. You should not feel responsible for what happened," she stressed, starting to repeat herself. "None of you should."

"Do you really believe everyone has a time to die?"

"Oh yes. Death is the one thing you can't escape. When it's your time to go, you will go."

I bit my lower lip. Did she believe it wasn't Dad's time to go? Was that why she didn't believe he was dead? Or was she just being delusional like Mrs. Rutledge claimed? I didn't dare ask.

After dinner, Mom disappeared upstairs. I was surprised when I didn't hear from Eirik. Sleep didn't come easily. I kept checking to see if Torin was home.

"Wake up, Raine."

Mom's voice reached me as though from afar. I squinted, trying to find her. "What?"

"You slept through your alarm, sweetie. You're going to be late for school."

I flung the covers aside and saw the time. I had twenty minutes to get my butt to school. I showered and changed in record time and raced downstairs. There were several texts from Eirik and one from Cora asking if I needed a ride. I called them back, but they were already at school.

"Do you want me to come get you?" Eirik asked.

I stared at my car and chewed my lower lip. He was so sweet, but I didn't want him to be late for his first class just because of the stupid runes on my car. "It's okay. I'll drive. See you later."

I closed my phone and slowly walked toward my car, staring at it like it was a viper. I could ask Mom for a ride, but she would want to know what was wrong with my car. Of course, finding out that it was okay would only reinforce her belief that something was wrong with me.

"Need a ride, Freckles?"

I exhaled and turned to face Torin. "No, thanks."

"I could get you to school in two minutes flat."

It took me ten minutes most mornings. "Is that before or after you get a speeding ticket?"

"The cops would have to see me to give me one," he bragged and extended his helmet toward me. "Unless of course you want to drive your car and learn firsthand the curse associated with those runes."

My stomach hollowed out. "Curse?"

"Or blessing. Depends on how you look at it. Come on." He disappeared inside his garage.

I studied my runes-covered car, then crossed our yards. He was playing with my head again, yet curiosity drew me to him. Could he really get me to school in two minutes? He was already straddling his bike when I reached him.

"How come you live on your own while Andris and his harem are living with a host family?"

"No one would have me."

Was he serious?

He grinned, and I knew he was teasing me again. "You should have seen your face. Don't ever feel sorry for me, Freckles. I have money and can afford to live on my own. Come here." He lifted the helmet.

My heart pounding, I moved closer. He placed the helmet over my head and tucked my hair behind my ear, the gesture so gentle and unlike the violent guy I knew him to be. He snapped the strap in place, then rolled a lock of my hair between his thumb and fingers.

"You have soft hair," he murmured in a husky voice.

I somehow found my voice and said, "Thank you."

He smiled. "Okay, uh, do you have a waist strap for your backpack?"

I nodded and secured it with hands that weren't steady. Usually, I went toe-to-toe with him on anything, but today, a shyness I couldn't explain had crept in on me, and I hated it. I glanced up and found him staring at me.

"It's going to be okay," he said, his voice gentle.

I believed him. I didn't think he'd hurt me or anything like that. It was just that being close to him messed with my head. Having to actually wrap my arms around him scared me. I straddled the bike and sat.

"Closer. I don't bite," he teased. "No, that's not true. I do, just not when nosey neighbors are watching."

I glanced over my shoulder at Mrs. Rutledge's and caught a movement behind a curtain. *Oh well, here's something for you to gossip about.* I scooted closer to Torin's back, our bodies touching, his warmth enveloping me. A shiver shot through me. I didn't understand this effect he had on me. It was both scary and exciting.

"Give me your hands," he said huskily. I did. He took my wrists and wrapped my arms around his waist. "Hold on tight."

I tightened my grip. He slipped on his sunglasses and started the engine. Talk about sitting on such a powerful machine and hugging an even more powerful one. The difference was a bike could be controlled. Torin couldn't. He was an unknown entity. Unpredictable. All muscles, heat, and forbidden desires.

Firm muscles flexed under my knuckles as he took off. The T-shirt he wore was so thin he might as well be shirtless. I tried my best to pretend he was Eirik, someone safe, loving, and kind. It wasn't happening. Both men had their special scents, and Torin's was intoxicating.

As soon as he hit Orchard Road, he picked up speed. My hands curled, grabbing his T-shirt since his jacket was unzipped. His broad shoulders made it impossible to see in front of us, so I felt rather than saw the runes. It was as though an electric shock shot through him and leaped to me, charging us both. Everything became blurry as he picked up speed. Soon it felt like we were moving at five times the speed of a rollercoaster. I closed my eyes and laughed. Instead of fear, I felt exhilarated, free, like I was one with the wind.

How could we move so fast without hitting something or someone? Just like he'd picked up speed, he slowed down. I opened my eyes and smiled. He was entering Riverside Boulevard, the street in front of our school. No wonder he'd appeared suddenly near Longmont Park the day of Ultimate Frisbee.

He found a place to park and turned off the engine. A few students hurrying to the school turned to look at us. I looked at my watch and grinned. Two minutes. "That was… wow. How can you ride like that and not hit something?"

"Practice." He unsnapped the helmet, lifted it from my head, and brushed hair away from my face, his knuckles lingering on my cheek.

I laughed to cover my hot cheeks and exhaled with relief when he turned and picked up his backpack. We walked toward school, so close our hands almost touched.

"You did great for your first ride," he said. "I heard you laugh."

"I closed my eyes."

"I know."

I rolled my eyes. "How?"

"Because I know everything there's to know about you, Lorraine Cooper."

"Yeah. Right."

"Ask me anything." He held the door and followed me into the main hall. The first bell rang, and the few students hanging around hurried away. I had no time to take my backpack to my locker. "I dare you," Torin added as we headed upstairs to our math class.

"I hate the name Freckles. Why?"

He chuckled. "Some idiot teased you about the cute ones on your nose."

Cute again. This time I forgave him. "Any two-bit shrink would know that. Tell me when, where, and by whom."

"At the playground, Kayville Elementary School, by Derrick Gregory, who had an awful crush on you and hated that you and Seville were best friends."

I'd stopped walking as soon he mentioned Derrick. How could he know such details of my life? First, the light signal Eirik and I used, now this? Could he read minds? See the past?

"How did you know?"

A wicked smile lifted the corner of his mouth, but all he did was push open the door to our math class. He indicated I walk ahead of him. Eyes followed us. Mrs. Bates was already in class. Frank Moffat pressed against the back of his chair, his eyes fixed warily on Torin. Yeah, Torin had definitely been behind Frank's meltdown. I sat at my desk while Torin continued to the back of the class.

How had he known about Derrick Gregory? I glanced back. He winked and indicated that I turn around. I wrinkled my nose and faced forward. I must have glanced back a hundred times and caught his twinkling eyes on me. I couldn't wait for class to be over.

"How did you know about Derrick?" I asked him when the class ended.

"That will have to wait." He glanced over my shoulder. "Golden Boy is waiting."

I turned and saw Eirik by the door. Dang. Sighing, I went to join him. Eirik slipped a possessive arm around my shoulders and pulled me closer, then glanced at Torin and nodded briefly. We moved away from the door and headed for the stairs.

"I didn't know Torin was in your class," he said. "Isn't he a senior?"

I shrugged. "I think so. I was surprised to see him in my class, too."

"What's up with the backpack?" he asked.

"I didn't have time to drop it off. So… what are you doing tonight?" I asked before he could bring up my car.

He shot me an easy smile. "Nothing. Want me to come over?"

"Sure. You can have dinner with us and, uh, bring your swim suit."

"We're going swimming?"

"Yeah, around seven thirty." The sound of giggles reached me, and I turned to find the source. Torin stood in the hallway surrounded by girls. I recognized a few cheerleaders and swimmers. Even though he was talking to them, his eyes were on us.

"How's your new neighbor?" Eirik asked, following my gaze.

His voice sounded strained, and I berated myself for letting Torin get to me. The problem was he was like a magnet. Not just to me, but to other girls from the looks of things.

"Torin is… Torin. He keeps to himself and causes a lot of ruckus with his bike. He's your typical high school guy." Yeah, right. Between ten years in Land of Mist and rune magic, he might be a lot older than he looked. An Immortal, whatever that meant. Eirik, on the other hand, was very much the guy next door, normal and human. He was also my boyfriend. I should've been happy, content.

Downstairs, we put my backpack in my locker, collected the rest of the books for my morning classes, and Eirik walked me to my next class, leaving me with a peck on my cheek. He was sweet. Safe. Why, then, was I drawn to Torin? He wasn't nice or even remotely safe.

***

Gina Lazlo, a student aid, walked into my computer tech class and handed the teacher a note. Mr. Finnegan looked around the classroom then walked to my row. "Lorraine Cooper, you're wanted in the main office."

My stomach hollowed out. Students turned to stare. We were rarely summoned to the office unless we'd done something wrong. I collected my books and hurried out of the class. I ran to catch up with Gina.

"What's going on, Gina?"

"I don't know, but Mrs. Underwood is with Principal Elliot."

Mrs. Underwood was my counselor. I hadn't done anything that would interest her. One tardy didn't count, and I wasn't failing any of my classes.

Inside the office, the secretary looked up and impatiently waved me in. My stomach churned faster. Principal Elliot stood when I entered the office, though Mrs. Underwood stayed seated.

"Lorraine, sit," the principal said, indicating the seat next to Mrs. Underwood's.

I sat on the edge of the chair and licked my lips, which had suddenly gone dry.

"How are you doing, Lorraine?" Principal Elliot asked.

"Fine." My hands clenched the books.

"How are things at home?"

Was this about my father? Was he back? Or had they found his body? I swallowed, heart pounding. "Uh-hmm, okay."

"We want you to know that we are here for you, Lorraine," Principal Elliot said. "If you need to talk, my office and Mrs. Underwood's are always open. We want what's best for you and all our students."

I nodded when he paused.

"But if a situation arises that makes it impossible for students to learn, it is our job to find out what's going on. If it's something we can take care of, we do it. If they need help coping, we help them cope."

This was definitely about my father, the one subject I didn't want to discuss with anyone at school. I bit my lower lip and hoped I wouldn't start crying. I wasn't a crier, but every time I thought of my father, the waterworks started.

"Is there something bothering you that you'd like to discuss with me or Mrs. Underwood?" Principal Elliot asked.

I shook my head. "No."

"Kate Hunsaker's accident was not your fault, despite what anyone says," the counselor said, shifting in her seat so she faced me.

"I know. My mother told me the same thing."

Mrs. Underwood's brow furrowed. "Do you talk to your mother a lot?"

I smiled. "Of course. With my father go... Yes, we talk," I finished quickly.

"There's still no news about your father?" Principal Elliot asked.

I blinked. "You know?"

"Yes, Lorraine," the principal said in a voice I'd never heard him use. It was gentle. Fatherly. "Your mother came to see me during registration and explained the situation."

I'd thought no one in school knew. I wasn't sure how I felt now. "No, there's no news."

"Do you ever talk to him when you're sad or scared?" Mrs. Underwood asked.

I frowned. "What do you mean?"

"Some people find relief when they talk to their diseased or absent family members, especially when they're upset," the counselor explained. "Yesterday, you were seen in the parking lot during the assembly yelling and talking to yourself."

Oh, crap. The thought that someone might have seen me talking to Torin never crossed my mind.

"Lorraine," Mrs. Underwood urged gently.

I couldn't tell them the truth, so that meant doing some damage control. I braced myself for the lie of the century. "I do that sometimes. Talk to my father." I stared at the principal, my eyes welling. The tears were real. I missed my father, missed talking to him. "He and I are close and often discussed school, my goals, and any problem I might have. He's always there for me. Even though he's not here, I feel like he can hear me, so I tend to pour out my heart to him. In my head."

"I understand." Mrs. Underwood nodded, pity in her eyes. I really hated to be pitied.

"I didn't know I was vocalizing my thoughts," I added, glancing at the principal. He squirmed. It was obvious he was uncomfortable with a student crying in his office. He slid a box of tissues toward me. "Thank you."

"Lorraine, I want you to try something else," the counselor said.

I nodded, dabbing at the tears.

"Whenever you feel like talking to him, write your thoughts down. Tell him everything just like you would if he were standing before you."

I was so happy to leave the office and go back to class. No more talking to Torin and his friends when they were covered in their runes.

***

Cora frowned as she studied me and Eirik across the cafeteria table. "So you're going swimming, too?"

"Yep." He glanced at me and winked.

"What's going on? There's something different about you two, something I can't put my finger on."

My face warmed. I hadn't had a chance to tell her that Eirik and I had kissed. From Eirik's smug smile, he hadn't said anything either. I bumped him with my shoulder.

"Tell me. I hate secrets, and you two are buzzing with one." Eyes narrowed, Cora scrunched her nose and leaned forward.

"You haven't heard?" Keith said, joining us. He sat next to Cora and planted a kiss on her lips. "They're dating."

"No, we're not," I said quickly. Eirik and I hadn't exactly discussed it and made it official.

"Absolutely not," Eirik added, but he spoiled it by smirking.

Keith looked confused. Cora gave me her 'I know you're lying' look. Then she glanced at Keith and pouted. "Do you have to volunteer tonight again?"

"My mom insists. She's on call this week, so I can't skip. I'll make it up to you next week." He looped an arm around her shoulder and gave her another kiss, a longer one.

"Get a room already," Eirik mumbled.

Cora gave him a saucy smile. Then she frowned, her gaze on something behind me. "Wow, Eel strikes again."

I glanced over my shoulder. Jessica Davenport was making goo-goo eyes at Torin, her arm linked with his, her annoyingly perfect smile at full throttle. Jess was a senior co-captain of the Trojans Swim Team. Her on and off-again relationship with Drake, Kayville High's bad boy, often played like reality TV. They usually had a public breakup and then an equally nauseating make-up session. Their last breakup was on the last day of school, which meant she was on the prowl for an interim boyfriend. Some say her nickname 'Eel' was because she moved like an eel under water. Cora insists it was because she was a predator. No guy was safe around her, and Torin fit her type to a T—athletic, gorgeous, bad attitude. From the smile on his face, she was his type, too.

I turned around and stared at my food, my chest tightening with an emotion I couldn't explain. I ate without tasting the food. Torin and Jess looked perfect together. They both had black hair and gorgeous, unusual eyes. Hers were violet.

"I thought she and Drake were back together again," Cora said, but no one responded. "Knowing her, she'd play with poor Torin's heart, then dump him and go back to Drake."

"So that's Torin," Keith said.

"Why do you say it like that?" Cora asked, going all defensive.

"He was the dude at the club." Keith glanced over at me with a frown. "The one who told you to stay upstairs, right?"

"Yes." *Please talk about something else.*

"Darrel said he also hauled out a guy who was bothering you," Keith continued like a derailed train.

"Whoa, who was bothering Raine? When?" Eirik asked.

"It was nothing," I said quickly.

Eirik frowned. "Where was I?"

"You'd gone for our drinks, and a guy came on to me. Torin happened to pass by and told him to get lost." My attempt to make it seem trivial failed to placate Eirik.

"Do I know this guy?" Eirik asked.

I rolled my eyes. "Will you forget about him? I didn't even recognize him under the crazy club lights."

Eirik glanced over his shoulder at Torin and scowled. "But Torin came to your rescue. He seems to be around a lot when you're in trouble."

Cora leaned forward, eyebrows cocked. "Really?"

"He's exaggerating," I said, even though I knew he was right.

"No, I'm not. At the park, at the club, and yesterday when you had a nose bleed. I don't know whether I should thank him or accuse him of stalking you." Eirik sounded annoyed, as though he was looking for an excuse to take on Torin.

"Sounds like a stalker," Keith said.

"Keith," Cora protested, but her eyes were on my face. "He's a nice guy *and* Raine's neighbor. Of course he'd want to help her if she's in trouble. Have you guys thought that maybe Torin likes Raine? I'd rather he dates her than Ms. Violet Eyes."

Silence followed Cora's statement. Keith's eyes moved back and forth between me and Eirik. I sat stiffly, listening to Jess' annoying giggles, wishing I could tell her to shut up.

Eirik took my hand and squeezed it. Then he smiled at Cora. "He can't date her because Raine and I are together now."

The smiled disappeared from Cora's lips and a wounded look crossed her face. Then she kicked me under the table.

"Hey, what was that for?" I protested.

"For keeping me out of the loop, that's what."

Lunch was awkward after that, and I didn't get to talk to Cora again until the end of the day. Her eyes were red as though she'd been crying. "You okay?"

"My life sucks." She closed her locker with so much force it rattled. "You, my best friend, are keeping secrets from me. Things are not working out between Keith and me. I want to dump him, but he's so nice and sweet and supportive."

"And an amazing kisser," I added. "You told me."

She made a face. "I might have exaggerated a bit to, you know, gross out Eirik. He was giving me one of his scornful looks." Her breath hitched. "Oh, let's not talk about me. Let's talk about you. Have you two kissed?"

I laughed and linked our arms. "Give me a ride home, and we'll talk. This is all new to me, so I'm not sure how much I should tell you."

"Everything." We barely left the parking lot when she said, "Okay, spill."

I leaned back, closed my eyes, and tried to relieve the kisses Eirik and I had exchanged. Instead of Eirik's face, I saw Torin. Torin laughing at something I'd said. Torin pushing my hair away from my face. Torin telling me I was beautiful. My stomach lurched, and my breathing quickened. Why was he intruding on my most cherished thoughts? He wasn't my boyfriend. Eirik was and he was perfect in every way. He was my best friend, the boy I'd loved since I became old enough to appreciate the difference between boys and girls.

I pushed images of Torin away and focused on Eirik. "We kissed for the first time at the club. It was so beautiful, Cora. Perfect." Kissing Eirik was like floating in the clouds, so comforting and pleasant. "Every time we kiss, I want to—"

The car swerved, yanking my attention to the road.

"Sorry about that. A dog dashed across the street out of nowhere." Cora's knuckles were tight on the steering wheel, her face pale. She looked pretty shaken.

"If you want me to drive—"

"No, I'm okay," she said through clenched teeth. "I hate it when people don't restrain their stupid dogs."

"Cats are worse. Anyway, back to Eirik—"

"You know what, I think I'll let you drive the rest of the way." She signaled and pulled up on the edge of the street."

We traded places. As soon as she sat, she removed her phone and texted Keith. For the rest of the drive, she kept busy texting. The subject of Eirik didn't come up again and became a non-issue when I entered our cul-de-sac. My car was gone.

CHAPTER 9. THE UNEXPECTED

"No," I moaned.

"What?" Cora asked.

"My car's missing." I parked and jumped out of Cora's. Who could have taken it? Mom? I reached into my pocket for my cell phone and speed dialed her number. *Please, let her be okay.* "Do you have my car, Mom?"

"Hey, sweetie. You didn't use it, so I took it in for inspection. The registration card's been sitting in my office for weeks, and the deadline is tomorrow. All's taken care of now. I'll bring it home."

I was so relieved she was fine, but I wasn't taking chances. "That's great, Mom. Can I just come over and pick it up? I need it now."

"Sure. Bring mine. The spare key's in the drawer. Oh, Mrs. Rutledge said you left with our new neighbor on his Harley this morning. When am I going to meet this young man?"

I swear I couldn't sneeze without that nosey hag saying something to somebody. "I don't know. Whenever. I'll see you in a few minutes, Mom." I hung up, looked at Cora, and grinned. "My mom took it in for inspection."

Cora rolled her eyes. "Of course she did, and you were acting like it's the end of the world. No one around here steals cars. Pick you up at seven fifteen," she added then reversed.

I waved and went inside the house to retrieve the spare key from the kitchen, my car keys, wallet, and laptop and headed to the garage. I almost collided with Torin, who was entering the cul-de-sac as I left. I ignored him even though my stomach did its usual flip-flop. I didn't understand my body and how it could ignore what I knew. Torin was bad for me on some many levels. It didn't matter that I melted every time he was within an inch of me or that the mere thought of him had the power to send my pulse leaping. He was trouble. I'd lied to the principal and my counselor today to protect him and his friends. Who would I lie to next? My friends? My mother?

Mom's store was on Center Street, one of the busiest streets in Kayville. I couldn't find a place to park, so I parked in one of the reserved lots in the back. My Sentra was there, runes squiggled all over it. I really hated those things.

The bell dinged when I opened the back door to enter the custom-framing and mirror store. I couldn't see Mom, but Jared waved from behind the service desk while the new girl, Deirdre, was busy talking to a customer at the other end of the store. I ran a hand along a baroque picture frame, peered at the designs, and frowned. No, it couldn't be. My crazy mind was seeing symbols that looked like runes in places they shouldn't be.

"Hey, Raine," Jared called out.

I moved closer and smiled. "Hey. Where's Mom?"

"With a customer, but she said you should wait for her. How's school?"

I shrugged. "Same. How are things here?"

"Crazy busy. We got a huge order from the museum that's keeping us busy."

That explained Mom's new schedule. Not only did she frame mirrors and print art for furniture stores, she started receiving orders from Portland Art Museum a year ago. I moved around the store, studying framed photographs and mirrors.

"There you are," Mom said from behind me, and I turned. As usual she was dressed in a colorful top and skirt. Then I saw who her customer was, and my smile disappeared. Eirik's mother. Despite not being related, she was tall with blonde hair like Eirik. Unlike him, she always dressed in an expensive, designer suit and was unapproachable.

"Hi, Mrs. Seville," I said.

"Lorraine." She gave me one of her stiff hugs. "We haven't seen you around the house lately."

Not when they were at home. She and her husband were cold and unwelcoming most of the time. "I've been kind of busy with school and swimming."

Mom hugged me and smiled. "And she does so much around the house, too. Where are you off to, sweetheart?"

"The Swim Shop for a fitting," I said. The swim team used different swimsuits each year. "Doc said he's already talked to them about this year's team suit. I also need a new pair of drag shorts, goggles, and fins."

Mom frowned. "Do you need more money?"

I shook my head. "I have my debit card."

Mom smiled. "Okay. Since it's almost three, why don't you go to the shop, then come pick me up for your check up?"

There was no way I was driving my car with her in it. Outside, I approached my car as though it was a viper. What if the car only acted weird when I was behind the wheel? Body tense, I slid behind the wheel, inserted the key in the ignition, and turned. The engine purred to life. Holding my breath, I backed out.

So far so good. Keeping below the speed limit, which wasn't hard on the busy Main Street, I indicated and exited the parking lot. By the time I reached The Swim Shop, I was sweating.

My drive back wouldn't be as traumatic, but with Mom in the car, I'd be crapping bricks again. I shoved the keys in my purse and went back to the store, reaching a decision.

"Can we take both cars, so I can go directly home after the checkup?"

Mom frowned, but she nodded. "I'm almost done here."

"I'll fill out the forms while I wait."

She gave me a blank look. "What forms?"

"For the swim team. I'll need our health insurance number and your signature. Actually, I can just type in your name."

"No, you will not, my little Ms. Independent." Mom pinched my nose and went to retrieve the insurance card. "I don't understand why we have to do this every year."

I chuckled and started on the forms. Mom did her motherly duty and signed it before we left for Kayville Medical Center. Dr. Sherry Carmichael was a member of Marlow Clinic, which was affiliated with the medical center. She'd been my doctor since birth, and there wasn't a thing she didn't know about me.

"Any aches that I should know about, Raine?" she asked, examining my legs.

I shook my head. "No."

"Are you looking forward to another swim year?" she asked.

I smiled and nodded.

"I heard about Kate Hunsaker," she added. "It's always sad to lose someone so young."

"Yes, such a terrible tragedy," my mother said, before changing the subject. "Do you think Raine's a little underweight, Dr. Carmichael? She hasn't been eating well lately."

"Mom?" I protested.

The doctor smiled. "She's fine, Mrs. Cooper. Her weight is within the range for someone her height." Dr. Carmichael signed the forms and handed them to Mom. "But if you're worried about anything, feel free to come see me. You, young lady," the doctor added, focusing on me, "should remember that you need about 4,500 to 5,000 calories a day, which includes your BMR. Remember to avoid fast foods and snacks. Eat lots of fruits and vegetables... nuts... small amounts of red meat... fish and chicken... breads and pastas... Eliminate sugar from your diet. Listen to your body. If you're hungry..."

I heard this every time I saw her, so I basically tuned her out. When we left her office, Mom took my arm. "That went well."

"Underweight, Mom? Really?"

"I had to say something to shut her up. Everyone I meet wants to know how *you* are dealing with Kate's loss." She humphed.

She was being overly sensitive about Kate's death because of my birthday party. "I'm okay, you know. I've accepted her death for what it is. A terrible tragedy." *Please let her believe me... please let her believe me...*

She cupped my face and kissed my cheeks. "That's my baby. Now, what do you want for dinner tonight?"

"We have enough leftover lasagna. I can toss a salad and make fresh garlic bread to go with it." She nodded. "Oh, can we have Eirik over for dinner?"

"Sure. I'll bring dessert."

"Didn't you hear the doctor? Cut down on sugar."

Mom laughed. She knew how I loved cookies, especially chocolate chip. I waited until she left before starting my car. Once again, the car behaved. No engine sputter, sudden stop in the middle of traffic, or anything out of the norm. I was grinning by the time I entered our street.

Torin's door opened as I drove past his place. By the time I pulled up and parked, he was crossing our lawn. My heartbeat picked up tempo. I stepped out of the car to find him leaning against the body of my car.

"Very courageous, Freckles," he said, a wicked smile on his sculptured lips. "But then again, I didn't expect anything less from you."

"I've no idea what you're talking about." I closed the door and stepped away from him, running from his intoxicating presence and his effect on me. He had a shadow on his chin, which made him look even yummier.

"Ride with me again," he said, hurrying ahead of me and turning to walk backwards so he could look at me.

My feet faltered. "What?"

"Take a ride with me."

"Why?"

"I want to show you something."

The wicked smile and twinkling sapphire eyes said he was up to something that could potentially get me in trouble. "I can't. I have homework. Tons of it."

"We'll be back before six. You'll have plenty of time to do your homework."

He made it so hard to say no, but going anywhere with him was wrong and unfair to Eirik. Eirik already didn't like the fact that Torin was always around whenever I needed help.

"I don't know." I started walking, forcing him to continue his backward walk.

"You can ask me anything."

"Anything?"

He squinted. "Within reason."

"That's not fair. There's always a limit on what you can tell me."

He stopped in front of my front door and crossed his arms, making it impossible for me to go inside. "I've already broken many rules for you, Freckles."

"Really?"

He nodded. "Really."

"Why?"

He frowned. "I don't know. I told myself I'd keep my distance from you. I tried, but there's something about you that calls to me."

I wanted to laugh, because that was the corniest line ever, but his eyes were serious like he was truly puzzled. I chewed on my lower lip as I thought about his offer.

"Come on. I promise to bring you home in one piece. "

That was the least of my worries. Eirik was coming to dinner. Seeing us would hurt him. Still… "Okay, but we have to be back *before* six. I have a date with Eirik." Torin's eyes flashed, and for one brief moment, I thought he'd say something, but he just nodded. "I'll get a jacket."

"Or you can borrow mine." He started to shrug off his leather jacket.

"No, thanks. I also need to put my laptop away." He continued to frown and realization hit me. He was worried I might change my mind if I went inside the house. "You can come inside and wait."

"Okay." He stepped aside, and I opened the door.

"Have a seat. I'll be right back." I ran upstairs, threw my laptop on the bed, and searched through my closet for a warm jacket, anticipation coursing through me. I shouldn't be feeling this way. Not with Torin. I was supposed to feel like this with Eirik. He was familiar, safe. Torin was opposite Eirik in every way. Impulsive, dangerous, yet I couldn't walk away from him.

I grabbed a furred-lined leather jacket and shrugged it on. Torin was waiting at the foot of the stairs when I started down. A tiny smile tugged the corner of his lips. He didn't move out of my way, forcing me to stop on the second to last step.

"Just a second." His eyes not leaving mine, he reached for my face, and my breath stalled in my chest. He lifted my hair and adjusted the collar of my jacket, his hand brushing my neck. Heat shot through me, and my legs grew weak. "You have beautiful eyes," he whispered. "They change with your mood. Golden-brown when you're relaxed, green when you're excited, like now."

I swallowed. "Don't."

"Don't what?"

"Say things like that." My face grew warm, and I knew a blush was coming. "Can we go now?"

"You don't like compliments?"

"That's not it," I stammered.

"You're not used to being complimented," he said with such certainty I didn't bother to contradict him. "What's wrong with Seville?"

"Nothing," I said quickly. "He's perfect."

He rolled his eyes and ran his knuckles along my cheek. "Your skin is warm satin."

My mind told me to move back and break the contact, but I couldn't move. I gripped the banister for support, my heart pounding so hard I was sure he could hear it.

"Your hair is pure silk." He speared his fingers through my hair and gripped the back of my head. I stopped breathing. He stepped on the first step and moved in, bringing with him heat and forbidden desires. His head lowered. "Lips perfect for—"

The ding-dong of the doorbell resounded in the house, breaking the sensual haze he'd created around us. I blinked. Torin growled, then he stepped down and indicated the door.

Somehow, I managed to get off the stairs and walked to the door. It was the crone from across the street. "Hi, Mrs. Rutledge."

"Lorraine," she said, then leaned sideways and waved with much more enthusiasm. "Hi there, Torin."

"Mrs. Rutledge," Torin said, coming to stand behind me. "You're looking lovely as usual."

"Thank you." She touched her hair and smiled. "I told you to call me Clare, Torin. Around here we're all informal with each other."

Yeah. Right. If I dared call her by her given name, she'd stare down her nose at me and call me impertinent.

"Then Clare it is," Torin said.

I almost jumped when his hand brushed against mine. At first I thought he'd done it by accident, but then I realized he knew exactly what he was doing when he rubbed his thumb back and forth across my wrist. I yanked my hand away and crossed my arms in front of my chest.

"What can I do for you, Mrs. Rutledge?" I asked.

"That silly mailman put some of your mail in our mailbox again." She thrust several bills at me. "I thought I'd drop them off."

"Thank you."

"Just being neighborly." Her focus shifted to Torin. "Do stop by for a cup of tea, my dear. I don't like seeing young people fend for themselves."

"I still have the meatloaf and the pie," he said.

"There's more where those came from."

I stared at her retreating back, then turned and faced Torin. "Wow, what's your secret? I've known that woman all my life and I still call her Mrs. Rutledge. She's never invited me over for tea or dropped off a pie at my house, and she disapproves of everything I do."

Torin flashed one of his bone melting grins. "I'm irresistible, and I don't call her a hag or a crone behind her back."

I frowned. "How do you know things like that? First the signal Eirik and I developed, then Derrick teasing me about my freckles, and now Mrs. Rutledge's nicknames? Do you read minds?"

"No. I just know things."

"How?"

"Magic." He grinned. "Can we go?"

"Yes, but—"

"But what?" He frowned.

"You're going to answer all my questions."

He shook his head.

"Most of them?"

"Yes."

"No mind games. I don't like it when you mess with my head."

He grinned wickedly.

"Do we have a deal?"

"Deal." He leaned closer until our faces were a few inches apart and whispered, "But you have permission to mess with my head any time you like."

My mouth went dry. He was so close if I moved an inch, our lips could touch. How would it feel to kiss him? My lips tingled.

"What makes you think I want to?" I asked.

"You don't have to want anything, Freckles. You just do." He shook his head as though puzzled. I couldn't tell whether he was confused by why I affected him or by my inability to understand how I affected him.

This time, I refused his help with the helmet. I was sure Mrs. Rutledge was cataloging everything we did. "This looks new," I said, adjusting the pink strap.

"I bought it for you."

That was sweet. "Thank you."

Another wicked grin from him, then he put on his helmet. Holding him was this morning all over again. His warmth sipped through our clothing and crept under my skin. I shuddered, hating the way my body betrayed me when I was with him, yet craving his nearness. Loving it.

"Freckles?"

"Let's go," I said in voice that sounded strangled to my ears.

He chuckled and started the engine. We went at a regular speed until we hit I-5 and headed north. Then he picked up speed, just like this morning, until the scenery became blurry again. I wasn't sure where we were going, and I didn't care.

When he slowed down, I saw the sign to Multnomah Falls, the tallest waterfalls in Oregon. It was about an hour's drive from Kayville, but Torin got us there under twenty minutes. Unlike regular waterfalls, Multnomah Falls fell in two drops. The upper and longer waterfall crashed halfway down the hill to a pool before falling again. It was one of my family's favorite spots, and the lodge at the base served amazing dishes.

As soon as we parked the Harley, Torin grabbed my hand. "Come on."

His excitement was contagious. I didn't complain or pull away. Holding his hand felt natural. Still, guilt followed as thoughts of Eirik crossed my mind. I pushed them aside as we ran toward the paved trail leading to Benson Bridge. The waterfalls were breathtaking against the colorful fall foliage, the climb to the bridge steep but exhilarating.

It was a short hike. On the bridge, I let go of Torin's hand, ran to the rail, and looked up at the top waterfall. Memories of family trips here washed over me, and my throat squeezed. I missed Dad. So much.

Arms wrapped around me from behind, offering me comfort. It was as though Torin knew I needed it. I let my head rest against his solid chest, my hands covering his. For a moment, we just watched the water cascade like a curtain of silk and crash below. When I was calm enough, I said, "It's beautiful."

"It is."

"How did you find it? I mean, you're new here."

He chuckled, and the sound rumbled through his chest and my body. The effect on me was weird. My knees grew weak, and I wondered if I would have crumpled on the ground if his arms hadn't tightened around me. "I've been across this area several times before."

"Doing what?"

"This and that," he said vaguely.

Of course he wasn't going to tell me. I turned, and his arms dropped to his sides. I felt cold without them and shivered. He'd pushed his sunglasses up in his hair, baring his brilliant blue eyes, but the wicked twinkle was gone. His gaze was intense as he studied my face. Then he looked away, but not before I saw the flash of pain in the depth of his eyes.

"What is it?" I asked.

"Rules suck." He glanced at me and smiled, but the smile didn't reach his eyes. "I want what I can't have and need what I shouldn't need."

The cryptic talk made no sense, but then I remembered his words to Andris that night at the club. *There's no room for love and sentiments in this business, just rules and punishment if you break them.*

"Whose rules?" I asked.

"My superiors." He snagged my hand again. "Come on, let's toss coins in the pool and make wishes." He pulled out mixed coins from his pocket and put some in my hand.

I walked to the other end of the bridge facing the lodge and threw a penny. Light bounced off the coin as it flipped through the air. It fell in the pool at the bottom of the second waterfall. *I wish I could help Torin, so he'd stop hurting.* When I turned, he was watching me with a peculiar expression. "What?"

"What was your wish?" he asked.

I cocked my brow. "If I tell you, it won't come true."

The wicked grin came back. He threw his coin and watched it sail to the bottom. Then he chose another, but I grabbed his hand. "Don't. One wish at a time. If you add more, you'll dilute the first one."

"Says who?"

"My father." I stared at the viewing area of the lodge, remembering the first time we came to the falls. I'd skipped to the lodge's viewing point, almost falling on the steps in my haste. My father had to carry me to the bridge. I smiled. "My family used to come here every summer. This is my first time here in the fall. It's even more beautiful."

"Do you miss him?"

I nodded, but I didn't want to discuss my father or I'd end up crying. "Eirik said you were an orphan. Do you miss your parents?"

He frowned. "Seville said that?"

Actually, he'd said Torin didn't have parents. "Yes. What happened to them?"

"My parents died a long time ago. Do I miss them?" He made a face. "No. I might have at one time. Whatever memories I had of them were erased a long time ago."

I frowned. "You make it sound like it's been gazillion years."

"About eight hundred." He crossed his arms, leaned against the bridge beams, and watched me expectantly. I opened my mouth then closed it without speaking. "I told you I'd give you answers. Ask me anything," he added.

"What do you mean by *about eight hundred?*"

"I'm an Immortal, which means I've lived for a very long time and will probably continue to do so for twice that long if I want to."

I tried to see if he was joking, but I couldn't read his expression. "Are you saying you are…?"

"Old."

I studied him, feeling hurt that once again, he was messing with my head. "Are you done poking fun at me?"

He sighed. "You don't believe me."

"Do you blame me?" Several people were walking toward us, so I stepped closer to the rail and stared at the waterfalls. Just once I wished he could be honest with me instead of playing games. Sometimes talking to him could be so frustrating.

"Which part don't you believe?" Torin asked, coming to stand beside me.

"All of it. Look at you. You are what? Eighteen?"

"I was turned when I was nineteen."

I blinked. 'Turn' was a word I'd heard him use before. He'd told Andris not to *turn* any more human girls. "Turned?"

"The moment I gave up my humanity and embraced immortality. I was born in England during the reign of King Richard the Lion-hearted. My father, Roger de Clare, was an earl and a favorite of the king, so I was able to join the army when England established a crusade to fight in the Holy War. It was an exciting time, and every nobleman wanted to be in the crusade or their sons to be part of it. I was only seventeen, and James, my brother, was nineteen. We traveled with King Richard, fought valiantly, and captured Cyprus. I was nineteen when James died saving my life. I gave up the de Clare surname and took up his name. He was a saint."

Of course, St. James. I studied his face, my heart sounding loud and erratic in my ears. No one could make all that up. "You're serious?"

He nodded.

He was 'turned'. "But you're not a vampire," I whispered.

"No."

I swallowed, trying to wrap my mind around everything he'd said, things he could do. "What are you?"

He sighed. "That's one question I can never answer. I've broken enough rules just talking to you. Just accept that I'm an Immortal."

"But you promised to answer my questions," I protested.

"Some. As for my real identity, you'll figure it out by yourself." He sounded sad, like he hated keeping secrets from me, which was very unlike him. He always acted like he got a kick out of shocking me.

"So St. James isn't really your last name," I murmured.

"It is now. The de Clare line died when I ceased to be Mortal."

"But you were a nobleman."

He shrugged. "That was a long time ago."

It explained the trace of British accent. "Now you roam the world as an Immortal doing what?"

He grinned. "This and that."

Once again, snippets of the conversation I'd overheard between him and Andris flashed in my head. "You, Andris, and the girls are here on some kind of a job, right?"

A wry smile titled the corners of his lips. "You could say that."

"And it has something to do with the swim team," I added.

Torin stiffened and glanced over his shoulder. Several people were walking toward us. He gripped my arm. "Let's head back to the lodge." We started toward the trail. "Who told you about the swim team?"

I couldn't tell him I'd eavesdropped on him and Andris. "Does it matter how I know?"

He became silent as he mulled over my question. "I guess not."

"Why are you after us?"

He frowned. "You could say we're scouts. You know, we search for talented, athletic people and recruit them."

Immortal scouts? Sounded surreal. From his expression, he was uncomfortable talking about it. Still, curiosity egged me on. "Recruit them for what?"

He shook his head. "I can't discuss that either. There's only so much I can tell you without breaking more rules. Ask me anything, except about my job."

I sighed with disappointment. "Who turned you?"

"A woman. She came to the battle field to treat the wounded. The first time I saw her, I thought she was an angel. She had a glow around her. I didn't know they came from the runes on her body. I'd just promised my brother I'd do my best to survive, yet there I was fatally wounded and dying." Torin stared into space as though reliving the moment, his expression hard to describe. There was sadness and regret. "She gave me two choices. I could either die peacefully and move on or agree to serve her and become an Immortal. I was stupid and cocky, and I wanted to be by my king's side when he won the Holy War and conquered Jerusalem. I chose immortality."

He became quiet as we walked around the lodge and headed to the parking lot, where he'd left his Harley. "She used the runes to heal you?" I asked, hoping he'd continue talking.

Torin nodded. "Yes. After that, my wounds would heal every time I was hurt. One night, after a gruesome battle, she told me it was time to intensify my training. While King Richard went home triumphant and my father and mother were given the news of my death, I went to her castle for further training. After several years of mastering the right skills, I became like her, moving from place to place, recruiting more able young men."

"What about women?" I asked.

He chuckled. "Don't give me that look. I didn't make the rules. Women weren't involved in wars. They stayed at home while their men went to war, so men were recruited. Things have changed now. Physical abilities aren't measured by how you wield a sword or how valiant you fight. Skills are tested in arenas, stadiums, and swimming pools. We've adapted, but the objective stayed the same, recruit as many people as we can for the cause."

"Which is?" I tried again to see if he would slip up.

Torin smiled and shook his head. "Nice try, Freckles. Telling you more than I already have has consequences I can't live with." He sounded serious, almost apprehensive.

"Okay, I won't push for answers. Do you live with her?" I asked, jealousy rearing its ugly head, surprising me.

"My maker? No. Once I finished my training, she provided me with a place to stay, a cache of gold for expenses, and left. If I had known what I'd signed up for..."

The loneliness in his voice was hard to hear. I found myself doing something I would not have thought of doing an hour ago. I slipped my hand through his. He froze, then smiled and squeezed my hand. Walking hand-in-hand, I didn't speak until we reached his Harley.

"Will you ever finish repaying your debt to her and become free?" I asked.

"No. This is a lifetime commitment." He let go of my hand, picked up the helmets, and handed me mine. Our excursion had started on such a happy note, and now all I felt was sadness. His situation was hopeless. Another thought crept into my mind, and a shiver ran up my spine.

"Did you turn me when you healed me? I mean, will I become like you?"

"Hel's Mist no," he murmured, peering at me. "I know you didn't believe me when I told you before. You would have died if I hadn't healed you, but I wasn't the first one to mark you. I was just as surprised when I saw the runes appear on your body. Unfortunately, they were protection runes against *mortal* accidents. They're completely useless against an attack by an Immortal. There are things I cannot share with you, Freckles, but I'd never lie to you about this."

Panic coursed through me. "Then who marked me?"

"I don't know. But I give you my word," he added, sounding so formal like the son of an English nobleman he once was. "I will never let you become like me."

CHAPTER 10. NORMAL

I'm not going to panic... I'm not going to panic...

I repeated the words during the ride back home, until Torin pulled up outside his house and turned off the engine. Eirik's Jeep wasn't parked outside my house, even though I was ten minutes late. I hoped I hadn't missed him. I needed to see him. Right now, he represented everything sane and normal.

"Thanks for everything," I said, giving Torin the helmet.

"Any time." He studied me intently. "Are you okay?"

"Yes. No. I don't know." I rubbed my eyes, my hands shaking, my mind starting to shut down. "I can't deal with all this, Torin."

"I understand. Maybe I shouldn't have told you the truth."

"No, I'm happy you did. I just remembered something else. I saw the runes on Andris *before* you healed me."

Torin frowned. "You sure?"

I nodded. "That kind of confirms that I was marked before, right?"

"Yes," he said slowly as though he was reevaluating everything he knew about me, which only made me feel worse. "Who did you meet first? Me or Andris?"

"You."

His frown deepened.

"What's that got to do with anything?"

"I was afraid he'd marked you and awakened your ability to see magical runes."

"And that would be... what? Bad?"

"Maliina is messed up because of how he turned her. He is..." He shook his head. "He's reckless."

This was all too much for me to handle. "I have to go. Eirik will be here any minute."

Something flickered in Torin eyes. Pain? Anger? I couldn't tell. He recovered and smiled. "Have fun. I hope he knows what a lucky guy he is."

I was the lucky one to have Eirik, someone I could depend on when my world was crumbling. I walked away and tried not to look back. No matter how fast I hurried, I couldn't outrun what Torin had told me. Someone had marked me before he arrived in town.

Who? Why? Would I end up like him? Alone? Roaming the world? Recruiting people for some secret organization? Probably. Tears rushed to my eyes. No, I refused to be like him. I was Lorraine Cooper, a normal teenager with a normal girl best friend and a normal boyfriend.

As soon as I entered the house, tears filled my eyes. I leaned against the door and slid down until I sat on the floor.

A knock rattled on my door. "Freckles?"

I ignored him, tears flowing faster and faster.

"Please, don't cry," he whispered.

I didn't know how he knew I was crying. I just wanted him to go away.

"Let me come inside, so we can talk."

"No." He could probably use his runes to walk through the door, but I didn't care. "Go away."

"I'm sorry."

Why should he be sorry? It wasn't his fault. I cried harder. I knew he didn't leave, knew he felt my pain and confusion on some fundamental level that defied explanation. It was one of those truths I didn't bother to question anymore. I wasn't sure how long I cried, but I felt rather than saw him leave. By then I was drained, completely spent.

Focus, Raine. This is not you. My father taught me to always look for solutions, not let a problem consume me to a point where I became useless. I had to do something. Anything. I looked around the house and focused on the familiar, ordinary things that were part of my daily, normal life.

I checked my cell phone. There was a text message from Eirik. He was running late. I texted him back then headed to the kitchen to start on dinner. Good thing we were having leftovers. I turned on the oven to warm up the lasagna then started collecting the ingredients for a salad.

This was normal. This was my life.

The doorbell rang, and I ran to answer it. Eirik grinned from the threshold, and I laughed. I had never been happier to see him. With his wavy, Chex Mix hair and warm amber eyes, he represented everything sane in my life.

"Sorry for being late," he said

"It doesn't matter. You're here now." I leaped in his arms and kissed him. Not a peck, but a full-blown, I'm-crazy-about-you kiss. When I pulled back, Mrs. Rutledge was watching us from her window with disapproval. Yeah, whatever. Eirik was my boyfriend. I pulled him inside the house and shut the door.

"I should be late more often." Grinning, he dropped his gym bag on the floor and looped his arms around my waist. "And that kiss makes what I'm about to ask a lot easier."

He tried to sound nonchalant, but I saw the uncertainty flicker in his amber eyes. "What?"

"Will you go to the Homecoming Dance with me?"

We'd skipped school dances the last two years because, well, he never asked me and I never really wanted to go with anyone else. "Are you sure? We don't do school dances."

"*Didn't* do school dance," he corrected. "It's different now."

"It is?"

He pressed his forehead against mine. "You're my girlfriend, and I want to show you off."

I loved it. Going to the Homecoming Dance was what normal teens did. "That sounds like I'm a trophy or something," I teased.

He gave me a sheepish smile. "Sorry. How about this? *You* take *me* to the Homecoming Dance and show *me* off to the entire school. I don't want other guys thinking you're available."

I rolled my eyes. "You're such a goofball, and yes, I'll take you to the dance and show you off as my trophy."

He laughed, lowered his head, and kissed me. This time, I let him lead. It started slow and grew intense fast. I put my arms around his shoulders and pulled him close. He was safe, dependable, normal, and a great kisser. My arms tightened.

"Wow," he murmured when we moved apart. "We should have started dating years ago."

"I don't think you were ready to see me as anything but your childhood friend," I teased, feeling bad the kiss didn't have the wow-factor for me.

"Oh, I've always liked you this way, but you seemed happy being just friends." He kissed me again, but I didn't let him deepen it. I slipped out of his arms, grabbed his hand, and pulled him to the kitchen.

"Better late than never. I was making salad. Want to help?"

He wiggled his fingers. Exchanging a grin, I gave him the tomatoes. He knew where everything was and retrieved the cutting board from the cabinet where it was kept. While he sliced the tomatoes, I washed romaine and red-leafed lettuce heads. The familiarity of the scene brought normalcy back to my crazy life.

When he got a can of black olives from the fridge, opened it, and popped one into his mouth, I pointed my knife at him. "No, you don't. You cut the onions, mister."

"I hate onions." He popped another olive into his mouth.

"I hate washing lettuce. Rules are rules. Tomatoes slicer does the onions, too."

It didn't matter how sharp the knife was, his eyes always teared up. I was laughing so hard by the time he finished. Tears ran down his face.

"I'm so going to make you do this next time," he vowed then went to the downstairs bathroom to wash his face.

We added whatever we found in the fridge—olives, pickles, almonds, feta cheese—then tossed it with Italian dressing. Mom was still not home. I placed a tray of garlic bread in the oven and wiped down the counters. Eirik always made a mess.

We were making out on the couch when I heard Mom's jiggling keys as she entered the house. We sprung apart.

"Hey, Mom," I said, hoping I didn't look as guilty as Eirik.

"Mrs. C," Eirik said in a weird voice. I suppressed a giggle.

"Good evening, lovely children." Mom dropped a kiss on my forehead then walked to the other end of the sofa and planted another on Eirik's. She gripped his chin. "No more jumping over the balcony and sneaking into Raine's bedroom, young man. You want to date my daughter? You do it the right way. You come *and* leave through the front door. No more spending the night in her bedroom either. The couch in the den opens into a queen bed. It's yours whenever you want it." She straightened and grinned. "I bought pumpkin pie."

We stared after her.

"How did she know?" Eirik whispered.

"Sixth sense or something," I said, jumping to my feet. "She's scary smart."

We followed Mom into the kitchen, where we'd set the table for three. I removed the lasagna from the oven and increased the temperature to make the garlic bread crispy. As we settled around the table, I had a feeling we were being watched. Torin. I glanced out the kitchen window several times, my emotions mixed. Part of me wished I could invite him over, even though I knew we were better off this way. He didn't belong in my world, and I'd never be part of his. The other part wanted me to close the window. But if I did, Eirik would know why and I'd hate for him to think he had to compete with Torin for my attention.

As we settled around the table and started eating, our conversation by the waterfalls returned to haunt me. "Mom, did I have an accident when I was young and almost die?"

Mom choked on her wine and started coughing.

"You okay, Mrs. C?" Eirik asked, getting up to thump her back.

"Thank you, sweetheart," she said, putting her glass down, her eyes on me. "Where did that come from?"

I couldn't tell her about the runes and the possibility that someone had saved my life by using them. It was the only explanation.

"Just a weird dream I've been having," I fibbed.

She frowned. "You've never been in an accident, sweetie. However," she added and my heart stopped, "before you were born, we never thought you'd make it."

"What do you mean?"

"From the first trimester, we thought we'd lose you. It started with the spotting."

"The spotting?" Eirik asked.

"Bleeding. Not heavy like periods, but just enough to cause Dr. Ellis to worry."

"Ew, Mom. We're eating." Eirik and I made eye contact and grimaced.

Mom chuckled. "You opened this can of worms, sweetie. Your father planned to tell you the story on your birthday or before you left for college, but I think you might as well know the truth."

"Unless something happened and I was miraculously brought back to life, we don't need the details," I said.

"Your father thought… thinks you should. He said there's a reason you survived."

I stopped eating and held my breath. She was no longer smiling. "What reason?"

"He said *you* would find out on your own. So many times we thought you wouldn't make it, even after the first trimester, but you were determined to live. Then you were born premature, and there were complications. While you were fighting for your life, I was busy fighting for mine. Your father insisted we both fought to stay with him, but the nurses told me a different story. He did everything to make you live, from feeding you to giving you the human contact you desperately needed. Every day, he'd let you lie on his chest while he massaged your tiny body." Her chin trembled as she smiled. "That's the kind of man your father is. A fighter. Nothing ever stops him. That's why I know he's alive, that he'll come back to us."

Silence followed. My eyes welled. Now I understood why Dad often called me his little warrior, why he and I were close. I grew up running to him with my problems. From scrapes to little fights I had with Eirik, I'd go to him instead of Mom. That didn't mean I didn't love her as much as I loved him. He and I just shared a special bond. Still, the story didn't explain the runes.

"I had no idea," I whispered, wiping the tears from my cheeks. "How come you never told me any of this?"

Mom squeezed my hand. "Because it's not a topic you discuss with a child or a rebellious teenager, who might think you're trying to make them feel guilty."

"I was never rebellious," I protested.

Mom laughed. "Oh, sweetie. But enough talking about the past. What plans do you two have for this evening?"

"Homework, then swimming as soon as Cora gets here," I said, my mind still mulling over what she'd told me. What if I survived because my father had help from someone like the one who'd turned Torin? "She volunteered to coach one of the new exchange students, and we're going to keep them company."

"That's sweet. Maybe this time we'll win state."

Chances of that happening were slim. A 6A title meant we would have to beat Lake Oswego and Jesuit High. They had the fastest swimmers in the state. Torin should be recruiting them, not us. Maybe he would see that at the Trojan Invitational Meet in a few weeks and leave. Both teams would be there. I frowned. The thought of Torin leaving left a hollow feeling in my stomach.

"Go finish your homework while I clear the table," Mom insisted after dinner. "And you'd better be doing homework up there."

I made a face and led the way upstairs.

"That was an amazing story," Eirik said when we reached my room.

"Yeah, who knew I almost killed my mother." I was going to get her something really special on Mother's Day next year.

"I'm not surprised you defied odds. You are a fighter." Eirik pulled me into his arms. "Remember how you gave Derrick Gregory a bloody nose in third grade?"

Derrick couldn't admit a girl had hit him, so he'd lied to the teacher by claiming he'd tripped and fallen. He never called me Freckles again. "He deserved it. Now, stop distracting me. I have homework."

Eirik reluctantly let go of me, took my laptop, and settled on my bed while I plodded through my homework. I still wasn't done when Cora entered my bedroom.

"Hey, Kayville's newest golden couple. Time to go." She walked to the window and peered outside. "I saw Torin tinkering with something in his garage when I drove up. Should we invite him to come with us?"

"No," Eirik and I said at the same time.

Cora made a face. "Okay. You don't have to bite my head off. What are you two doing anyway?" She glanced over my shoulder. "Homework? You're usually done by now."

"I have three more math questions." History would have to wait until later. I tuned out Cora and Eirik, who were having an argument over something online, until she tapped me on my shoulder.

"Come on. It's seven twenty." Cora slapped Eirik's foot on her way out. "Move it, mister."

Wishing I hadn't committed to going, I put my pen down.

"You could always tell her no," Eirik said, scooting to the edge of the bed and picking up his shoes. "I'd rather just hang out here with you."

"No, she needs us."

"Why?"

"I don't like the girl she's helping."

He slipped on his shoes and followed me downstairs where Cora was talking to Mom. I got my swim bag from the laundry room. "See you later, Mom."

"Drive carefully," she said.

"I always do, Mrs. C," Cora said.

Outside, we piled inside her car. Eirik sprawled in the back, while I took the front passenger seat. As Cora drove past Torin's, she pressed her horn. He looked up and waved.

"Hey, guess who's going to the Homecoming Dance," I said.

Cora laughed. "You two? Really?"

"Yep. Eirik asked me. Can we go with you and Keith?"

She frowned. "I guess so."

I nudged her. "Where's the enthusiasm? You guys are going, right?"

"I don't know. Keith hasn't asked me yet."

I remembered our conversation outside the lockers. She'd hinted they might be breaking up. Not wanting to discuss it in front of Eirik, I dropped the topic.

"Let's go shopping on Saturday," she said. "I might not be going, but I want to make sure you make an impression."

I hadn't thought about what I'd wear. "Sure."

In no time, she was pulling up outside the club. In the summer, no one blinked twice at skimpily dressed swimmers parading around the pool or the foyer of Total Fitness Club. In the fall, they were a rare sight. Ingrid, in a skimpy one-piece swimsuit, was pacing and drawing attention when we arrived.

"I thought you stood me up," she said with a pout, her accent more pronounced once again. "Oh, and you brought friends."

Eirik, typical guy, ogled her. I jabbed him with my elbow. He smirked. At least he hadn't brought his camera to immortalize her. After checking in, we disappeared in the women's locker room while he headed to the men's. Cora was still spraying leave-in condition to protect her hair against chlorine when I finished getting ready. Ingrid watched her impatiently through the mirror. An insane idea popped in my head, and I moved closer to her.

"How come you're here alone?" I asked.

She ignored me for a few seconds then shrugged. "I can do things without Maliina, and Andris is gone."

"Gone where? Hel's Mist?"

She shuddered. "How do you know about Hel?"

"I'm learning a lot about your world. Maybe you can help me decode some runes."

She studied me with narrowed eyes. "You're trying to trick me." She glanced at Cora and whispered, "We are not supposed to teach runes to Mortals."

"I'm not like other Mortals," I pushed, noting that her accent was all but gone.

"Then ask whoever taught you about Hel."

I was getting nowhere with her. Cora was putting her things away and would soon join us. "You probably don't know anyway. Well, I hope you and Maliina are happy with what you did to my car."

Ingrid scowled. "Your car?"

"Yeah, the stupid runes you drew all over it. Now I can't drive it without worrying. Thanks a lot." I turned and headed toward the door leading to the pool deck.

Ingrid followed. "We didn't draw runes on your car."

"Maybe you didn't, but I wouldn't put it past your sister." I reached the swimming pool and waved to Eirik. He was already in the water. "I bet she's also the one who caused the blackout."

"She did not," Ingrid protested. "It was meant to happen."

"And Kate just happened to wear a dress like mine, had brown hair like me, and was about my heights. Just because she killed someone else instead of me, she had to put a whammy on my car. If anything happens to me—"

"Show me the runes," she hissed.

I had her. I knelt, dipped a finger in the pool water, and used it to draw the runes on the dry concrete floor.

Ingrid laughed. "Your sketches are terrible, and no, Maliina didn't do it. Those are protection runes, and she'd never protect any woman Andris wants."

I rolled my eyes. "I don't want him. Doesn't that mean anything to her?"

"Then why is he protecting you? We saw the runes at your school. She knows Andris drew them," Ingrid whispered harshly.

"Him? Why?"

She studied the sketches. "The middle rune is for Goddess Freya. She's Andris' protector."

"Is she Torin's?"

She made a face as if I was nuts and dived into the pool. I stared after her, mulling over what she'd told me.

"Coming?" Cora asked as she walked past.

I followed her and joined Eirik. I tried to have fun, raced him and goofed around while Cora worked with Ingrid, but at the back of my mind I replayed the conversation I'd had with the Immortal. They were protected by deities, and I shared a protector with Andris. Was that why he'd asked me to join his team?

Screams filled the air, and I turned to find the source. We weren't the only ones frolicking in the pool. A family with younger and noisier kids was in the smaller, warmer pool the club used for senior therapy. We left the pool for the hot tub.

"I'll be back," Eirik said and disappeared toward the restrooms.

As though she'd timed it, Maliina entered the pool deck. Dressed in black skinny jeans, knee-length heeled boots, and a soft-pink sweater, she paused and glanced around. Her eyes narrowed when our eyes met. Then she continued searching until she found Ingrid and Cora. A smug smile lifted the corner of her mouth. She went to the side of the pool to talk to Ingrid, interrupting their lessons, but her focus changed when Eirik entered the pool room.

Still talking to Ingrid, she watched him as though he was her favorite dish and she hadn't eaten in decades. I clenched my fist. That viper had better not go after him.

"Eirik?" she called out, and he turned around.

My stomach clenched. What did she want with him? I stood and hurried out of the hot tub. I couldn't hear their conversation because of the noisy kids, but I wasn't taking chances. Grabbing a towel, I wrapped it around my shoulders and went to join them.

"Maliina," I said, coming to stand beside Eirik. He put his arm around my shoulder and pulled me closer.

"I was just leaving, Raine. Catch you later, Eirik Seville." She turned and sashayed away. I counted slowly from ten to one, but I was still pissed. The girl rubbed me the wrong way.

"What was that about?" Eirik asked.

"I can't stand her. She came to my birthday party at the club and was a total bitch. What did she want?"

"I'm not exactly sure." Eirik frowned as we walked back to the hot tub. "She asked me some very weird questions. Do I live with my parents? Was I adopted? Do you remember those weird birthmarks I had on my back?"

I nodded. Pink bumpy marks used to crisscross his back, but they were gone now. They'd disappeared by the time we were in third grade.

"She asked about them. How did she know? And *who* asks such personal questions?"

An Immortal who was up to no good. I glanced back and caught her watching us with a calculating gleam in her pale-blue eyes. Would she hurt Eirik to get back at me? How had she known about Eirik's birthmarks? Torin knew personal facts about me, too. Maybe they had background info on every member of the swim team.

"She's weird. Promise to stay away from her."

He grinned and pulled me closer. "Jealous?"

If playing the jealous girlfriend would keep him safe, then I'd play. "A little. She's kind of hot."

"She's not my kind. Why would I want her when I have you?" He kissed me, taking his time. I poured all my fears into the kiss. When we eased off, I rested my head on his shoulder and closed my eyes, savoring the moment, until I realized he had gone quiet. Eirik was a talker.

I leaned back and caught his frown, so I turned and followed his gaze. Cora was laughing at something Ingrid had said. The two were out of the pool.

"How did Cora connect with Maliina's sister?" Eirik asked.

I explained the meeting at The Hub as Cora started toward us. Ingrid and Maliina headed toward the changing rooms.

"How did it go?" I asked when Cora joined us.

"Great. She's really nice. Oh, this feels good," Cora said, slipping in the churning water.

"Did you tell her it was a one-time thing?"

Cora shrugged. "No. She asked if we could do it again tomorrow. I said I'd call her."

I sighed. "Cora."

"I know that her sister is not nice, but Ingrid is different. She misses home. Her sister hangs out with her boyfriend all the time and leaves her alone. Blaine doesn't have any sisters for her to hang out with." Her eyes flashed. I knew that look. It meant she was going to be stubborn.

I raised my hands in the universal sign of surrender. "Okay. Work with her, but I'll be here to keep an eye on Maliina."

Cora rolled her eyes. "You don't have to. I mean, she's kind of mean, but she's hardly a serial killer. I don't need you babysitting me."

"Fine. Have it your way."

"I always do," she retorted.

I wanted to shake some sense into her. She could be so annoyingly stubborn sometimes, but this time, she was dealing with forces beyond her understanding. I glanced at Eirik. He wore a puzzled expression like he'd landed in the Twilight Zone.

"What's going on?" he mouthed.

I just shook my head. "We should go. I still have history homework."

Tension was heavy in the air as we changed and during the drive home. I hated it. Cora and I were tight and rarely fought. This was the Immortals' fault. Their presence was disrupting every fabric of my life. I clung to my seat and hoped Cora didn't kill us.

She careened into Orchard Street without slowing down, totally forgetting the yield sign and almost hitting another car. She jerked the wheel, swerved, and kept going. I held on to the dashboard and opened my mouth to tell her to slow down, but Eirik beat me to it.

"Damn it, Cora!" he yelled. "Slow down."

"Why? That wasn't my fault," she snapped, veering to the left to overtake another car. "Idiot! Slow pokes!" She overtook another, almost colliding with an oncoming truck.

I was queasy by the time she screeched to a halt outside my house, barely missing our mailbox. I stared at her with wide eyes, but she didn't bother to look at me. "I've gotta go, so out of the car."

"You can't drive if you're pissed off about something, Cora," I said, my stomach still roiling.

"Last time I checked, this was my car, so get the hell out," she said rudely.

Eirik leaned forward. "Cora—"

"Out!" she screamed.

We scrambled out of her car, and she threw the car into gear. We stared after her as the taillights disappeared around the corner. Cora was usually a careful driver. What had gotten into her?

"What the hell was that about?" Eirik asked. "Did you two have a fight that I missed? Because nothing makes sense. Why was she driving like a lunatic? We almost got into an accident," Eirik snarled, still freaking out.

I had no answer for him. Instead, I pulled out my cell phone and texted Cora, then glanced at Torin's. The lights were on in the upstairs bedroom, which meant he was home. He might know what Maliina and her sister had done to cause Cora to act so reckless. She'd almost gotten us killed. "I have to go."

"Do you want me to stay?" Eirik asked as he walked me to the door, making me wonder if he'd caught the way I'd glanced at Torin's.

"That would be nice, but I won't finish my homework," I whispered back.

He gave in without an argument and gave me a brief kiss. "I'll see you at school tomorrow. I have to go in early for a meeting with Drexel."

Drexel was his art teacher and Visual Arts Club advisor. I checked my cell phone as soon as Eirik left, but there was no message from Cora. Not that I expected any. Sighing, I locked the door and headed upstairs. Mom was still awake when I walked past her door.

"How was it?" she called out.

I popped my head inside her room. She had a large book on her lap and receipts all over her bed. She was doing her finances.

"You do know there's software for such things," I teased, no longer feeling queasy.

"I'm too old fashioned for computers." She continued to scribble.

"I can help if you'd like. I took computer applications last year, which covered Microsoft Excel."

"No, sweetie. I'll stick with what I know while you…" She studied me with a knowing smile. "You focus on your school work, being a teenager, and finding a guy that puts stars in your eyes."

"Eirik puts stars in my eyes." I fluttered my eyelashes.

"Then I'd like to hear more than 'okay' after an evening out with him."

My face grew warm.

"Don't worry, sweetie. You'll meet the right guy someday and you'll understand."

I shook my head. "Goodnight, Mom."

"Night, sweetheart."

In my room, I changed into my pajamas and was getting ready to start my homework when I got a text from Eirik. He'd stopped by Cora's to make sure she was okay. She got home safely but was still acting crazy. I hope whatever had gotten into her would wear off by tomorrow or Maliina was going to get an earful from me.

I barely finished my homework when the lights in Torin's bedroom flashed on and off. My heart skipped, but I ignored the signal and turned on the computer. I'd wait until tomorrow and see how Cora was doing before talking to him. Right now, I was dying to meet Goddess Freya, my protector.

CHAPTER 11. BEING IGNORED SUCKED

The beautiful Freya was the goddess of love, beauty, fertility, war, and wealth. She was also the guardian of feminine magic and a patroness of women who attain wisdom and power. She was part of the older Norse pantheon known as the Vanir, while Odin, Thor, and Loki were part of the younger gods, the Aesir. Reading how the Aesir fought Vanir gods and took over reminded me of how Zeus and the Olympians fought the Titans in Greek mythology. The only difference was Odin and the Asgardians embraced the Vanir gods and goddesses afterwards.

Odin might have received magical runes, but Freya taught the gods sorcery, spells, and charms when she moved to Asgard. The interesting part was, when soldiers died in battle, she received half of the dead heroes while the other half went to Odin in Valhalla. These soldiers then trained for the final battle between the gods and their evil enemies, when our world would be flooded and destroyed.

The more I read about the goddess, the more I wanted to learn. I had to remind myself she wasn't just a mythological goddess. Torin and his immortal friends believed in her and other Norse pantheon, and the runes associated with them gave them real powers.

Remembering Ingrid's scathing words about my sketches, I traced the two runes associated with Goddess Freya several times in a notebook.

Once again, the lights in Torin's bedroom flashed. I ignored the signal and crawled into bed. Half the night, my mind went in circles with the things I'd learned.

Mom took one look at me in the morning and frowned. "What happened?"

"I couldn't sleep."

"Is this still about Kate?"

"No, homework… tests…" I escaped behind a bowl of cereal before she could question me anymore.

I drove to school without worrying about accidents or something bad happening to me. That didn't mean I ignored the runes on my car.

I planned to find out who wrote them and why they felt I needed protection. After Cora's crazed driving last night, maybe I could ask whoever it was to protect her, too. Or I could do it myself now that I knew how to sketch the runes. The problem was my runes would freak her out. I didn't have the invisible ink Torin and his people used, and I had no plan of talking to them or asking them for help.

Lady Luck wasn't on my side, though. The first people I saw when I arrived at school were Ingrid and Maliina as they stepped out of Blaine's SUV. Like a magnet, Maliina found me. She said something to Blaine then crossed the parking lot and cut me off.

"Lorraine."

"Maliina." I kept walking.

"Do you really think those runes will protect you from me?"

"I try not to think about you, Maliina."

"You know what they say about keeping your enemies closer? I perfected it. Last time Andris showed interest in another girl, I took care of her." A cruel smile twisted her lips as she glanced at her sister.

"You turned your own sister?"

"No, but I made sure Andris did, so stay away from him."

"Only if you stay away from *my* friends," I retorted.

She laughed. "Your friend is an idiot, gullible. I hope she had a nice drive home last night."

"Yeah, thanks to Goddess Freya," I bragged, lying through my teeth. "She not only protects me. She protects anyone close to me." The smile disappeared from Maliina's lips. I wasn't sure whether it was because I'd mentioned the goddess or something else.

"You can't be with your friends all the time, Mortal. She might just be a pawn in this game we're playing, but Eirik Seville is much more. He intrigues me."

"Stay away from him."

"Or what? What can you possibly do to me?" She chuckled gleefully and took off. I stared after her then released a shaky breath. What a sicko. She'd done something to Cora, or her car. For what? An obsession with a guy?

Torin pulled up as I crossed the street. I thought I heard him call my name, but I kept going. My sanity demanded I stay away from him and his kind. Cora was waiting for me by the lockers, her expression contrite.

"I don't know what happened," she said, hugging me. "I was horrible to you, and I can't even explain why."

I could. I checked her face and the back of her hands for runes. There were none. "I've seen you at your worst."

"I know. Dad took my car keys when I had a fender bender and threatened he'd take my car until I leave for college if I got into another accident. I'm going with the original plan. One lesson and I'm done. I'll text Ingrid and explain."

"Good. Did she or her sister do or say anything to you before they left the pool last night?"

Cora frowned. "Not really."

"Are you sure?"

"I know I acted like I was crazy or something, but it had nothing to do with them. All Maliina did was show me this really cool pen that's shaped like a dagger. She accidently scratched my arm, but it was nothing. There was no blood. Where's Eirik? I owe him an apology, too. He stopped by my house to check on me and I went loco on his poor head."

"You had a bad moment. I'm sure he'll understand. He came early to see his art teacher about something."

We turned a corner and almost bumped into Torin and Jess with her sidekicks—Danielle, Savanna, and Vera. The four girls, all seniors, had been the relay *Dream Team* before I joined varsity. I replaced Vera in my freshman year, and they never forgave me.

Jess was plastered to Torin's side like a wet rag, one hand rubbing his chest absentmindedly as she talked. I wanted to yank her arm from its socket and drag him away from her. Our eyes met, and my breath froze in my chest. Blue fire flashed in the depth of his sapphire eyes. He was pissed, yet when Jess reached up and touched his cheek to draw his attention, his expression softened as he stared down at her. I couldn't explain why it hurt to see them together. I had no claim on Torin. He could date whoever he liked. Looking away, I tried to control my emotions. Luckily, we were close to the restrooms.

"I'll be right out," I said and slipped inside.

"Did you see that?" Cora hissed, following me. "Torin totally ignored us like we were invisible or something."

I didn't speak. Instead, I found an empty bathroom and ignored Cora's rant from the other side of the door. Why did it hurt to see Torin with someone else? I didn't want him or own him. I had Eirik.

Besides, Jess was the senior co-captain of the swim team and knew our best swimmers. Since Torin wanted to recruit our best swimmers, he would need her help.

"We'll never ever be part of that crowd, and he's been here… what? A week and he's already one of them? So unfair," Cora ranted on.

"We have our friends, Cora." I opened the door and washed my hands even though I hadn't used the bathroom. "And he obviously belongs with them."

"Belongs, my butt. You should have snagged him the day he moved next door."

That was never going to happen. I rinsed and dried my hands. "He's not my type."

Cora laughed.

"What?" I snapped, getting irritated by her attitude.

"Torin St. James is every girl's type," Cora said as we stepped out of the restroom.

"Should I be jealous?" Keith said from behind us.

Cora turned and slipped her arms around him. "No, you shouldn't, silly. I'm crazy about you."

Keith kissed her. "I should hope so, because I'm crazy about you, too."

I shook my head at their show of affection. Yesterday, she was talking about breaking up with him and this morning she was crazy about him? Cora could be so unpredictable.

Eirik caught up with me before I reached my math class. Torin and Jess were already by the door. She was draped all over him as they made goo-goo eyes at each other and he played with her hair.

"Your hair is like silk," he'd told me. Did he think Jess' perfect hair was silky, too?

The kiss Eirik pressed on my lips felt awkward. Or maybe it was just me. He nodded at Torin and took off. I was halfway to my seat when Jess stuck her head in class and said, "Nice to see you two finally got your act together and stopped acting like brother and sister, Raine."

I didn't bother to answer her. She wasn't worth my time. Besides, I knew her dislike of me went beyond swimming. Her friend Danielle had had a thing for Eirik, for like forever, and got nowhere.

"We thought you were into girls or something," she added.

I stopped. I didn't need another viper coming after me. Maliina was enough. If I could, I'd walk back and shut Jess up with a slap, but physical violence wasn't encoded in my DNA.

Instead, I turned and smiled. "It's nice to know you can actually think, Jess. *I thought there was nothing but air between your ears.*"

She blinked and opened her mouth, but I was already turning away. Snickers followed. Face red, I slid behind my desk and opened my math textbook. I couldn't believe I just did that.

"Way to go, Raine," someone said.

Torin entered the class, and I couldn't help looking up. I braced myself for his anger. After all, I had insulted his new girlfriend. His eyes twinkled with a devilish delight. Why was he happy? I'd just pissed off the meanest girl on the swim team, which meant she was going to make my life hell. As a senior co-captain, she helped the coach with seating arrangements on the bus when we traveled to meets and assigned rooms for overnights stays. I could already see her making me sit and room with freshmen.

When he paused by my desk, I looked down. *Please, go away.*

"We need to talk," he said.

"No, we don't."

"Yes, we do. Wait for me after class," he added.

For the rest of the period, I was aware of his eyes on me. I didn't wait when the class ended. Part of me knew I wasn't just running away from Torin. I was running from my growing feelings for him. From my reaction when I saw him with Jess, my feelings were stronger that I'd thought.

Luckily, Eirik was waiting by the door. Unfortunately, so was Jess. Someone forgot to tell her only desperate girls walked guys to their classes and waited around for them like a groupie. She shot me nasty look. As we walked away, I heard her annoying high-pitched voice as she whined to Torin. How could he stand her voice?

Oblivious to my yo-yoing emotions, Eirik talked about his meeting with his art teacher. Mr. Drexel was sending some of his photographs to some national photography contests.

"Oh, that's great," I mumbled, not really paying him the attention he deserved. His photographs always made it to nationals every year. Maybe they would win this year. If he noticed my inattentiveness, he didn't show it.

I gawked when Torin stood at the entrance of my physics class and looked around. I slouched lower, trying to be invisible. He found me anyway, then sauntered to the front of the class and handed Mr. Allred a piece of paper.

"You're three weeks behind, St. James, and will need to work hard to catch up. Saturday classes are always an option if you find yourself struggling."

"I have a friend in this class who's agreed to tutor me. There she is. Hey, Raine." He waved enthusiastically.

Seriously? I wanted to kill him.

Mr. Allred studied me with his mismatched eyes, one brown and the other blue. I always got the willies when he looked me. "Fine, St. James. I'll get you a textbook after class, but in the meantime, share a textbook with Cooper." The chair beside mine happened to be conveniently empty. Great! Torin sat and scooted his chair closer.

"Hey," he said, grinning.

"What are you doing?" I whispered.

"Getting ready to learn, uh… What class is this?"

Argh, he was so annoying. Having him seated so close made it impossible for me to focus. Half the time, I studied him from the corner of my eyes. He slouched in his seat, his arm resting on the desk. He had beautiful hands, the fine, dark hair on the back of his arms intriguing. I wanted to reach out and touch him.

Okay, I'm officially insane. Certifiably loony. Ixnay on touching.

When the class ended, I practically ran out of the room. But I might as well have not bothered. I could only stare when Torin entered my history class. Mr. Finney was the youngest and cutest of all my teachers and seemed to genuinely love teaching. The problem was I sucked at history. Finney started every class with a question and a heated discussion, and today was no different. At least Torin ended up at the back of the class.

"All wars and conflicts are started because of one thing," Finney said, grinning. "It has four letters. Go."

"Fear," someone yelled.

"Hate," said another.

"Envy."

"Lust."

"Sex."

The class laughed.

"Sex, Ricks?" Mr. Finney chuckled. "Nice try. Any more guesses? Come on, people. Think. Be creative."

"Gold."

"Need."

"Love."

"All of you are wrong." Mr. Finney grinned. "Drum roll, please. The answer is… land. Pretty simple, isn't it? L-A-N-D."

"I disagree," a single voice of contention rose from the back, and everyone turned to find the speaker. I recognized Torin's voice and slid lower in my seat.

"Who said that?" Mr. Finney asked. Torin must have raised his hand because the teacher said, "Ah, the new face in my class." He picked up the piece of paper Torin had given him and read it. "Torin St. James. Why am I wrong, St. James?"

"Because you are the product of an educational system which recycles historical facts written by the victors whose perceptions are often skewed and self-serving."

A collective gasp filled the room.

Mr. Finney's eyes narrowed as he walked past me. "Is that so?"

"You believe land is the cause of all wars because humans need to eat and live, and that means they need resources, which come from land. The fact is wars have been fought over many things, from nationalism to religion, jingoism to pure stupidity, but the underlying cause stays the same."

The class was so quiet a feather dropping would have been heard. No one ever stood up to Mr. Finney. Me? I just wanted die. Why was Torin doing this? Why was he stalking me?

"What is the underlying reason, St. James?"

"Greed. G-R-E-E-D. Five letter word, Mr. Finney. Not four."

Mr. Finney laughed. "Okay. I'm listening. Explain your reasoning."

"Humans are by nature self-centered. It doesn't matter how civilized or primitive they are. If they want something, they'll find a way to get it or take it. The old empires used land, women, religion, pride in one's nationality, or preservation of their culture as an excuse to start war. Presently, you use technology, world policing, expanding markets, and protecting national interest, but the underlying theme has never changed. As long as there are greedy people in this world, there will always be wars."

Mr. Finney chuckled when I'd expected him to be pissed. It must be the debate-loving side of him. He was in charge of Debate Club.

"You speak as though you're above all this, St. James," he said, sounding impressed.

"Absolutely, Mr. Finney. I am an evolved human being."

"So what drives you, young man, if not greed like the rest of us?" Mr. Finney asked.

Silence followed the question and against my will, I found myself turning my head and glancing at Torin. His eyes locked with mine and a wicked smile tilted the corner of his mouth.

"Love," he said. "To give and receive love is the essence for my existence. It is what drives and motivates me."

Warmth rushed to my face. Several people laughed, some followed his gaze to me. I just wanted the floor to open up and swallow me. He was cocky and impossible. I spent the rest of the period plotting his demise.

At the end of class, one student asked, "What is jingoism?"

"I'll let St. James answer that," Mr. Finney said, crossing his arms and propping his butt on his desk.

"It is the extreme level a country is willing to go to protect its so called national interest. Some even declare war on other countries."

He was still talking when the bell rang. I ducked out of the room, hoping he didn't know what my next class was. I was dead wrong. He appeared in the doorway of my next class, grim determination on his gorgeous face.

I jumped up and marched to him. "Follow me."

He grinned. "Finally. I thought I'd have to go to all your classes before you stopped ignoring me."

My stomach knotted with tension, anger, and tingly feelings I'd come to associate with him. I yanked open a broom closet and pulled him inside. There was hardly any space between us, and his scent and warmth wrapped around me. If I wasn't so pissed, having him this close would have royally messed with my head.

"What are you doing?" I said through clenched teeth.

He glanced around and cocked his brow. "Hiding in a broom closet with you. Do people really make out in tight places like this?"

Oh, he thought he was cute. "Why are you stalking me?"

"I don't like to be ignored."

I rolled my eyes. "So you humiliated my history teacher to get my attention?"

He grinned. "It worked, didn't it? And no, I didn't humiliate Mr. Finney. I challenged him. He's actually a smart guy. Tomorrow he'll be armed with facts to refute everything I said, which was all bullshit anyway. I'm looking forward to another—"

"No, you're not coming to my classes tomorrow, Torin."

"If you ignore me again—"

I sighed. "What do you want from me?"

"Everything." Blue flames burned in the depth of his eyes. Then as though he hadn't meant to say that, he shook his head. "We need to talk. I'll wait for you outside during lunch."

"I can't. I'm meeting Eirik."

He cursed softly under his breath. "Fine. Then have dinner with me."

I shook my head. "I can't do this, Torin. I want my old life back. It was sane, predictable, maybe a little boring—"

"A little?" He rolled his eyes.

"But it was mine, and I loved it," I finished as though he hadn't spoken. "I don't want to be hauled in front of the principal because I'm talking to people no one else can see. I don't want weird writings appearing on my body whenever I'm hurt. I don't want to travel at abnormal speed. I want a normal life with normal people."

"But you're…" His voice trailed off.

"I'm what?"

He didn't speak, his expression begging me to understand. I hated that there were things he couldn't share with me. "You can't even tell me what I am, let alone what you are, can you? You know what, it doesn't matter. I'll find out on my own."

"Stay away from Andris and the girls," he warned.

"Why? You scared they might tell me the truth? Like why I'm under the protection of Goddess Freya?" He scowled. "Yeah, I learned that last night from Ingrid. Imagine what I'll know by tomorrow. Stay away from me and my friends." I reached for the doorknob.

He pressed his hand on the door and stopped me from opening it, his expression serious. "I can't. I promised to protect you, and I plan to keep my promise. Maliina is unhinged and fixated on you, and without Andris to keep an eye on her, there's no telling how far she'll go to hurt you. I can't let that happen. I *won't* let that happen. I know I said things that scared you, and I'm sorry I did." His voice sounded bleak. "You want space to deal with what you've learned? Fine. I'll give you space. But please, don't ask me to stay away from you or walk away. My greatest fear is Maliina will learn where you live and attack you when I'm not there."

I swallowed, imagining that psycho bitch standing over me while I slept. "I'll be fine."

"No, you won't. You're not an Immortal. There's just so much self-healing you can do before your body shuts down."

I wasn't sure what to say. Part of me wanted to let him deal with my problems, but the other part knew I had to learn as much as I could about what was happening to me. Ignorance wasn't bliss. It could get me killed. Then there was Torin. My fears went beyond the runes and weird supernatural stuff he could do. He made me feel things I'd never felt before. Made me want things I couldn't articulate. Crave with intensity that was all consuming. I didn't know how to deal with any of them.

"Who will protect me from you, Torin?" I whispered.

His eyes widened. He stared at me as though I'd reached up and stabbed him. I felt terrible. "I'd never hurt you, Freckles. I would condemn myself to eternal servitude to Hel than harm a single strand of your hair."

Tears rushed to my eyes at his vow, yet he'd hurt me without him knowing it. Seeing him with Jess had felt like someone had reached inside my chest and yanked out my heart. I never wanted to feel like that again.

"I have to go," I whispered.

The door swung open before I touched the doorknob, and Officer Randolph, the school security officer, stared down at me with narrowed eyes. Oh crap. Mom was going to go ballistic when the school called her about this.

"What are you doing in a broom closet," Officer Randolph looked behind me, "alone?"

I glanced over my shoulder, and my eyes widened. Torin stood there with a wicked grin on his handsome face, glowing runes on his cheeks, forehead, and hands. He looked other worldly, beautiful, and invisible to the guard. For the first time, I wished I could pull that trick, too.

"Step out of the closet," Officer Randolph ordered.

Taking a shaky breath, I stepped into the hallway. There were no students, thank goodness. The last thing I wanted was for the entire school to know I'd been busted by the guard in a closet.

Officer Randolph slammed the door shut. "To the office, miss."

Torin walked through the solid door as though it was made of air, a broad grin on his face. "Start crying and tell him you were hiding from a bully," he said.

"I can't do that," I murmured.

"Excuse me?" Officer Randolph asked. He obviously had heard and misunderstood my words.

"Sorry, I, uh, wasn't talking to you," I said lamely, my face warming up.

Officer Randolph scowled. "You make a habit of talking to yourself, don't you? You were in the parking lot a few days ago talking to yourself, too. I informed the office, but they obviously chose to ignore me."

"You were seen?" Torin asked.

"Of course I was," I said through clenched teeth. Once again, Officer Randolph assumed I was talking to him.

"Okay, young lady. That's it. Let's go." He grabbed my arm and whipped me around.

Torin's entire demeanor changed. Eyes flashed and more runes appeared along his neck. He reached inside his pants' back pocket and pulled out a dagger. It was all black with the nastiest looking runes on its blade, and I knew he was going to attack the officer.

"Don't," I cried.

"He can't treat you like that." Torin moved fast. One second he was twirling the dagger, the next the tip of the blade skidded on the back of the officer's hand. He moved back, and I saw the cuts. Instead of bleeding out, the blood disappeared into the wounds, leaving behind black runes. The officer didn't even realize he had been marked. He was busy looking at me like I should be locked up in maximum security loony bin. Then his eyes became unfocused as though his thoughts were elsewhere. He let me go, hand dropping to his side. Then he turned and walked away.

I stared after him with wide eyes. "What did you do to him?"

"Marked him with forgetful runes." Torin grinned.

"Forget what?"

"That he saw you. He'll be okay in a few minutes. Will I see you later?"

I shook my head. "No. I need space to deal with… you and everything else."

He studied me with narrowed eyes then nodded. He didn't look happy, but he accepted my decision. The runes on his body glowed, and he disappeared through the door. Swallowing, I reached out and touched the door. My finger sank into the wood. I pulled my hand back, completely spooked, and took off.

Not only did I get a tardy, I missed a quiz.

***

Cora dropped her tray across from mine, sat, and demanded, "Start talking, missy, and do not leave anything out."

"Talk about what?" I asked, praying she wasn't talking about the closet and Torin. No one had seen us, other than the security guard.

"Jess Davenport. Did you really call her a skank and threaten to kick her butt from here to the Grand Canyon."

My jaw dropped. "I did not."

"I heard you called her an airhead," Keith said.

"That I did." Laughing, I looked up, and my eyes met with Jess'. She, Torin, and her entourage just entered the cafeteria. She clung to him like he was her lifeline and tried to kill me with her eyes again. Yeah, right back at you. I couldn't bring myself to look at Torin.

"When did this happen?" Eirik asked.

I shook my head. "It doesn't matter. Let's discuss something else. Did you get the e-mail Doc sent out about the meeting on Friday?"

The mood at our table changed. Cora nodded and stared at her plate. Eirik's lips pressed into a straight line. Keith looked at us and frowned. "That's the swim coach, right?"

"Yeah." Eirik glanced at me. "I think the meeting is about Kate's funeral. I heard it's on Saturday. They have the first wake on Friday morning at ten and the second Saturday morning before the service."

"Are you going?" Cora asked, looking at me with teary eyes.

I nodded. "Saturday for the wake and the funeral, unless Doc asks us to go as a team."

"Eirik?" Cora asked.

He nodded. "I'm going on Saturday, too. I went through my photographs and found quite a few of her pictures. I might make a slideshow, burn it on a CD, and give it to her parents." His gaze swung from me to Cora then back to me again, a slight flush on his cheeks. "I know they probably have home movies, but this will be different. You know, it will be something from the swim team."

I squeezed Eirik's hand. I didn't know any guy who'd think of doing something that special for someone else, but that was Eirik. He was amazing. From the way Cora stared at him, I wasn't the only one who thought so.

"I think we should use Movie Maker and add comments." I glanced at Cora. "You're good with the software."

Cora grinned, her mood improving. "I can add fancy animation, zoom in and out, and make her the focus on every picture. You can add pithy captions, Raine."

As the three of us discussed what we could do to make the presentation memorable, Keith cleared his throat and cut in. "What can I do to help?"

"Oh, we didn't mean to leave you out," Cora said, laying her head on his arm. "You can inspire us by feeding us. Since my parents still limit my computer time and I've been forced to abuse my poor cell phone, we can meet at..." She glanced at me then Eirik.

"My place," I said. We hardly ever went to Eirik's when his parents were around. "Should we start tonight?"

"I can't," Cora said. "My family is going to my aunt's for dinner."

"Tomorrow?" I asked, and everyone nodded. "Keith, do you still volunteer at the hospital?"

"Yeah." He bit into his burrito, chewed, and swallowed. He washed it down with soda. "I'll be there Friday after school and possibly on Saturday."

"Do you know anyone in Records?"

"Yeah. Debbie. Why?"

"I'm trying to see my medical records, maybe find the identity of the nurses who took care of me in the ICU after I was born."

"Your doctor should have your medical record on file, but if he doesn't, come and see me on the first floor, Orthopedic Wing. I'll take you to Debbie."

"Whoa, what's going on?" Cora asked. "What's this about your birth record?"

"My mother said I was a preemie, and I want to thank the nurses who took care of me. I plan to nominate them for the Daisy Award."

"What the heck is the Daisy Award?" Cora nudged Keith's arm. "And who's Debbie and why is she willing to help *you*?"

While Keith reassured Cora of his feelings, my gaze connected with Torin's. I was desperate for answers he couldn't give me. It didn't matter how far I had to go to find them. Somebody somewhere must know if I miraculously recovered from a near fatal condition in the last seventeen years. It was the only explanation for the runes.

As soon as I got home that evening, I called Dr. Carmichael's office. Her nurse wasn't helpful. "I'm sorry, Miss Cooper. We don't give out medical records to minors."

"But these are *my* medical records. All I want is the name of the nurses who took care of me when I was born. I'm thinking of nominating them for the Daisy Award," I added, hoping to wow her.

"Bring your mother with you, Ms. Cooper," the woman said, clearly not impressed. "Both of you must have picture IDs and a copy of your birth certificate to prove she is who she claims to be. We've had problems with adopted children trying to track down their birth mothers, so we are very cautious and thorough when it comes to these things."

"Thanks." *For nothing.* There was no way I could ask Mom to take me to the hospital without explaining my reasons. She might think I was obsessed with my birth and haul me to a shrink's office.

CHAPTER 12. PARTY PLANNERS

I entered Doc's geography classroom and looked around for Eirik and Cora. Our coach also taught geography and psychology, and most members of the swim team often hung out in his class before the first bell.

Today they were in the back of the room, where Torin and the Dahl sisters were holding court in opposite corners. Cora was among the girls surrounding Torin. Jess hadn't arrived yet, but as soon as she did, the other girls would melt away. Eirik and a few guys lounged in front of the class, so I headed their way.

He pulled me down onto his lap, his arm possessively around my waist.

"What's going on?" I asked.

"St. James is throwing a swim party tomorrow at his place and *they*," he nodded toward the corner where Maliina and Ingrid were charming mostly guys, "are throwing one, too. They have a pool; he doesn't." Eirik grinned. "Can't wait to see how this plays out."

From the large group of girls surrounding Torin, Maliina and Ingrid didn't have a chance of luring more students to their party. Guys tended to go where the girls were. Andris was still missing since the fight with Torin, so he'd be no help. Where had the silver-haired Immortal disappeared to anyway?

My eyes met Torin's, and my stomach contracted. His expression was hard to read. I hadn't spoken to him since the closet fiasco, and I felt like crap. It was as though a part of me was missing. As though someone had carved a hole inside my chest and every day it expanded.

He, on the hand, seemed to be enjoying himself with Jess. They were inseparable. He didn't attend any of my other classes except math, but she always walked him to class. I had tried to keep from staring at them, especially during lunch, but like someone compelled, I always did. Each time, I'd find him staring at me. Part of me longed for him, wished I was with him, while another part knew it was better this way. I only hoped the pain would lessen with time.

I didn't see him at home either anymore, except for the purr of his Harley as he came and went. Every time, I wondered whether he was going to Jess' place or if he had been with her. At least he hadn't taken her to his place. That would kill me.

As if dealing with the two of them that wasn't bad enough, there was Maliina. Every time I turned around, she was watching me, waiting. Sometimes I wanted to yell at her to do her worst. Maybe then Torin would come to my rescue and my self-imposed exile would end.

"I'll go with St. James," Tim, a junior freestyle sprinter, said.

"He's badass, so there might be booze," someone else added.

"I just want to check out his Harley," another said. "That ride is hot."

"Aw, come on," Tim said. "You're going 'cause he has the girls." They high-fived each other.

"Which party, Seville?" someone asked.

"Neither. I've plans." Eirik's arms tightened around my waist.

I heard him, but my eyes were on Jess who'd just entered the room. She headed straight to Torin, the other girls moving out of her way. She kissed him, and a sharp sting of pain sliced through me. I'd never seen them kiss before. Watching them hurt so much I couldn't breathe.

As though aware of my reaction, Torin glanced at me, and I saw something in his eyes I hadn't seen before—pain, an echo of the same pain crashing through me. Next second, he was back gazing into Jess' eyes, smiling.

I was the one who'd pushed him away, demanded space, yet I was so miserable. From what I'd just seen, he was miserable, too. The saddest part was there was nothing we could do about it. I'd never hurt Eirik, not even to be happy.

I leaned against Eirik's chest and shut everything out, until Coach Fletcher entered the room. Everyone moved away from the back and grabbed seats. He waited until there was silence before he spoke.

"Most of you know that Kate's funeral is tomorrow morning. The wake and service will be at Grandview Baptist Church on Fulton before we head to Northridge Cemetery. I'd like to see the swim team represented, so if you plan on attending, please sign up now. The wake will start at nine and the service at eleven." He walked around and passed out clipboards, which had several signup sheets and pens. "I need the exact number of students attending the service so the school can provide us with transportation."

He walked to the front of the class, gesturing to the students who'd just arrived to take seats. "The bus will meet here at eight-thirty. We'll leave at ten-to-nine for the church. The bus will bring everyone back here from the cemetery. The transportation to and from school will be your responsibility. Any questions?"

No one spoke.

"Okay. Try to dress appropriately, which means black or dark colors. I know eulogies are hard to give, but it would be nice to have a student or two say something during the service." He studied us. "Any volunteers?"

Silence. I wasn't surprised no one wanted to speak. Kate had been one of those students we ignored. Shy and quiet, she'd blended with the background, except during meets when she shined brightly. Unfortunately, as soon as she stepped out of the pool, she would become invisible again. Now I felt guilty for having ignored her.

I glanced around, but no one raised their hand. My eyes met Cora's from where she sat in the back. She mouthed, "Do it."

I made a face. I hated talking in front of people. Seconds ticked past. It wasn't fair. Kate was getting the same treatment she'd received while alive. Ignored.

"Going once… twice…" Coach Fletcher said, in an auctioneer's voice, trying to lighten the mood.

Sighing, I raised my hand.

"Sold to Miss Cooper. Happy to know I won't be the only one on the podium. If anyone else decides to join us, e-mail me. Okay, give me the clipboards on your way out."

We got to our feet and filed out of the room. Cora caught up with us in the parking lot.

"Are we going to Torin's party tomorrow night?" Cora asked, her eyes sparkling with excitement.

"I don't know." Eirik caught my eyes. "Do you want to go?"

My priority was seeing my medical records and writing a nice eulogy. "Depends on how I feel tomorrow."

Cora rolled her eyes. "We're going if I have to drag your sorry butts there. You are neighbors for crying out loud. How do you think he'd feel if you don't go?" She glared at Eirik. "Your parents know his people and—"

"I don't care how he feels," Eirik retorted. I had a feeling he'd noticed the way Torin always stared at me.

"Can we talk about our plans for tonight? We have to work on the slideshow presentation, and I'll need help with the eulogy." I was already regretting volunteering.

"I'll stop by your place in an hour or so," Eirik said. "Are you two going to the hospital?"

I nodded. "Keith said to meet him around four."

"I can come with you guys if you'd like," he offered.

"We *can* do things without your exulted presence, Pretty Boy," Cora teased.

Eirik shot her an annoyed look. "I wasn't talking to you."

I bumped him with my shoulder, hating that they were back at each other's throats again. "We'll be fine. One, you're late for the meeting with the other editors, and two, you hate hospitals. I'll fill you in later."

"I just remembered we're going dress-shopping for Raine's Homecoming dress tomorrow afternoon," Cora cut in, glancing at Eirik. "You're coming with us, right?"

Eirik made a face. "No, thanks. No shopping. I'll take you guys to Torin's party." He kissed me and ran off toward the media center.

Cora laughed. "Gah, men are so easy."

"How did you know he'd choose the party?"

She linked our arms. "'Cause I happen to know which buttons to push. I don't understand why he hates shopping with us. He gets the front row seat to a private fashion show. Any man would kill for that."

"Eirik is not most guys."

Cora grinned. "I know."

I looked at my watch. "Let's stop by the Creperie for lattes then leave your car at my place before going to the hospital. No need to take both cars."

***

An hour later, we sat in the hospital's parking lot, sipping our lattes and listening to the radio. My ring tone started. Mom. I pressed the green button and brought the phone to my ear. "Did you get my message about tonight?"

"Yes, I did. Don't worry about it. I'll bring you guys something to eat for dinner."

I grinned. "You're the best, Mom."

She chuckled. "I'll see you tonight."

I turned off my cell just as a song ended. "Is that Taylor's latest hit?"

Cora stared at me blankly. "I don't know. I wasn't really paying attention. What time is it?"

"Three forty-five. You're worried about this Debbie girl for nothing, you know. Keith's crazy about you."

"Then why hasn't he asked me to the dance?"

"Maybe he just assumed you'd go together or he's waiting for you to ask him."

She widened her eyes. "That's dumb. Men always do the asking."

"You asked him out," I reminded her.

Cora grinned. "That's 'cause he was taking forever when it was obvious he liked me." She sighed. "I could go with you guys, but I hate being a third wheel. Oh, let's go get this over with. Debbie can have him for all I care."

We threw our paper cups in the bin by the entrance then stepped through the sliding, circular automatic doors. The ladies behind the desk at the physical therapy entrance were nice, but Keith frowned when he saw Cora. Maybe she had a reason to worry.

"What?" Cora asked with attitude.

"My mother's here." Keith glanced over his shoulder and hustled us away from the desk.

Cora frowned. "So what? She knows we're dating."

"Yes, but she doesn't approve of my girlfriends coming to my place of work."

"Girlfriends? Just how many—"

Keith pulled her toward him and shut her up with a kiss. "I'll come to your place tonight. There's something I need to ask you. Right now, I have to introduce Raine to Debbie then go back to work before my mother finds out I'm gone. She's big on work ethics. Get it?"

Cora grinned. "Got it."

"Good." He planted another kiss on her lips. "This way."

He led us down a set of stairs and along a hallway to a door. He opened it to reveal an office with several workstations, but only one was occupied by a heavy-set, middle-aged woman. She waved to us. I elbowed Cora, who grinned.

"Debbie, this is Lorraine Cooper, the friend I told you about, and her friend Cora. Girls, this is Deborah Keegan," Keith said when we stopped by the woman's desk. "Thanks for agreeing to help them, Debbie." He squeezed her shoulder and turned to Cora. "See you tonight."

Debbie didn't wait for him to leave the room before she tapped on the keyboard then glanced at me. "What's your social security number?"

I recited the nine-digit number and waited with anticipation as she typed. She glanced at me. "Just the names of the nurses?"

"Yes."

She tilted the screen away from us as a page popped on the screen. She scrolled down, clicked, and scrolled some more, then picked up a pen, scribbled something on a piece of paper, and handed it to me. "Anything else?"

"No, thank you." I studied the names—Gabrielle Guillaume, Kayla Jemison, and Sally Mullin. I wanted to ask her if they'd retired, but I doubted she would appreciate it. From her cold demeanor, it was obvious she was only helping us because of Keith.

We were by the door when I whispered, "I wish I could ask her if they still worked here."

"Go ahead and do it," Cora said.

I glanced at Debbie from the corner of my eye. "I don't know. She didn't seem thrilled to be helping us."

"Oh, whatever. Are they all retired?" Cora asked, turning to face Debbie.

The woman looked up and scowled. "Excuse me?"

"The nurses," Cora said. "Are they retired, dead, or still around?"

Debbie sighed. "There's a Gabby Guillaume upstairs at the Women's Center," she said. "But I don't know if it's the same nurse."

We were grinning as we left the basement and headed for the elevator. I couldn't believe I was actually going to talk to one of the nurses who had taken care of me. "Thanks for asking her."

Cora shrugged. "Are you excited?"

"Oh yeah." Scared, too. I wasn't sure what to expect.

We followed the signs to the double doors of the Women's Center. Inside was a spacious, spa-like waiting room with soft background music, comfortable furniture with fluffy pillows, and ottomans. I shivered. Someone must have cranked up the air conditioner because the temperature in the room was cooler than outside. Through the glass walls, I could see women lounging in beds, some with their babies. A young nurse who reminded me of Marj from the swim team sat behind the large, circular nurses' station. She wore fashionable blue floral scrubs, and her braids were in a bun. We approached her.

"Hi. We're looking for Gabby Guillaume."

She frowned, her eyes volleying between Cora and me. "I'm Gabby. How can I help you?"

Cora and I exchanged a glance. She was too young to have taken care of me seventeen years ago. "I think someone made a mistake. We're looking for Gabrielle Guillaume who worked here seventeen years ago?"

The nurse frowned. "That was my aunt. I'm named after her. What is this about?"

I explained about my birth and wanting to thank her aunt. The nurse's expression changed as I spoke, from confusion to surprise then finally wariness.

"Ooh, that's sweet," another nurse overheard us and said. She was short and curvy and had a kind smile. A third nurse had her back to us and was busy punching the keyboard.

"She's thinking of nominating her for an award," Cora said.

"The Daisy Award," I explained.

Nurse Guillaume smiled, but it didn't reach her eyes. "She would have loved that, but my aunt is retired now and moved back to Louisiana. If you leave your number, I can give it to her and explain what you want. If she wants to talk to you, she'll give you a call."

"That would be great. Thank you." I scribbled my cell number and name on the piece of paper. "Um, you don't happen to know Kayla Jemison and Sally Mullin, do you? They worked here with her."

Nurse Guillaume shook her head. "That was before my time, but Aunt Gabby might know. I'll ask her if she knows how to contact the other two."

"Thank you." We left the Women's Center and entered the elevator, but I couldn't get rid of a weird feeling about the nurse. "Do you think she reacted kind of weird?"

Cora frowned. "What do you mean?"

"I don't know. Maybe I'm just being paranoid, but she seemed almost reluctant to help us."

We headed to the parking lot, but just before the car started, I thought I heard a motorcycle engine roar to life. I looked around, but there was no biker. Not that I expected to catch a glimpse of Torin. He probably used rune magic to move at a super speed.

***

Eirik was talking to Torin when we arrived at my house. While Eirik crossed over to our place, my eyes connected with Torin's. There was a flash of something in his eyes. Anger? Grim determination? I wasn't sure.

"Hey, what took you guys?" Eirik slipped his arms around my waist and kissed my temple.

Aware of both Torin and Cora watching us, I closed my eyes and tried to savor the feel of Eirik. I'd always loved the way he smelled. Now I craved a different scent. I imagined different arms holding me, different lips kissing me. My senses leaped at my thoughts and guilt followed.

Eirik turned me around, cupped my face, and kissed me. He angled his head and deepened the contact. I welcomed the invasion of his tongue and clung to him, desperately using him to erase Torin from my mind. It didn't work. My body knew he was just a substitute. Instead of passion, I found comfort. Instead of heat, I got warmth.

Eirik eased off the kiss and looked over my shoulder. I knew then that he'd kissed me to warn Torin off or prove something. "Let's go inside."

Cora disappeared with Torin while Eirik and I walked to my house. Once I finished explaining our visit at the hospital, we worked on uploading the photographs onto his computer and cropping them. When Cora finally joined us, she was quiet. Too quiet.

"You okay?" I asked, but she just shrugged.

While the two of them finished with the slideshow, I worked on the eulogy.

"I'm home," Mom called a while later. The scent of fresh pizza reached us before she popped her head into my room. "Pizza, drinks, and wings for my hardworking crew."

Eirik jumped up, took the box, and kissed her cheek. "Thanks, Mrs. C. I was starving."

"You're growing," she teased him then gave me the bottle of soda and plastic cups.

"Thanks, Mom."

"How's it going?" she asked.

"Take a look." Cora turned the laptop and tapped a key. The slides showed pictures of Kate with other swimmers—in the pool swimming, at meets, doing team cheer, at parties and dinners my coach loved to have before meets, and around town during fundraising gigs for the team.

Mom smiled and patted Cora's shoulder. "That was beautiful. I'm sure Kate's parents will appreciate all the hard work you guys put into it."

"Yeah, I wish I could say the same about my eulogy," I mumbled. I had half a page written, and it sounded pathetic.

"You're giving a eulogy?" Mom asked, not masking her surprise.

I sighed. "Yeah, I don't know what I was thinking when I volunteered."

"I'm sure it will come to you, sweetie." Mom squeezed my shoulder and disappeared downstairs.

Thirty minutes later, I threw the pencil down. "I need help, people. Desperately."

Cora scrunched her face. "Don't look at me. I didn't know her."

"You urged me to volunteer, you traitor," I retorted.

"Since when do you listen to me?"

"Since always." I threw a pillow at her, and she blocked it with her greasy hands. "Eew, you got pizza sauce on my pillow."

"Serves you right for throwing it." She kicked the pillow out of the way and glanced at Eirik. "Are you going to help or just demolish the food like a starved ex-convict?"

Eirik licked his fingers then reached for another chicken wing. "I don't talk when I eat."

"Grrr-ross," Cora said, watching him suck the flesh off the bones.

He smacked his lips and winked at her then glanced my way. "Maybe you should just say a line or two and let the slideshow speak for you, Raine."

"We'll see." I jumped up. "Anyone want anything else? I'm going downstairs to talk to Mom. She's good with people and always knows what to say."

"About everything," Cora said.

"And everyone," Eirik added.

Laughing, I headed downstairs. I reached the bottom and froze. Mom wasn't alone. A familiar voice mingled with her softer voice, and my heart leaped. Torin.

As though aware of my presence, Torin looked up and stood. I swallowed, my senses soaking him as though I hadn't seen him earlier. I walked toward them, my heart racing so hard I felt lightheaded.

"Did you finish your eulogy, sweetie?" Mom asked.

"No, I need help. Kate wasn't very outgoing, so we know next to nothing about her," I said absentmindedly, my eyes not leaving Torin's. I wanted to look away, but couldn't. His eyes held me spellbound. He watched me as though every expression on my face was of utter importance to him. "I didn't know you two had met," I added, my voice breathless.

"Your mother and I met a few days ago," he said, cocking his eyebrows. "I hope you don't mind."

"Why should I?" My face grew warm, the conversation we'd had in the closet at school flashing in my head.

"Torin wants to know if it's okay for him to throw a party tomorrow night for the swim team. Isn't that thoughtful of him to ask all the neighbors first?" Mom said.

"Just being neighborly, Mrs. Cooper."

I dragged my eyes from Torin and glanced at Mom. She wore an innocent grin, which didn't fool me one little bit. I couldn't help but wonder why she hadn't told me the two of them had met. Taking a deep breath to calm my pounding heart, I focused on their conversation. "Have you spoken with Mr. Peterson yet?"

Torin chuckled. "Yeah, he's a funny guy. He said it was no problem at all, that we should have parties around here more often."

"Really?"

"Really. We met the day I arrived and hit it off." He grinned. "We share a passion for unique mailboxes."

I giggled.

Torin grinned back. "I came over to personally invite you to my party, Freckles."

"Me? I, uh..." Did he just call me Freckles in front of my mother?

He bowed stiffly and proper like an English gentleman. "Please. It will be an honor to have you there."

"I, uh, okay. I'll be there. I mean, we'll be there." A chuckle drew my attention to Mom, and I blushed. I had completely forgotten her presence.

"It's been a pleasure talking to you again, Mrs. Cooper," Torin said. "I better head home. I've a lot to do between now and tomorrow."

"You should ask Raine to help. She's good with parties."

I glared at Mom. "I can't. We have Kate's funeral in the morning and shopping for a Homecoming Dance dress in the afternoon."

"That's okay, Mrs. Cooper. I have a few friends coming over to help."

Who? I wanted to ask, feeling jealous, but he was still talking.

"I promise to keep the noise to a minimum, but if the music becomes too loud, please, feel free to stop by and let me know."

Mom chuckled. "Oh, don't worry about me. I can sleep through a tornado."

I snorted at the lie. Everybody appeared to be bending over backwards to be nice to Torin. He must have drawn be-nice-to-the-new-neighbor runes on them or something.

"Do walk Torin to the door, sweetheart," Mom added.

I gave her a sharp glance, but she just smiled. The challenging look in Torin's eyes told me he wouldn't move until I escorted him to the door. Sighing, I led the way to the front entrance, my eyes darting upstairs when I reached the foyer.

"Don't worry. Golden Boy doesn't know I'm here," Torin whispered. "Not that I care if he does."

"You should. If you haven't noticed, he doesn't particularly like you." I opened the door and stepped aside for him to pass.

"That's because he knows he's not worthy of you," Torin whispered as he walked past me. Then he turned and added, "I wish you didn't have to bring him tomorrow night, but I'm willing to have you anyway I can."

His boldness didn't surprise me anymore, but his words thrilled me even though I knew they shouldn't. "You shouldn't say things like that."

"Why not? They're true. Come on, walk me to the driveway."

I frowned. "Why?"

"I've missed you."

I'd missed him so much I wanted to close the gap between us and touch him. I opened my mouth to tell him how I felt but the words got trapped in my throat. Instead, I stared helplessly at him. The yellow security light danced on his chiseled cheekbones, the sculptured lips, the lock of black hair on his forehead, and his impossibly gorgeous eyes.

"I also know a thing or two about Kate that you might find useful." When I still hesitated, he added, "Scaredy-cat."

"Not."

"What do you think I'm going to do with your mother a few feet away and Mrs. Rutledge peering at us from behind her curtain?"

Sure enough, I caught the subtle movement behind our neighbor's curtain. I rolled my eyes and closed the door behind us. "Nosey crone," I mumbled.

"Be nice," Torin said. "So? Did you find any answers at the hospital?"

I smiled, getting my equilibrium back. "So that *was* you on the bike. Are you stalking me again?"

"It's called guarding, Freckles. So what did you learn?"

"You want me to share info? Start by telling me what you know."

He stopped, crossed his arms, and studied me with a wicked smirk. "Okay. Kate Hunsaker was the person behind the nicknames."

"What?" The switch in topic caught me off guard.

"Kate was the one who came up with nicknames for your teammates."

"Yeah. Right."

"You are called Slinky because of your favorite slinky toy. Cora makes funny expressions when bored so she's Eyezz. Eirik is Houdini because he pulls disappearing acts during practice. Jimmy Baines is Condor because he looks like a condor when he does butterfly. Jess is Eel…"

I stared at him with round eyes as he listed the nicknames of all the swimmers on my team and the stories behind the names, most of which I didn't even know.

"I had no idea. How did you know? Never mind. You probably got all that from talking to other swimmers."

He chuckled, the sound low and sexy. "Actually, no. When I recruit, I come prepared with background info on everyone on my list. So? What were you doing at the hospital?"

Still absorbing what he'd just said, which explained why he knew so much about me, I studied him. "Where do you get your information?"

"From my superiors."

"So you know everything about me?"

"Nope, just relevant stuff. Quit procrastinating and tell me why you went to the hospital."

"I figured that if you didn't mark me, then someone must have." I quickly explained what my mother had told me about my birth. "Did you know about that?"

He made a face. "No-oo. Go on."

"My doctor didn't have any answers, so I went to the hospital to find the identities of the nurses who took care of me. Unfortunately, they don't live here anymore." I explained about the three nurses and what we learned from Nurse Guillaume. "I got strange vibes from her, but..." I shrugged. "I could be wrong."

"No, always trust your instincts. What are the three nurses' names?"

"Why?"

"So I can track them down."

"Without me?" I asked.

"I work better alone."

"Not this time," I protested. "My birth, my investigation, so wherever you go, I go."

"You do know I can go to the hospital and get the information on my own, like that." He snapped his fingers.

He'd have to go through Debbie first. I grinned. "Yeah, good luck with that."

He frowned. "You know something that I don't?"

I gave him a toothy grin. "Oh yeah and loving it."

"One day you'll come to trust me, Freckles." He caressed my nose. "See you tomorrow."

I could still feel the heat from his finger on my nose as I entered the house, closed the door, and went to join Mom. She'd been watching something on TV but turned it down.

"Freckles?" she teased.

"I hate that name."

She chuckled. "Yeah, I could tell."

I made a face. "Are you going to help me with the eulogy?"

Mom patted the stool next to her. "Tell me what you know about Kate?"

I sat and sighed. "Hmm, she was quiet and shy. When you talked to her, she'd just clam up."

"Put a positive spin on these things that defined her. Quiet and shy becomes thoughtful. Clamming up just means she was a good listener."

When Mom finished, I was grinning. I hugged her. "You're the best, Mom."

"Raine?" she called as I ran toward the stairs.

"Yeah?" I turned and walked backwards.

"It's nice to see stars in your eyes."

I made a face. "I'm going to pretend I don't know what you mean."

"As long as you understand what you're getting into. Have you thought of what you're going to do about it?"

I shook my head. "No."

"Be careful."

Seriously, mothers shouldn't be involved in their daughters' love lives.

CHAPTER 13. AN OBSESSION

Kate's wake and funeral service were beautiful. Not that a funeral could ever be deemed a thing of beauty, but her family made it memorable. There were flowers inside and outside the church, colorful balloons, teddy bears, and swim-themed stuff placed near the entrance. A photo montage cycled on the video screens as soft religious tunes played over the speakers. Photos and a photo board were also set up next to Kate's coffin at the front of the room. The turnout was huge, which made me dread my turn at the podium even more.

The pastor spoke first, followed by various relatives and friends. Doc gave a beautiful eulogy. By the time he was done, there was not a single dry eye. My turn arrived too soon.

Taking a deep breath, I walked to the front.

For one brief moment, everything I had rehearsed flew right out of my head as I studied the audience. What had I gotten myself into? I glanced at the cards in my hand. They had talking points, but I couldn't focus on a single one. Panicking, I glanced at Eirik. He nodded encouragingly. Cora gave me two thumbs up.

As though on cue, Torin entered the church. He leaned against the back wall and crossed his arms. I hadn't expected him to attend the funeral even though I'd seen Jess and her friends on the bus. As usual, my heart skipped. He smiled, and the weirdest thing happened. I felt a boost of confidence, like I could conquer the world. The smile didn't just have the ability to make me weak in the knees. It said he believed in me.

Exhaling, I glanced at the top card. "First, I'd like to offer my condolences to the Hunsaker family," I read. "It's not easy losing someone you love. Kate and I first met in junior high when we swam for the Kayville Dolphins. Two years later, we both made varsity as freshmen." I frowned, hating the way my speech sounded stiff and rehearsed.

I flipped the cards upside down and pushed them aside, then focused my attention somewhere above everyone's heads—the golden rule of public speaking. Or imagining everyone naked, which would be iffy since Kate's grandparents were seated right in front of me. Without intending to, my eyes locked with Torin's.

"I had an entire speech rehearsed and written down, but I've decided it's not good enough. Rehearsed speeches are boring, something Kate wasn't. Kate was full of surprises. She was the glue that held the swim team together even though some of us didn't know it." Warming up to the subject and becoming less nervous, I made eye contact with Kate's grandparents and talked to them. "You see, in any sport, there's something the teammates do that makes everyone feel special and part of the group, makes new members feel welcome. We give each other nicknames. We put these special names on kickboards and jackets, flippers and trophies. Parents don't hear anyone scream their daughters' and sons' name at meets. Instead you hear Condor and Slinky, Houdini and Sparkplug…"

Chuckles came from the students. I glanced at them.

"These unique names define us out there in the water during meets. What you may not know…" I made eye contact with Kate's parents then glanced at the section with the swimmers. "What most of us *didn't* know was the identity of the person behind these names. The person who listened, observed, and came up with the perfect nickname for each and every one of us." I paused for effect. "Kate."

Excited murmurs came from my friends again. Some turned and looked at each other in surprise.

"The coolest thing is there's always a story behind whatever she picked. My name is Slinky. I wish it's because I'm fast or smooth under water. My father bought me a slinky toy, which I'd take to meets to calm my nerves when I was with the Dolphins. Kate remembered." My eyes smarted as thoughts of my father intruded. I swallowed and pushed them aside. I pointed at Marj. "Marj is Zoomer because it took her forever to master the use of her Finis Zoomer fins. Randy over there," I pointed at another swimmer, "is Stoner. He *acts* high after practice because chlorine messes with his head."

Giggles came from the students.

My gaze met with Jimmy Baines. "Jimmy is Condor because he has the perfect form when he swims butterfly, like a condor. Coach Fletcher is Doc because he's been working on his PhD, like…"

"Forever?" someone yelled from the audience, and laughter followed.

"And Kate was Shelly, because she was quiet and shy until she was in the pool. Then she crawled out of her shell and shined like the star she was. I can list more things that made Kate special. From setting records in her freshman year to how she was always the first one in the pool and the last one out, but it won't take away the pain of losing her, of knowing…" My voice shook, and tears filled my eyes, thoughts of my father returning and blindsiding me. I cleared my throat and blinked rapidly to stop the tears from falling. "The heartache of knowing that someone you love has been taken from you so suddenly, that you'll never see him… her…"

More images of my father flashed through my head, and the floodgate opened. The harder I tried to stop crying, the faster the tears flowed. Through the haze, I saw two people move toward the stage. The next minute Eirik and Cora flanked me.

While Eirik finished my speech, Cora led me outside to the church's stoop. She held me while I cried. She mumbled something over and over, but I didn't hear her. The tears kept flowing. Kate's parents had no idea how lucky they were to have closure. Not knowing whether my father was alive or dead just made everything worse.

A second thought crept in. I'd broken down in front of everyone. That was beyond humiliating. The thought of riding the bus to the cemetery then to school with them only made me feel worse.

"I wish we could leave before the others come out," I whispered.

"I can give you a ride home," Torin said from behind me.

I wasn't sure I should. "We still have to go to the cemetery."

"Go with him, Raine," Cora urged. "Everyone will understand."

I hugged Cora and started toward Torin's bike. We didn't speak during the brief walk. He wiped some of the wetness from my cheeks before snapping the helmet into place, his expression filled with concern. More tears threatened to fall. I hated it when people pitied me. It was as though their pity made things seem worse.

Needing his warmth, I wrapped my arms around him and closed my eyes, for once not stressing about holding him. As though he knew it, he gripped my hands before starting the engine. When we got home, he walked me to the door, his hand reassuring on my arm.

"Thanks for the ride," I said.

"Anytime. If you want to talk, I'm a good listener," he said softly.

I did want to talk. "Okay. Come inside."

Mom was gone, but she'd left the TV on. I switched it off, removed my coat, and draped it on the back of a dining room chair. I glanced at Torin. "Would you like something to drink?"

He shook his head and waited until I got bottled water and sat on a stool before he did, his eyes not leaving me. "I wish you wouldn't stare at me like that," I whispered.

"Sorry." He still didn't look away. "You miss him, don't you?"

"What?"

"Your father."

I blinked. "Yes. How did you know?"

"Something you said in your speech. The tears and the pain I see in your eyes are more personal."

I stared at him, amazed at how well he could read me.

"Tell me about him."

I remembered what he'd said last night about knowing those he recruited. "But you already know about him."

"All I know is that he was flying home from a business trip when his plane crashed. It's been months, and they still haven't found his body."

"The last time we spoke, he was at the airport," I started, but soon I was talking about my childhood, the things we used to do, places we went as a family, the way he was always there for me. I talked until my voice was hoarse. "Mom believes he's alive," I whispered. "But I'm scared she's deluding herself, maybe losing it."

"Why do you say that?"

"She talks to herself. I mean, she stands in front of that," I waved toward the living room mirror, "and pretends she's talking to him. I can't afford to lose her, too. She's all I have." I didn't realize I was crying until Torin reached out and wiped the tears from my cheeks. I swiped at my cheeks, too. "I'm sorry. I don't usually break down like this."

"Don't apologize." He tugged me into his arm. "Cry all you want. I'm here for you for as long as you want me."

Needing the comfort, I clung to him. I was surprised I had tears left. When he leaned back and ran his knuckles along my cheekbones, drying the wetness, his touch was so gentle. My heart picked up tempo, and I struggled to breathe.

"Freckles," he said softly, his voice low and urgent. "Look at me."

I looked up and immediately wished I hadn't. Blue flamed flickered in the depth of his eyes, their intensity taking my breath away.

"You feel it, don't you?" he said. "This *thing* between us."

'Thing' didn't begin to describe how I felt about him. He was an obsession, a craving. I had Eirik whom I'd loved since we were children, and that wasn't about to change. But Torin affected me in ways I couldn't begin to describe. I was miserable without him, yet when with him my emotions were all over the place. He made me mad one minute and euphoric the next.

"I, uh, I need to wash up." I moved out of his arms and went to the downstairs bathroom. I couldn't look at myself in the mirror without feeling like a fraud. How could I love Eirik and want Torin? It didn't make sense.

Taking a deep breath, I left the bathroom. Torin stood in front of the mirror in the living room, the same one Mom often talked to. He turned and smiled, but the smile didn't reach his eyes. "Feeling better?"

"Yeah, thanks."

He closed the gap between us. "Could you do me a favor?"

I nodded warily. "Sure."

"Give your mother the benefit of the doubt when it comes to your father."

"What do you mean? Do you know something you're not telling me?"

"True love transcends logic, Freckles. It's a blending of minds and souls." He stared into my eyes, and at that moment I knew he could see right through my bullshit to what I really felt for him. "It makes us feel and see things in ways that normal people don't. You don't question it or try to understand it. You just accept it for the gift it is. So if she believes he's still alive, give her the benefit of the doubt."

"Okay."

"Good. I, uh, better go. I have guests." He ran his knuckles along the side of my face then headed out the door.

I ran to the window, expecting to see Jess and her friends. Instead, a furniture truck was backing into his driveway. Cora and Eirik arrived while the people were still carrying huge boxes into Torin's house.

"You okay?" Eirik asked. I nodded, but we didn't discuss my breakdown. "Come on. I'll buy you two ladies lunch," he said, placing one arm around Cora's shoulder and the other around me.

"Does that mean you're going shopping with us, too?" Cora asked.

Eirik laughed. "In your dreams."

***

"Come out and give me your honest opinion," Cora called out.

I poked my head out of the changing room and studied her. She preened in front of the three panel mirror at the corner, turning left and right, the pink dress frothing around her knees. "I love it, but it's a bit tight across the chest."

"I know." She tugged at the neckline. "I love the color, though. Did I mention that Keith came to my place last night and asked me to the dance?"

"No, you didn't. So we'll go together?"

"Absolutely. He had a surprise for me, too. He's made the final list for Homecoming King."

With everything going on in my life, I had completely forgotten the tradition my school took so seriously. "That's great. With everything he does, he might beat Blaine hands down. It would be nice to have a king who wasn't a quarterback."

"I know. Go try the green dress. I want to see how you look."

I disappeared inside the changing room and slipped on the emerald-green dress. I studied my reflection and grinned. I loved it even though I was worried about the back. It had a plunging neckline, which meant I'd have to wear it without a bra. Also, it was way above my budget.

"Well?" Cora called out.

"It's cute," I said.

"Cute? Your first Homecoming Dance deserves a dress that's more than cute. I want to see it."

Rolling my eyes, I stepped out of the changing room, but she was still in her changing room. I walked to the mirror she'd been using before and studied my back.

"You look stunning."

I whipped around, my heart skipping. Torin leaned against the wall, a heated look in his sapphire eyes. "What are you doing here?"

"Looking for you." His eyes ran along my shoulders, left bare by the thin straps, a wicked smile curling his lips. My body reacted as though he'd reached out and touched me. He pushed against the wall and moved closer. My heartbeat picked up tempo. "Following your essence hasn't been easy. You've been all over the mall."

"My essence?"

"Yes, your essence. Andris is back, so I thought I'd give you a heads up."

"Where was he?"

"He took a friend home." His voice deepened with each word as he continued. "You take my breath away, Freckles. You always have, but in that dress... I want to claim you and to Hel with the consequences."

His voice washed over, and the adoring look in his eyes held me spellbound. He came and stood in front of me, his eyes locked with mine. "The color adds green flecks to your eyes, and the material," he leaned back and gave me a once over, "hugs your lush curves in just the right places."

I swallowed, my face burning. I wanted to say something witty, but my mind had gone blank, and my tongue stayed glued to the roof of my mouth. His hands rested on my hips and slowly pulled me closer until our bodies touched. I quit breathing all together.

"If you were mine," he whispered, "we'd have a private dance for just the two of us before I shared you with the world." Suddenly, runes appeared on his cheeks and forehead.

"Who are you talking to?" Cora asked from behind me. She'd stuck her head out of the changing room. Torin's hands dropped from my waist, but he didn't move away.

"I, uh, I was talking to myself," I stammered.

"How could you say that is cute? You look fabulous," Cora gushed. "Turn around."

I turned, aware of Torin watching my every move, his eyes gleaming. He reached out and ran a finger down my back. Heat shot up my spine, and my knees nearly gave away. But he was there, tugging me against him so my back rested against his chest. He was tormenting me whether he knew it or not, and worse, I couldn't scold him without looking and sounding like a lunatic.

"You okay?" Cora asked. "You just stumbled."

I blinked. "I did? I must be more tired than I thought."

"Then let's finish here. Oh, and you're buying that dress or I'm never shopping with you *ever*," Cora threatened, moving closer to the mirror to study her own reflection.

"I'll shop with you," Torin whispered. "You can buy anything you want." He dropped his head and kissed my shoulder. I trembled, shocked by his boldness and the sensations rocking my body. He was seducing me right in front of Cora. Worse, I didn't want him to stop. His lips moved along my neck. I moaned and closed my eyes, tilting my neck to give him better access.

"What are you doing?" Cora asked, studying me through the mirror.

My eyes snapped open. "I'm, uh, imagining I'm dancing in this dress," I said in a squeaky voice then tried to put some distance between me and Torin, but he wasn't ready to let me go. "I'd love to buy it, but it's outside my price range."

"Charge it," Cora said. "Your mother gave you a credit card, didn't she?"

"No, just the debit," I corrected her.

"I have money, Freckles. Plenty of it. I'll buy it for you," Torin offered, his voice seductive and hypnotic. "You can wear it just for me."

"Okay, I'll buy it," I said, answering both of them. Torin chuckled and stepped back from me, while Cora grinned as though she'd won the argument. If only she knew.

I ran into the changing room, expecting Torin to follow. He was so bold I wouldn't be surprised if he did. I wanted him to. I could still feel his lips on my skin. A delicious shiver shot up my spine.

"You didn't tell me what you thought of my dress," Cora called out.

"I'll be out in a second." By the time I pulled on my jeans and stepped out, I was calmer and Torin was gone. Disappointed, I studied Cora's outfit. "It's nice, but I like the blue one better."

"Me, too," she said. She disappeared inside her changing room. "Be out in a second."

We paid for our purchases and headed home. Marj, Catie, and Jeannette, the three girls who'd helped Eirik and Cora with my birthday party, were getting groceries from an SUV outside Torin's house. They saw us and waved.

Marj walked over, her curly hair rolled up in a bun. As I studied her, she looked more and more like the nurse at the hospital. It was spooky. I shivered a bit.

"We didn't know you and Torin were neighbors," Marj said.

"I'm not, Raine is," Cora said. "What are you guys doing?"

"Helping Torin. He's gone all out, and his place is amazing. Are you guys coming over to help?"

"I will," Cora said. She glanced at me and cocked her brow.

I shook my head, just as Torin stepped out of his house. Our eyes met and heat sizzled between us, my senses remembering the incident at the mall. He grinned as though he'd read my thoughts. Cora, oblivious to the undercurrent, walked over to chat with him.

"I guess we'll see you tonight," Marj said.

"Sure. Uh, Marj? Are you by any chance related to the Guillaumes? I met a nurse at the hospital by the name of Gabrielle, and you two could be sisters."

She blinked. "Yeah, uh, we're cousins," she said, laughing. "But I look nothing like her. See you later."

As I watched her go, I wished I had agreed to help with the party just so I could ask her about her cousin and aunt. On the other hand, one second in Torin's presence and they'd all know how I felt about him.

Sitting on the window seat, I started on something I had put off since our visit to the hospital. I pulled out the phone book and tried to track down the other two nurses.

Mullin was a common local name and yet I still couldn't find a Sally Mullin or anyone who'd known her. Kayla Jemison wasn't even listed.

***

"Have fun," Mom called out hours later.

Even though she smiled at the three of us—Cora, Eirik, and me—I knew she was talking to me. My heart picked up tempo the closer we got to Torin's. Along with the excitement was worry. What if Jess was there and she saw me staring at Torin like a love-struck idiot? I wasn't even sure what I felt for him was love. All I knew was that I wanted him. Needed him. He made feel alive, special.

Some students lounged on the front porch while others were in the backyard, plastic cups in their hands. The thrumming music didn't seem loud, until we entered the house. Sketches of runes in neon ink ran across the walls. Maybe they had something to do with the dampening effect of the music.

I searched for Torin among the dancers in the living room, but didn't see him. Jess wasn't around either. Were they making out somewhere? I had no idea where the thought had come from, but it made me sick.

Pushing aside the thought of the two of them together, I looked around. Instead of the single couch I'd seen before, several lined the wall. A band played on the large flat-screen TV above the fireplace, giving the illusion of a live show. For someone who didn't like technology, he'd sure gone all out on the latest gadgets.

Loud laughter drew us to the kitchen. The L-shaped kitchen counter and the island had chips and dips, crackers and cheese, and pitchers of drinks. Some students sat on the stairs leading to the second floor. Others were crowded in the family room across from the kitchen, watching a four-player game on another large-screen TV.

"Happy you could make it, guys," Torin said from behind us, and we turned. Jess clung to his arm like a leech.

"We won't stay for long," Eirik said, his arm tightening around my shoulders.

"Then help yourselves to anything and have fun." His gaze lingered on my face, or maybe it was just my imagination.

"I hope you don't mind, Jess, but Torin promised me a dance." Cora grabbed his hand and tugged until Jess let him go. She pulled him toward the living room.

Jess stared after them, then turned and faced us. Her friends, Danielle, Savanna, and Vera stood behind her like courtly entourage.

"Hi, Eirik," Danielle said sweetly.

"Danielle. Excuse us, girls." He started to lead me way.

"That was a beautiful eulogy, Raine," Jess said.

I stiffened. A compliment from Jess? I didn't think so. She was buttering me up for something. "Thanks. It was a group effort."

"Group effort?" she asked, her eyebrow lifted.

"She means we worked on it together, Jess," Eirik said in a hard voice. "Excuse us." He started forward, forcing Jess and the other two girls to move aside. Danielle wasn't easily intimidated, even though she was petite.

"Dance with me, Eirik," Danielle said, wrapping her hands around his other arm, completely ignoring me.

Eirik freed his arm from hers. "Maybe next time. Right now, I need to dance with my girlfriend." He shuddered as we walked away. "Piranhas. How can Torin stand them?"

I had no response for him. Coming to Torin's party had been a terrible idea. This afternoon he had looked at me like I meant everything to him, and now he was with Jess. My chest hurt just thinking about them together. I wanted to go home and cry my eyes out. The problem was if I left, Eirik would want to know why.

Determined to act normal, I smiled and pretended everything was okay. We got drinks, nibbled on cheese, and mingled. The turnout was huge, and from the animated faces, everyone appeared to be having fun. I was miserable.

I focused on the house, noting the changes from before when Eirik's family had lived here. The old den was now a mini-gym with weight racks, several machines, and a workout bench. A few guys were messing around with dumbbells. Upstairs, two doors were locked. One led to Eirik's parents' old bedroom. The other was Eirik's old bedroom, now Torin's. The other rooms were empty, but not for long. Students had a way of finding all the cool niches to make-out.

Back downstairs, some of the guys dragged Eirik to the video game. He gave me a helpless look, and I found myself smiling.

"I'll be fine," I reassured him and headed outside where Marj and a group of people sat on the trampoline. Eirik's parents had gotten rid of the jungle gym when he became too old to use it, but left the trampoline alone.

Intent on attracting Marj's attention, I didn't see Jess and her friends until I stepped on the back porch. "All alone?" Danielle asked. "Did Eirik desert you?"

I ignored them and tried to walk around them, but they blocked my path.

"I guess it's just you and us now," Jess said.

"What do you want, Jess?" I asked, injecting as much venom as I could in the single question. I wasn't scared of her or her friends.

"Stop ogling her boyfriend," Vera snarled.

I blinked. "Excuse me?"

"You don't think we haven't noticed the way you're always staring at Torin?" Danielle added. "You already have Eirik."

"As for the fake tears in church today, we saw right through them. You wanted him to feel sorry for you and take you home," Jess said. "You're so pathetic."

"Actually, you three are the pathetic ones," a familiar voice intruded. I looked over Danielle's shoulder at Andris, his silver hair spiked, brown eyes twinkling. He winked at me. "Hey, sweetheart. Miss me?"

"No." For the first time since we'd met, I was actually happy to see him, not that I'd let him know it. He sat on the porch rail with his back against a pole, legs crossed and a bottle of a clear liquid in his hand.

"Who are you?" Jess asked.

"Get lost," Andris said rudely, then waved me over and patted the rail. "Join me, Raine."

I slid past the three girls and moved to his side. "Don't call me sweetheart."

"I rescue you from these…" he studied Jess and her friends and dismissed them with an eye roll, "and you're giving me attitude?"

"I didn't need rescuing," I said.

"You can't talk to me like that," Jess snarled at the same time. "This is my boyfriend's house."

"Boyfriend?" Andris laughed. "Not only are you stupid, you're delusional. One word from me and St. James will throw your sorry ass out of here. Now beat it and take your groupies with you." He dismissed them again with a flicker of his hand.

"Oh, we'll see who gets thrown out," Jess said peevishly and stomped away. Her friends followed.

Andris focused on me and smirked. "Did you miss me even a little bit?"

I ignored the question. "Where's Maliina?"

"Home on a timeout. She's been a very naughty girl."

That was an understatement. "You can't put her on a timeout. She's not a child."

"No, she's not, and I'm crazy about her. However, I had a lot of explaining and groveling to do because of her. That's why I was gone for so long, just in case you're wondering. Want a sip?" He offered me his drink.

I wrinkled my nose. "No, thanks. If you're crazy about her, why don't you show her? She only acts out because she needs reassurance that you love her."

"I know, but when you've been together for a couple of centuries, you do what you can to spice things up. A little jealousy goes a long way, and the makeup sex is amazing." He wiggled his brow.

My face heated. "That's a stupid reason to chase Mortals."

"I *pretend* to chase Mortals, except in your case. You're special."

"Yeah. Right."

"That's him," Jess said from the doorway and pointed at Andris. Torin stepped on the porch behind Jess, followed by Vera, Savanna, and Danielle. Torin's gaze swung from me to Andris, his eyes narrowing.

"What are you doing here?" Torin asked. He sounded too calm.

"Doing *your* job, big brother. I rescued Raine from your... whatever they are." Andris studied Jess and her friends and made a face. "They ganged up on her, the skanks," he added with mock outrage.

Skanks? I almost laughed, until I saw Torin's expression. He looked thunderous as his eyes shifted from me to Jess. "You did what?"

Jess blinked. "I, uh..."

"Come with me," he snapped.

Jess frowned, confusion on her face, and she followed him.

Andris snorted. "She's like a puppy, isn't she? Run along," he added to the other three girls. As they turned and scurried away, I almost felt sorry for them.

"Are you always this rude to people you plan to recruit?"

"Absolutely. I don't like Mortals, especially those not on my list." He sipped his drink. "No, that's not true. I prefer them," he hopped down, leaned toward me, and whispered, "dead." He laughed, bathing my face with alcoholic fumes. I leaned back. "You should see your face. Classic. Later, sweetheart." He entered the house, still chuckling.

He was nuts, just like Maliina. I had no idea how I fit in their grand scheme of things, but I was done with this party. I went in search of Eirik, but he was busy playing whatever game they had on the screen. The crowd watching had grown larger and louder. Not sure whether to leave without telling him or not, I paused behind the couch.

Then my heart tripped as I felt Torin's presence. It was as though I was wired to sense him or something.

"Dance with me," he whispered, his breath brushing my ear.

I swallowed. "Where's Jess?"

"She doesn't matter. You do."

I wanted to believe him, wanted to look into his eyes and see if he meant it. It was impossible to explain how he'd come to mean so much to me so fast. "You marked her with de-skanking runes?"

He chuckled. "She and I have an understanding now."

The back of his hand brushed against mine, and I sucked in a breath. For a moment he traced squiggles on the back of my hand, his caress light and hypnotic.

I closed my eyes, savoring his touch. He shifted, the tips of his fingers running up and down my palm, inviting me to play with him. Heart pounding, I went for it. Fingers caressed my palm. It was the most erotic foreplay ever. He gently stroked my arm, and I trembled. He wasn't playing fair. Finally, he looped his pinky around mine. Since we stood so close with the back of the couch in front of us, I hoped no one could tell we were touching.

"Don't just stand there watching them," Cora said, coming to stand beside me. She fanned her face. "Go dance."

I yanked my hand from Torin's and turned to face her. "I don't mind."

"Really? What's the game about?" she challenged and cocked her brow.

I stared blankly at her. "I don't know, but Eirik seems to enjoy it and I don't want to pull him away."

"You don't have to dance with him." She grabbed Torin's arm. "Dance with Torin."

Cora could be so bossy sometimes. I glanced at Torin and found him trying hard not to laugh. Once again, they were ganging up on me without knowing it. I wanted to go with him. Eirik was into the video game and wouldn't miss me. Besides, it was just a dance. No need to feel guilty.

I led the way to the living room. As though on cue, the music changed to a slow tune. The dancers on the floor went with the flow. I hesitated. Torin didn't give me a chance to escape. He took my hands and placed them on his shoulders.

"Did you change the music?" I asked.

"What do you think?" He flashed a wicked grin, looped his arm around my waist, and pulled me closer.

If it were possible to melt, I'd be a pool of goo on the floor. Time lost meaning. Wrong and right ceased to matter. The twig of guilt at leaving Eirik disappeared. We moved even closer, my check resting on Torin's chest.

"Let's get out of here," he said, his voice husky.

I didn't say yes, but neither did I say no. The music was still playing when he maneuvered us to the side door leading to the garage, opened it, and closed the door behind us. The lights turned on automatically. I looked around. His Harley looked majestic in the middle of the garage.

"Alone at last," he said.

"What are we doing in here?" I asked, walking toward his bike.

"Escaping the noise. Techno music is just not my thing."

I laughed and glanced his way. He watched me with a naughty gleam in his eyes. I swallowed, trying to focus on our conversation. "Then why play it."

"This generation seems to enjoy it, and faking interest in the same music creates trust." He followed me, his gait slow like a predator stalking its prey.

"So, it is important to gain our trust?"

He shrugged. "Not really, but it makes my work easier."

"You still won't tell me why you need to recruit athletes?"

A pained expression crossed his handsome face. "I can't."

Andris had hinted Jess and her friends weren't on his list. "Do you have a list of recruits?"

He laughed. "No."

"Will I be on yours?"

A look of utter horror crossed his face. "No way."

His reaction hurt. "Why not? Am I not good enough?"

He shook his head, a lock of hair falling over his forehead. He pushed it back, and I could tell he hated discussing his work. "That's not it."

"Maybe I'm on Andris' list."

"He wouldn't dare without telling me," Torin ground out.

Silence followed. I might not know why they were after the swim team, but his attitude sucked. "I should go back inside," I said weakly, though I didn't make a move to leave. "Eirik's probably looking for me."

"Don't go," he said softly, walking around the Harley. He stood behind me, bringing his intoxicating warmth. "I didn't bring you in here to talk about my work."

"Why then?"

"I wanted us to be alone."

I released a shaky breath. "I saw you earlier."

"It wasn't enough. Call me greedy, but I need more." He ran his knuckles up and down my arm. I shivered. His hands rested on my hips. Then he lowered his head and pressed his face into my hair. "I didn't expect you when I came here, Freckles. This was supposed to be a routine job, yet now it's much more."

I leaned against him, wanting to ease the pain in his voice even though I didn't know how. "But I'm with Eirik."

"He's not right for you." His voice was low, intense.

"I've known him all my life. He understands me."

"Does he make you tremble with a touch?" He ran the tips of his fingers up my bare arm, his touch feather light, yet it lit a fire inside me. I closed my eyes, my entire body trembling. He lifted hair from my neck, lowered his head, and pressed a kiss on my exposed neck. Warmth pulsed through me. "Is he the first person you think about when you wake up in the morning and the last one you think about before you fall asleep?"

Torin was the one I thought about every night and every morning. I opened my mouth to tell him he was the one. That he was all I'd ever wanted in a guy, but I couldn't speak.

"Do you know what I want to do to him every time I see him touch you? Every time he kisses you? I want to rip his head off." He turned me around and brought me against him.

I looked into his beautiful sapphire eyes and found myself drowning, melting. He traced my jaw line then my lips with his finger. Unparalleled craving rocked through me, and I grabbed a handful of his shirt to keep from falling. He lowered his head, and I stopped breathing. All my senses focused on him.

Then our lips met.

A tingling started on my lips and skidded under my skin. His teeth nipped my lip, and I gasped, giving him access to my mouth. He gently soothed the bite with his tongue then slipped past my lips to find my tongue. The first taste of him and my world exploded. I ceased to exist. I became part of something bigger, better, and brighter.

He groaned and deepened the kiss, his arm tightening around me and pulling me closer. I let go of his shirt, reached up, and cupped his face, holding him in place. This was what I had craved ever since he stopped outside my house, this feeling of completeness. He let go of my mouth long enough to rain kisses all over my face and down my neck, but I wasn't ready to let him go. I grabbed his head and brought his mouth back to mine, my head spinning, my entire body on the verge of something I didn't understand.

He tore his mouth from mine and looked at me with burning eyes, his breathing heavy. I loved that he was affected by the kiss.

"You are mine, Freckles," he vowed.

A chuckle filled the room. "This is very entertaining—"

Torin growled. "Get lost, Andris."

"I plan to, big brother, but her love-struck boyfriend will be here any second. He's looking for her and getting frantic."

I stared at Torin in horror. Eirik. What was I going to do? "I have to talk to him."

"No. We'll talk to him together."

I shook my head. "No. I have to do it alone."

"I agree with her," Andris butted in again. "Duty calls, big brother."

Blue ice flashed in Torin's eyes, but he ignored Andris. "Freckles—"

"This whole place is about to go ka-boom, Torin," Andris cut in.

"What?" Torin glared at Andris, his arm tightening around me.

"What do you mean ka-boom?" I asked, my senses still humming from the kiss, but reality returning like a splash of cold water.

"Maliina is here, and she's on the war path. I think she broke a gas pipe or something. You might not smell it in here, but inside reeks of it. I thought you'd want to know."

Torin cursed. "You said you bound her with runes."

Andris shrugged. "Ingrid must have released her. Don't worry. I'll find her and take her home."

"Like Hel you will," Torin snapped, runes appearing on his body, their glow visible through his dark clothes. "I'll deal with her myself. Take Raine to safety."

"No, I have to warn my friends," I protested.

"Let her," Andris added. "Why do we have to do everything by the book? Mortals and Immortals working together sounds great."

One second Torin was beside me, the next his hand was wrapped around Andris' neck. "I'm entrusting you with her life, *little brother.* Anything happens to her and your life is mine for eternity. Get it?"

Andris nodded, but a huge grin settled on his face.

"Good. Now get her out of here." The runes glowed brighter, and Torin went through the door.

I ran after him, fear making my insides shaky. I reached for the door knob. I had to find the others. If anything happened to Cora or Eirik…

Andris grabbed my wrist before my hand closed on the knob. "Where do you think you're going, sweetheart?"

I yanked my arm. "Let go, you psycho. I have to find my friends."

"No, you don't." He wrapped his arms around my mid-section and lifted me toward the side door leading out of the garage. I kicked and struggled, but he just laughed. "One thing you're going to learn is that St. James is like a one-man army."

"I know this house," I snapped, still trying to break free. "I know where some of the people are making out. He'll need our help to get everyone out."

For a brief moment, I thought Andris would disobey Torin when he put me down. I turned, and he snugged me, slung me on his shoulder like I was a sack of potatoes, and left the garage. I hit his back, kicked. Cool night air slapped my heated cheeks as he moved away from Torin's house so fast everything was blurry. "Put me down."

He did, but didn't let go of me. We were under my tree.

"Do you know how big this is?" he asked.

I ignored him, studying the students pouring out of Torin's house and trying to find Cora and Eirik.

"He trusted me with the most important thing in his life," Andris added.

Seriously? He was the most self-absorbed guy I'd ever met. "This is not about you, Andris. Your girlfriend is about to kill my friends and for what?"

"For thinking you can take him from me," Maliina snarled, and the next thing I knew I was airborne. Arms flailing, I tried to find something to grab onto. I found nothing but air. My head slammed against the wall. Stars exploded behind my eyes, and spears of white pain shot across my skull.

Disoriented, I struggled to keep my eyes open and move away from her. She landed on my chest with so much force I nearly blacked out. Air whooshed from my lungs like they were popped balloons. Pain radiated across my chest. I tried to breathe but couldn't. It hurt too much.

Through a haze of pain, I saw Andris and Ingrid struggling. Then Maliina's rage-twisted face blocked them from my line of vision. Her fingers, spread like claws, moved toward my face. I tried to raise my arms to block her, but she'd trapped them with her thighs.

She was about to finish me. I couldn't even fight back because every movement sent sharp pain across my chest and lungs. One second I was struggling to stay alive, the next someone yanked her from me and sent her flying.

CHAPTER 14. MEMORIES

Why wasn't I self-healing? My head pounded, and my lungs hurt, each breath sending needles of white-hot pain through me. Arms cradled me close, and gentle fingers pushed hair away from my face. I recognized Torin's familiar scent, his voice. He was talking, but a ringing in my ears made it impossible to hear him properly. I only caught the tail end of his sentence.

"...be okay," Torin vowed.

"No, she won't. Heal her... start the transformation... together forever and..." Andris' voice ebbed, but I didn't mistake his words. Forever with Torin sounded great.

"No," Torin snapped.

"Why deny yourself..." I didn't hear the rest of Andris' words. The ringing in my ears grew louder and louder. Then suddenly it stopped.

"It doesn't matter what I need," Torin ground out, his voice clear. "It's about what *she* wants. The last time I healed her, she hated it. I won't do that to her again."

"You're a fool. If you can't heal her, then let her die," Andris said. "At least then you can—"

"Damn it, Andris," Torin swore. "Don't you get it? I gave her my word. I won't let her become like us."

I opened my mouth to tell him I didn't care as long as we were together, but Andris interrupted. "This is no time to develop a conscience," he said.

"Go. Find Maliina and stay with her. I'll deal with her later."

"Heal me, Torin," I whispered, my words slurred, my breathing shallow. A weird pressure started on my temple, but my eyes sought his.

He stroked my temple and shook his head. "No, Freckles. You can't make a decision like that now. We'll talk later."

"It hurts. Make the pain go away," I begged.

"I can't," he whispered achingly, before pressing a kiss on my forehead. "Don't try to move. Help's on its way."

"Why can't I self-heal?"

"Your injuries are too extensive." His voice dropped to an anguished whisper. "You need new healing runes."

"Do it. Rune me. Please."

"Don't ask me to do this. I can't sentence you to a life like mine unless you know everything, yet I can't tell you much because I'm bound by an oath."

"I don't care what you are. I trust you. Please…" Pain speared across my skull, and my vision blurred. There was pounding all around me like running footsteps. It grew louder and louder, making the pressure in my head worse. "My head. Make it stop."

"What happened?" Eirik demanded, his voice echoing eerily.

"She was climbing the tree and fell," Torin said.

"Did you call 9-1-1?" Eirik dropped beside me.

"What do you think?" Torin snapped.

"That you might have healed her again," Eirik snarled.

How did Eirik know about Torin? I struggled to keep my eyes open. "How…?"

"Don't talk," Eirik said softly. "I'm here now."

"Is she okay?" Cora knelt near my feet. "Where does it hurt?"

"My chest." My eyes sought Torin's, hoping he'd take the pain away. He shook his head. My vision grew hazy again. I blinked to clear it, my eyes clinging to his. There was so much pain and despair in his eyes. Part of me was angry with him for refusing to help me while the other just wanted him to hold me. Then there was Eirik. He knew about Torin healing me and never said anything. The shrill sound of an ambulance pierced the air, adding to the ringing in my ears.

"Why does she keep blinking?" Eirik asked.

Torin answered, but I didn't hear his words. Darkness pulled me under again.

***

When I came around, someone was lifting my eyelids and flashing light on and off into my eyes. I tried to protest, but I couldn't speak. I tried to sit up, but something held me down. I was trapped. Voices filtered through my foggy head, and once again, I strained to hear.

"CT scan… hematoma… broken ribs…"

A sob followed. Mom. I wanted to reassure her, but I kept slipping in and out of consciousness. Voices came and went—Mom, Torin,

Eirik, Cora. They urged me to wake up, told me they loved me. Then there were the three women. I wasn't sure who they were or what they wanted, but they hovered in the background, silent, watching, waiting. It was impossible to see their features. They kept changing, hazy one minute, transparent the next. At times they looked ancient, other times young like regular teens. Something about them was familiar, but I couldn't tell what.

It was dark when I woke up again. My neck was stiff, and my chest and head throbbed. At least the pain was dull. I tried to open my eyes, but I couldn't and panicked. A beeping sound went off.

"Shh, it's okay," a familiar voice said in the void. Torin.

I managed to open my eyes, turned my head to find him, and winced when a spasm of pain radiated across my chest. A bright light drew my attention to the corner of the room. The light came from the glowing runes on Torin's face and body. He got up, the light from his body bathing Mom, who was asleep on a chair by my bed. No, not my bed. A hospital bed. I tried to remember how I got to the hospital, but I couldn't recall anything that happened after Maliina hit me. Now beeping machines monitored my vitals, and my body felt like I'd been run over by a truck.

A nurse entered the room and fussed over me and the machines. She checked my vitals, flashing light into my eyes, asking if I knew my name and my pain level. She adjusted the IV and fed me ice cubes from a cup. My throat was dry and painful, and the ice felt nice, but I wanted her gone so I could be alone with Torin.

"Thank you," I managed to say.

As soon as she left the room, my eyes found Torin again. The glow from the runes made his blue eyes hypnotic. He moved closer, scooped up an ice cube from the cup, and fed it to me.

"Why am I here?" I whispered hoarsely.

He frowned. "Maliina attacked you, but I pulled her off before she seriously hurt you." He fed me another ice cube. "I shouldn't have trusted Andris to watch over you. He's completely useless."

Memories of the events at the party trickled in. "No, he took care of me, Torin. He carried me from your place, but Maliina appeared out of nowhere and attacked." I glanced around the room. There were flowers and 'Get Well Soon' balloons. "How long have I been here?"

"About thirty hours."

"The gas leak at your place, was anyone hurt?"

He smiled. "No, but we cut things short. Actually, quite a number of students followed the ambulance here and camped in the waiting room until you left the operating room."

"I had surgery? Where?"

"Your brain." He stroked my forehead, but my skin felt weird. I tried to lift my hand to find out why, but Torin pressed my hand down. "Don't. You've broken several ribs and mustn't move too much. Do you want more ice?"

I searched his face. "I don't understand. You said I wasn't seriously hurt, yet I had surgery and broke my ribs. Why didn't you just heal me?"

"What's the last thing you remember?" he asked instead of answering.

"Maliina attacking me. I don't know what happened afterwards, until I woke up just now." Panic surged to the surface. "What happened? Why can't I remember?"

"You had bleeding in your brain, which caused you to lose consciousness. The doctor stopped the bleeding and told your mom you'll be okay, but some of your recent memories may be affected."

He tried to feed me more ice, but I turned my head away, my mind racing. I couldn't remember anything that happened after the attack, yet something about Torin and Eirik teased my mind.

"Was Eirik there?" I asked.

"Yes. He and Cora were here until a couple of hours ago when your mother insisted they go home. They have school tomorrow."

I glanced at Mom. She was usually a light sleeper. She must have been up the last thirty hours to be so tired. Who was taking care of her?

"Don't worry about her," Torin said as though reading my thoughts. "She's a lot stronger than you think. Go back to sleep, Freckles. I'll be here when you wake up." He put the cup of ice down and covered my hand.

He fell asleep before I did, his head resting on the bed beside my hip. I stroked his hair, happy despite my banged up body and missing memories. As the pain meds worked their magic, I relived every moment Torin and I had spent together just before Maliina attacked. The kiss, so beautiful and perfect. The feeling of completeness. He hadn't said he loved me, but he'd claimed me as his. I planned to claim him too as soon as I broke off things with Eirik.

Thoughts of Eirik filled me with sadness. He loved me, but my love for him was not enough. It wasn't comparable to my feelings for Torin. Maybe there was someone out there for him, someone who'd love him like he deserved. I was still thinking about how I'd break up with him when sleep tugged at my senses and I closed my eyes.

***

It was daytime when I woke up again. The first person I saw was Mom seated on the chair, a magazine on her lap. She looked so miserable. Torin sat in the corner, arms crossed, runes making him invisible to everyone but me.

He smiled and mouthed, "Good morning, Freckles."

"Good morning." I didn't realize I'd spoken out loud until Mom looked up and gasped.

"Oh, honey. You're awake." She jumped up, and the magazine fell from her lap. "The nurses told me you woke up last night and talked, but I didn't believe them. They should have woken me up. How are you feeling? Are you in pain? Do you want me to call the nurse?"

I managed a smile. "No, Mom. I'm fine."

Tears filled her eyes, and a sob escaped her lips. She covered her mouth. "I was so scared when they told me you were bleeding in your brain. Then they drilled a hole into your skull and… and… I'm sorry I'm going on, but I'm just happy you're okay." She sniffled and wiped her cheeks. Then she reached out with a trembling hand as though to touch my head. At the last minute, she stopped, fisted her hand, and gave me a tiny apologetic smile. "Look at me, crying like a baby when you're finally awake. That cursed tree is being chopped down tomorrow. I already made an appointment with a landscape company." She turned to pull the chair closer to the bed.

I glanced at Torin in confusion.

"I told her you fell from the tree," he explained. "It was the only explanation I could give her and the EMT."

"Don't blame the tree or cut it down, Mom," I whispered. "Dad planted it."

"Your father will understand. Every time I see it, I'll be reminded of how close I came to losing you. You were right to be wary about climbing it all these years. It's dangerous."

There was no point arguing with her once she made up her mind. She could be as stubborn as me. I reached for the water.

"No, don't move. The doctor said you must not exert yourself." She picked up the cup and held the straw to my lips. "Are you hungry?"

I nodded.

"I'll see what the nurses can rustle up." She disappeared out the door.

Torin moved closer and stroked my hand. "How are you feeling?"

"Better."

"You missed Eirik and Cora this morning, so don't be surprised if they come back during lunch."

Before I could respond, Mom came back. Torin moved back to the corner and watched us with a tiny smile as she fussed over me and talked about the surgery. She reassured me about my hair and the scar. Apparently, they had to shave an area near my ear for the surgery, but my chopped off hair was the least of my problems. The hospital food, when it finally arrived, was awful, and I could barely hold it down.

"Do you want me to get you something else to eat?" Torin asked.

Happy I could see him and talk to him without Mom knowing, I nodded. He left and returned a little later with breakfast—egg and sausage sandwiches and hot chocolate for both of us. By then, Mom had left for home to change. We ate. Then he left so I could rest. He came back hours later with lunch. A few minutes after he arrived, I heard the cheer chant for the Trojan swim team.

We are the Trojans. Oh Yeah
Kayville High top guns. Oh Yeah
When in the pool. Oh Yeah
We are so cool. Oh Yeah

When at a meet. Oh Yeah
We bring the heat. Oh Yeah
We've got the hold. Oh Yeah
On all the gold. Oh Yeah

I grinned, recognizing Cora and Eirik's voices. Even though they weren't yelling, I was surprised the nurses didn't kick them out or tell them to zip it. They danced into my hospital room, both of them in

Trojan crimson and gold swim pants, jackets, and T-shirts, swim goggles on their foreheads. They continued to chant.

> *Cause when we race. Oh Yeah*
> *We set the pace. Oh Yeah*
> *We're number 1. Oh Yeah*
> *The only one. Oh Yeah*
> *Oh Yeah, Oh Yeah, Oh Yeah, Oh Yeah*

They finished and posed. Torin stared at them as though they'd lost their minds, but he was trying hard not to laugh. They looked ridiculous, but it was Homecoming week.

"First day of Spirit Week is…?" Cora asked, hands on her hips, head cocked to the side.

"Sports Day," I said.

Cora's chin trembled, tears springing to her eyes. "Tomorrow is…?"

"Neon Day, then Wacky Tacky," I added, my eyes welling, too. "Then my favorite… Character Day."

"You remembered. That means you're okay, right? Your brain is working fine." She closed the gap between us, tears racing down her face.

I lifted my hand toward her, and she gripped it, both of us crying. "They might have drilled a hole into my skull, but I can never forget how crazy you act during Spirit Week. What floor did we get?"

"Second floor, west wing," Eirik said, grinning.

"We decorated it with blue balloons and streamers, water-themed…" Cora swallowed a sob and glared at me. "Don't ever scare me like that again. I thought I'd lost you and… and… I want to hug you, but I'm scared of hurting your ribs." She swiped at her cheeks. "I'll say it again. Don't ever, *ever* scare me like that again." She glanced at Eirik. "Okay, it's his turn. I'll wait outside, where I can sob like an idiot without making you cry, too."

I stared after her and shook my head. She was such a drama queen, and I loved her to death. My eyes connected with Torin's, but he didn't make a move to leave. In fact, he leaned back and got comfortable, his expression saying he wasn't going anywhere. Sighing, I ignored him and focused on Eirik.

Eirik planted a kiss on my forehead, then sat in Mom's chair and reached for my hand. My eyes went to Torin to see his reaction. Blue ice flashed in his eyes, his annoyance obvious. I knew his display of jealousy shouldn't please me, but it did anyway.

"Do you want me to get you anything? Something to eat other than hospital food? Bust you out of here?" Eirik asked.

"I have our food here, bonehead," Torin said.

Once again, I ignored Torin. "That's sweet, Eirik, but I'm okay food-wise and leaving right now is against the surgeon's orders."

Eirik's smile disappeared. "I'm so sorry I screwed up, Raine."

"You? What do you mean?"

"It's my fault you were hurt."

I frowned. "No, it's not. Why would you say that?"

"If I hadn't left you alone to play that stupid game, you wouldn't have been bored and decided to go home." He pressed a kiss on my knuckles, and Torin leaned forward as though he wanted to dive across the room and maul him. "You know that I love you."

Torin growled.

I shot him a warning look, but answered Eirik. "I know."

"And that I would do anything for you," Eirik added.

"I know that, too."

"I let you down, Raine, and I'm really sorry."

I sighed. "Eirik, don't—"

"No, let me finish. If you want to change our relationship and go back to being just friends, I'll understand," he continued.

Torin sat up and I could only guess at what he was thinking—here was my chance to cut ties with Eirik. But I couldn't take the coward's way out and blame Eirik for something he hadn't done.

"You're not my keeper, Eirik, and I won't let you blame yourself for something that wasn't your fault."

"You're sure?"

I nodded. "I tried to climb the tree to get to my bedroom because I didn't want to wake up Mom. It was my fault, not yours." My gaze connected with Torin. He didn't look happy. Eirik, on the other hand, sighed with relief and flashed his famous sunny smile.

"Good, because I wasn't about to give up on us without a fight," he said. Then he frowned. "Did Torin have anything to do with you leaving the party?"

"Why do you say that?" I tried not to look at Torin.

"Cora said you were dancing with him. Did he say or do something to make you leave his place? Because if he did—"

"No, he didn't." I shook my head. "We danced."

"And kissed," Torin added from the corner of the room.

"Was it Jess?"

I shook my head. "No. No one is to blame for what happened to me, Eirik."

***

"I want to hold you while you sleep," Torin whispered that night after everyone left.

I scooted to create room for him. Since the incision on my head was behind my right ear, I spent most of the time on my left side. He curled behind me in the narrow bed, his hand resting around my waist. "Let me know if anywhere hurts."

"I don't care."

"I do." His thumb touched my lips as though to stop me from speaking, but the effect on me was instant. My lips tingled. "I want to kiss you, but I'm afraid of hurting you."

I wanted to kiss him, too. "You could never hurt me. Not with a kiss."

He chuckled. "I'll not want to stop, so let's not try it. Go to sleep, Freckles."

The next morning, I opened my eyes and looked into his beautiful eyes. It was still dark outside, and it sounded like the nurses were changing rotations. He cupped my face and gently stroked my cheek. Only one rune glowed on his forehead. He had an amazing ability to control them, I'd noticed.

"I'll be back later with breakfast," he whispered.

For the rest of the week, Eirik and Cora stopped by in crazy Spirit Week outfits. Eirik came during lunch and sat with me. In the evenings, he stayed after Cora left, did his homework, and even watched a little TV. Torin left whenever Eirik appeared, but he hated it. I saw it in his eyes, yet I couldn't bring myself to tell Eirik the truth yet.

Night was my time with Torin. We spent every night together. I didn't know if he used runes to stay invisible or if he enchanted my room so the nurses saw only what he wanted them to see. I didn't care. I loved sleeping in his arms.

While he was at school, I tried to stay active by walking around. My doctor encouraged it. Often, I crossed from Surgical to the Women's Center to see the newborns. It was as though a force I couldn't explain pulled me there.

"Is one of them yours?" a man asked me.

I laughed at the thought of me with a child. "No. I'm only seventeen."

"What happened to you?" he asked, his gaze on the bandage around my head.

"I fell from a tree and injured my ribs and head. Which one is yours?"

He grinned with pride and pointed to a puny baby in an incubator. "His name is Jeffrey. He came out early, but he's a fighter."

Tears rushed to my eyes. The pride in his voice made me think of my father. "I was a preemie, too," I whispered. "My father said I fought to live, but holding and massaging me helped a lot. They say human contact is good for preemies."

"Is that so?" The man thanked me and walked away.

On Friday, I got enough courage to approach the nurses' station at the Women's Center and asked for Nurse Guillaume.

The nurse behind the desk frowned. "Who?"

"Gabby Guillaume. I just wanted to say hi."

The nurse shook her head. "You must be mistaken, honey. We don't have a nurse by that name working at this center."

I frowned. "Are you sure? My friend and I were here a week ago and talked to her. She was behind the counter and… and her aunt worked here seventeen years ago, too."

"It's okay. Calm down." The nurse reached across the desk and patted my hand. "What floor are you from?"

"Not the crazy ward," I retorted and yanked my hand from under hers. I was annoyed and, to be honest, spooked. Had I imagined visiting the hospital with Cora and meeting with the Gabby Guillaume?

"Just a second. Could you describe her?" the nurse called out.

I debated whether to keep walking, but I needed answers. Someone was messing with my head. "Medium height, brown skin, and braids. I think she's Creole. Her cousin goes to my school."

She quickly typed on her keyboard. "I'm sorry, but someone played a cruel joke on you, honey. We've never had the person you just described work here. Maybe she works at a different center."

"Even seventeen years ago?"

"I can't say for sure, but Records would have that information." She gave me a smile filled with pity. Not only had the fake nurse lied to me, Marj had, too.

Puzzled, I turned to leave and almost missed the father of the preemie I'd spoken to a few days ago. He was with his wife in one of the rooms and in his arms was little Jeffrey. Smiling, I left the center.

That night, I told Torin what I'd learned about the fake nurse. "That means Marj lied to me."

"Marj? Who's Marj?"

"Marjorie LeBlanc. She, Jeannette, and Catie helped you with your party last Saturday."

Torin sat up and came around the bed so I could see his face. "What are you talking about?"

"When Cora and I came back from shopping, Marj and her friends were helping you get groceries from an SUV."

He chuckled and shook his head. "I think your memories are a little off, Freckles. I used a catering company to help with the party. They sent three women, and if I recall correctly, not one of them was called Marj or Marjorie, and I don't recall the names of the other two."

"I talked to Marj, Torin," I insisted, trying not to panic. "She's on the swim team. The three of them are. They also helped Eirik with my birthday party at the club." A foreboding feeling washed over me. What if all my memories were false and things I thought had happened never did?

Torin frowned. The next second, he was pacing room. He paused and said, "Describe them."

"Marj is brown-skinned, Creole, I think, with dark-brown eyes. Catie has black hair, hazel eyes, and tan skin, and Jeannette has blonde hair and gray eyes. They're about the same height, five-seven or eight, neither skinny nor fat. They all transferred to our school last year and became fast friends. I've never asked them, but I always assumed they knew each other before they came to our school."

"Norns," he whispered.

"What?"

He paused and looked undecided, then came back and sat on the edge of my bed. "I'm sorry there're things I cannot share with you yet, but I promise to tell you everything once I know whether we're dealing with good or bad ones."

"Did you say *norms*?"

His frown deepened. "No, Norns. Don't bother looking for the three nurses who took care of you when you were born, because you won't find them. If we're dealing with Norns, it might explain their presence."

***

Armed with a list of instructions from my doctor, Mom checked me out of the hospital on Saturday. Eirik stood outside my house with flowers, 'Welcome Home' balloons, and a broad smile. My gaze went to Torin's, but his garage was closed, which meant he wasn't home. Had he found anything on the Norns—whatever they were?

The first thing I did when I got to my room was shower. Even though I'd showered at the hospital, using my own shampoo and soap made me feel a lot better. I studied the already healing wound on my head. The bumps of titanium plates and screws holding the bone together under my skin felt a little weird. At least the area was perfectly hidden by my hair and no one would notice it unless I put my hair up in a ponytail.

Standing naked in front of the mirror, I studied the yellowish bruises on my chest. It still hurt whenever I took deep breaths. Unfortunately, I had to take deep breaths as part of my daily exercise to prevent my lungs from collapsing.

Eirik was waiting in my room when I finished in the bathroom. Just like old times, he'd pulled out the spare bed from under mine and was lying on it. The thought of breaking off our relationship and hurting him made me feel terrible. I lay on my left side and tried to see his face as we talked.

"I want to ask you something," I said as soon as I settled on my bed.

He cocked his eyebrows. "Okay. Shoot."

"I know this is going to sound strange, but it's a test to see if my memories are intact or not."

He wore a skeptical look. "You remembered Homecoming week themes."

"I'm serious, Eirik. The doctor said people tend to have short-term memory loss after a brain trauma. Homecoming is an old memory."

He sobered up fast and sat up. "Okay."

"Who helped you with my birthday at the club?"

"What do you mean?" he asked, frowning.

"You gave me a surprise birthday party, right?"

He nodded. "At L.A. Connection. Cora and I planned it."

"Who else helped you organize it?"

"Some woman in charge of parties at the club. We worked with her and her friends."

"What about Marj, Jeannette, and Catie?"

He frowned. "Who?"

"Marjorie LeBlanc, Jeannette Wilkes, and Catie Vivanco. They're on our swim team."

Eirik scrubbed his face. "Raine, there's no one on the swim team called Marjorie LeBlanc, or Jeannette Wilkes, or Catie Vivanco."

I swallowed panic. How could I remember them so clearly when everyone else couldn't? Either I was going crazy or Torin was right. Norns, whoever they were, were messing with my head.

"Hey," Eirik said, gripping my hand. "You okay?"

"Yeah. I thought we had three new girls on the team." I described them and explained their arrival last year, but Eirik kept shaking his head. Two down. If Cora didn't know who they were either, then I'd know for sure something was wrong with me. "I have a friend called Cora though, right?"

Eirik scowled. "That's not funny."

I grabbed his hand when he plopped back on the pullout bed. "I mean it. Do I have a friend called Cora?"

"Yes. In fact, I'm going to call her right now, so you can talk to her. I'm happy you remembered me." He pulled out his cellphone and punched in numbers.

How many people and incidents had I forgotten or imagined? "You're going to the Homecoming Dance, right?"

He shook his head. "Wrong. The whole point of going in the first place was for *you* to show *me* off. You can't do that when you just came back from the hospital and your memories are messed up."

"You can go without me," I begged him.

"Not interested." He brought the phone to his ear. "I'm going to pick up your favorite movies and something to eat. Then we'll hang out. Here, talk to Cora." He gave me a brief kiss, then left. I had a feeling that seeing me so confused and vulnerable bothered him too much.

As he walked away, part of me knew I wasn't being fair to him. I still wasn't sure how to tell him it was over between us. He loved me and just wanted to spend time with me, while I wanted him out of the way, so I could spend my first night at home with Torin.

I finished with Cora, who said she'd stop by later. Then I sat by my window, booted my laptop, and waited for Torin to come home. He didn't. Not worried, I went online and started researching Norns. Mom kept interrupting me, wanting to know my opinion on one thing or the other. I saw through her excuses. She was still worried about me and was checking on me on the sly. In between her visits, I managed to do some reading.

Norns were Norse female deities in charge of the destiny of Mortals. They were like Fates in Greek mythology, only more powerful. They even decided the fates of the gods. The more I read about them, the more I could see why Torin had freaked out. While there were only three Fates, Norns were many but tended to work in groups of threes. They often appeared when a person was born to determine their future. The good ones were kind and protective, while the evil ones were behind tragic events.

We had to be dealing with evil Norns—Marj, Catie, and Jeannette. It explained why they were always there *before* something bad happened. The night of my party, they'd helped Eirik and we'd had a blackout. The night I got hurt, they'd helped Torin with his party. What if they were at the Homecoming Dance tonight?

Trying not to panic, I went back to reading.

Of the three Norns that appeared when someone was born, one was in charge of the past, the second one was concerned with the present, and the third was in charge of the future. If Marj and her friends were Norns, they might have messed with everyone else's memories and left mine intact. It might explain why I remembered them when no one else did. They might also have been there when I was born. Had they saved my life or tried to kill me then? Everything was so confusing. If only Torin was around to give me some answers.

Cora pulled up before Eirik returned. She wasn't dressed for the dance and didn't carry her garment bag or makeup tote either. Weird. In a few minutes, I heard her voice and Mom's outside my door.

"Look who's here to see you, honey," Mom said in a cheerful voice. "Eirik called. He's running late, but he'll be here with dinner. In the meantime, if you girls need anything, let me know."

"Thanks, Mom. Shouldn't you be getting ready for the dance?" I asked as soon as Mom left.

Cora snorted and slumped on the window seat. "Like I'd go without you? So how are you feeling?"

"Fine. What about Keith? Isn't he expecting you to go with him?"

"He wasn't too thrilled when I told him I couldn't, but he understood."

My friends were annoyingly loyal. Sighing, I walked to the closet and removed the green dress I'd bought for the Homecoming Dance.

"What are you doing?" Cora asked, standing up.

"Getting ready for the dance. Did Marj swim this week?"

"Marj? Who's Marj?"

"Never mind." Three down, confirming I was the only one who could remember them, which meant I was the only one who could stop them from causing more mayhem. I chose a pair of shoes from my closet.

"Seriously, what are you doing?" Cora demanded.

"If you and Eirik insist on hanging out with me, we might as well do it at the dance. It'll do me good to be up and about." She stared at me as though I'd gone crazy. "Go get your outfit, Cora Jemison. Homecoming Dance, here we come. You can do my hair and makeup."

"Hold up, crazy lady. You just came back from the hospital," she protested. "You can't just go to the dance. I won't let you."

"I'm not going to dance. I'll dance vicariously through you." I grinned. She frowned. "Look, I've been staring at the walls for a whole week, and Mom is beginning to drive me nuts. She uses some lame reason to check on me every ten minutes. I need a break or I'll go crazy."

Cora chewed on her lower lip. "She won't go for it."

"Oh, she will. Doctor's orders. Go get your stuff." I shooed her with my hands. "Oh, text Eirik and tell him about our change of plans. I have no idea where my cell phone is. Wherever it is, the battery's probably dead anyway." I waited until she left then went to Mom's bedroom. "Is it okay if I go out with Eirik and Cora for a few hours?"

Mom frowned. She put down the book she'd been scribbling in and walked to where I stood. "Go where, honey?"

"The Homecoming Dance. I promise not to push myself."

She sighed. "I don't know."

"But the doctor said—"

"That you shouldn't sit for long periods of time, I know. I just hate the idea of you going anywhere right now." She touched my cheek. "Every moment you're out of my sight, I worry."

"Mom," I said and sighed.

"I know. I'm being everything I hate in a parent. Clingy and nagging." She smiled then pressed a kiss on my temple. "Fine. Go, but if you feel dizzy or have any of the symptoms the doctor mentioned, you come straight home. No driving, no lifting anything, no alcohol, no—"

I laughed and kissed her, then walked back to my bedroom to change. Hopefully, Torin would be back before we left.

CHAPTER 15. A CENTURY OR TWO

"Wow, look at this place," Cora said when we entered the gym. "The décor's better than last year's."

I had no idea what the theme was last year, but the transformation was amazing. The room was done in Trojan colors—gold and crimson. From stretched arches for taking commemorative pictures and gold and crimson gossamer curtains flowing from floor to ceiling to strings of twinkly lights and oriental lanterns hanging from the ceiling. Gold and crimson balloons littered the floor, and tall, lighted luminescent columns covered in black with gold streamers were strategically positioned around the dance floor. I searched for Torin among the dancers.

"That no good, lying, cheating bastard!" Cora snarled.

I turned and followed her gaze. She was staring at Keith, who was making out with some girl on the dance floor.

"He said he'd come alone, that he'd miss me. Yeah, groping another girl is the new missing me," Cora continued with her rant.

Eirik laughed then faked seriousness when she glared at him. "Do you want me to go punch him?"

"Yes," Cora said with glee, eyes flashing. She looked amazing in her blue dress, her hair teased and her makeup perfect. Eirik kept staring at her. "Go. Avenge my honor."

"No, go talk to him," I said. "Keith might only be with her because you ditched him to stay with me."

"Oh, please. Don't make excuses for him," Cora snapped. "I should go over there and rip him a new one."

I pushed Eirik toward Cora. "Dance with her. I'll *talk* to Keith."

Cora and Eirik eyed each other, but they didn't make a move to join the dancers. I rolled my eyes as I walked toward Keith and his date and tapped on his shoulder.

Keith turned around and frowned. "Raine? What are you doing he—oh crap," he added, looking past me.

"Yeah, she's pissed, so you'd better have a really good explanation." Cora looked ready to commit murder. Then she grabbed Eirik's hand and dragged him to the dance floor. Keith scrubbed his face, glanced at his date apologetically, and looked at Cora and Eirik.

"Good luck," I whispered and walked away, continuing my search.

Staying on the outskirts of the dance floor, I searched for Marj, Catie, and Jeannette among the dancers. They weren't here. A few times I thought I felt a zing, the tingling feeling I always associated with Torin's eyes on me, but when I turned around, he wasn't there.

The news about my accident must have spread because people turned to stare as I walked past. Usually too much attention bugged me, but this time I didn't care. I couldn't afford to feel self-conscious. Some members of the swim team and band even stopped me and asked how I was doing.

"Raine."

I stiffened, recognizing Jess' voice. *Please, don't let Torin be with her... don't let Torin be with her...* I turned.

She was with her friends and four other guys, two from the swim team and two I'd seen hang around her and her friends. None had shaggy black hair and sapphire eyes or the smile with a punch. I sighed with relief.

"You look amazing," she said.

Jess being nice was, I don't know, disturbing. "Thank you."

"What are you doing here?" she asked.

"It's the Homecoming Dance," I said politely, trying not to be rude.

"I mean you were hospitalized with brain injury. Are you sure you should be at a dance?"

Her concern blindsided me because it seemed genuine. "Yeah, the doctor said I should stay active. It's good for my brain." Despite her niceness, I couldn't bring myself to ask her if she'd seen Torin. "Uh, have fun, Jess."

I left the gym through one of the side doors and headed outside. The Sports Complex housing the basketball court, the pool, and exercise room was separated from the school's main building by a large patio with a waist-length wall and a parking lot. The crowd on the patio was even larger, but the chaperones were everywhere, so students didn't disappear in their cars to make out.

I shivered, wishing I'd worn my coat instead of leaving it inside. It was cooler outside than inside the gym. Then a prickly feeling I often associated with being watched washed over me, and I turned.

Ingrid floated toward me. She wore a white, vintage dress, the hem touching the ground as she moved. Her blue eye shadow matched her eyes, and her blonde hair was piled up, wisps near the ears framing her face.

"He wants to see you," she said.

I frowned. "Who?"

"Torin."

My heart fluttered. "Where is he?"

"This way." She headed back inside the Sports Complex, using a door that led into the broad hallway that cut across the building. We walked past the inner entrance to the gym and kept going. Two chaperones—a teacher and unfamiliar woman who was probably a parent—stared at us, but didn't try to stop us. I started to worry. Ingrid had never done anything to show that she hated me, so there was no need for me to be afraid. Still, I wasn't sure about going anywhere. Maybe I should find Eirik and Cora first or text them.

"Do you have a phone?" I asked.

Ingrid chuckled. "We have no need for modern technology, Raine."

"I should tell my friends where we're going," I said.

She stopped. "Listen, you can either come or not. I don't care. But you should know that he's leaving."

My stomach dropped. "Leaving? What do you mean?"

Ingrid shook her head and continued down the hallway. "Did you think he'd stay here forever? He has a job, you know. He does it, like all of us, then moves on to the next one." She turned a corner.

I hurried after her, my heart pounding. Torin wouldn't leave me. Wherever his job took him, he'd come back to be with me. I followed Ingrid into one of the girls' restrooms.

"What are we doing in here?" I asked.

She ignored me and checked the stalls to make sure they were all empty. One wasn't. She rattled on the door. "Move it. This bathroom is being closed. Use the ones closer to the gym." A girl dashed out of the stall. Ingrid indicated the exit. "Go!" Then she locked the door behind her.

I stared at Ingrid with wide eyes, fear slowly beginning to trickle through me. "What's going on?"

She ignored my question again and lifted the hem of her dress to reveal a black, leather thigh-strap with pouches. She pulled a rune dagger from one of them. This one was different from the one Maliina had used to draw runes on her skin. Ingrid stepped in front of the full-length mirror and started sketching. The dagger was some kind of sketching tool. The runes blended with the mirror. She stepped back, her eyes glowing.

"What are you do...?" My voice trailed off when the mirror moved and shimmered, until it no longer showed our reflection. The surface became less grainy. It rippled like the surface of water. Panic slithered up my spine. "What is that?"

"A portal," she said. "It is how we move from place to place. Come on."

I took a step back. "No, I'm not going in there. I'll get a ride... home." My gaze was transfixed on the portal. The watery surface peeled back to reveal a short hallway. The walls and the floor now had that weird watery look, and at the end was a room that looked vaguely familiar.

"Don't you recognize the room?" Ingrid asked.

I nodded. "Eirik's parents' bedroom had the same wallpaper and carpet."

"It's the same room and you know it's in Torin's house. See, I'm not trying to hurt you. My sister might have, but she was under the influence of forces we've never dealt with before." Ingrid extended a hand toward me. I still hesitated.

Runes appeared on her arms. The next second, she'd grabbed my arm and was moving toward the portal. I closed my eyes, expecting the worst, but instead, there was a gentle brush of cool air on my skin, and my feet landed on a solid surface. The coolness disappeared, and we stopped moving.

Ingrid chuckled. "You can open your eyes now."

I did, slowly. Behind me, the portal closed, the watery surface shifting and remolding into a floor-to-ceiling mirror, which I recognized immediately. It used to be in Eirik's parents' bedroom when they'd lived next door. They must have left it behind. Were they part of Torin's world?

Heart pounding, I swallowed. "Do you use only mirrors as portals?"

"Any surface where we can draw runes can do, but we prefer mirrors. They're more efficient."

She walked to the door and unlocked it. During the party, the door to this particular room had been locked. Was the portal the reason? The door to Torin's bedroom was ajar. There was no furniture, no sign that he'd ever slept there.

My insides tightened with dread. He wouldn't leave without me. My stomach churned at the thought and nausea rose to my throat. I followed Ingrid downstairs, almost tripping in my haste. Downstairs, the furniture he'd used for the party was gone. The emptiness closed around me like suffocating fumes.

"Where is he?" I asked in a voice I didn't recognize, fear constricting my throat. "Torin!"

"He's not here," a familiar voice said, and I whipped around. Andris closed the fridge and faced me. He carried a bottle with a clear liquid, his eyes glazed and his silver hair disheveled as though he'd run his fingers through it.

"Where is he?" I asked.

"Gone. Maliina, too, and they're never coming back," he said, his words slurring.

Air left my lungs, and dizziness washed over me. I gripped the rail. "I don't believe you."

"Look around you, sweetheart," he snarled, making the endearment sound like an insult. "Do you see any furniture? Does this look like a place he plans to return to? No, he's gone, and he took my mate with him."

His anger was like a slap on the face. The last time we talked, he'd been polite, nice. "Where did he go?"

"Hel's disease-ridden realm or worse."

Torin hated Hel's Mist. I swallowed past a knot of panic. "What could possibly be worse than Hel's world?"

"Being indebted to evil Norns put in charge of death and mayhem while you slowly become like them... cold, cruel, dead inside. No one challenges Norns without paying a price, yet he decided to do it for you, Lorraine Cooper. Once a destiny has been set, no one messes with it. Torin changed yours. He broke the ultimate law." He twisted the lid off the bottle, threw it, and watched it bounce off the wall, then guzzled some of the drink. He swallowed, made a face, and shook his head. "You," he pointed the bottle at me, "my lovely, should have died at the park. That was your destiny. He did the unthinkable. He saved your life and changed it. Then on your birthday, he intervened again. Saving you and changing your destiny meant saving the others and changing theirs. Then at his house last weekend, he intervened again."

"But these were accidents started by Maliina—"

"Who was being used by evil Norns," he snarled, his eyes glistening. "Bitter old hags. If I'd known, I would have saved her." He rubbed his eyes, and for one brief moment, I thought he was crying. "There's a reason why we don't interact with Norns, Raine. They screw with people's heads. Mortals, Immortals, gods, it doesn't matter. They control all destinies. Now my mate is gone because of them, because of you. Something about you drove her insane with jealousy."

He hadn't minded Maliina's jealousy last weekend during Torin's party. Not sure what he wanted now, I stepped back and glanced at Ingrid. She wore an unreadable expression, but she blocked my path to the front door and huge boxes blocked the back door. There was no escape.

"I don't understand what my dying has to do with your job."

Andris smirked. "You were on our list, Raine, and everyone on our list leaves with us. Torin changed that because he couldn't resist you. He crossed you out and, by doing that, sealed his fate." He walked toward me, guzzling his drink, his face twisted with anger. No, not just anger. Grief, too. He really loved Maliina. "The worst part of this is you have no idea what's going on. You're just a Mortal girl who thinks she's in love, or in lust, or whatever you think you feel for Torin. From what I remember, Mortals' love never lasts. It comes and goes on a whim."

"That's not true," I protested. "I love Torin."

"Really? What about your love-struck boyfriend? Does he know you don't love him, or were you stringing him along in case Torin left?"

My chest squeezed. "Is that what Torin thinks? That I don't love him?"

Andris shook his head. "I have eyes and ears. I stopped by the hospital several times and watched him eat his heart out while you laughed with that love-struck idiot. Do you know how amazing it is he let you get away with so much? For centuries, he did everything by the book. He got the job done without losing sleep or caring about anyone on his list, never letting anyone get close. Women were just a means to an end. Then he met you." Andris walked around me, his gaze assessing. "I can see why any guy might find you irresistible. You have a timeless beauty. You're graceful, smart, loyal, funny, but for him, it went beyond the physical. Something about you pierced his cold, hard exterior. He should have done what he always does—seduced you and moved on, but he wanted more. Maybe your protection runes and ability to see us started it. I don't know. When you were hurt, I begged him to heal you and start your transformation into an Immortal, but he refused. Do you know why?"

I shook my head, his words and accusations piercing my heart.

"He gave you his word. What kind of crazy ass argument is that? You could have had a century or two together, and he would have made it up to you a thousand times. But no, a few centuries weren't good enough. The worst part of it is he doesn't even trust Mortal doctors, yet he refused to heal you and left you in their hands." Andris slammed the empty bottle on the counter. "Stubborn fool."

I stared at him with wide eyes. He seemed to alternate between anger toward Torin and bitterness at me. I wasn't exactly sure what he wanted. Did he plan to take me with him? Kill me?

"Please, tell me what to do to fix this," I said in a tiny voice.

Andris' eyes glowed eerily. "Short of dying, nothing. The funniest thing is I begged him to let you die. At least then he would have escorted your soul home, visited you every time he took new ones, but I guess that wasn't good enough either. I still don't understand why saving your life was so important when it stopped him from having what he wanted. You."

Escorted my soul? "What are you?"

He laughed bitterly. "For such a smart girl, you're a little slow."

"Torin told me you recruit athletes for your secret organization," I protested weakly.

Andris chuckled. "He does have a way with words, doesn't he?" He reached inside the fridge, removed another bottle, and twisted the lid. "No, Raine. We don't *recruit* athletes. That's the saddest part of this situation. Torin is willing to sacrifice everything so you can live your pitiful Mortal life and you don't even know what he is. Had you died when you were supposed to, you would have known and all this explanation would be unnecessary."

"Just tell me what you are," I begged.

"We're reapers, Raine. Soul collectors. We find strong, athletic men and women, wait for them to die, then whisk them to Valhalla and Falkvang to train for the final battle between good and evil, the destruction of the gods and your world, the beginning of a new one, yada, yada, yada."

I stared at him with round eyes. I'd read enough about Norse mythology to guess at their identity. "You can't be Valkyries," I whispered. "Valkyries are women."

He shook his head. "Mortal books are always behind the times. Originally all Valkyries were women. Men went to battle while their women stayed at home, so it was only logical to have female Valkyries collecting slain soldiers from battle fields. In death, as in life, opposites attract. Women soldiers are likely to follow a handsome male Valkyrie. Teens follow teen Valkyries. As more women joined combat, Valkyries started recruiting men, the younger and more handsome the better." He spread his arms as though to indicate himself. "The world changed, and we changed with it. Soldiers are no longer found in fields. We get them at sporting event, arenas, swimming pools, and anywhere an athlete meets his or her untimely death."

Everything fell into place. Torin might not have revealed his identity, but he'd given me clues. I just never connected the dots.

"You weren't just after me," I whispered. "You were here for the swim team."

"Finally, you're catching on. Just because we're leaving doesn't mean they're safe. Torin just bought them time. They might have a day, a week, a month, but eventually, other Valkyries will come for them. They can't escape death."

Anguish gripped my chest. "Is that why you brought me here? To tell me my friends are going to die? Torin said you're not supposed to tell Mortals about your world."

Andris leaned toward me and smirked. Alcoholic fumes bathed my face. "No, we're not. When we do tell or you notice us, we make sure you don't remember a thing, but I think you deserve to know everything, Raine."

I blinked at the anger in his voice. "Why?"

He rocked on his heels, his eyes glassy and watery. "Because of you, I've lost Maliina. Because of you, Torin is rotting in Hel's Mist or turning evil. Knowing death is stalking your friends and you can't do anything about it is a small burden to carry, don't you think? So here's to you, sweetheart." He lifted his bottle and drained it, then threw the empty bottle. It smashed against the wall, shards of glass flying everywhere. "Come on, Ingrid."

Runes appeared on their skin. I could swear there was pity in Ingrid's eyes as she turned away. Their blurry forms zipped upstairs, presumably to use the mirror portal. I watched them go, dizziness washing over me, my knees threatening to give out.

I staggered backwards and gripped the banister. Torin was gone, and it was my fault. He'd sacrificed his existence, his soul, so I could live. Worse, my friends were in danger and there was not a thing I could do to change it.

I didn't know how I did it, but one second I was inside Torin's empty house, the next I was outside my house, warm tears racing down my face. I opened the door.

"Raine!" Mom ran toward me and yelled over her shoulder. "Cora... Eirik... she's home. What happened? Where have you been? We've been worried sick." She cupped my face. "You're frozen, shaking... crying. What's wrong? Are you in pain?"

Cora and Eirik ran from the kitchen.

"Come on upstairs." Mom put her arms around me. "Cora, run her a hot bath."

I forced myself to snap out of the cloying numbness. "No. I need... need to lie down. My head hurts. I need to rest."

Mom helped me under the blankets and gave me some meds, but nothing could ease my pain. It was deep and vast, like someone had punched a hole inside me and filled it with nothingness. I curled under the blanket, wishing Torin was around to hold me, reassure me that everything would be okay.

Mom must have sent Cora and Eirik away because soon it was just the two of us. She curled behind me and stroked my hair, but I wished she was Torin. I missed his arms. Missed his scent. I wanted him back. My chest hurt, and the thought that I'd never see him again filled me with such anguish I couldn't breathe. Sobbing silently, warm tears raced down my face.

***

Monday arrived too soon. I had shut everyone out, even Mom, and now I had to deal with school. I wished I didn't have to go, wished I could stay in bed and never leave my room, but hiding wouldn't bring Torin back.

I ate without tasting the food while Mom watched me from across the table with a worried expression. "Are you sure about going to school today? You don't look too good. Maybe we should go see the doctor first."

I shook my head and forced myself to smile. "I'd rather stay busy. Is Eirik coming to pick me up?"

"No, I'll drive you to school myself."

I couldn't remember the last time she drove me to school. Kindergarten? In elementary school and junior high, Dad would give me rides whenever I needed, but I often used the school bus.

Eirik and Cora were waiting for me outside the school. He carried my backpack. According to my doctor, I wasn't allowed to carry anything heavier than a two-liter bottle of soda. Cora opened the door and held it for me. Seeing the runes on the entrance sent a rush of anguish through me. Would everything I saw remind me of Torin? The walk to my locker happened in a haze. It didn't sink in that Torin was really gone until my math class started and he didn't appear.

"Do you need to see the nurse?" Mrs. Bates asked.

I stared at her with unseeing eyes. "No."

She leaned closer and whispered, "You're crying, Ms. Cooper. If you're in pain, go home or take your meds. If you need a moment, go to the restroom and calm yourself down."

I calmed down, but I couldn't wait for the day to be over. Eirik was attentive, always outside my classrooms, walking me to class after class. When the bell rang and signaled the end of the day, I headed to his car. The closer we got to home, the tighter my stomach became. All I needed to see was Torin's garage door. If it was open, then I'd know he was home.

The garage door was closed.

Days rolled by, his absence a festering wound that ate at me. A few times, I could have sworn I felt him, but it was only wishful thinking. Every time I turned around and searched the crowd for a pair of brilliant blue eyes and a wicked grin, the empty hole inside me grew.

At night, I cried myself to sleep, missing him. I wasn't allowed to do any physical activities, so I couldn't go swimming. Eirik and Cora filled me in on what was happening during practice. They came to my house most evenings after dinner. Not once did they mention Torin. Part of me appreciated it, while the other part resented them for not caring he was gone.

Eirik was attentive, loving, and patient. I couldn't have made it through the week without him. He became my anchor. As for the swim team, I didn't know what to do about them. The thought of either Eirik or Cora dying chewed my insides, but warning them wouldn't change a thing. Cora had ditched Keith after the Homecoming Dance, but she didn't seem too broken up about it. In fact, she seemed happier. He'd already moved on and had a new girlfriend.

On Friday, we entered the cafeteria, and the first people I noticed were Marj, Catie, and Jeannette. The three Norns were back. The swim team's time was up. Fear rose to my throat and stifled me while they laughed and acted normal.

"You okay, Raine?" Eirik asked.

I shook my head, dizzy with dread. "Do you guys know those three over there?"

Cora and Eirik turned and followed my gaze. Marj and her friends were staring at us now. Eirik nodded at them. Cora waved.

"Yeah, we met them yesterday during practice," she said. "They're transfers from Doc's old high school. They're starting on Monday because we have the Crimson versus Gold meet tonight. Why do you ask?"

I shrugged. I didn't have an answer for them. What could I tell them anyway? That another accident was about to happen? Without Torin to stop it, more people would be killed. My stomach churned, and my mind raced with possible things I could do to stop them. Would they strike tonight during the intrasquad meet?

"If I was a new student, I wouldn't want to join the team now," Cora said, drawing my attention to the conversation she was having with Eirik.

"Don't start with that again," he said.

"I'm not the only person thinking it," she retorted.

Eirik rolled his eyes.

"Thinking what?" I asked.

"Doc tried to organize a dinner party, but there were no takers," Eirik explained.

We always looked forward to team dinners. "Why?"

"After the incident at the club and last weekend, everyone thinks the team is jinxed or something," Cora said.

Or something.

"Excuse me." I stood on shaky legs and started across the cafeteria. I had no idea what I was going to tell the three Norns, but I had to try and reason with them. By the time I reached their table, I was shaking with fear and anger. The alarming coldness I always felt in their presence threatened to overwhelm me. I ignored it, leaned down and looked into Marj's eyes. "Bring Torin back."

She stared blankly at me. "What?"

"I want Torin back."

She looked at the other two then pinned me with a glare. "Who are you?"

"You know who I am, just like I know who you are, Marj LeBlanc." I glanced at the one with black hair and tan complexion. "Catie Vivanco." Finally, my eyes connected with the blonde's. "And you, Jeannette Wilkes. It doesn't matter what names you're using now. You are Norns. You were there when I was born. You were recently at the hospital when I got hurt, though I thought I was dreaming, and now you're back. What do you want?"

They didn't hide their shock, but Marj recovered first.

"You're crazy," she snapped. "We're new here. We've never met you before."

"Oh, stop it, Marj," Catie said. "She can see right through our lies."

Jeannette glared at Catie. "And whose fault is that? You just had to save her. She's going to be impossible to control just like her—"

"Don't," Marj snapped and gripped Jeannette's hand.

"My what? My father? My mother?" Catie smiled. She seemed to be nicer than the other two, but I wasn't ready to play nice. "I won't let you kill my friends or keep Torin and me apart."

Marj's brown eyes glowed eerily. "*You* won't let us?"

I swallowed against a rising panic. "That's right. My friend has a vlog that most students around here watch and millions more online watch. Starting tomorrow, I'll use it to do an exposé on you, your world, and what you do." They stared at me, then each other, and then back at me again. "Leave my friends alone, and bring Torin back."

I turned to leave and bumped into Eirik and Cora. They'd followed me and were looking at me like I was nuts. How much had they heard?

"What's a Torin?" Cora asked.

CHAPTER 16. A SURPRISE

How could she not remember Torin? I glanced at Marj and her Norn buddies. Their expressions were watchful as though daring me to confess.

"*Toe ring*," I improvised and shrugged when Cora gave me a you've-got-to-be-kidding look. "It was special. They came to the hospital when I was sick and stole everything from me."

I didn't know whether I convinced them or not, but I couldn't eat after that. I munched on an apple without tasting it. What was I thinking challenging Norns? Especially after Andris had told me no one got away with it. I was tempted to glance over my shoulder at their table to see what they were doing. Since I didn't dare, I forced myself to listen to Cora whine about the meet with our archrivals, Jesuit High and Lake Oswego. Would the Norns strike then?

"With our luck, we'll lose and be thoroughly humiliated," she said.

Eirik didn't say much, but he kept glancing at me. I could tell he was worried.

"So what was that about a toe ring? I've never seen you wear one before," he said as he walked me to my next class.

I tried to smile and act nonchalant even though he'd probably see through my lie, which meant I had to distract him. "Dad bought it for my birthday and left it with Mom. Did the cops ever find the person behind the blackout at L.A. Connection?"

Eirik shook his head. "No. The investigation hit a dead end."

"Do you remember how people got out of the club?"

"Someone broke down the doors. The bouncers or cops, I don't remember."

Torin had saved them, I wanted to remind him. Andris hadn't lied. The Norns had wiped everyone's memories. "When I hurt myself last weekend, were we hanging out at my house?"

"No, my old house. It was a dumb idea to have party there to begin with. Why are you asking me all these questions? You still don't remember?"

I shook my head. "No, but I keep hoping."

Outside my next class, Eirik tucked a lock of my hair behind my ear, the gesture so Torin's that my heart squeezed. "Listen, the editorial team is meeting after school," he said, "but I'll only stay for about five minutes, so wait for me."

"Okay. Think you can give me a ride to the pool, too? I want to watch the Gold and Crimson showdown."

"Sure." He bent down, kissed me gently on the lips, and took off. I stared after him and sighed. Part of me wanted to finish things with him, but part of me was reluctant to let him go. I needed him now more than ever. Maybe Andris had been right. Maybe I was holding on to Eirik and his love for me in case Torin didn't come back. What did that make me? Selfish?

Focusing in each class became difficult as the hours passed. I couldn't stop worrying about Marj and her friends. Would they go after my friends tonight at the meet? What could I do to stop them? I cringed when the bell rang. For the first time in days, I hated that school was over.

Since I couldn't carry my heavy backpack with all of the books, I made several trips to and from my locker to the front of the school, carrying a few books at a time. I was in the band room picking up my oboe when I felt the now familiar suffocating coldness and froze. Slowly, I turned.

Marj, Catie, and Jeannette stood just inside the room. Jeannette, who was closest to the door, waved her hand and the door closed on its own as though she'd pushed it. Then they just stood there, staring, waiting. Waiting for what? My heart pounded with fear.

"What do you want?" I asked with false bravado.

"You," Marj said coldly. I swallowed against the fear threatening to overwhelm me when she stepped forward and the others followed. "We don't take kindly to snooty, smart-alecky, little girls threatening us."

"Especially when they think they know what's good for them better than we do," Jeannette added.

My first instinct was to run, but they stood between me and the door. Behind me was a window. Could I throw the oboe and crash it? They do it in movies. No, I was standing my ground. My grip tightened on the case's handle, my heart pounding.

"You've taken people I love from me," I said, my voice shaking. "First my father, now Torin."

"Your father?" Catie asked, her eyebrows shooting up in surprise.

"He's been gone for months, and we don't know whether he's alive or dead."

Catie glanced at the other two. They shrugged indifferently.

Anger surged through me. "He might not mean anything to you, but he has people who love him and want him back."

"Let me guess, you?" Jeannette said with a cruel smile.

I really didn't like this Norn. She was right behind Marj on my hate list. The jury was still out on Catie. "Yes. Me, my mother, and Eirik."

"Eirik?" Catie asked.

"Don't start celebrating yet," Jeannette snapped and glared at her.

"Sourpuss," Catie muttered.

"Crone," Jeannette retorted.

"Girls, focus!" Marj snapped then glared at me. "We don't negotiate with Mortals."

"Or Immortals," Jeannette said. "What makes you think we would with you?"

Catie's laugh echoed around the room. The other two glared at her.

"I'll give you what you want in exchange for Torin's punishment and bringing my father home," I said.

"What could you possibly have that we would want?" Marj asked.

"Me." A fierce intensity entered their eyes, and I shivered. "Torin saved me when I was supposed to die, and it's obvious that's what you want. If I go with you, it makes what he did null and void." My voice grew stronger. "So take me, and let him go."

"How does she know—?"

Marj raised her hand and cut off Jeannette. "She doesn't. She's guessing, but we'll see if she's willing to go through with it." She angled her head. "Someone's coming. Let's go."

They grew hazy until I could see through them. Then they disappeared. My legs gave out under me, and I sat on the nearest chair just as one of the custodial workers walked in.

"You okay, miss?" he asked.

"Yes, thanks." I clasped my oboe against my chest and left the room, surprised my legs could carry me. Eirik was pacing the front hall when I arrived. During our walk to his Jeep, he talked about a Trojan

Gazette special edition they planned to print. I must have made appropriate responses because he didn't ask if I was okay.

I slouched in my seat and got lost in my screwed up world as Eirik started the engine. A month ago I was just your average teenager. Now I had a date with death. A date I'd made. For the guy I loved. Eirik didn't say much during the drive home, until he turned onto my cul-de-sac. "Looks like my parents found a new tenant."

My eyes flew to Torin's house, and I sat up, my heart tripping. A moving van stood in the driveway, blocking the entrance to the garage door. I couldn't tell whether the motorcycle was inside the garage or not.

Torin. Please, let him be home.

I jumped out of the Jeep before Eirik switched off the engine. "When are you picking me up?"

"I was planning on waiting for you, then going to my place and picking up my stuff." He stepped out of the car, lifted my backpack from the backseat, and noticed I was staring at Torin's place. He followed my gaze, his expression puzzled. "You've met your new neighbors?"

"No, but, uh, could you just pick me up *after* you collect your swim stuff? I have to do some of the exercises the doctor recommended. You know, for my wacky memories." I made a goofy face, picked up my oboe, and raced toward the house.

"Whoa, slow down." He ran after me and wrapped his arm around my waist. "I'm happy to see the sparkle back in your eyes, Ms. Wacky Memories." He planted a kiss on my temple. "I'll be back in twenty minutes, and you'd better still be smiling. I've missed the way your face crunches up when you smile."

"That's insulting." I unlocked the door. "My face doesn't..." Something familiar prickled my senses as I stepped into the foyer. A scent. Footsteps. "Mom? What are you doing home...?"

A tall man appeared in the doorway of the study.

"Dad?" The oboe fell from my hand. I closed my eyes, praying I wasn't imagining him, then opened them just as fast. He was still there, smiling, walking toward me. I flew across the room, straight into his arms. He groaned and laughed when he almost lost his balance.

"It's okay, my little warrior," he murmured into my hair.

I didn't know how long he held me while I cried before I leaned back and looked at him. "Where were you? We were worried and scared. I almost gave up, but Mom…" She stood behind him in the doorway, her hand covering her mouth, tears running down her face. "She never gave up. Never doubted you'd come back. You lost weight."

He laughed and pressed a kiss on my forehead. "And you climbed your tree without waiting for me to catch you. Thank you for taking care of her while I was gone, son," he added and extended a hand toward Eirik, who was still standing in the entry with a stupefied expression on his face.

"It wasn't easy, so it's good to have you home, sir." They did their manly hug. It was great to have Dad back. It was a miracle, or maybe not. The Norns must have responded to my threat, which meant Torin was back, too. Telling them goodbye was going to be painful.

"Where was he, Mom?" I asked.

"A commercial fishing boat rescued him from the ocean. He's been unconscious all this time at a hospital in, uh, somewhere in Central America."

"But it's been months. Why didn't they call the airline? The police? The crash made international news."

"Sweetie." She cupped my face. "I'm sure the people on the boat had their reasons for not wanting the police involved, but he's home now and that's all that matters." Mom kissed my forehead, patted my cheek, and went to pick up my oboe from the floor. "Were you two going somewhere?"

"A swim meet," Eirik said, glancing at me. "Do you still want me to pick you up?"

"No. I want to talk to Dad first." Then go to Torin's.

"No, pumpkin," Dad interrupted. "Go with Eirik. I'll be here when you come back."

"But I want to know what happened and…" I noticed the way Mom clung to his side, and it hit me. They probably wanted to be alone. I glanced at Eirik. "Okay. Pick me up in twenty minutes."

"Nice to have you back, Mr. C." Eirik yanked the door and disappeared outside.

I ran to the kitchen and looked out the window. The moving van was gone. How was I going to go next door without an explanation? I turned and found my parents watching me with indulgent expressions.

"Is he gone?" Dad teased.

He knows about Torin? "What?"

"Eirik. Since when do you watch him drive away?" he teased.

My faced warmed. If only he knew. I hugged him again. "I'm so happy you're home, Daddy. I still want to hear details of what happened, okay?"

He grinned. "Absolutely."

"We have a new neighbor, Mom," I added, heading for the stairs. In my room, I knelt on the window seat and stared across at Torin's window.

"Torin," I whispered. "Please, come to the window. Give me a sign you're back."

"Hey, Freckles."

I froze. So scared I was imagining him again, my heart threatening to pound right out of my chest, I slowly turned around. He wasn't a figment of my imagination. He stood by the closet's full-length mirror as though he'd just stepped through it. He probably had. Dressed in his usual black, his hands shoved in his front pants pockets, he looked so breathtakingly beautiful. The lock of raven hair brushing his forehead was as familiar as the wicked smile that often curled his lips, except the smile was missing this time.

"You're back," I whispered.

Blue flames leaped in his eyes, his gaze roaming my face hungrily. "I had to."

"My father is back, too."

"I know. I found him."

"You? I thought the Norns—"

"They don't care enough. I'd risk anything for you, Freckles," he whispered, his voice low and intense. "I'd do anything to make you happy, and that's why I found him."

One second he was across my room, the next, he'd pulled me into his arms. His mouth found mine, hungrily molding it and every sense in my body to his will. I grabbed his shirt and hung on for the ride. I was drowning in sensations, the haze of pleasure so intense I groaned. He became the focus of my existence. His scent, his addictive taste, the feel of his hard, hot body.

He growled something under his breath and pulled me closer, his hand caressing my sides, moving around to my chest. I stopped breathing. He tore his lips from mine, his breathing harsh, eyes intense as he stared at me. I sucked air into my starved lungs and smiled. He opened his mouth to speak and closed it without saying anything, stark pain flashing in his eyes.

"What is it?" I asked.

"I can't do this," he whispered achingly. "I thought I'd come here, see you one last time, and say goodbye, but it's not enough. You make me feel things I've never felt before, Freckles. Make me want and crave the impossible. When I'm with you, the rules cease to matter. The reason for my existence becomes you." He cradled my face. "Yet I know I'm not right for you."

"You are." I reached up and gripped his hands.

He shook his head, his expression wreathed with torment. "No, you can't live in my world," he said in a hoarse whisper. "To do that, you must be like me, and I'll never let that happen."

I pressed my fingers on his lips to stop him from saying anymore. "I know what you are, Torin. Andris told me everything."

He frowned. "When?"

"The night of the Homecoming Dance." I searched his face. "I don't care that you are a Valkyrie. Why didn't you heal me when you had a chance and start turning me into an Immortal?"

Torin closed his eyes and pressed his forehead against mine. "I couldn't do it any more than I could let you die. You're not some unhappy girl in a bad situation that needs to be rescued like Maliina and her sister. You have a wonderful life, Freckles. People who love you."

"I don't care."

"Don't say that when you know it's not true. You care." He cupped my face, caressed my cheeks. "I ignored their existence because I loved how I felt when I'm around you. You made me laugh, chased the loneliness away. For once, I was willing to ignore the rules and go after what I wanted. What I needed. But then I saw how your friends rallied around you when you were at the hospital, saw the look in your mother's eyes when she thought she'd lost you, learned about what she's been through for you, and I couldn't ignore them anymore. I knew this was where you belonged. With them. Alive." Sounds came from downstairs. He stepped back, his hands falling to his side, runes appearing on his perfectly chiseled face. Behind him, my mirror became smoky. "I have to go now."

My knees threatened to give out as I stepped toward him. My attempt to save him had failed. "You can't leave me."

"Don't make this more difficult than it already is, Freckles." Desperation clouded his brilliant eyes and more runes appeared on his skin. The mirror was now swirling gray smoke. It was nothing like the portal Ingrid had created. "You have a chance to live a normal life with your father and mother. Do it. Enjoy it. Make my sacrifice mean something."

"But you promised…" My voice trailed off, and tears sprang to my eyes. The portal formed. I couldn't see where it led. It was a murky, dark mass of nothing. "You promised you'd do anything to make me happy."

"Anything but take you away from your family. They love you as much as you love them. They need you."

"I need you."

"You'll be fine. You're strong. Be happy. For me." He stared at me one last time as though memorizing my face. The runes started to glow, highlighting his handsome face, his raven hair, and sapphire eyes. Then he turned and walked toward the portal. Smoky tendrils leaped from the dark walls and grabbed him. As I watched, the darkness swirled around him, swallowing him. Then the mirror reformed.

My knees gave out, and I folded on the floor like a wet cloth. My breathing hitched, tears racing down my face. I curled up my legs and wrapped my arms around them as though to make myself small and invisible, but my pain was big, consuming. Torin had shattered my heart into tiny pieces. No, he'd ripped it from my chest and left with it, leaving behind nothing but a giant hole. It hurt to breathe, to think, to imagine my life without him.

It was a while before I noticed the chill. It crawled under my skin, causing me to shiver. Soon, I couldn't feel the cold either as numbness crept through me.

CHAPTER 17. CHOICES

It seemed like forever before a knock resounded on my door.

"Just a minute." I swiped at my cheek and struggled to my feet, my movement sluggish and automatic, like a robot. I went to the bathroom and splashed water on my face. My eyes were red. One look at me and anyone would know I'd been crying.

"Pumpkin, Eirik's downstairs," Dad said from the other side of my door.

I didn't really want to go, but if I stayed, I'd have to explain why to my parents, especially Dad. I'd never been able to hide anything from him. Then there was Eirik. He and I might have a special relationship, but he deserved more. I had to break things off with him. Tonight. He was a wonderful guy who deserved a girl who was crazy about him. I wasn't that girl.

"Raine?"

"I'll be out in a second, Dad," I called.

I changed my shirt, brushed my hair, and put on sunglasses. Downstairs, Dad studied my face and frowned. *Please, don't ask me what's wrong.* If he did, I'd start crying again.

"Love you, Dad. So happy you're home." I gave him another tight squeeze, kissed Mom, then joined Eirik. We ran to the Jeep. It was raining, typical fall weather in Oregon.

"It's great to have your dad home, isn't it?" Eirik said instead of starting the engine.

"Yeah. It's a miracle." My voice shook.

Eirik lifted the sunglasses from my nose. "You don't have to hide behind the sunglasses, Raine. I know you've been crying. I also choked up when I saw him."

I laughed, faking amusement. But having Eirik believe I'd been crying because my father had returned was a relief. I took the glasses from his hand and threw them on the tray between our seats. "Okay, let's go. Warm ups will start in," he checked his watch, "five minutes."

He started the engine and took off.

I didn't bother to glance at Torin's house as we drove by. He was gone. It didn't matter how much it hurt, I had to learn to live with the fact that he was gone and was never coming back. Tears filled my eyes again. Eirik reached for my hand and squeezed it.

***

We parked behind Draper Building, which housed Walkersville University's pool, racquetball courts, indoor basketball and tennis courts, and the gym. College students were everywhere. Inside the building, I headed to the balcony while Eirik disappeared in the boys' locker room.

Since this was an intrasquad meet, the bleachers were empty except for the girlfriends and boyfriends of some of the swimmers. I ignored them and moved to the lower row of seats. Some of the swimmers were in the pool, warming up. Others had towels around their waists or shoulders and were busy talking. I spied Cora. She was in the pool and hadn't seen me yet.

I pulled out my phone and headphones. Right in the middle of checking my music playlist, I felt the telltale prickly feeling on the back of my neck. Someone was watching me. I turned my head, checking my right then left. My eyes widened when I saw Andris and Ingrid.

What were they doing here? Was Torin around, too?

I searched past the few students seated behind me to the top of the bleachers. My stomach dropped. Marj, Catie, and Jeannette stared at me with unreadable expressions. Norns and Valkyries in one place meant bad news, but I didn't care anymore. Marj and her friends had turned down my deal and taken Torin, so let them do their worst. In fact, they could all go rot in hell. The real hell with eternal suffering and Lucifer, not theirs run by some goddess living in a fancy-shmancy hall.

Ignoring them, I turned around. Eirik entered the pool deck, and I tried to catch his attention, but he was staring at someone. I followed his gaze and frowned. He was staring at Cora with a weird expression. She'd just pulled herself out of the pool.

I blinked, not sure if I was reading him correctly. He'd never looked at me like that. Could Eirik be into Cora? Had I been blinded by our friendship and not seen something right under my nose? Or maybe I was imagining things. His expression soured, and I saw why.

Cora was hugging one of the senior swimmers and laughing at something he'd just said. Wow, Eirik was definitely into Cora.

Jaw tense, Eirik turned and looked toward the bleachers, obviously searching for me. I waved. He saw me and waved back. I reached a decision. Just because my heart was broken and my dreams were shattered didn't mean I'd let my friends die. Eirik deserved a chance to win Cora's heart, and I planned to bring them together.

I glanced to my left, and my eyes collided with Andris. He scowled. Another turn of my head and I had a stare down with Marj. She looked away first, then glanced at the skylight above the pool. I followed her glance and wondered what they were planning. It was still raining, but it was just a drizzle.

You're not winning, crone.

She smiled as though she'd heard my thoughts. I got up.

"Where are you going?" Andris asked, appearing suddenly beside me. Ingrid appeared on my other side.

"What do you want, Andris?" I asked rudely.

"To reap the souls of your friends, that's what." He gripped my arm and pulled me down on the bench beside him. "You shouldn't be here, Raine. I already told you. No one can change their destiny."

I yanked my arm from his hand. "How are they going to do it? Another electrical outage? A gas leak? Why am I asking you anyway? Death is not your department." I glanced at the three Norns and called out, "What is it going to be, Marj? Mass electrocution? Gassing?" Several students turned to see who I was talking to, but I didn't care that they couldn't see the three Norns.

"Who are you talking to?" Andris asked.

"The three Norns in the back row."

Andris and Ingrid followed my glance.

"There's no one there, sweetheart," Andris said.

If the Norns could make Torin forget meeting them, they could easily be invisible to Andris. "Believe me, they're here. I can't believe I tried to make a deal with them."

"You did what?"

Something in Andris' voice had me dragging my eyes back to him. "I tried to make a deal with them. You know, me for Torin's punishment."

"Why would you do such a stupid thing?" Andris ground out.

I glared at him. "It's my fault Torin's in trouble. Isn't that what you suggested I should do in order to save him?"

"I did not," Andris protested, fear flashing in his eyes.

"Actually, you did say it was the only solution when I brought her to see you last weekend," Ingrid said. "You'd been drinking," she added.

He frowned. "I must have been wasted. You didn't tell Torin, did you?" There was fear in his voice now.

"Of course not. Not that it matters. They didn't take the deal. Torin's gone, and they're here to finish off my friends." I glanced over my shoulder and found the three Norns staring at the skylight above the pool with unnerving intensity. I followed their gazes and gasped. The skylight was moving, shifting, and changing color. "A portal is opening."

"About time," Andris said with glee, and I wanted to smack him. No one should be that excited about people dying.

Like the portal on my mirror, this one was grayish. The ominous, swirling mass churned faster and faster. Unaware of the mayhem about to be unleashed, Doc blew the whistle, and the first race began.

"Doc! Stop!" I yelled, but the cheering students swallowed my words.

I jumped up, ran to the end of the row, and down the stairs to the pool deck. Andris yelled something behind me, but I wasn't listening. I ignored the stares and went straight to the coach. "Cancel the meet, Doc."

His brow rose. "Why?"

"Something bad is about to happen."

He beckoned frantically to someone, grabbed my arm, and led me away from the other students. Andris shook his head when our eyes met. The Norns watched the portal. The gray core was forming some kind of a tunnel.

"Raine—"

"No, listen to me, Doc. Get everyone out of here before it's too late."

He peered into my eyes. "No, you listen. You're recovering from a head trauma, and I think you should take things easy. You know, take more time to fully recover before coming back to the team."

"This has nothing to do with my accident or me being on the team," I snapped, my voice rising. "The whole swim team is in danger. Please. Tell them to leave."

Eirik appeared beside us. Coach nodded to him. "Get her out of here. Her behavior is scaring the other swimmers."

"Come, Raine," Eirik said.

"No! Go." I pushed him away and jumped into the shallow end of the pool fully clothed, boots and all. Walking slowly, I moved toward the middle, bumping into swimmers and forcing them to stop. "Get out of the pool. Now! You're in danger!"

Some kept swimming. Others stood and stared at me in shock before looking at the coach.

"Don't look at him. Move! Go!" The entire roof was now an endless black tunnel, just like the one that had sucked Torin away. Bolts of light zipped along its walls, and thunder rumbled eerily at its core. It was only a matter of minutes before one of the bolts changed trajectory and hit the pool. On the deck, the swimmers stared, whispered, and pointed at me. A few of their words reached me.

"What's she doing?"

"She's crazy—"

"I guess she never recovered from her accident."

"Raine! Get out of there," Cora demanded.

I glanced at her. She was cradling Eirik, who seemed to have passed out at the corner of the deck. The other students continued to stand around with towels around their shoulders, shock on their faces as they watched me, pointed, and continued to whisper. Chances were they saw the skylight above the pool instead of the hellish tunnel I could see.

Coach Fletcher yelled frantically at someone on the phone. Andris and Ingrid waited near the rail separating the bottom row of bleachers and the pool deck. He was smirking as though everything was pure entertainment. The Norns stood beside them, watching, waiting.

Tears filled my eyes. "I tried but—"

A bolt of white light shot through the portal and hit the wet pool deck with an ear-splitting crack, then fanned out along the floor like tentacles. Chaos broke out as students ran, or tried to, but they couldn't outrun electricity. Bodies twitched as high voltage shot through them. Screams filled the air.

"Help them," I yelled to Andris and Ingrid. They didn't move from the bleachers or look away from the screaming students. Marj and her friends had moved and now stood near Eirik and Cora, their eyes glowing, their gazes on me. "Please, stop this."

Marj walked to the edge of the pool and extended her hand toward me. "Come with us, Raine."

"No," I cried out, tears racing down my face. "Stop this first."

"We're not the ones doing this. They are." She pointed at the portal.

I looked up and tried to see who or what she meant, but I couldn't see anything beyond the dark tunnel and crackling lightning.

"I don't see anything. Make them stop." Even as the words left my mouth, more bolts zipped from the depth of the portal to the pool deck, catching students in mid-run. Bodies were knocked into the air before they fell on the deck or into the pool, the echoes of death horrifying. The lucky ones made it to the bleachers, but I couldn't see past the flashing lights to see how many survived.

Andris and Ingrid walked among the fallen, collecting souls of the dead. Two other Valkyries were with them. Grief squeezed my heart, knowing the two were Torin's replacement. At least I couldn't see the souls.

"Give me your hand, Raine," Marj urged. "I'll get you out of here alive."

The urge to ignore her was there, but I was tired. Defeated. I had tried and failed. My friends were either dead or dying. Wading through the water, I started for the edge of the pool.

"NO, RAINE. DON'T!"

"Mom?" I froze and looked around, frantically searching for her.

"Stay away from her," Mom screamed.

"Stay back," I yelled, searching for her at the entrance, where students were huddled together. I couldn't see her. I had to stop her from coming on the deck. I reached for Marj's hand.

"No, Raine. Don't touch her."

Then I saw Mom walking through the field of death, runes glowing on her face and hands. More were visible through her Bohemian skirt and top. She glared at Marj and snarled, "You have some nerve coming for my daughter behind my back. Leave her alone."

Marj took a step back. "You're not supposed to see us anymore."

"Think again, Norn," Mom snarled. "A mother's love and instinct to protect her child is stronger than all the magic and all the powers in the world. I heard her cry for help and came. And I'll always see your true form no matter what disguise you wear. Now go."

I didn't bother to check if Marj and the others left or not. I stared at Mom with wide eyes. "How?"

"We'll talk later. Give me your hand."

I blacked out before our fingers touched.

***

Voices filtered through the fog in my head. I was feeling toasty, which meant someone had removed my wet clothes and replaced them with dry, warm ones.

"How's she doing, Mrs. C?" Eirik asked.

"Good. She stopped shivering. Why don't you wait downstairs? I'll call you when she wakes up. If Tristan wakes up from his nap and wanders downstairs, keep him there. I don't want him to see her like this."

The click of the closing door followed. I didn't want to deal with what I knew was coming—more of Mom's revelations, how many friends I'd lost tonight.

"You'll have to open your eyes sometime, sweetie," Mom said.

Sighing, I slowly lifted my eyelids and stared at her. Her hazel eyes twinkled. Only she could still smile in the face of a catastrophe. That was how I saw my life. A huge disaster. I sat up, the covers slipping to my waist. "Why didn't you tell me you were a Valkyrie?"

"I wanted you to have a normal life for as long as possible. I didn't know Norns would try to recruit you this early," Mom said. "You're not even eighteen."

"Is that what you call it? Recruit? Mom, they killed my friends and tried to kill me, too."

"No, no, sweetie. It was your friends' time to go, not yours. I would have known. Like I told you before, no one can escape death when their time's up. The Norns just used the opportunity to attempt to lure you to their side. The fact that they didn't wait until you were a Valkyrie tells me you're very special, but then again, I always knew you were." She smiled. I didn't feel like smiling.

"Is Cora okay?" I spoke slowly, scared to know the answer yet I had to.

Mom nodded. "Eirik said you saved him and Cora."

I blinked. "I did?"

"You pushed him hard, and he slipped on the wet deck, banged his head, and blacked out. He landed on the dry part of the deck, and Cora stayed with him. The lightning didn't come anywhere near them."

I remembered pushing him and seeing Cora cradling him near a wall. I focused on my mother. "Is Dad a Valkyrie, too?"

Sadness tinged her smile this time. "No, sweetie. It was one of the stipulations from the Norns. If I couldn't follow my destiny and become one of them, I couldn't turn the man I fell in love with."

I thoroughly hated Norns. "Stipulations?"

Mom sighed. "There's no time to give you details of our history. You'll learn all that in the coming year, but here's the shorter version. We come from a line of powerful Valkyries. Or maybe I should say powerful spiritual Mortals, who become Valkyries. We even have a few Norns in our family tree. I had started training as a Norn when I realized I was in love with your father and couldn't imagine a life without him. Norns or would-be Norns are not supposed to fall in love. They're maidens dedicated to shaping destinies and nothing else. Their duties leave no room for romance, husbands, or kids. So when I chose your father, they stripped me of my powers and bound me to earth. That means I can never go to the Realm of the gods." She rolled her eyes and shrugged. "I don't care. I've been very happy with your father."

I could only stare at her. I still couldn't wrap my head around the fact that my mother was a Valkyrie. I had so many questions. How old was she? How did one become a Valkyrie? "So I wasn't supposed to die?"

"No, or I would have known." She leaned forward and added, "I still have friends back in Valhalla, and they would have told me. Come on, your friends are waiting downstairs."

"But I have so many questions," I protested, but stood anyway. "Can you explain the mirrors at your store? Are some of them portals? Because I swear I noticed runes on some of their frames." Another thought occurred to me. "The mirror downstairs is a portal too, isn't it?"

She chuckled. "Yes, I use it to communicate with my friends. And it's true. Some of the mirrors at the store are portals. Your father owned the store when we met twenty years ago. In fact, I was his regular customer for a while." She blushed. "Now I use the business to create portals, which we ship all over the world. With the runes already sketched on frames, Valkyries can use them wherever they are without sketching runes on them."

Eirik's parents knew Torin before he arrived in our town, and they had a mirror portal in their old bedroom. "Are Eirik's parents Valkyries, too?"

Mom chuckled. "Yes, but they don't reap souls. They have special duties here on earth."

"So when they told Eirik they were going home, they meant," I pointed up, "the Realm of the, uh, gods?"

She nodded. "Yes, and that's why I was surprised."

Eirik was adopted, so he was obviously human. They must be using him to blend in. "Does Eirik know about them?"

Mom chuckled and looped her arm around mine. "Oh, sweetie, I know you have questions, but there's just so much I can tell you because of rules and whatnot. When your trainer gets here, all your questions will be answered."

Trainer? Everything was happening fast, and I wasn't sure I was ready to start training. "You should've told me, Mom, especially when I saw the runes on my car and freaked out."

She sighed. "I'm so sorry, baby. But like I said, there's a limit to how much I can tell you. I'd hoped you'd learn the truth about us and your legacy from your trainer when you turned eighteen. As for the runes on your car, I had to protect you somehow when you started driving. You know me. I don't trust Mortal machines."

I laughed. I couldn't help it. Her aversion to computers now made sense. Then what she'd said registered. "If you sketched the runes last year, how come I didn't see them until now?"

"Something happened to open your eyes and mind to magic. It might have been a physical, mental, emotional, or spiritual link with something or someone from our world."

Torin. I'd started seeing the runes after I met him.

"Actually, you started seeing them earlier than normal. You're not supposed to have the sight until you're eighteen."

I frowned. "The sight?"

"The ability to see past the rune veil. It was probably the Norns' presence," Mom continued. "They should be ashamed of themselves, trying to lure you to their side when you're so young and vulnerable." She chuckled. "But you showed them, didn't you? Just as I chose your Dad over joining them, you chose your friends and Torin."

My eyes widened. "You know about Torin?"

"Oh, sweetie. There's still runic magic left in these old bones for me to know when a Valkyrie moves next door."

My throat closed, images of Torin flashing through my head. "He found Dad."

"I know. He's an amazing young man. He came to the store to get me as soon as he brought your father home. We'll talk some more later. Right now, go on downstairs and talk to your friends. The longer we stay up here, the more they'll worry." Rubbing my arms, she opened the door. "I'll always be here for you. I don't know who they will assign to teach you runic magic or when they'll get here, but keep an eye out for Norns. They come in many forms, but always in threes. They put me through trials worse than a trip to Hel's Hall to prove I loved your father before they gave up. They're not going to make it easy for you and Torin either."

My heart leaped. "He's back?"

She smiled and patted my cheek. "I should hope so. If he's your true love…"

"He is," I said.

"Then don't let the Norns win. Fight for him. Now go."

"Love you, Mom." I gave her a big hug, then raced downstairs. Eirik had his arms around Cora. From her red eyes, she'd been crying.

Eirik cocked his brow when he saw me. "Are you okay?"

I nodded, joined them, and we hugged. "I'll live. You guys?"

"We were on the dry part of the deck and got lucky," he said.

"I don't know if I can take it anymore," Cora said between sniffles, and Eirik's arm tightened around her. "So many swimmers dying. I already told Mom I'm quitting the team."

I rubbed her arm. "No one will blame you. How many died?"

"Eight from the last text we received from Kicker," Eirik explained. "We just wanted to make sure you were okay before heading to the hospital."

I looked down at my fleece pants and shirt and fuzzy, bootie slippers. "Can you guys wait for me while I put on regular boots and a jacket?" They didn't speak, and when our eyes met, they looked uneasy. "What?"

"People are talking," Cora said, visibly cringing.

"But we don't care," Eirik said. "Grab your stuff and let's go."

I frowned. "What are they saying?"

"It doesn't matter," Eirik insisted.

I ignored him and focused on Cora. "What are they saying, Cora?"

"Um, you knew something was about to happen and warned us," she said slowly, her face red. "So everyone is really scared."

I swallowed. "Of me?"

She winced again and nodded. "How did you know something was about to happen?"

"I just did, and now I'm officially a freak." Mom was right. The Norns let this happen. They could have easily erased everyone's memory like they'd done before. Cora and Eirik studied me with concern. "Maybe we can tell them something happened to me when I hurt my head and now I have superpowers," I added flippantly.

Cora stared at me with wide eyes. "That makes sense."

I threw her a disgusted look. "I was kidding, Cora."

"No, this is good," Eirik cut in. "It's the perfect explanation. Once we tell them about your accident and the superpowers, they'll stop acting weird."

I shook my head. "No, don't. If my presence will bother them, then I don't have to go."

"Who cares what they think. You're Raine. You never let anything or anyone stop you from doing the right thing. If they want to treat you differently, screw them. Powers or not, you're our friend."

"Eirik's right," Cora added, but I could tell she was uneasy.

"I really shouldn't go anyway." I touched my temple for emphasis. "I'm feeling a bit woozy. Come on, I'll walk you guys to the car." I sighed with relief when they didn't argue. As soon as I opened the door, the powerful sound of a Harley reached my ears. My heart pounding, I reached the driveway before Cora and Eirik and stared toward the entrance of the cul-de-sac.

Torin entered the cul-de-sac just as Eirik and Cora were leaving it. By the time he pulled into his driveway, I was crossing our lawn at a run.

He removed his helmet, stepped away from the bike and pushed the lock of raven-black hair away from his forehead. When he turned, I hurled myself at him.

His arms opened and caught me. I wrapped my arms and legs around him, never ever wanting to let go. The feel of his body, his scent, his warmth was heavenly. A delicious shiver rolled through me, and my heart responded to his nearness, leaping and thundering. I leaned back and drank him in, the naughty glint in his brilliant blue eyes, the wicked smile curling his perfectly sculptured lips.

"Let me guess," he said in a husky voice, his arms tightening around me. "You're the Neighborhood Welcoming Committee?"

I giggled. I wanted to tell him how happy I was to see him, to have him back, but I couldn't speak. If I tried, I'd start crying, so I showed him. I grabbed his face, pulled his head down, and kissed him, pouring all my love into the kiss. A groan escaped him as he took over and deepened the contact. When he leaned back, I tightened my arms around his neck and buried my face into his shirt. Laughter rumbled through his chest.

"Okay, sweetheart, this has been very enjoyable," he said in a husky voice. "But I'd like to know the name of a girl before I kiss her."

At first I wasn't sure I'd heard him right. A sickening feeling settled in my stomach. I leaned back and searched his eyes for signs of teasing. "What?"

"May I at least know your name before we continue this inside?"

No. Please no. I wiggled out of his arms, my face flaming. "Are you saying you don't recognize me?"

He studied me the same way he'd done when we first met, with amused interest and slight condescension. A smile tugged the corner of his lips, his eyes roaming my face before settling on my lips. "I would definitely remember you if we'd met before."

The Norns had erased his memories. How could they be so cruel? It was bad enough the swim team thought I was a freak. Now the guy I loved couldn't remember me.

"I'm Torin St. James." He stuck out his hand. "And you are?"

I looked at his hand then his beautiful, familiar face, and a sob escaped my lips. I covered my mouth, horrified, tears welling in my eyes.

"No, no, please don't cry. I didn't mean to make you cry." He reached for me, genuine distress on his face.

I shook my head, turned on shaking legs, and ran like demons were chasing me, tears racing down my face. I didn't stop until I was inside my room. I slammed the door, slid on the floor, and covered my mouth as sobs shook my body.

My life didn't just suck. It had taken a left turn into Crap Town.

THE END

THE RUNES SERIES READING ORDER

Thank you for reading RUNES. If you enjoyed it, please consider writing a review. Reviews can make a difference in the ranking of a book. The links are available here:

Runes: http://bit.ly/RunesbyEdnahWalters

Check out the other books in The Runes series (See below) and what book is next in the series. I've also included a bonus chapter for GODS as a thank you for pre-ordering HEROES, Eirik Book 2.

I still have one more Echo/Cora book and Torin/Raine book to release in 2016. To be updated on more Runes exclusives, the next book in Eirik's story, giveaways, teasers, and deleted scenes, join my newsletter.

http://bit.ly/EdnahWNewsletter

For the discussion about the series, join my private page on FB:

http://bit.ly/EdnahsEliteValkyries

READING ORDER

Runes: http://bit.ly/RunesbyEdnahWalters
Immortals: http://bit.ly/ImmortalsbyEdnahWalters
Grimnirs: http://bit.ly/GrimnirsbyEdnahWalters
Seeress: http://bit.ly/SeeressbyEdnahWalters
Souls: http://bit.ly/SoulsbyEdnahWalters
Witches: http://bit.ly/WitchesbyEdnahWalters
Demons: http://bit.ly/DemonsbyEdnahwalters
Heroes: http://bit.ly/HeroesbyEdnahWalters
Gods: http://bit.ly/GodsByEdnahWalters

PRE-ORDER THE NEXT IN THE SERIES

Gods, A Runes Companion Novel.
(Eirik Book3.)

To be released on June 14th, 2016.
http://bit.ly/GodsByEdnahWalters

NOTES FROM THE AUTHOR

In Runes, readers are introduced to three best friends, Raine, Cora, and Eirik. Runes, Immortals, Seeress, and Witches chronicles Raine's story and her journey to fulfill her destiny and find true love with Torin St. James, a Valkyrie (there's one more story left). Grimnirs and Souls chronicles Cora's journey to fulfill her destiny and find love with Echo, a Grimnir. There's one more story left in their story.

Eirik's story ends with Gods and I promise you, you won't be disappointed, so buy your copy NOW. It is only fair that Eirik gets the same love as Cora and Raine, and I'm sure by now you have fallen in love with him and Celestia, so don't waste another moment and pre-order Gods coming June 2016. Why did I write Eirik's stories before finishing Raine/Torin and Cora/Echo? Torin and Raine are going to need him and his connections in Hel to kick some serious Norn booties.

ABOUT THE AUTHOR

Ednah Walters holds a PhD in Chemistry and is a stay-at-home mother of five. She is also a USA Today bestselling author. She writes about flawed heroes and the women who love them.

Her award-winning YA Paranormal Romance—Runes Series—started with Runes and has a total of 7 books to date. The next one, Heroes, will be released in March 2016. Her last book, Witches, was a Readers' Favorite Awards winner.

She writes YA Urban Fantasy series—The Guardian Legacy Series, which focuses on the Nephilim, children of the fallen angels. GL Series started with Awakened and has a total of 4 books. The latest book in the series, Forgotten, was released in June 2015. The GL series is published by Spencer Hill Press (Beaufort Books)

Ednah also writes Contemporary Romance as E.B. Walters. Her contemporary works started with The Fitzgerald Family series, which has six books, to her USA Today bestselling series, Infinitus Billionaires.

Whether she's writing about Valkyries, Norns, and Grimnirs, or Guardians, Demons, and Archangels, or even contemporary Irish family in the west coast, love, family, and friendship play crucial roles in all her books.

To stay up to date with her work, exclusives, giveaways, teasers, and deleted scenes, join my newsletter.

EDNAH WALTERS' LINKS:

YA/Ednah Walters': http://bit.ly/EdnahWNewsletter
For the discussion about her series, join her private pages on FB:
RUNES and GL: http://bit.ly/EdnahsEliteValkyries
Ednah Walters' Website: http://www.ednahwalters.com
Ednah Walters in Facebook: http://bit.ly/EdnahWFans
Ednah Walters on Twitter: http://bit.ly/EdnahTwitter
Facebook Fanpage:
https://www.facebook.com/AuthorEdnahwalters
Instagram: http://bit.ly/EdnahW-Instagram
Tumblr: http://bit.ly/EdnahWaltersTumblr
Blog: http://ednahwalters.blogspot.com

E.B. WALTERS' LINKS:

E.B.'s mailing list.
http://bit.ly/EdnahsNewsletter
Discussion group about her billionaires, join her private page:
http://bit.ly/LetsTalkBillionaires
E. B. Walters' Website: www.author-ebwalters.com
Facebook Fanpage: https://www.facebook.com/AuthorEBWalters
Twitter: https://twitter.com/eb_walters
Blog: http://enwalters.blogspot.com

20079617R00151

Printed in Great Britain
by Amazon